I0822883

NEWEARTH:
Justine Awakens

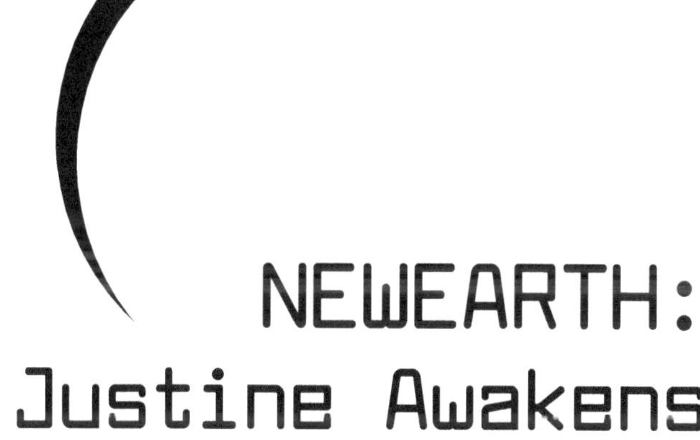

NEWEARTH: Justine Awakens

A. K. FRAILEY

FRAILEY BOOKS

A. K. Frailey Books
110 Possum Lane
Fillmore, IL 62032

Cover and Interior: Trese Gloriod • DESIGNproChristus.com

ISBN: 979-8-9861803-4-2

THE WRITINGS OF A. K. FRAILEY

Books for the Mind and Spirit

https://akfrailey.com/

Contact: akfrailey@yahoo.com

Historical Science Fiction Novels

OldEarth ARAM Encounter https://amzn.to/2KLhlsN

OldEarth Ishtar Encounter https://amzn.to/2OAkDQF

OldEarth Neb Encounter https://amzn.to/3iGqGlQ

OldEarth Georgios Encounter https://amzn.to/3v7w8oI

OldEarth Melchior Encounter https://amzn.to/3nyfkEJ

Science Fiction Novels

Homestead https://amzn.to/3DcTuhz

Last of Her Kind http://amzn.to/2y1HJvg

Newearth Justine Awakens http://amzn.to/2pq0vWN

Newearth A Hero's Crime https://amzn.to/3S4rROI

Short Stories

It Might Have Been—And Other Short Stories 2nd Edition

https://amzn.to/2XXdDDz

One Day at a Time and Other Stories https://amzn.to/2YFtQ5r

Encounter Science Fiction Short Stories & Novella **2nd Edition**

https://amzn.to/3dq6q5l

Inspirational Non-Fiction

My Road Goes Ever On—Spiritual Being, Human Journey **2nd Edition**

https://amzn.to/2KvF3Ll

My Road Goes Ever On—A Timeless Journey https://amzn.to/3v5BlOM

The Road Goes Ever On—A Christian Journey Through The Lord of the Rings

https://amzn.to/3rtAy6S

Children's Book

The Adventures of Tally-Ho http://amzn.to/2sLfcI5

Poetry

Hope's Embrace & Other Poems **2nd Edition** https://amzn.to/3cn22X8

ALIEN RACES

Bhuac: A gelatinous race with no set "form" from the planet Helm. They can mold themselves into the likeness of a variety of races.

Cresta: A techno-organic race from the planet Crestar with long, soft bodies, tentacles, and large, watery eyes. They speak in a synthesized voice, and their large "brain sack" lays hidden behind a spiral shell. They wear breathing helms when not on their own water-based planet.

Ingot: A cyborg race from planet Ingilium that wears bulky techno-organic armor and breather helms built directly into their bodies.

Luxonian: Light beings from the planet Lux. Luxonians send out Guardians on a regular basis to observe alien cultures in order to protect their interests in the region.

Uanyi: Small, slim creatures from the planet Sectine, standing about four to five feet tall, insect-like, with soft, rubbery exoskeletons, enormous eyes, and wear a breathing mask that covers their crab-like mandibles.

PROLOGUE

Cerulean, a Luxonian light being, prayed to an unknown God amid the swirling masses. The tips of his fingers touched steeple style as he appeared in his favorite form: a muscular, middle-aged man with soulful, blue eyes and a determined chin. He sat on a dais facing a massive assembly and squared his shoulders. The crowded, domed hall decorated with statues of long dead but never-to-be-forgotten members of the Inter-Alien Alliance Committee resonated with numerous murmuring conversations. As his gaze flowed over the squirming court of very-much-alive representatives of six races, Cerulean's mind slipped back to the love of his life, Anne Smith, whom he had buried under a blooming apple tree on Oldearth twenty-three years before.

He closed his eyes to the memory. After a deep breath, he reopened them to face the trial of another woman of interest: Justine Santana, an android and one of the most notorious weapons ever used during the Intergalactic Oskilth War.

After a despairing human remnant abandoned Earth and fled to Lux, Cerulean crafted a resettlement plan for Newearth, but war intervened. Now, after the last war crimes trial, he would finally be free to help humanity resettle on Newearth.

But this trial must come first. After all, Justine was human too....

CHAPTER ONE

All My Sins Remembered

"We have definite..." The Luxonian Supreme Judge in a trim human form and dressed in a dark blue robe, stirred in her seat, "...proof that you assassinated well over a hundred and fifty beings on the troop transport called..." She glanced down at a datapad, "...the *Generous Sharon*." She fixed her black-eyed gaze on the lone figure standing on the floating dock with narrowed eyes.

Well over fifty delegates had gathered at Bothmal Criminal Court and sat on comfortable chairs, each tailored for a particular species. Every sentient race on the Inter-Alien Alliance Committee, including Ingots, Uanyi, Crestas, Luxonians, Bhuacs, and humans had at least one representative in attendance. No race wanted to be absent from this trial. Hundreds more sat in the court's upper wings, savoring the spectacle while millions watched the unfolding drama on holoscreens.

The figure standing silently at the center of this hurricane of watchful emotion was a biomechanical hybrid, an android built in female form, in this case, human. Long black hair fell like a cascading waterfall down her back; her blue eyes stared straight ahead, peering into shadows. Massive cuffs, secured with powerful magnets and chains, were locked tightly about her wrists and ankles.

The android moved slightly, shifting her weight from one leg to the other. An expectant hush settled over the assembly. The silvery rattle and clanking of chains broke the quiet.

"Well?" The Supreme Judge leaned forward in her chair, fixing the prisoner with narrowed eyes and lowered brows.

"Yes." The word was a sigh, not of regret, but of weariness or boredom. "Yes, I killed them." She glanced up at the massive holoscreen hovering over the assembly. On its curved surface the security recordings from the *Generous Sharon* played on a constant loop. "My guilt is...pretty obvious. There's no point denying it." A small smile curved at the corners of her lips.

Cerulean shifted to the edge of his seat and coughed lightly into his hand. "If I may ask, why?"

Pondering a moment, the android straightened. "They were in my way." Her musical, almost bell-like voice would have been lost in the echoing chamber if not for the amplifiers.

"Justine, correct?" Cerulean folded his hands into his long robes, leaning forward.

"That is my name."

"It was necessary, you say. Did you feel no...revulsion? Pity? Empathy? How could it be necessary to end the lives of over a hundred beings?"

Justine placed her shackled hands on the dock's rails. "You work in this hall. Did you ask the building permission to occupy it? What its feelings were?"

Two delegates, a Cresta and a human, spoke at once.

"So, you compare yourself to an inanimate object?"

"Are you suggesting that you, as an android, cannot be sentient?" The human representative's fingers nervously played with a datapad.

Cerulean raised his hand. "Justine, I've read the reports, your psychological profile." He cocked his head. "You've made jokes, noted ironies—shown a full range of emotions. Are you suggesting that, like an inanimate object, you can't feel or rather, that you had no choice?"

Justine looked at the human, turning slightly. "The Inter-Alien Commission declared that it is impossible for a robot to be sentient. That is your belief. I say nothing about my own." She fastened her cold, blue eyes on the Cresta. "I am the product of fetal tissue and a computer. How much choice do I have?" Her lips curved mockingly.

"Well, we know she appreciates sarcasm." The Cresta's dry wit drew a chuckle from the crowd.

The Supreme Judge rapped her gavel on the metallic podium. "Order! Order!"

Silence fell as the Cresta representative raised his voice to speak once more. "What are we doing here?" The silence continued as the Cresta chair detached from its mooring and floated before the assembly. "Does no one here appreciate the irony that we are, in fact, holding a trial for a gun?" The chair slowly revolved as the Cresta looked at each of the delegates in turn. "Thousands of machines, robots, and androids were used on both sides of the late Oskilth Civil War. This particular gun," The Cresta gestured with a free tentacle, "just happened to kill its targets more effectively than most."

The android remained still, her mouth drawn in a hard line.

"No, the real reason we're here is because the ringleaders of the war escaped, and now, like hatchlings, you stage an elaborate show, desperate to vent your frustrations on *something*." The Cresta floated back, locking his chair in place, his tentacles wiggling smugly.

The courtroom erupted into roars; many in the assembly leapt to their feet.

"Bold words, coming from you who never suffered an invasion!" The Bhuac representative shimmered as he struggled to maintain his human form.

The Cresta snorted water through his breathing helm dismissively. "To be frank, I don't care what you do with it. Let's wipe its memories and be done with it."

"Memories make us who we are! Wiping her memories is a death sentence." Cerulean's voice reflected stern determination in contrast to the discord all around.

"Order! Order!" The hard smack of the gavel echoed over the uproar. "Any further disturbance and this courtroom will be cleared!" Noise subsided as the judge's sharp gaze scoured the room. "The fate of the accused will be decided by the jury at the proper time."

"If I may speak before they adjourn?" Cerulean rose to his feet.

The Supreme Judge nodded.

"Thank you." Cerulean's chair floated before the assembly. He paused a moment. "Fellow beings, I have studied many different sentient races, my own included." He looked down at the android, who continued to stare off into space.

"I believe that this being calling herself Justine Santana is both sentient and aware, although," he raised his hand as the human delegate jumped to her feet, "I'm also aware that this is only my opinion. I believe that she was not fully responsible for her actions. My argument against the death sentence, or memory wipe, is not based on opinion, however." His back straight, he gazed into the throng, his hands gripping the guard-rail. "Once destroyed, her memories are gone—forever beyond our reach."

The Cresta representative's tentacles gently caressed his bio-suit, his eyes fixed intently on the Luxonian, his tendrils wiggling thoughtfully.

"Who knows when, or how, the data stored in her brain could benefit one of us." Bowing, Cerulean returned his chair to its original location.

No one in the massive courtroom noticed the subtle flicker in Justine's eyes as she appraised the Luxonian before he sat down, storing his features in her data files.

Many of the delegates muttered and whispered, while expressions of indecision crossed their faces.

"If no one else has anything to say…." The Supreme Judge's head swiveled, appraising the vast crowd. "No one? Very well—" she pointed to the assembly of six beings representing each race sitting at her left "the jury may now adjourn."

Justine sat alone in a Bothmal holding cell, lit only by a dim, red light. Her chains had not been removed, but they did not hinder her as she dabbed paint, faster than the eye could follow, on a bare, white board.

With a hissing squeak a small, thickly barred window opened in the fat cell door.

"You." Her hand continued to flicker over the white board. She remained focused on her work.

"Yes, me." The Luxonian tilted his head, peering down through the bars. "You draw?" He nodded at the rapidly filling canvas.

"Paint." She tilted her head, lips pursed. "It helps pass the time. A cheap means to keep the prisoner quiet. You have the advantage. You know my name, but I don't know yours."

"Cerulean."

"Thank you, Cerulean."

"You're thanking me for...?"

"I may be an unrepentant murderer, but I still appreciate those who aid me." Her brush paused mid-stroke. "Your speech out there is the only reason they're having any discussion about my fate at all." Her brush continued to dance across the board.

"I read the full reports."

"Really?"

"I was probably the only one to do so."

Justine's sigh was barely audible. "This trial was pure politics."

Cerulean wrapped his fingers around the bars, tilting his head to view as much of Justine's face as possible. "Your objective was to disable the troop carrier?"

She shrugged. "Yes."

Cerulean's voice rose slightly. "I've seen the carrier's blueprints. Deck forty-two A and rooms thirty-two C and B were nowhere near the command room. I saw where you breached the ship. You doubled back and deliberately searched those rooms. Why?"

Justine smiled coldly, her hand moving a bit faster, the tip of the brush a blur. "Maybe I just like to kill."

Cerulean pursed his lips. "Then why were troopers Alex and Jerrod left alive?"

Her mouth drew into a tight line. "Maybe I missed them. Maybe I thought they were already dead."

"I read your specs. Enhanced senses, hearing, sight.... You can hear a heartbeat from a hundred meters away."

The brush moved faster.

"Trooper Jerrod thought it was a miracle that the escape pod managed to fire on autopilot."

Justine's mouth twisted into a mocking smile. "So, what's your explanation?"

"You resent humans, hate them, and by extension their allies. You saw it as payback, didn't you, as justice? But when you saw trooper Jerrod trying to stanch his comrade's wound, even as he was bleeding out himself, you couldn't bring yourself to press the trigger. Even though it went against orders, you lowered your gun."

"A charming story. But why wasn't that...story used to play to the court's sympathy?" The brush tip filled in tiny details.

"Unlike the Cresta, I don't see a gun. I don't see a cold, calculating machine." His voice softened. "I see a very scared woman who desperately wants to seem strong in her final moments."

The brush froze. Justine's head lowered, and for a second, the proud shoulders sagged. The moment passed as her head lifted again, a confident smile playing on her face. "Really?" She raised an eyebrow. "I have no idea what you're talking about." She carefully laid the brush aside. "It's finished. What do you think?" She displayed the panting in the crook of her arm.

His eyes widening, Cerulean stared into a portrait of himself, true to life on even the tiniest of hair ends. "It's...beautifully done."

"Thank you. Keep it." She set the painting aside before making eye contact with Cerulean for the first time.

Cerulean swallowed a lump in his throat. "I don't know what to say. I'm honored."

“You can hang it on your wall or throw it in the trash. Whichever you prefer.” Justine rose. “Anything else?”

Cerulean stood thoughtfully before he shook his head. “No.”

“Then goodbye.”

Cerulean turned to go. He closed his eyes as a sudden wave of dizziness swept over him. Squaring his shoulders, he forced open his eyes and marched down the long, dim hall.

Justine called after him. “You know, if I had killed them and blown up the ship, there wouldn’t have been anything to identify me. I wouldn’t be here right now.” Justine’s voice echoed down the tunnel, her face and hands pressed against the bars. “No good deed goes unpunished, right?”

Cerulean stopped in midstride and looked back. “Everything we do has consequences. Alex and Jerrod are still alive.”

Silence.

“I hope you find happiness.” Justine’s fingers rubbed against the bars as the window slowly moved.

“You too.”

“Not likely.”

The window shut with a clang. Cerulean stood in the dim, red light, his hands clasped, his head bowed.

“This jury has found you guilty.” The Supreme Judge craned her neck.

Justine stood alone on the floating dock, her wrists and ankles bound with chains.

“Do you have anything to say?”

A mocking grin formed at the corners of Justine’s lips. “I regret nothing.”

“Very well.” The Supreme Judge frowned. “I will read your sentence. You are to be turned off, and your body will be locked in Bothmal Penal Internment forever or until such time as the information encrypted into your brain is deemed useful. Do you understand?”

"I do."

Two security drones placed heavy hands on Justine's shoulders and led her from the room.

One by one, the delegates filed out and the vast wings emptied. The courtroom grew dark as millions of holoscreens switched to yet another stream. Within a few days, the delegates and judge would relegate these memories to deep storage or utter forgetfulness.

Cerulean stood at the head of a large, metal table. He was the only one in the small, red-lit room that wasn't a prisoner, guard, or a technician.

"You came." Justine lay flat on the table. Large metal bands secured her legs, arms, and neck. She twisted her head slightly, smiling crookedly at Cerulean. "To sleep, perchance to dream; aye, there's the rub…all my sins remembered."

"Oldearth poetry?"

"A point well made. 'To be or not to be….'"

Cerulean patted the helpless hand. "It'll be…all right."

A frown puckered Justine's brow. "Being turned off isn't like going to sleep, you know." She turned away. "When a human sleeps, their mind is turning, working, dreaming. When a robot is turned off, its mind is completely inert. Dead." She gazed fixedly ahead, her mouth set in a grim line.

Cerulean sucked in a breath. "But this way, there's at least a chance…for you to…come back."

"Thanks."

A technician cleared his throat. "It's time. Sorry."

Justine's fingers gripped the air, her hand opening and closing, her jaws clenched. Her voice became a whisper. "I'm… scared…."

Cerulean placed his hands on hers.

The technician swiped a bar on his datapad.

Cerulean watched Justine's eyes widen and freeze, her mechanical body jerking against the restraints like a living thing. Her hand fell limp and no longer gripped his. His jaw clenched as he swallowed hard. "Goodbye, Justine."

"Sir?" The technician looked up from his datapad, a puzzled frown on his face.

The table slid into a receiving hole in the wall.

"Nothing." Cerulean turned away.

"It wasn't human. Sir…?"

The door clanged behind Cerulean.

CHAPTER TWO

For One Purpose

Seventy Years Later

Slowly, deliberately, a light scalpel moved over cold flesh. "Tell me, do you fear death?" Mitholie, a brilliant Cresta renowned throughout the interplanetary scientific community, fixed his companion with a hard gaze as they stood in the bright-lit Crestar laboratory.

Taug, an up-and-coming apprentice, let a tentacle drift through the warm salt water of his bio-suit. His large, golden, watery eyes gazed coolly at the specimen lying suspended in the examination tube. "No. Why should I fear a void?" His eyes slowly rose to meet the elder's scrutiny.

"Well—" Sensitive tentacles curled about the delicate equipment as Mitholie's green eyes returned to the subject of their examination. "—your sociological profile says you...dislike death." The light scalpel cut deeper, revealing bone. Mitholie's mouth orifice lit up in a pleased smile.

Taug moved his bio-suit slightly nearer, bending over the examination tube. His eyes, lit by the dim, icy-blue lighting, flickered over the specimen. "I don't fear death. I see it as a waste."

"A waste?"

"Yes. I calculate waste on how hard it is to retrieve lost data." Taug sucked in water letting it drift slowly over his gills. "A brain sack once destroyed is gone, forever beyond our reach."

Mitholie scanned each of the specimen's organs carefully, individually. "But what if I no longer need that mind?"

"It's hard to tell when and how something might be useful, or even worse, necessary."

"You have an...intriguing mind." Mitholie turned a lump of flesh in his tentacles.

Taug watched intently. "Beyond that, there is practical reality. I'm neither a trained soldier nor an assassin." He gestured with waving tentacles, "Like you, science is my passion."

"Your father's pet project has been identified—alive." Mitholie's eyes remained fixed on his work, ignoring Taug.

Taug slowly exhaled water. "I would say that was impossible, but I know the High Tribunal must be certain or else you wouldn't have told me." His mouth orifice remained in a fixed smile. "Is this a favor? Am I being offered a chance to commit suicide before the messy business of torture, trial, and execution?"

Mitholie spasmed, his long body wiggling with glee, "No such dramatics, no." His tentacles released the delicate equipment; he looked Taug in the eye. "The High Tribunal simply wishes you to...purge your father's unfortunate experiment. That done, I'm sure this messy business can be consigned to the dark waters."

Taug's tentacles curled thoughtfully. "Forgotten?"

"And forgiven."

"I'll need its location."

With a flick of a tentacle to his bio-suit, Mitholie effected a transaction. "I'm transferring the data now. By the way, hiring another Cresta to kill it is...unadvised. The High Tribunal wishes the waves of the 'humons' to be kept tranquil, at least for now. Besides, you have contacts? Yes?"

Taug's eyes moved swiftly, scanning the long streams of data crossing before his eyes. "Yes...."

Mitholie laid down his knife and stepped back. "Very good. I'll go with you to the harbor dock."

Taug stepped aside. "Thank you."

Together they moved down the sterile, rounded, white hallway, deep in secretive conversation. Plugging their bio-suits into the wall jacks, they shed them, and came out on the other side of the wall free, gliding through dark water.

The human specimen floated in the examination tube, alone.

Floating in deep space, Bothmal Penal Internment was left deliberately unmarked on any space charts. Its layout was confusing and disorienting; carved from an asteroid, it stood as a grim reminder of what could happen to one if you angered enough powerful beings. Many sentient races held a similar vision of hell, and those imprisoned at Bothmal all agreed that if it wasn't hell—it was right next-door.

Zenith stood beside the docking bay port, scanning a list of names being streamed to him. Long ago, he had been fully human, but the allure of immortality had led him to enhancing most of his body with synthetic replacements, including his eyes. He would celebrate his four hundredth birthday this year, if he continued the practice. A heavy trans-platinum chest guard protected his vital organs. Over this he wore a synth-weave robe with a hefty handgun resting on his hip.

As the Chief Warden of Bothmal, Zenith knew the tangled structure like the back of his bio-metal hand and had several backup maps downloaded to his brain, just in case.

An interstellar ship, several times larger than the skyscrapers of Oldearth, docked nearby with its boarding tube neatly extended. Only one passenger exited the ship.

Taug moved slowly down the platform, flexing his tentacles in his new bio-suit. Biomechanical three-toed feet moved him smoothly over the floor, keeping his center of gravity low.

"Ah...Taug." Zenith deftly pronounced the name that popped

up in his holo-vision. "Pleased to meet you." He inclined his head, motioning with his arm. "This way, if you please."

Taug mimicked the bow and moved silently after his host.

"I hope you'll forgive us for giving you this guided tour rather than allowing you to down-stream your own maps." Zenith turned slightly. "Security, you know."

Taug spoke, his voice synthesized. "I do."

"You're here on business?"

Taug's brow furrowed.

Zenith's grin turned malicious, "You're not here to visit a relative...?"

"Certainly not! As you say, it's business. I simply need to see if someone is still...available."

The burly, six-foot human guard was not happy to see the large, soft-bodied Cresta in a gleaming black mechanical exoskeleton lumber toward him. His squint-eyed frown kept pleasantries to a minimum.

Taug strode forward. His tentacles arched stiffly at his side as he assumed the air of a harassed official, which was not off the mark. The journey to Bothmal had been long and exhausting. He hated the tough, unrelenting metallic form that allowed him to move and breathe on land, but he had little choice. Terrestrials dominated the universe. He felt out of sorts and hungry, but this part of his plan could not be delayed.

"I have an appointment." Taug pinched a computer chip with his tentacle and dropped it on to the guard's palm.

The guard inserted it into his datapad. Scowling, he jerked his head toward the back room. "Oh, it's you. I was wondering who in darkness would want it. After all these years, it's probably not any good. I'd start fresh if I were you."

Taug shook his head, the water in his breathing helm swishing with each motion. Water dripped down the side of his face. "Good thing you're not me."

The guard sneered his reply.

The two shuffled through the doorway into a back room where Justine lay immobile on a steel table, the same table where she had been turned off. Taug stared at the figure and appraised its strength, noting its perfect symmetry and conjecturing on its intelligence. He turned to the guard.

"Now, please."

The guard hesitated. "Like I said, it's probably no good, but if you want to waste your time—"

Taug cleared his throat.

The guard punched some numbers into his datapad and swiped it with two fingers.

Justine jerked.

The guard jumped back but threw out his hand protectively in front of Taug. "You never can tell how these things'll react. She could go bloody ballistic, if you know what I mean."

Taug stood motionless. His eyes narrowed as he studied Justine's response.

She opened her eyes, turned her head, and stared first at Taug and then at the guard.

Taug nodded. "She is awake. Everything looks fine. You may leave us."

The guard shook his head. "You sure? She could sit up and throttle you as soon as I walk out the door."

"Will you throttle me, Justine?"

Justine sat up, her gaze fixed on Taug. "Should I?"

The guard stifled a laugh.

Taug ignored the guard and returned Justine's intense stare. "No."

"Then I won't."

Taug's gaze shifted back to the guard. "Thank you. You may leave."

With a shrug, the guard shuffled to toward the doorway. "Okay, it's your neck. If I hear a scream…or something…I'll—"

Justine flicked her gaze to the guard. "You wouldn't have time."

The guard stalked out the door.

Taug stepped back, allowing Justine room to shift herself off the bed. She stood and appeared to be appraising her internal workings.

"Are you all right?"

"It appears so."

Taug meandered toward a conference table and a pair of comfortable chairs. "Please, let's sit. You can hardly imagine what I've been through to get here. Interminable bureaucrats... but, never mind." Taug lowered his stiff body onto a chair and sighed. He sniffed into the breathing helm and allowed the briny liquid to play over his face.

Justine strode over and stood by him. "I'd rather pace if you don't mind. I've been lying around for...how long?"

"Approximately seventy years, give or take, depending on whose calendar you use these days. Since we'll be settling on Newearth, you might as well get used to their systems of measurement."

"Why? I mean, why have you...?"

"Turned you back on?"

"I would have said awakened."

"Yes, I suspected as much. You seem to consider yourself... human. I hope that won't be a problem."

Justine did not break her stride. "You haven't answered my question."

"I awakened you because I need you."

Justine paced across the cylindrical room.

Taug's eyes followed her. "What do you know about Crestar?"

Justine stopped and peered inward. She refocused her gaze on Taug. "Apparently, my databank remains intact. No memory wipe of any kind?"

Taug shrugged. "A very persuasive advocate advised against it. A Luxonian, I believe."

With a stiff nod, Justine clasped her hands behind her back and resumed a professional mode. "Crestar, home of over twenty-seven billion life forms. A water planet ruled by a coalition of seven leading scientists, called the Ingal. Notorious for unprecedented experimentation on other beings—"

Two tentacles admonished Justine into silence. "Stop. You've been brainwashed by those on the Inter-Alien Alliance—"

Justine leaned forward, her eyes flashing. "No!" She glared down at Taug. "I am incapable of being brainwashed. Especially not by the very beings that nearly destroyed me."

Taug nodded. "Good to know. Please...." He nodded toward the chair. "Sit."

Justine perched on the edge of the available chair, her back straight and uncompromising.

Taug sighed. "You must understand my position. I am a Cresta caught between worlds. I believe in my culture, but at the same time, I fear we are heading to our doom."

Justine pursed her lips. She folded her hands in her lap, her gaze fixed on Taug.

"I have a plan to assist my race, but I need your help to see it through. During your long sleep, a new force has arisen in the universe. It is called by the remarkably unimaginative name 'Newearth.' Do you happen to know anything about Oldearth?"

Justine's gaze hardened. "I am party composed of human DNA."

"That was not my question."

"I know everything about their history and downfall up until I was shut down."

Taug nodded and struggled out of his chair. "That would be year twenty-three of what the human remnant calls their 'Hidden Years.'" He padded to a wall screen and pushed a button. A light flared and the screen illuminated the starry universe.

"They stayed on Lux for forty years, resettled Newearth, and lived in relative obscurity until our leadership recognized an opportunity." Taug tapped a keypad and the image zoomed through space until it focused on Newearth spinning in all its blue-green glory. "We invaded successfully until the Luxonians took the humans' part and negotiated a peace treaty called the Inter-Alien Alliance." He tapped again and the image refocused on a human city. Low lying buildings dotted the landscape, and humans bustled about in self-made importance.

Justine stared at the screen in unblinking fascination.

Taug looked from Justine to the image. "I've been ordered to serve in a city called Vandi and accomplish a, shall we say, *delicate* task. It is hoped that I will learn ways to secure a stronger position for my government in the alliance."

Justine's gaze slid to Taug's face. Her lips stiffened. "I am not for hire."

Taug shrugged. He flicked off the image, breaking the trance. "I didn't say you were. I simply have plans for myself...and Newearth."

"What plans?"

"They can't be shared at this early stage. I just need someone with your abilities at my disposal."

"Why?"

"I may be forced to kill someone, a mixed-breed accident, but I'm not particularly suited to committing acts of murder. Especially since no one can discover an association between me and the—"

"Object?"

"Yes, I guess you could say that. Though he does have a name." Taug folded his tentacles together in a meditative motion. "You see, he does not appear to be a threat at the moment, but he could become one. I need to consider the situation carefully. In the meantime, I must be ready to act—if necessary."

"What's its name?"

"He is not an *it*, though I suppose.... Still, I object. His name is Derik Erland, and you are to treat him with respect. He is part human, part Cresta."

"So, I'm an assassin—again?"

"If need be."

Justine tapped her thigh as she circled the room. "Why not make it easy on yourself? Give me a description and its location and I'll take care of it. After all, you just gave me back my life. I ought to do a little...something."

Taug chuckled. "You'll have me convinced that you are sentient before long. No, I can't simply kill Derik. After all, he may be worth more alive. My father, Taurgon, created him. He believed, quite naively, that once races begin interbreeding, then divisions melt away. I'm not such a fool."

"So? What's the mixed-breed worth to you?"

"He might be the answer to every Cresta's deepest aspiration—immortality and nearly infinite power. Once we are able to successfully graft our intellect onto other beings, we can simply regenerate ourselves as often as need be."

"There are creatures that do something similar. I believe they are called parasites."

"Ah, but there would be a difference. We would not simply live off our host; we would become more…a greater being in our own right. We might even rival the creator in time."

"Who?"

Taug raised a tentacle. "I've already said too much." He rose stiffly to his feet. "I have awakened you for one purpose: to be of service to me. At some point the High Council might have decided that they needed your bed, and then where would you be? Recycled perhaps? That would be a shame. You have a lot of history tucked into that synthetic brain of yours. You might become much more than an assassin. Again, I'll have to wait and see. In the meantime, come with me."

Taug led the way toward the door where the guard snorted with irritation.

Justine took one final glance at the abandoned, steel bed and marched after Taug. "Where are we going?"

"Newearth. It's my home for now. You may call it what you wish."

CHAPTER THREE

The Mingling Throng

Cerulean stared up at the lofty two-storied cabin with large gabled windows and wide surrounding porch and grinned. It was everything he had dreamed of and more. Turning his head, his gaze swept over the lofty panorama, skimming across the waters of the great lake. Huge, white geese flew high above the bubbling crests that rolled upon the shore on this fine, summer evening.

He was exhausted, but he was getting used to that sensation. Ever since he won his last great tussle with the Inter-Alien Alliance Committee, he had promised himself a retreat and a rest to build up his depleted reserves. He had been fighting Luxonians, humans—and pretty much everyone else—for far too long.

Even as his shoulders relaxed, shuffled footsteps forced him to turn his gaze from the blue-green water, across the pine-strewn forests, and back to the front of his cabin. There, on the dirt trail, a small assembly of men and women came to a huddled stop. His whole body stiffened and he frowned. *Who the—?*

The eldest figure spoke first. "Excuse us, sir. We hate to bother you, but are you Cerulean, the Luxonian leader of the Inter-Alien—?"

Cerulean sighed, his shoulders drooping. *Oh, God.* He peered into their tanned faces, appraised their homespun clothing and work-roughened hands, and repented his impatience. *Give me strength*. "I'm not the leader of anything anymore. I've retired."

A tall, extremely thin representative of the group stepped forward. He strangled a straw hat in his hands and shuffled his feet. "But you are that Luxonian?"

Cerulean shrugged. "I helped patch together the Inter-Alien Alliance on Newearth, yes." His gaze roved over the group as a baby, hidden from site, squalled. "Is there something I can do for you?"

The tall man took another hesitant step forward, his brown-eyed gaze looking up the slope and into Cerulean's piercing eyes. "My name is Able, and you see, we're settlers here, neighbors, kind of. We call ourselves the Amens. Separatists. We want to return to the ways of our ancestors and live in union with God's created world."

A wavering grin played on Cerulean's lips. "The Bhuac would love you."

Able's face brightened as a smile broke the straight line of his mouth. "Yes, sir, we know of them, and they do support our dream, but they have their own struggles. They've been persecuted too."

"Someone's persecuting you?" Cerulean pursed his lips. "Listen, this is no way to get acquainted. Please, step up here. The porch is large enough, and I have a few chairs. I've even got some food inside, if you like."

The two women offered sidelong glances and grinned as the elder one shifted her baby from under a blanket onto her hip. The other men started forward. Able put up his hand. "We wouldn't think of disturbing you, but it would be a kindness to speak in the shade. The sun is hot, though the breeze you have up here is a real blessing."

Cerulean opened his hands in a welcoming gesture, and the group filed past and climbed the four wooden steps. In quick jerking motions, he dragged chairs forward. "I just moved in, and I haven't gotten everything set up yet."

Able waved his hand anxiously. "Please, we only want a few

moments of your time to explain our mission and why we need your help—if you don't mind."

Cerulean leaned against a post, suppressed a sigh, and nodded.

The three men moved into the background, while the two women settled into the available chairs. The mother rocked her baby with a relieved smile.

Able continued to wring his hat as he focused his attention on Cerulean. "You see, we were granted immigration status four years back, but it took time to organize our people and buy the right plot of land. We don't want to trouble anybody, and we have no prejudice against any race, but we do have rules we must abide by. We choose to live simply and in union with nature. That's why we moved into this wilderness over a year ago. At first, everything went along as planned. We built homes for our members and worked the land so that we could plant, and we even made a few contacts with businesses in Waukee."

Cerulean saluted Able with an appreciative nod. "Sounds like you're a marvel of planning and industry."

Able accepted the compliment with a shy smile before his face sobered. "Well, we aren't afraid of hard work, but we are afraid of death threats."

"Death threats?"

"About six months ago, a mob of Uanyi showed up and told us to move on, that we're not welcome in this district. I told them that we had the authorization of the Inter-Alien Alliance Committee to buy land here and that we have full human rights to form our own society as we see fit. I even showed them our data chip authorizing—"

"They ignored it, didn't they? Uanyi don't much care for humans. They'll continue trying to intimidate you if they think they can get away with it."

"They did a whole lot more than intimidate. They beat three of our men senseless and threatened to come back and kill our women and children if we didn't leave."

Cerulean's frown deepened as he pushed off from the post.

"Did you inform the Human Rights Bureau? Get any Interventionists out here?"

Able sighed. "A couple of Interventionists flew in and took down our complaint. But they told us that since we didn't have any hard evidence, it's going to be difficult to follow up. I went all the way to Vandi and issued a formal complaint, but the Human Rights detective I met said that threats against humans were too numerous to deal with. Humans are the minority and what with the Cresta, Uanyi, Ingot, and Luxonians—pardon me, sir, but not all Luxonians are like you—we find that we have very few rights and even fewer friends. At least not anyone who can help to defend us against a band of unruly Uanyi."

Cerulean sat on the top step and rubbed his hands over his face. He let his gaze absorb the vast beauty before him and took a deep breath. Craning his neck, he looked back at the assembly.

Able blinked and glanced away. "You can't help us?"

Cerulean rose and strode to the woman and the now sleeping infant. He smiled at the bright pink face nestled against his mother's enfolding body. With a gentle finger, he caressed the tousled, straw-colored hair and peered into the mother's eyes. "I'll do everything I can. I have friends. Just give me a few days to track down these Uanyi idiots, and I might be able to convince them that it'll be in their best interests to leave you alone."

Relieved smiles broke across every face. The mother's eyes filled with tears as she reached out and gripped Cerulean's hand, her voice a shy whisper. "Thank you."

Cerulean nodded. "Well, I don't know about you, but solving problems makes me hungry. How about you come in and I'll scratch up…something?"

A burst of laughter followed this as the two women shuffled to their feet. Able gripped Cerulean's shoulder. "On the contrary, you'll be our guest tonight, if you'll do us the honor. My wife is one of the best cooks on the planet, and her sister can brew the finest tea this side of the moon."

Cerulean grinned at Able's soft, delighted eyes. "I can hardly wait to meet them."

Perching his rumpled hat jauntily on his head, Able grinned back. "You already have." The small troop shuffled down the steps with Able guiding the woman and baby. He looked back at Cerulean as he stopped on the trail, the rest of the group traipsing down the incline. "I'll come back at sunset and lead you over. We'll gather everyone to celebrate."

Cerulean sighed. "I hope you aren't counting on me too much. I'll do the best I can, but you know, trouble is part of life here on Newearth."

Able bobbed his head in agreement and turned away with a wave. "True, true, but we've got the best reason in the universe to be glad. It isn't every day that you meet a new friend."

Cerulean's gaze followed the small group as they traipsed away. An odd sensation made him look down. His legs were shaking. In fact, his whole body shook. Collapsing on the bottom step, he held his head in his hands and groaned.

Stopping just outside the Vandi Transport Center, Justine stared. Her eyes dilated for maximum reception. Humans wearing every assortment of casual and formal attire, insect-like Uanyi with their soft, rubbery exoskeletons, Ingots in their bulky techno-organic armor and breather helms, Crestas with their tentacles and mechanical exoskeletons, and Bhuacs, appearing like fairies from an Oldearth storybook, all bustled about, intermingling on an ordinary city street.

So this is Newearth? Justine smiled to herself. *At least I am free of Taug for a few hours. Pity the universe hasn't improved its business class accommodations. Still, I won't complain. I am alive, after all.*

Moving forward, Justine fell into step with the scurrying mix of life forms. Her heightened sense of hearing and sight allowed her to absorb vast and complex information with relative ease. After crisscrossing the main sections of the developing city, she recorded a perfect map of each of the important structures: hospitals, schools, shops, assorted businesses, and government buildings. Each alien race had an embassy suited to its specific needs.

The Crestar structure enclosed a two-hundred-meter pool filled with imported Crestonian water and loaded with the best livestock that Crestar officials could afford.

The Uanyi embassy was built half-underground with a smooth, rounded surface, which appeared much like an enormous anthill, meeting the needs of the insect-like race perfectly but sending their human neighbors into fits of disgust.

The Ingots, being fond of straight lines and geometric shapes, devised their structure so that it looked very much like a computer chip, which created a startling contrast to the rest of the Vandi environment.

The Bhuacs' obsessive devotion to nature compelled them to build their embassy on the outskirts of the city, imitating the trees and hills so perfectly that many citizens simply passed by, never realizing that the structure was anything more than the natural environment.

At Vandi Central Park, Justine stopped at the sound of laughter. A small group of children swung on a swing set that allowed them to fly high into the air, jump, and fall into a safety net. An older boy encouraged a younger child to let go and free fall.

"It's safe. You saw me do it, Joe. Go on. Let go! You'll love it."

Two younger girls watched in mesmerized fascination as Joe flew higher and higher, his grip tightening on the swing.

Justine's gaze swept the assembly. A mirrored smile crept across her features at the children's enthusiasm. It did look like fun.

Suddenly, Justine's eye caught the glint of a ragged piece of metal. She focused her gaze on the top bolt that held the structure together, attaching the swing structure to the welcoming net. Snap!

Pounding across the short grass, Justine reached out for the child just as he finally gained the courage to let go. As he flew up, Justine dived. With her arms out stretched, she slid across the gravel towards the small falling body. A snapping crack rent the air as the structure broke completely. Shrieks filled the park, and Justine felt the heavy thud as the child landed in her arms. She leaned into the fall and allowed its momentum to skid her further along the gravel. She'd have to make repairs before she met with Taug this evening.

When the last pebble skidded to a halt, Justine gazed into the small crumpled face, the eyes squeezed shut, lips wobbling. She folded her arms protectively around the child. His piercing blue eyes opened wide, startled, amazed. His expression of gratitude touched the depth of her being.

A pudgy, tanned hand pressed on her shoulder.

Justine, forced to unlock her gaze, glanced back, following the trail of the arm, the shoulder, and then another face, wide-eyed and blanched with fear. She sucked in a breath and offered a small grin. Straightening, she shifted the boy from her arms onto his own shaky feet.

His hand gripped hers tightly, squeezing her thumb.

With a comforting pat, she rose to her knees and looked him in the eyes again. "You're okay. That was a close call. Lucky I saw the hinge break."

The older boy pressed closer, putting his arm around little Joe. He peered deep into Justine's eyes, shaking his head. "You moved so fast. It was—I don't know. I never saw anything like it. He could've broke his neck if you hadn't caught him."

Justine quickly brushed her pant legs, covering the tears and the lack of blood. She straightened to her full height and tilted her head as she appraised the elder boy. "You would have done the same, if you had seen it in time."

The elder boy shook his head again. The girls shuffled closer, their gazes shifting between Joe and Justine. The smaller girl touched Joe's arm, stroking him like a cat, while the other pointed to Justine's legs.

“That must hurt. You want to go to a doctor and get it looked at? My mom’ll pay. You saved Joe.”

Justine’s face twitched in the glimmering, late afternoon sunlight. The sounds of the bustling city carried on as usual. “I’m fine. A little scrape doesn’t bother me.” She stepped away from the small group and glanced back. “Glad to help.”

She turned and, sweeping her long legs across the street, entered the mingling throng.

CHAPTER FOUR

Good Fortune

Clare shielded the sunlight from her somber brown eyes as she stared in fixed fascination. A Bald Eagle soared into the azure sky with a snake dangling from its beak. Shivers ran through her slim figure. *Lord, how awful! And I don't even like snakes…yet he's glorious, can't deny that.* The twin sensations of revulsion and admiration warred within until she heard a screech in the distance, forcing her gaze from the sky.

Dawn had just broken, and a vast array of beings had already flooded Vandi, ready to face another late summer day. The contrast between the conflicting races, working and living together, each jostling for their place of primacy, filled her with a fresh sense of purpose. She was one of the lucky ones. At least she had a career, something she loved and could devote her life to…not like some of these alien slugs who were merely fulfilling a politician's promise, a diplomat's dream, or worse yet, a bureaucrat's nightmare.

She studied the screeching being. The human wasn't hurt. The Cresta's autoskimmer hadn't even touched him, but you'd think his leg had been taken off by the way he reacted. Such a lot of screaming! A crowd was gathering.

"Creepy Cresta! What'da'ya think you're doing? Swimming

across the street? You can't fishtail like that and expect—"

With no obvious expectations in mind except to stop the human's tongue, the Cresta moved in for a grab.

Using mosquito-like quickness, the human offered a stinging slap to the Cresta's hindquarters and dodged away, whining.

That did it. The Cresta's usually controlled demeanor devolved into a snorting catastrophe.

The crowd laughed.

Clare strode away from the gathering crowd as the whirling blades of the Interventionists copter approached.

A woman's voice rang shrill above the noise. "Flip him on his back, boys, then they can haul him off easier!"

Score one for the home team! Clare grinned and shook her head at the irony of it all. She hated mindless blood sports, but she couldn't help cheering every time a human got the better of an alien.

She sailed across the street, scrolling through her datapad. Her smile faded. Mrs. Lane Hoggsworth had been found dead in her home late last night, Day 73, Year 53 Newearth reckoning. Clare's brows furrowed in irritation. If the woman had been more important, Human Services would have pulled in a high-profile investigator, but as it stood, she was only important to her family, and they didn't have much money or influence. After all, the deplorably dark saying, "It's only a human," held sway in a world where humans were the minority and considered, by some, to rate only slightly above their wildlife counterparts—like snakes and eagles.

She checked the time and her scowl deepened. If Bala showed up late for his first big assignment, there'd be trouble. She wasn't going to blow this case, not for him and his silly-fool addiction to hearth and home. Not that she minded his family-ties mindset. Everyone had a right to an obsession. She planned to build a safe house in the wilderness someday. She had even saved up for flying lessons. But with each new case, she realized there was no escaping Newearth reality. Not even on an island.

Clare rounded the corner and ducked into The Breakfast Nook, nearly colliding with Bala's skinny frame. "You're late!"

"Am not!" Bala held up his datapad and smirked. "Thirty seconds to go." He tapped his finger on his wrist screen, his copper-colored face breaking into a wide smile. "Good thing I have a timer, or I might've been. You should have seen Kendra jump when the alarm went off. I set it so loud the whole street could hear it."

Clare shook her head and waved him through the door. "It amazes me that you manage to keep your head attached. Some folks don't take kindly to loud noises. How about if—"A seven-foot Ingot hostess with thick bio-armor and leathery skin ushered them to a booth in the back. "—A Bhuac took offence? You know how irritable they get with high-pitched sounds. One could have slipped over and picked off half of your family."

Bala grimaced. "You're always exaggerating! It so happens that we do have a shape-shifter down the way, but we've been on very good terms ever since I saved one of their pod-thingys from submersion. How it got in the gutter—don't even ask—but I was in the right place at the right time and, you know, as secretive as they can be, they really do have a deep capacity for gratitude."

"Oh, please!" Clare looked up at the impatient hostess. "Coffee, strong as you can make it while still keeping it liquid, a honey-grain bar, large energizer salad, and fruit of the day."

The hostess turned her full black-eyed glare upon Bala who was perusing the menu as if he hadn't memorized it long ago. "Coffee, cream, toast and...some bacon and eggs."

The hostess lunged. She gripped Bala's heavy plaid shirt and hauled his whole body into the air, leaving Clare stunned into gasping silence.

With arms flailing helplessly, Bala had just enough air to beg. "Just a joke! Really. Kidding. I didn't mean anything... seriously. Let me down. Please?"

The hostess dropped him and shook her datapad in his face. Her techno-organic armor glistened a reddish-purple as her breathing helm hissed. “You want to order, then order. No sick jokes. Eggs and bacon! What next? You think it’s funny to talk like that, but there are some who wouldn’t mind eating you!”

Bala rubbed his neck and sniffed in a long cleansing breath. “You’re right, it was stupid of me. Really… quite insensitive. I’d just been reading some Oldearth novels, you know. Fiction? Stories? Anyway, they made everything sound so delicious— Sorry! I didn’t mean that. I just—”

Clare’s glare could have melted a polar cap. “Would you order before you get us both killed?”

“Coffee, chocolate pudding, and a raisin-nut bar, extra-large.”

The hostess pounded away, huffing.

“You are such an idiot sometimes, you know that? What was I thinking when I hired you?”

Bala’s eyes twinkled mischievously. “Oh, you were thanking God above that I’m going to save you from the hideous fate of trying to solve all of humanity’s problems single-handedly. It is funny how we don’t recognize our good fortune when it’s staring right at us.” Bala’s grin practically engulfed his face.

Slapping her hand on the table, Clare leaned in and hissed, “Good fortune? It was pity, pure and simple. I couldn’t let that lovely wife of yours and your brood of—how many is it now—six? Six helpless humanoids suffer from the sad fate of having *you* as the head of provisions.”

Bala turned his less-than-symmetrical face aside to display his profile. “At least I’m as handsome as a Greek god, you’ve gotta give me that.”

The hostess returned and slammed down two mugs of steaming coffee, slopping a little on Bala’s hand.

Bala slipped his hand into his lap with a stifled “Ooo-ahh,” looking every which way but at the hostess.

Clare nodded her appreciation and waited till the hostess stomped off.

“As I was saying, we have a job to do. Mrs. Hoggsworth didn’t blow a hole through herself. Her husband is nearly suicidal and her son wants revenge. Neither of them have much money, but the son has connections to the Michigan territories. I've got my eye on a little spot over there. If we can work out a deal, I might be able to find a place for my island getaway, and you might get a little stretch in the woodlands on the northern coast. It'd be away from the usual madness, and you could raise your clan in relative safety." Clare clapped her hand on her forehead. "So long as you don't go around ordering bacon and eggs."

Bala leaned in, returning her earlier hiss. "Listen, there are those of us who believe that meat and eggs are not off the menu. There's nothing wrong with a bit of animal flesh, so long as it isn't from one of the sentient beings."

"Tell that to one of the Race Relation Councilors, and you'll find yourself in treatment, boy-o."

The hostess slipped two metal plates with their breakfast assortment in front of them and twitched as another customer snapped for her attention.

Bala and Clare stared at the plates, switched them, and began to eat. Bala talked around chews. "So where do we begin?"

"At the house. The Hoggsworths live on Memory Lane near the shore, right across from the University. I went by there earlier to make some initial inquiries. As I said, Mr. Hoggsworth is near despair while his son, Tim, is ready to kill someone. I promised we'd be back, so I want to swing by first and talk to the neighbors, review the facts, and see I missed any other bio samples." Dusting away the crumbs from her grain bar, Clare tucked into her salad.

"And me?"

"Oh, this is good!" Clare took a long sip of her coffee. "You're going to take the samples back to the lab, run them, and do a background check on everyone near the scene. Ordinary stuff. I'm convinced the history professor, Baltimore, is guilty. He got into an exchange with Mrs. Hoggsworth over a history paper he assigned Junior. I guess he's into revisionist history, rewriting the past age, and making things look nice for the present." Clare's gaze scrolled down her datapad. "Mrs. Hoggsworth apparently took exception. Not surprising, though she was a fool to make it so obvious. Everyone knows that the professors are protected." She glanced at Bala. "I doubt Old Baltimore killed her himself. He's human with a bad back and skinny arms. Hardly the type to face an enraged mother one-on-one. " She wiped her lips and pushed her plate aside. "My guess is, he hired a thug, probably one of those— "

The hostess slammed down a metallic fist and stared at Clare. "You paying?"

Clare's eyebrows rose. "I always do."

"The cashier's broken. You'll have to pay me directly."

Clare tilted her head sideways and scanned the room. It was nearly empty. *Stupid! You're supposed to be better trained than this!* Kicking Bala under the table, she placed both hands on the table edge and the two of them flung the light structure into the hostess' chest.

Jumping to her feet, Clare called for the owner. "Hey, Riko! Your help wants me to pay her directly. That okay with you?"

Riko, a slim Uanyi marched forward. His soft, rubbery exoskeleton gleamed through a crisp, white shirt. His enormous eyes bulged as his crab-like mandibles twitched under his breathing mask. "I told you last time, it'd be the salvage yard if you tried it again!"

Clare dashed to the cashier in attendance, a pretty, human-looking Bhuac. In a matter of seconds, Clare paid her bill and tugged at Bala's sleeve.

"You don't want to see this. Really."

Bala stared, fascinated. "You think he'll really—?"

"That's not our concern. We're humans, remember?"

"Yeah, but where I grew up, we all got along. We helped out when— "

"You were living off-planet in some airy-fairy religious fantasyland. This is Newearth, boy-o, this is the real world, and here, you don't get involved with other species. Let's go."

Bala turned as a loud hiss issued from the backroom, where

Riko had ushered the hostess moments before. Clare stepped on the threshold when a hand stopped her.

"Excuse me. But are you Detective Smith?"

Clare appraised the thirty-something man in front of her. He was tall, with dark curly hair, chocolate brown eyes, a jutting chin, massive chest, and large hands. He certainly wouldn't be up for any "ideal specimen" awards, but then again, you never knew. There was that hideous guy from Old-Chicago. Women fell for him right and left. *Funny that. Not that I'm looking—* Clare shook herself.

"What can I do for you?"

"Can we talk somewhere...privately?"

Clare checked her datapad and flashed a glance at Bala. "We have an appointment in a few minutes, but if you want, I can meet you later."

"Where?"

"How about the Coliseum? The government types will be leaving about dusk."

"That'll work. Could I buy you dinner?"

"I never eat with prospective clients. But I'll take some coffee—decaf or I'll never sleep."

"Fine."

Clare turned away but then stopped herself. "Is it a murder case?"

"No, a missing person."

"Okay. You got a name? Maybe I can look something up when I have a free moment."

"You can't. He's not missing—yet."

As Derik stood in front of the Oldearth-styled restaurant known as the Coliseum, the city slowed to an evening pace. Derik ran his fingers up and down his arms. The bulges were definitely larger. He wiped sweat from his brow and wondered again about the sea scent that followed him everywhere.

The rosy sunset settled behind the silhouetted trees in the park, sweeping his anxieties aside. He marveled at the simple beauty that arrived with glorious regularity each day. If only—

"Hi! Have you been waiting long?"

Derik nearly jumped out of his skin, though he realized with a tinge of fear that his skin no longer felt like his own. "Uh, no. I've— I've just been admiring—the sunset." He waited for the smirk… the bewildered stare.

Clare turned and joined him, facing west. A sudden breeze caught her hair, sending wisps cascading against her pink cheeks.

Derik marveled. How could such stern, uncompromising lips be transformed into such soft, inviting— "Uh? What?"

Clare frowned. "I said, I wonder why God keeps painting such beautiful pictures for such an unappreciative audience."

Derik swallowed. Had she read his mind? "I was just thinking the same thing. Amazing."

"Not really. After all, it's true." Her gaze rolled over him, apparently making a professional appraisal.

Derik cringed at what those eyes would tell her brain. Yeah, he was a big guy, "relative to an elephant" his foster mother used to say. He felt more related to a mouse.

"Well, for starters, I'd like a name. I can't just say, hey you, all the time."

"Yes, of course. My name is Derik, Derik Erland. I'm from the Wisconsin Territories. You ever been there?"

"Yeah, I did some training there. I love the coastal area. So, you want some coffee?"

Derik nodded and led the way up a long flight of stone steps toward the Coliseum's grand structure with its nine-foot metal doors. Without breaking a sweat, he pulled the door open and stepped aside with a curt bow.

After a moment's hesitation, Clare strode into the foyer.

A host in his mid-twenties, clean-shaven and with dark hair and darker eyes, wearing a toga-style outfit, ushered up to them. "At your service."

Clare waved a lazy index finger. "Just coffee, and maybe some of those nut muffins."

The host bowed and gestured toward a side room. Low tables with enormous pillows were arranged sporadically around the perimeter, while round, dark wood tables polished to a high gloss stood in each corner. A low balcony overlooked a huge sports arena where teams vied for a bloody first-place, day and night.

Derik dashed ahead and nearly knocked Clare down in his effort to pull a chair out for her.

Clare's eyebrows rose.

Derik heaved a sigh and offered a weak grin. "Sorry. Don't know my own strength. Still a growing boy, Mom used to say."

"You? You don't look like any boys I know. How old are you?"

Derik cleared his throat, pulling on his shirt collar. "Thirty-five."

Clare sat, her wide-eyed stare appraising his stature. "Your parents had—what? Germanic DNA?"

"Can't say. I was adopted."

Clare's gaze flickered to the sports scene. A hockey game in full swing swirled around the ice, while a five-person fight broke out in the corner. After closing her eyes for a moment, she refastened them on Derik. "Used to?" Clare grimaced. "You said your mom used to say...."

"She's been gone ten years now. She passed away six months after dad."

Clare's eyes softened. "Ouch."

Derik shrugged away old losses and nodded with a quick smile to a small group of middle-aged men who strolled to a table on their left.

Clare leaned back, apparently relaxed. "You know this place pretty well."

"My dad used to bring me here when we were traveling. I love Oldearth history, and he thought...well, let's just say, he always hoped that I'd be inspired by the warrior spirit."

With a twisted smile, Clare sniffed. “With that body, you don’t need to prove anything.”

A puck slammed into a net, followed by a shout, and ten players pummeled the goalie.

Derik grinned at the players’ antics. “If I were just up against humans, that’d be true. But around here—”

The slump-shouldered host set the platter before them. Clare took a sip, darting a glance at the game as a player was dragged off the floor, a trail of blood streaming behind. She pushed the muffin plate away. “So, you want to tell me about the missing person…who isn’t missing…yet?”

Derik picked a muffin to shreds. With an intake of breath, he steadied himself. “It’s me. I’m the missing person.”

Clare chewed her lip, brushed imaginary crumbs from her fingers daintily, and sighed. “Look, if this is some kind of joke or a really weird pick-up routine, I’m going to be seriously disappointed.”

“I’m not joking and, though you are definitely—well, it’s not that.” Derik wrung his hands in a furious twist. “I need to know who I am. I’m not who I thought I was. Or who my parents said I was. Heck, at the moment…I’m not even sure I’m human!”

As the game ended and the players lined up to shake hands, Clare shook her head. “Oookay, I’ll go along for the ride. But I need more. I feel like I just picked up in the middle—”

“James and Monica Erland adopted me as a baby. The official report said that I was a human abandoned at birth at the Wisconsin Center for Human Services. My parents raised me, even homeschooled me so that I wouldn’t have to deal with all the Exos and their prejudices. My dad studied Oldearth history—a great man.”

“Sounds good. But that hardly explains—”

“I was getting to that. My parents noticed that I grew larger and faster than most kids. They figured I came from some Nordic or Germanic strain. They did a test, but when the results came back, they only joked that my DNA broke their machine.

I worried that there was more to it—I was always different." He rubbed his arms. "A few months ago, I noticed a change—a significant change. I'm long past adolescence, but I feel like I'm just now coming into my own. I feel powerful. And my skin—"

A cleanup crew began mopping up the blood as another team assembled on the stadium floor. This time club-wielding Uanyi players lined up against humans armed with Tasers.

Clare's wide eyes swiveled from the stadium to Derik. She frowned. "Your skin...?"

Derik pushed up his sleeve and revealed a thick arm coated in what appeared to be a rubbery shell.

Clare reached out a tentative finger and tapped it. "What is it?"

"I don't know. You see?" Derik leaned in and whispered, huskily. "I'm not human...or at least not pure. I might be a mixed—"

Up flew Clare's hand. "Sheesh! Keep your voice down. Don't even say that!" Blowing air between her lips, she ignored the metallic clang announcing the start of the next game. "I see your problem. I'm just not sure how I can help. You're not really missing. You're clearly not dead. Perhaps you should see a doctor. This might just be some kind of odd skin condition."

Derik shook his head like an obstinate ox. "I can't show this to a doctor! They'd be bound to report it to the authorities." He leaned back and slouched. "How about if I am...mixed? I'm not supposed to exist."

Clare frowned, rubbing her eyes. Screams echoed from the side as cheerleaders from opposing teams tried to out shout each other. "I'm just not sure what to do."

"You're an investigator. So—investigate. I have a little money. I'll pay you myself, and once I know the truth..."

Clare sighed heavily and clasped her hands together. "Listen. No one else knows about your little problem, right? Why not just ignore this? Keep your *irregularities* a secret and pretend you're human. You've made it this far thinking that."

"I can't ignore this!" Derik hissed. "How about if I'm an Ingot or a Uanyi? Do you think I'll be able to keep that a secret? Or worse, how about if I'm a Cresta or some off-world creature I don't even know about?" Closing his eyes a moment, Derik clenched his hands so tightly they shook. "I've always wondered if—"

"Don't! Don't go there! By the Divide, you want to get experimented on, killed...and then experimented on some more? I'll tell you right now; nice beings don't do that kinda stuff. Finding out who's behind this could be very risky."

Derik threw up his hands in surrender. "You're right. I should never have asked you. This is too dangerous, and I've no right to involve anyone else." Derik looked away, blinking back despair. "I'm just glad my parents are gone."

Clare rolled her eyes. "Oh, please! I feel guilty enough. Common sense tells me to run out that door." She waged a finger at the nearest exit to make her point abundantly clear. "Still, I've never been one to shirk a challenge." Clenching her jaw against a deep okay-I-give-in sigh, she straightened and pulled out her datapad. "But listen, if I don't discover anything helpful within a month, I'm dropping your case. I might know someone else who could take it, but he's...well, he's kind of—" Clare reached across the table and patted Derik's hand. "I'll do what I can—promise."

As Derik returned her smile, a Uanyi player clubbed a human across the back. Another human rushed in and started Tasering the Uanyi long past the three-second limit. Whistles blasted from all sides as referees struggled to separate the furious players.

Derik and Clare stared, dumbfounded.

The host returned, his depression replaced by rage. He glared at Derik's arm and pursed his lips.

Derik straightened his sleeve and huffed back. "My account, please."

CHAPTER FIVE

Who Cares?

With a brown bag pressed to his chest, Cerulean savored the sweet taste in his mouth. No matter how long he lived among humans, he never ceased to marvel at the sheer variety of sense stimulations. Oatmeal-raisin-chocolate chip cookies had to be near the top of his personal list of favorites.

The sun lowered toward the horizon, casting long shadows. Gray clouds crisscrossed the sky while gnarled, old trees adorned their leafy tops with shades of pale yellow and brilliant orange. Flocks of geese gathered on the water's edge and made final preparations for their hurried flights to warmer and sunnier climates.

Relaxing on his porch, Cerulean peered down into the valley and watched the miniature forms of his neighbors chop a felled tree into manageable pieces. The distant echo of the axe thwacking to the rhythmic ebb and flow of their alternating strokes comforted him. No one could be sick on such a beautiful day in such a vibrant world. Especially not him.

As he was one of the founders of Newearth, he'd had first pick of the land. He had considered settling on Anne's old homestead, but the emotionally-charged memories overwhelmed him. Instead, he had moved north, into Wisconsin Territory, on property bordering a great lake. It had once been the site of an extensive stone and wood mansion. He had found enough ruins bearing testimony to the past owner's investment to assure him that he was not the first to value this particular view. The blue lake spread majestically before him, while a verdant valley lay to the east. Thick woods shrouded the northwest.

Cerulean sighed. He had accepted the protector role with weary hesitation, but even in their short acquaintance, he had come to love and respect these honest families and the lives they crafted in natural simplicity. Giving in to the innocent pleasure of a sweet morsel, he leaned back and closed his eyes.

"Hey, handsome. Got time for a world-weary detective?"

Cerulean choked on his cookie as he jerked forward.

Clare, looking not unlike her great-great aunt Jackie, stared at him through teasing eyes.

Brushing away imaginary crumbs to regain his stricken dignity, Cerulean glared at her. "Why do you always sneak up on me like that?"

"It's in my job description...being sneaky. How else am I going to find the latest killer?"

Cerulean nudged the other rocker in her direction with his toe. "Yeah, killer-catcher. Here, sit down. Tell me about it. Life has been quiet of late."

Clare plopped down with a heavy sigh, her gaze absorbing the gorgeous scene. "I wish I had a retreat like this."

"You can retreat here—anytime. You know that." Cerulean eyed the dark circles under Clare's eyes and her furrowed brow. "I thought you loved your work. You've wanted to become a Human Services Detective for so long—"

Clare leaned forward, slapping her hands over her eyes and groaned. "Oh, Cerulean, if only you knew!"

Rising, Cerulean shuffled to Clare's side. "Hey, now, it can't be that bad. There's no war declared...that I know of. You're in one piece." Cerulean stroked her hair.

Clare sniffed, raised her head, and rubbed her eyes. "Sorry. It's just that sometimes—"

With a grin, Cerulean waved her explanation aside. "Trust me, I understand—more than you know." He reached for his paper bag. "Want a cookie?"

Clare sighed and pulled out a sample.

"I can do even better than that. See those fellows down there? Their wives grow the best tea this side of the Divide. It's great for the nerves and helps you sleep. How about I brew some?"

A flock of birds settled in the trees off to the left, chirping their last songs of the day. The lake turned from blue to gray-black as clouds marshaled their forces overhead and the sunlight faded into twilight.

"Yeah, sure. I could use something."

Cerulean led the way into a spacious, wood-beamed, country kitchen. He took a canister from the shelf and pried off the top. He motioned to an assortment of cups on the dish rack. "Go ahead; pick one. I'll get the water on."

A puzzle lay strewn across a large, oak table, framed by matching benches. After setting everything in order, Cerulean sat across Clare and motioned to the partially assembled picture of the Luxonian skyline. "It helps pass the time. Feel free."

Clare slid onto the bench and picked up a red border and slid it into an empty slot. It fit perfectly. She shrugged. "Beginner's luck."

Cerulean picked up another piece and considered his options. "So, tell me, why can't you sleep?"

Clare closed her eyes, clenching her hands. "It's these dreams. You remember when my parents died? Everyone said it was an accident, but I never believed that. My mom knew her fungi. She'd never make a mushroom soup out of those poisonous things. The whole thing reeked of foul play."

Cerulean tried to force a piece into place. "Why would anyone want to poison your parents? They had no known enemies. There weren't any aliens around their place for a hundred kilometers. Frankly, I could never make any sense out of their deaths either. It could've been an accident."

Clare linked three pieces together, puckering her brow as

she considered where to put them. "Shortly before their deaths, I started having dreams. Something...someone came to me at night, a mind visitor of sorts. He had a husky voice, like he was using a translator or something. He seemed to want to be my friend—at first. He told me he was lonely." Clare dropped the pieces and they fell apart. She shuddered. "I was just a little kid; I believed him. My parents used to talk about how Great-Aunt Anne thought you were a guardian angel. And when I asked what an angel was they described a heavenly spirit. So, I thought—"

Cerulean swallowed. His face paled as he stopped trying to force the piece and considered it more closely. "So, what happened to him?"

Clare fiddled with the pieces she had dropped. "Nothing much. He'd come every now and again and ask me how I felt. Weird. He liked it when I described my feelings. He knew a lot about me, but he always wanted more."

"Comforting you?"

"No." Clare shook her head, wisps of disheveled hair falling into her eyes. "He just wanted to know how I felt—no matter how bad. I told my parents, but they thought I'd been dreaming. And I figured they must be right—until the day they died. He hadn't communicated with me for a while and I'd thought he was gone, but that night, he came back. He wanted to know how it felt to see my parents dead." Tears slipped down Clare's cheeks. "I told him to go away and never come back."

Cerulean's gaze fixed on Clare. "Did he?"

"He tried a few more times...but I closed my mind. I recited math formulas, sang snatches of songs, prayers...anything to block him out. Eventually he...it gave up." Clare heaved a sigh as she surveyed the puzzle again.

The kettle whistled. Cerulean rose and poured steamy, hot water into the teapot. He nudged the sugar towards Clare and returned to his bench. "I wish I had something a bit stronger."

Wearily, Clare poured the fresh brew into her cup. She took a tentative sip and forced a smile. "It's good."

Cerulean poured himself a cup and blew a cleansing breath. "So, what's brought all this back now? Has he returned?"

"Not exactly. It's just that I'm working for this guy, Derik. He's supposed to be human but now...well, it looks like he's the product of some kind of a mixed-race experiment. From everything I've discovered, and I've been doing a lot of digging, there have been only two other cases of this kind, and they were hushed up real quick. All evidence was destroyed and everyone pretended that it never happened. Lucky for me, I have friends, so I was able to interview some key people."

"You think this guy is related somehow to the voice you heard?"

"I don't know. All I know is that I've carried this secret with me for twenty years, and this guy's been lied to all his life. As far as some races are concerned, we're nothing but pests, for others, we're lab rats."

"Very illegal."

"Oh, but it happens. Don't bat your innocent blue eyes at me. I know you don't like to think about it, but even Luxonians...."

Cerulean frowned. "That was a long time ago and only *some* Luxonians."

Clare picked up another puzzle piece and waved it in the air. "I know, and I'm not trying to be unfair. It's just that I really want to help this guy, but I'm afraid of what I'm up against."

Cerulean snapped his piece into place. "Once you have identified his DNA, what more can you do? You figured that out, right?"

"Yeah, he's part Cresta. Poor guy. I don't even want to tell him. The lab reports came to my office yesterday. He's a nice guy, but I wonder what this'll do to him."

Cerulean nodded and rose. He peered into a black bay window, which reflected his somber face. "That's not the worst, I assure you."

Clare stared at his back. "Why?"

Turning around, Cerulean met Clare's demanding gaze. "He's illegal."

Clare slid off the bench. "Well, that's hardly his fault. It's against the law to murder a sentient being, no matter its heritage."

"I doubt his creators will care."

"Oh—" Clare's eyes widened, horror struck. "If anyone else finds out what I've done, and it leads back— I've got to warn him!" Clare raced to the door.

Cerulean grabbed her by the arm. "You'll do no such thing! You're already in over your head. Wait and let me think. That voice you heard—that scares me more than your friend's story."

"But I can't abandon Derik! He needs me."

"You won't. We won't. I have friends too, you know." Cerulean rescued the puzzle piece from Clare's hand and placed it on the table. "We'll figure this out—together."

Clare sat in her living room in the small farming town of Waukee and stared at the DNA report on her computer screen. Derik Erland: 37% Cresta, 63% human. "Well, at least the human part outweighs the Cresta." She pounded the desk. "Damn! He might end up *all* Cresta."

Blaring music pounded from her neighbor's house. Clare glared at the open window. Part of the reason she had moved into this ramshackle, country house was to avoid the crush of the city and revel in open spaces. Most of her neighbors were the typical farmer-types, quiet and with little nightlife. She had assumed that also meant little music-life, but this particular neighbor clashed with rural tradition. As a middle-aged musician, she would float strands of haunting Oldearth classical music into the somnolent darkness at midnight, then turn around and blare Newearth jingles by day, and throw in an eclectic mix of alien-tunes at odd moments to startle everyone. Clare sighed.

After striding to the open window, she considered shutting out the sound, but she knew from experience that would only mute the cacophony to an irritating thump. There was no way to solve a stupid neighbor problem, other than put up with it until fate intervened. She hoped that fate had nimble feet.

She shuffled back to her computer and shook her head at the open file. If she abandoned Derik's case, she might as well abandon a dozen others. None of them were safe. Being human wasn't safe. So why did she want to let this case slip by? She pictured Derik's face and smiled, but then she remembered his Cresta DNA and shivered.

Someone outside yelled. "Hey, honey, you keep that music so loud, you'll attract a nest of Ugani and you'll have a par-ty on your hands."

The music stopped.

Clare ran to the front door and swung it open. Bala's wife, Kendra, stood on the doorstep, a dish pressed to her chest. "I thought I'd bring this back since I was in the neighborhood." She glanced at the neighbor's house. "Whoo hoo! You weren't exaggerating. I should send Bala over with a warrant. That woman should be locked up in isolation for a month. Nothing will cure a person of foolishness faster than having to keep themselves sane."

Clare blinked as she relieved Kendra of the casserole dish and squeezed her in a quick hug. "Come on in. I could use someone with common sense."

Kendra bounced into the kitchen and laughed. "Oh good! You got someone with common sense inside? Can't wait to meet 'em...been waiting my whole life."

Clare shut the door and led Kendra to her small, single counter. "Want something?"

"Water would be a blessing. I thought I'd melt with pity, leaving Bala with the kids. He was being buried under little bodies as I stepped out the door..."

"Bala's as capable of manhandling that mob of yours as anyone I know. If you're not careful, he'll have them all practicing to be good little soldiers in God's army and have the whole house swept and polished by the time you get back."

Kendra's eyes twinkled as she accepted the glass of water.

"It would be like him. Dear, skinny man." Kendra took a long drink and then ran an appraising gaze over Clare. "So what's going on with you? Bala said you practically abandoned him, leaving him to handle the Hoggsworth case while you took sole control of this mixed race—"

"He told you!" A fierce blush ran rampant over Clare's face. "About Derik being mixed race? He wasn't supposed to tell anybody!"

"Oh, don't worry. Bala tells me everything, and I tell him practically nothing. I'm not about to get your poor Derik killed. That's not why I'm here."

Clare's eyes narrowed. "So? Why *are* you here?"

Pointing to the counter, Kendra sniffed. "Casserole dish." She clapped her hands, discharging the heavy weight of responsibility. "I hate leftover dishes, especially the Oldearth ceramic kind. I get all paranoid that it'll break and I'll have to buy a new one, except they don't make that kind anymore so I'll have to take some stupid ceramic class, and it'll take me about twenty years to figure out how they do that glazing thing, and by then I'll be in my grave doing time you-know-where for breaking the blinking thing in the first place." Kendra glanced at her datapad. "Oh, and I have a package to get out. When does your transport close?"

Clare eyed her computer. "In about ten minutes."

"Oh, glory! Come on. It's a wedding present...and the wedding's tomorrow. My name will be synonymous with mud if I don't hold up the family's honor with the perfect gift. You know."

Kendra rushed out of the house, snatched a package out of her autoskimmer, and looked wildly for the Trans-station.

Clare hustled out the door after Kendra. "Down one block, on the right. Here, I'll show you. Stop floundering and hurry."

Kendra jogged in step with Clare, who frowned in concentration as if thinking about it would get them there that much faster.

Matching her frown to Clare's, Kendra waved her free hand. "Dark skies, you look sour! My name might be ruined, but that's no reason for you to look so grim. What's going on?"

Clare slowed her pace and nodded to the yellow stone building in front of them. "It's Derik. I like the guy well enough, but I'd rather not deal with this mess. After all, he's over thirty percent Cresta. Who knows—?"

Kendra's eyebrows rose as she took the steps two at a time. "You want to restate that?"

Clare kept pace. "Don't worry, they'll stay open for us." She pushed open the door and entered the Trans-station. A Bhuac looking very much like an enchanted fairy stood behind the counter. Kendra deposited her package, allowing the Bhuac to calculate the cost. She turned and faced Clare, her raised eyebrows returning to their previous subject.

Clare leaned on the counter. "Oh, come on. We've been dealing with Crestas all our lives. They're not misunderstood good guys. When we finally find a case where a Cresta is actually innocent, I still wish I could arrest him since I know that he'll probably commit a crime first chance he gets."

The Bhuac cleared his throat. "That'll be 1.23 units."

Kendra grinned. "Better than I hoped. It'll get there tomorrow?"

The Bhuac nodded. "By sunrise."

"You just saved my life."

The perfect, almond-shaped eyes twinkled. "Glad to be of service."

Kendra winked at the Bhuac as she left. Sauntering down the steps, she whispered, "They are so cute! Don't you just want to pick them up and hug'em?"

"I don't think that would be…understood."

"Oh, you know what I mean. They're so adorable—"

"Bhuacs love idealized forms of creation. They discovered an equivalent tendency in our Oldearth fairies, nymphs, and elves. So, whenever they take on human form, they maintain a bit of the fairy-tale style. Haven't you ever noticed? You can always tell a Bhuac that way."

Kendra slapped her face in fascination. "The things you

learn as a detective! But—clue me in—when, exactly, did you get infused with the wisdom of God?"

Clare stopped mid-step and turned to face Kendra. "What?"

Kendra mimicked Clare's inflection perfectly: "After all, he's over thirty percent Cresta."

"I'm just telling it like it is."

Kendra nodded and strode toward her autoskimmer. "So, Derik's guilty by DNA?"

"You're putting words in my mouth."

"I'd rather put sense in your head. Look, Clare, I understand your aversion to Crestas. I feel it too. But I fight against it. Crestas have formed agreements with us and, for the most part, they've kept up their end. There are traitors. There're always traitors, but that's not the point."

Clare crossed her arms over her chest. "What is the point? What makes me unfit to judge another race?"

"Free choice."

"Free choice? That's what gives me the right—"

"Condemning a whole race is easy, a lunatic's response. Only the best of us remember our humanity."

Clare stopped beside Kendra's autoskimmer and sighed. "Maybe you're right. My DNA isn't so perfect. Only human, after all…."

"Aw, you just need to find the right match. Nothing does so much for a woman's good sense as looking after a husband." Kendra hugged Clare, climbed on her autoskimmer, and slipped a pair of pink goggles over her eyes. "Now, I'd better hurry back to my match…and see if I can scrape him off the floor."

Standing in his apartment bathroom, Derik peered at his reflection in the mirror and appraised what he saw in cold honesty. He had no doubt the DNA reports were correct. Surely his parents had suspected. *Why didn't they tell me?* He rubbed his weary, puffy eyes. *They probably hoped it would stay dor-*

mant so I'd go to my grave never knowing.

A scuffle outside his door made him turn and frown at the offending sound. After a brave attempt to fix his autoskimmer nearly blew him to bits, he realized that he'd best not attempt any serious home repairs. So he had chosen to live on the second story of a well-managed apartment building. All had gone well, until recently.

A noisy pair of Crestas had moved in on the floor above, and they had a never-ending stream of late-night visitors. If he believed Crestas capable of romance, he would have smiled the incidents away. But Cresta mating procedures were legal affairs and occurred at set times in very specific locations. Midnight interludes with a lady friend simply didn't enter the Cresta imagination. Though.... Derik riffled through some books he had ordered on Cresta life and culture. He had read something about it being a very passionate, almost deadly event. Apparently Cresta females—Derik closed his eyes. No. He didn't want to think about it.

Tiptoeing to the door, he pressed his ear against the thin wood and listened. The hissing of a breather helm was plain. Someone, probably a Cresta, stood right outside his door. Derik closed his eyes. *Dang! Dang! Dang!*

A muffled tap startled him.

In a sudden fit of passion, Derik kicked the door. The armored shoe he had taken to wearing to protect his now nearly boneless feet bashed right through the thin composite door.

"Hello?" The mechanical voice sounded curious.

Derik tried to extricate his foot, pushing on the frame as the hinges loosened. "Dang, cheap stuff! I pay good rent and—" With a quick, furious jerk, Derik stood before a wide-eyed Cresta, the door still attached to his foot, hanging at a crazy angle. He chose to ignore the door and struck a casual attitude. "Yes? Can I help you?"

The Cresta barely suppressed a smile. "I believe you can. But may I help you first?" He gripped the door and held it steady.

Derik jiggled his foot until it was free. A long bloody smear showed where a splinter had scratched his leg.

The Cresta pointed with a tentacle. "That looks painful… and dangerous. We should do something."

Derik backed up, nearly tripping. "Ah, no, it's nothing. I get scraped all the time. I just ignore it." A clown would have envied his lopsided grin.

The Cresta lumbered into Derik's apartment, neatly side-stepping the splinters. "Definitely a bad idea. Infections can lead to sepsis and that will cause death. I've seen it before. That's why I wear this." He gestured forlornly to his bio-suit. "You see; I know how it feels to be vulnerable."

Derik propped himself against his bookshelf, clasping his shaking hands. Sweat trickled down the side of his face. "Do I know you…from somewhere?"

The Cresta stumped to Derik's enormous fish tank and with a wide, childlike grin, he dipped a tentacle into the water. "Beautiful! I should've thought…." He turned and faced Derik. "But no, you don't know me. I, however, know all about you." The Cresta waved a tentacle in the air. "Please, let's sit. Something this important should not be rushed."

Derik's eyes darted to Cresta-shaped shadows in the open doorway.

"Don't worry. I asked a couple of my associates to see that no one interrupts us." The Cresta waved his tentacle again. "Please sit. You're like an unschooled hatchling." He chuckled, softly.

Derik stood immobile, his fingers white and bloodless. "Look, I hate to be rude, but I don't particularly like it when people show up at my door uninvited and then—"

"You had better see to that cut. You will bleed all over your clothes."

Derik pulled up his pant leg and forced back a gasp. Closing his eyes he swayed and then sat down. He squeezed his hand over the wound.

The Cresta gestured airily with a tentacle. "Where do you keep your bandages?"

Derik winced and nodded to the left. "In the bathroom."

The Cresta shuffled off.

Derik studied his leg. "Great! Clumsy as a Cresta, but I bleed like a human."

The Cresta returned with a white package and a small scissors in its tentacles. "Here we are. We'll have you fixed up in no time." He motioned for Derik to move over on the couch.

Derik did as directed and looked away during the procedure. He hated to see the tentacles working across his bare flesh, though he had to admit that the Cresta's touch was very light, and he felt not a particle of pain.

"Done! Good as new." The Cresta's golden eyes glowed with the pride of a job well done.

Derik remembered his manners. "Thanks."

Depositing the last of the bandage roll on the coffee table, the Cresta leaned back and folded its tentacles. "My name is Taug, and I've been sent here to kill you."

Derik's whole body jerked, his eyes wide and staring.

Taug reached out protectively. "Don't. There's no need to panic. I haven't decided to follow orders—yet." Taug resituated his tentacles on his lap, attempting to find a comfortable position for what promised to be a serious chat. "You see, you are the result of my father's dream. But Crestas signed an agreement years ago with the Inter-Alien Commission to never perform crossbreed experiments. That doesn't mean we don't perform other experiments, but it does mean that obvious proof of our breaking the law would put us—shall we say—in dark waters. So, you, as a mixed-breed human, are in need of aide and advice. I am here to give that."

Derik was trying hard not to swallow his heart, which had somehow managed to climb into his throat. "Mr. Taug, I appreciate—"

"Just call me Taug."

"Well, Taug...." Derik wrapped his arms around his body and tried not throw up. "I appreciate what you are trying to do—I think. But the fact is—" He jumped to his feet and winced.

Pacing around the room, he hugged himself to keep the shakes from rattling him into a million pieces. "Humans won't accept me and, as you say, I'm an embarrassing mistake to Crestas." He stopped and stared at Taug defiantly. "If I had an ounce of courage, I'd drown myself."

"Ah, that would be difficult. You're growing gills—the Cresta in you, I'm afraid."

Derik hung his head. Tears welled in his eyes, but he forced himself to maintain control with a violent shudder.

Taug appraised Derik with concern. "You are unwell. I understand that this is a shock. Though you must have known that you were not fully human for some time now. Crestas begin to mature at about thirty."

"I'm thirty-five."

Waving the difference away like an indulgent father, Taug attempted a soothing tone. "Nothing to be embarrassed about. Some develop a little slower than others."

"Oh, God."

Taug blinked as he turned his full gaze upon Derik. "I came here to appraise the true situation. It's not your fault that you were created by a well-meaning being who misjudged the generosity of his race."

Derik raised his head. "Excuse me?"

Taug's tentacles spread benevolently before him. "That's why I've come. You have a right to know. Even if we are forced to...eliminate you, at least you have a right to understand why you were created, and perhaps, why you must die."

A tear slid down Derik's cheek. "You know, it sounds awful when you say it, but in a way, I'm relieved. I wanted to know. And I appreciate the decency in you to be willing to explain."

Taug bowed his head and tapped two tentacles together meditatively. "My father was a scientist and a dreamer. My mother found certain aspects of his personality...challenging. She said he ought to write fiction." Taug wiggled gleefully. "They were like that, playful insults swirling through the water at all hours. But I digress.

"My father believed that Newearth embodied the ideal experimental environment. He knew, all too well, that inter-alien conflicts waste tremendous resources. He felt that there had to be a better way. So, he approached our scientific leadership with the idea of creating crossbreeds to ensure better relations, but the Inter-Alien Commission had just signed a treaty to desist from crossbreeding with humans. Seems that humans can't see protein for what it is...but that's another debate.

"My father decided to create one crossbreed in secret, hoping that if he could raise the thing, it would prove his theory. Apparently two others, quite inferior, were created, soon discovered, and quickly destroyed. Then you were created, but not long after, my father died. I have always wondered if—but, again, I digress.

"Someone—I have long suspected my mother—stole you away and placed you in an adoption agency. You have lived, hidden in plain sight these thirty-five years. Only recently were we made aware that you were beginning to develop. My superiors approached me with clear instructions."

"To kill me."

"To eliminate my father's mistake." Taug patted Derik on the knee with one tentacle. "But you know, there are many ways to approach the word *eliminate*. Now that I've met you, I want to consider matters more deeply before taking action."

"You mean—you're not going to kill me?"

"Not today." Taug rose to his feet. "You must understand. If it gets out that we broke our word and, worse yet, that we kept the result hidden after we discovered our mistake, it would look very bad, indeed. No one would trust us again. And trust is what makes the world go round, they say."

Derik's eyes begged. "But I'm an innocent man."

"Yes, there's that too." Taug lumbered toward the broken door. "I have much to consider. There are more beings than myself involved. You understand?"

Derik shuffled in step with Taug. He stared absently at the splintered frame.

"You'll need to get that fixed. Oh, and take care of that wound. We don't want that to fester."

Derik ran a finger along the ragged edge. "Who cares?"

Stepping through the doorway, Taug murmured. "I do."

CHAPTER SIX

A Small Matter

A sudden cold blast swirled orange and yellow leaves around like a graceful tornado. The leaden sky foretold a storm to come.

Justine strode through gleaming glass doors into the Cresta science building, a stark structure with little ornamentation, aside from brilliant white walls painted with intertwining blue-green waves, undulating in swirls along the corridor.

Justine didn't try to hide the smirk that broke the usual straight line of her mouth as she entered. *Scientists to their flabby cores. Why do they bother with primitive art?*

Eschewing the lift to the fifteenth floor, she ascended the steps at a rapid pace. An overweight man with graying temples and slumped shoulders huffed his way down the steps and almost smacked into Justine, forcing her to stop. His dark-circled eyes widened in surprise, and then just as quickly, crinkled into appreciative desire.

Without hesitation, Justine took the steps three at a time, disappearing from view within seconds. By the time she reached Taug's floor, she looked down the circular staircase and beheld the speck of a man still standing there. Her smirk turned into a headshaking frown.

"Taug?" Justine entered the laboratory and appraised the expensive medical equipment standing, hanging, and lying on steel tables. An examination tube extended from the wall while an obscured dissection victim floated in amber liquid and patiently laid in wait. *A Cresta's vision of Heaven.*

A shuffling noise turned her attention to the curved wall that narrowed into a tunnel on the left.

Taug padded into view. He looked up, and his puffy lips broke into a broad grin. "You are on time. Excellent! I should've had more trust. I was just pondering what to do if you didn't show up."

Justine fingered a long tube that ended in a spray gun, her eyes wandering the length, as if to judge how far it would reach. "And?"

Taug lumbered up and waved her hand off the tube. "Careful, that's not mine. I'm here as a guest. It would cost more than I will earn in a Cresta year to pay the fine if anything were broken." His winning grin softened the chastisement.

Justine slid her hand down the tube and turned toward a six-foot window facing the bustling city below. "What would you have done?"

Taug shook a tentacle playfully as his watery brown eyes gleamed in appreciation. "You have wit and persistence. Two traits I admire very much." He turned toward the dissection tube. "I would have sent out a bulletin describing you down to your nano-cells, alerting the public that a dangerous android was on the loose and must be destroyed by order of the Inter-Alien Commission."

"A lie that you could never explain away."

"I wouldn't have to. As far as the Inter-Alien Commission knows, you don't exist. I could make up an extravagant lie, and they would have no knowledge to refute my argument. I would win by default."

Justine took a step nearer the bulky form. Her eyes narrowed. "You. Are. Dangerous."

Taug's grin twisted, offering a one-shouldered shrug. "True.

But that makes two of us. You see now why I'm so happy you came." He padded to the window and nodded toward the milling throng appearing as multicolored dots to his Cresta eyes. "They mostly do as they are told because they lack the imagination to do otherwise." His gaze flitted back to Justine. "Not the case with you."

"You, a Cresta scientist, dare to flatter me?"

Taug's shoulders shook with mirth. One tentacle reached out and patted Justine's shoulder. "You delight me."

Justine rebutted his twinkling gaze with glowering eyes and a set jaw.

"Yes, well." He waddled to a desk set against the wall and pulled out an extra-large datapad, useful for beings with poor eyesight. "While you were out familiarizing yourself with your new home, I was busy at work introducing myself to my—"

"Victim?"

Taug's eyes darkened as his fixed smile stiffened. "No, my patient. I intend to study him. My instructions are deceptively simple, but I'm not sure that anyone really understands what they mean."

"So, why am I here? I have no interest in your studies or your instructions."

"*Your interest* is beside the point. I must keep my options open. Above all, I must appear to be following orders. You will assure me of success, no matter what happens."

"How?"

"If necessary, you will kill my patient."

"If I would rather not?"

"Why would you not? He's nothing to you. You care for no one, remember?"

"When did I say that?"

"You have lived that way your whole existence."

"I might have changed."

Taug lifted his datapad. "I am not offering you your past. I am offering you a future." He tapped on the screen and a hologram of Justine appeared in front of them. The spaces designated for name and biography were blank. "Once this task is complete, you will be free to become whomever you wish."

Justine paced to the window and peered at the milling throng. She could see every grimace, laugh, and furrowed brow. The image of a small crumpled face and wobbling lips forced her to close her eyes.

Taug twitched behind her.

Justine opened her eyes, turned, and locked onto his gaze. "As you say, I do not lack imagination."

Taug beamed.

In a calf-length, billowing dress, Justine stood as still as a statue on the Vandi city sidewalk beside a red and yellow lettered sign alerting the pubic to the Book Nook's "*Out of This World Sale*."

Derik bustled by, nearly knocking it into the street.

Justine's eyes monitored his every motion as he neared the busy intersection. Scrolling through a Cresta-sized datapad, he did not see a teen weaving through the crowd in his direction. Suddenly, the boy sprang between him and a waiting Bhuac and then darted forward.

As he was jostled, Derik frowned and looked up in time to see the boy sprint in front of an on-coming autoskimmer. Derik gripped the teen's arm and yanked him onto his backside.

Justine's eyes narrowed.

Within seconds, Derik was at the teen's side, concern etched across his brow.

The teen nodded and bounced to his feet.

Derik patted him on the back. In another moment, the teen was pacing away while Derik's attention returned to his datapad.

Pursing her lips in determination, Justine marched ahead of Derik, placed herself just within his field of vision, and proceeded to step in front of an oncoming autoskimmer.

Screams set the crowd into action. A Bhuac shrieked for medical assistance, while a Cresta caught the autoskimmer driver—a shaking human with horrified eyes—in a death grip. "Reckless driver!"

The driver protested her innocence, writhing in misery.

Lying prone, Justine looked away and waited.

Derik hobbled over. "Can I help?"

Relief animated Justine's face. She rose to a sitting position. "I'm all right, just shaken." She jutted her chin in the direction of the driver and the outraged Cresta. "It wasn't her fault. I wasn't looking." She darted a glance at the driver with a shrug. "Sorry. My mistake."

The woman huffed, shook off the offending tentacles, and retreated to her vehicle. "Be more careful, would you? Could've gotten us both killed."

Justine nodded. Her eyes skipped back to Derik, and she tilted her head charmingly. She peered into Derik's brown orbs. Smattered offers of assistance faded into the background. "Could you find me a place to rest?"

Derik glanced about. "Vandi Park is just across the street."

With a regal-like wave of the hand, she gestured her acceptance. "Please."

Grinning, Derik led his damsel-in-distress through the gawking crowd. He motioned to a forest-green bench picturesquely placed underneath a golden-red maple tree.

Justine crossed her beautifully shaped legs, threw back her head as the cool autumn breeze caressed her hair, and closed her eyes.

Derik leaned against the tree, his eyes traveling over her perfect form.

Justine opened her violet eyes and caught Derik's admiring gaze. "You're a gentleman, sir. Most people get very excited but are of little use in a crisis."

Raking his fingers through his hair, Derik shrugged. "I like to help when I can."

Justine's gaze traveled down Derik's body, landing unceremoniously on his Cresta-style boots.

After swallowing, Derik coughed and looked away. "I've never seen you before. I work at the housing department, so I see almost everyone every couple years when they renew their permits. You live around here?"

Justine shook her head and searched Derik's pensive face. "Not yet. I just arrived a few days ago. If you have any suggestions—?"

Derik returned his gaze to her with a twinkling grin. "How about dinner and we discuss possibilities?"

Justine's eyebrows rose. Yes, she had to agree with Taug, this mixed breed might be worth getting to know.

A solid knock shattered Derik's free-spirited humming. His hand froze over the top button of his dress shirt as he darted a scowl from the hall mirror to the new three-paneled door. Five indecisive seconds passed before he marched over and swung the door wide. "What?"

Cerulean, straight shouldered and dressed in a casual jacket and slacks, stood before him, one eyebrow raised. "Please tell me you don't do that every time someone knocks on your door."

Derik's scowl darkened. "What's it to you?"

Cerulean pointed into the living room. "May I? This isn't the kind of thing I like to discuss in the hallway."

Derik threw up his hands. "Why not? Seems like everyone feels more comfortable in my living room."

Cerulean appraised the large bookshelves, the assortment of Oldearth artifacts, and two very good oil paintings.

"You're not here to tell me that you plan to kill me? Are you?"

Cerulean spun around. "No. Why do you ask?"

"It's been done once this week. It'd get boring if we repeated it."

Cerulean heaved a sigh. "That's what I was afraid of. I told Clare this was too big for her."

"You know Clare? The detective for Human Services?"

"She's a friend of mine. My name is Cerulean." He offered his hand.

Derik's gaze shifted aside, passing up the offer. "Yeah, well, she's a friend of mine too, but she can't help me now." Reflexively, Derik smoothed down his shirtsleeves.

"Why is that?"

"Listen, you just barge in here acting like you know all about me and—wait, what do you know?"

Cerulean nodded toward the couch. "May I?"

Waving his hand in impatience, Derik tramped across the room. "Just sit, would you? Now talk!"

With an ill-boding creak, the couch sagged as Cerulean sat precariously on the edge and laced his fingers. "It's not complicated. Clare told me about your predicament. She's gotten the DNA results back and—"

Retreating to the hall mirror, Derik made quick adjustments. He sucked in his gut, tucked his shirttails, and straightened his collar. "I got the results too. Some Cresta brain created me in his lab, and it turns out that his son—Taug by name—has been sent to eliminate his father's—shall we say—indiscretion."

Cerulean rose, his face flushed. "How'd you find out about Taug? I had to pull a lot of strings to learn that. It was a Taugron who created you."

Turning from side to side, Derik nodded approval at his appearance. "Well, Taugron must be Taug's dad because he told me that his father created me." A quick run through with the brush, and Derik stood in front of Cerulean. "He explained the whole thing very nicely...considering."

The sun could have just imploded from the expression on Cerulean's face. "Taug was here?"

"Sat on that very same couch. He was actually pretty nice, even bandaged—anyway, he's not planning on eliminating me—today."

Cerulean slapped his hand to his cheek and paced across the room. "I don't understand. Why reveal himself?" He spun around. "What did he want?"

White knuckling the edge of the couch, Derik tried to pass off a lighthearted shrug. "To tell me the truth. He figured that if I understood why I was created, maybe I'd be able to accept the need to eliminate me."

"What?" Cerulean gripped Derik's arm. "And you believe him? He's a Cresta!"

His affected composure failing, Derik jerked his arm free. "He cares about me!"

Cerulean snorted as he backed off. "Crestas don't care about anyone outside their own race."

Pulling himself up to full height, Derik rolled up one sleeve and revealed his darkened, enlarged arms. "I'm Cresta, remember?"

"Only thirty-seven percent—remember?"

A sharp knock on the door froze them in place. With a shake, Derik glared at Cerulean and marched to the door.

Cerulean stepped in his way. "Be careful. You don't know who's out there."

Derik nudged Cerulean aside. "My days of being careful are over. Besides, I have a date, and I'm not about to be late."

Derik flung open the door and faced Justine's perfect face and form.

Her violet eyes peered into his. "I thought we were supposed to meet at the Coliseum an hour ago. You didn't show up so I—"

"An hour ago?" Derik fumbled to retrieve his datapad from a deep pocket. His eyes widened. "It's dead! I thought these never died. I mean—sorry, come in. I appreciate your concern." He glared Cerulean. "Some other day, eh?" He flashed a lopsided grin at Justine. "I'll just grab my jacket." Derik hurried down the hall, speaking over his shoulder. "Bye, Cerulean."

Cerulean wandered closer to the woman, mesmerized.

Justine stood her ground, her gaze roaming freely over Cerulean. An image of him standing over her filled her mind. She felt the warmth of his touch—"Cerulean?"

"Justine?"

Derik reentered the room glancing from Justine to Cerulean. "Still here?" He sidestepped the older man. "If you want to stay, fine. There's not much to steal but lock up when you leave." He took Justine's arm. "Let's go." Suddenly he frowned and stopped in mid-step. "Wait. How'd you know where I lived?"

Justine smiled brilliantly as she wrapped his bulky arm around hers. "You said you worked at the Housing Department. I looked you up. Easy."

Derik continued his forward momentum. "Oh, yeah. Sorry. Getting paranoid."

Justine glanced into Cerulean's eyes as she passed. "Bye, Cerulean."

Cerulean nodded. "Justine."

Mitholie's relaxed, dripping face appeared on a wide holo-screen. His tentacles rested on the hard edge of a murky green pool. He beamed. "Hello, my friend! How do you like your new home?"

With aching feet and chaffed skin, Taug stood stiffly in front of a stark wall-sized screen in the laboratory and smirked in retaliation. "Newearth has been very pleasant, though it's always a challenge getting accustomed to the necessary adaptations."

"Ah, yes. I hate the suits. Life out of water." The smug grin widened. "But never mind; you were made for adventure. I assume you have news?"

Taug huffed through his breather helm, his tentacles clenched around his middle as if holding back spontaneous combustion. "I have made contact and arranged for a skilled professional to attend to the situation."

Mitholie's upper body wiggled in exuberance. "Wonderful! Wonderful! The dark waters will converge, covering everything. Your father's memory will be only that—a memory."

Taug's tentacles squeezed tighter. "Thank you."

A grand wave dismissed Taug's humility. "Don't thank me. I just want to see you home again. Soon. There are changes planned." Mitholie's eyes glittered, reflecting rainbows dancing off the gentle waves.

"I will see to matters."

"Good! Very good! I know it's annoying, but the High Council—"

"Understood."

Mitholie readied himself for an exuberant dive. "After all, it's a small matter." He nodded to the pool. "The water calls."

Taug unwrapped his tentacles, spreading them wide in obeisance as he bowed his head.

The screen blinked into blackness.

As he stood alone in the dry, dark room, Taug's head rose, his shoulders straightened, and a gleam sparkled from his half-lidded eyes.

CHAPTER SEVEN

Humanity

Derik sat across from Justine, marveling at the vision of loveliness before him. His hand trembled as he laid it on the immaculate tablecloth in front of hers.

A crowd roared in the background. Three opposing teams rushed onto a hard floor, swinging metal balls at the end of stout poles.

Justine flicked a glance at the game before returning to Derik's gaze.

Derik shakily touched her fingertips.

Justine observed his imploring hand, mesmerized. Slowly, she extended her hand and intertwined her fingers with his.

Inside the Breakfast Nook, the Ingot hostess pounded across the room. Clare, settled at a long bench, scrolled through her datapad and tapped her fingers on the smooth tabletop.

Derik bustled through the doorway, dark circles under his eyes, searching the room. When he saw Clare, he exhaled in relief and rushed over. "Here you are. I woke up late and couldn't find this place again. I thought I'd miss—"

The hostess clumped back to the table. "Order?"

Derik swallowed as he appraised the huge Ingot. "Just coffee and a sweet roll—please."

The hostess charged off.

Derik shook his head. "Is she always so charming?"

"Only when she doesn't know you."

Derik tugged at his collar. "You have something to tell me?"

Clare sipped her coffee, assessing him over the lip of the cup. By the time she leaned back, she had made a decision. "You got the report I sent about your DNA results and the ramifications?" Returning his nod, she continued. "You'll have to deal with some heavy Cresta fallout. You'll likely be a pretty smart guy as your brain capacity increases, and you'll live a whole lot longer than the rest of us."

Derik shrugged. "Yeah, I read all that. But it doesn't really change anything. I'm still Derik Erlandson. As a matter of fact, I've met someone. She's...well, she's beautiful, brainy, and has a working knowledge of Oldearth poetry. Wild, eh? But what's really weird, she likes me."

"I take it you like her." Clare's expression remained neutral, an impartial judge assessing the latest case.

A nonchalant wave of the hand and an airy tone understated his exuberance. "We're going out again tonight."

Clare slapped down her mug and leaned forward. "Listen, I don't want to make you paranoid or anything, but just so you know, there're a lot of female hired guns. They get close to their victims and then—"

As if jolted by lightning, Derik jerked forward. "Justine isn't a hired gun!" Taking a deep breath, he scrambled for a hold on his emotions as his gaze ping-ponged off the walls. "She's wonderful and beautiful and perfect in every way. So what if she has a mysterious past?"

"Uh huh."

Derik rubbed his chin nervously. "I tried looking her up, and I couldn't find anything."

Clare's eyebrows rose. "That does not bode well. You

checked everywhere?"

Derik bit his lip. "Everywhere that's legal."

Clare flicked out her datapad. "Well, just to be on the safe side, let me look into it. What's her name?"

"Justine."

"Justine what?"

"Just Justine. She said she didn't believe in last names."

"Better and better...." Tucking a wisp of hair back into place, Clare stared into Derik's eyes. "Okay, I had every intention of telling you that I can't help you because, to be honest, I don't think I can. I asked a friend about you, and he wasn't too happy. Good guy, just a little protective. Don't worry, he's old country, a Luxonian from way back. Anyway, he advised me to drop the case and let him look into it. Last time I talked with him, he gave me the most annoying answers, full of tell-me-nothings. But I trust him. He'd warn me if—"

"Cerulean, right? I met him. Nice enough, but the guy has really bad timing. You talk about me a lot?"

"You met him?"

"He came by my place, warned me to be careful. Like I needed a warning."

Clare folded her arms across her chest, ready for her next lecture. "Listen, Derik, Cerulean's a pretty important man—Luxonian—I mean. He pointed out—"

"He's Luxonian?"

"The one who pounded together the Inter-Alien-Alliance."

"He's either as brave as an intergalactic trader or an utter fool."

Clare smashed her hands together into one clenched fist as her tone rose in intensity. "Anyway, he told me that it'd be in everyone's best interest if I try to keep you alive and well."

"Why?"

"What do you mean 'why?'"

"Taug has a point—"

"Perhaps you should have your head examined! Don't confuse me! I had this all figured out. Do you remember the old stories about when Oldearth was being polluted, these environmentalists convinced people to change their ways by showing them how a healthy planet would help everyone?"

Derik raked his fingers through his hair as he dropped his weary head onto his hand. "Your point?"

"Well, if the world isn't safe for you—is it safe for anyone?"

Derik tilted his head in a reflective attitude. "Am I worth all this trouble? I just want to be happy a while and let fate have its way. I'm tired of fighting this."

Clare put her hand over Derik's. "How about Justine?"

"She doesn't need me."

"Doesn't she?"

"She's already perfect. I'm only a mixed—"

"Maybe she needs someone to love. Maybe she isn't attracted to your biology but your humanity."

Derik snorted, his gaze turning inward. "Depends on how you define humanity."

Clare slid off the bench and stared down at Derik. "My point exactly."

The sun slipped behind the horizon hours ago, but Bala wasn't ready to return to hearth and home quite yet. A single lamp pooled light on a large, mahogany desk. A framed lace embroidered with the words "Hoggsworth Family" hung at his right. Bala accidentally tilted it as he leaned over, searching through Mrs. Hoggsworth's computer database.

Governor Jane Right? What about Jane Right? A bigwig in the Inter-Alien Alliance Committee, she had recently made a splash on Universal News by discovering a cache of old files that proved that her already illustrious family had a new cause to strut their stuff. He scrolled through the information and frowned. But here was a completely different take on that particular family history from a source named Justine. Hmm....

Bala sat down and ran through the files again, mumbling to

himself. "Who's Justine? Whoa, if this little lady were alive today, she'd be a cache of information. Governor Jane Right better not believe in ghosts."

Bala ran at full speed, his lungs ready to burst from the effort. He slid past playing children, a speeding autoskimmer, and an amorous Uanyi couple before he reached home. He slammed through the door, skirted past a tail-waving dog, and just managed to slip onto his chair before Kendra placed a steaming plate of rice and vegetables on the table.

She glanced at him out of the corner of her eye. "Man-of-mine, if you insist on being late to everything, including my fine dinners, I'm going to tie a string to you and yank when I want you home."

Bala surveyed the table full of wide-eyed children, his eyes twinkling as he mimicked being yanked by an invisible cord. He fell to the floor, writhing, sending the children into fits of laughter.

Kendra nudged him with her foot, her eyes rolling. "Get up before it gets cold."

Bala returned to his seat, but his bright eyes dimmed at the sight of vegetables and rice.

Kendra lifted her hand in warning. "Don't start with your steak and egg fantasies. I've got young-uns to raise. You want us to get hauled before an Inter-Alien Sensitivity Commission? No, siree!"

"I didn't say anything."

"You were thinking it and that's just as bad."

Bala gripped his fork like a warrior facing battle and set his jaw. He peered at the table full of children. "Remember, I'm doing this for you."

Bala leaned back against a maple tree aglow with fiery autumn colors and wrapped his arms around his knees, studying the sunset through falling leaves.

Kendra strolled over.

Bala's gaze stayed fixed straight ahead. "They in bed?"

With a muted groan, she slid down next to him. "Every last, blessed one of them."

Bala put his arm around Kendra and drew her close. "You're one fine mama."

"That I am." She appraised his somber profile. "You're not a bad papa."

"I try."

Kendra shared the sunset. "What's it this time?"

He turned his gaze, and the failing sunlight played hide and seek over his features. "Hmmm?"

Caressing Bala's furrowed brow, Kendra locked onto his gaze. "That expression. I'd know it on the dark side of the moon. You're worried about something."

Bala sighed and played with Kendra's fingers, lacing his with hers. "You know, I like puzzles as much as the next man, but sometimes I hate the picture after I've put it all together."

"Want to tell me about it?"

"I want to, but I'm not sure I should. Some pretty important people might be involved."

"By important, you mean...."

"They have resources. I don't."

Kendra leaned in so that their noses almost touched. "In all the time I've known you, Bala, you have never shirked from a challenge. Remember the First All-Species Olympics?"

A half grin peeked out of Bala's crooked smile. "That was only in fun."

"You almost killed yourself. Iceberg climbing, they called it; idiotic, I called it. And you all scared the penguins witless."

With a deep breath, Bala blinked back the sudden moisture in his eyes. "Back then, I didn't think about it. I was just playing. But now—"

A child's wail pierced the evening.

Kendra shot to her feet nearly as fast as Bala. She patted his arm in restraint. "You're worried about us. I understand; I worry about us, too. But, man-o-mine, you've got to live. If you tie your spirit to safety, you'll have to lock yourself at home. Not that you'd be safe here—"

The crying rose a decibel. Kendra strode forward. "Coming, baby." She peered over her shoulder at Bala's barely discernible outline against the falling night. "God made us of strong stuff. But remember, you got to the top by building steps."

Bala's eyes glowed as he watched Kendra retreat inside. When the shrieking stopped abruptly, a slow smile spread wide across his face.

CHAPTER EIGHT

Just the Beginning

"Come along, big fellow, keep up with me. For your large size, you take such tiny steps." Governor Jane Right forged ahead of Taug down the long, bright hallway of the Territorial Capitol.

Taug's somber gaze dropped to the floor. "It's the boots. They aren't built for a quick pace."

Austere nameplates with gold lettering testified to the worthiness of the inhabitants secreted behind ornate doors on the top floor.

Taug ignored the doors and concentrated on his balance as he tried to stay close enough to the governor to have a word with her. "I thought I was going to meet you *inside* your office."

She didn't bother looking back as he trailed along behind. "What? And have every tongue wagging about Governor Right's private meetings with an unknown Cresta? No, that wouldn't do. It's much better that you state your business out here while we walk. Keep your secrets in plain sight, I always say."

"But couldn't someone—"

"Eavesdrop? In the office, more likely. Listening devices

planted from floor to ceiling, I'm sure. No one ever thinks of bugging the hallway. Besides, until I know what you want, I can't waste my time."

"A laboratory." Taug huffed, attempting to adjust his breathing helm. *Never in all the deepest waters....*

"A laboratory? What for? We have plenty of labs in the hospitals, and I believe Central University has the best on the planet." A simper twitched across her face. "Being a bit greedy, aren't you?"

Taug slowed his pace as they neared a narrow, circular stairway extending from the blue, star-spackled, domed ceiling down to a brightly lit, green-tiled floor, creating the illusion of descending from a brilliant night sky to sunny Newearth.

One tentacle stroked Taug's chin doubtfully. "Not at all. I have an idea that cannot be shared, except with a chosen few."

"Huh." Governor Right pointed to the steep steps. "Can you handle these?"

Taug hesitated. "Possibly, if we go slow enough."

"Here give me your hand... or a tentacle. Whatever."

Taug placed a tentacle inside Governor Right's surprisingly strong grip and held on for dear life.

Concentrating on Taug's every step, like a mother taking her toddler into deep waters, the middle-aged woman furrowed her brow. "I need to know who's giving the party and why."

Taug laid each mechanical boot firmly on the step before lifting the other free. A sudden flashback of struggling onto land for the first time as a hatchling flashed through his mind.

"There is no *party*, I assure you. Only me and one other. I will have to hire a few assistants, but they will be completely in the dark as to the grander purpose."

"So what's the grand purpose?"

"To create crossbreeds."

Governor Right shook her head apparently at both their slow descent and the comment. "Whatever for?"

"To become invincible. Why else?"

The governor's eyes never strayed from his boots as Taug

inched himself down. "Invincible? How?"

"If I can blend Cresta intelligence with human, terrestrial capability, I can cultivate the brilliance of each species in the service of those who know how to manage a planet."

"Any others?"

Taug glanced up, an eyebrow raised, his mouth orifice puckered.

An eye-roll communicated the governor's impatience with Taug's obtuse understanding. "Why not Cresta with Uanyi? Or human with Ingot?"

Taug shrugged off the governor's unbounded ambition. "There are no limits to the possibilities, but Cresta and human would be the best combination to begin with."

Governor Right's hand flew out protectively as Taug stumbled. Her voice hardened. "Something could go wrong, and we'd have a mess on our hands."

The green-tiled floor was only one step away and Taug beamed. "Many things could go right, and we'd have the most versatile, powerful beings in our grasp."

The governor's tight lips broke into a mirrored grin as she assisted Taug onto solid footing. "Now, that wasn't so bad, was it?"

Taug wiggled his tentacle free of Governor Right's grasp. "Thank you."

Glancing around before starting forward, Governor Right beckoned him to stay close. "What'll I get?"

"Whatever you need." Taug wrapped his tentacles around his middle as he negotiated his way across the crowded floor. Even a minor slap with a tentacle could have serious consequences.

Her grin turned ironic. She glanced back. "Your Cresta word of honor?"

Taug offered a slight bow as he hustled out a wide doorway behind her.

A cool breeze played havoc with the governor's coiffured hair. "Thought as much. I want a full report each month, in person. Nothing written, of course." Halting on a busy sidewalk, she scanned the street.

Pedestrians rushed at a city pace on either side as the Vandi traffic roared in urbane, noonday routine.

"Naturally."

Never taking her eyes off her environment, Governor Right leaned over and whispered. "Oh, and I want to meet one, as soon as you have it ready."

Taug stiffened. "Would that be necessary?"

"No. But it'd be thrilling. Everyone needs some excitement now and again."

Taug bowed to the inscrutable.

With a new light in her eye, the governor lifted her arm and waved with broad, commanding strokes. "Ah, here comes my secretary. I have a meeting with the Inter-Alien Alliance committee in a few minutes. Pay attention now." She wiggled two beckoning fingers at a man crossing traffic. "George! Here!" She again leaned toward Taug. "My *private* secretary. Contact him when you need something."

Taug extracted a datapad from his bio-suit. "I have a list."

Snorting back her laugh, the governor beckoned George again. "How very efficient of you. So Cresta."

A snappy dresser with black hair, brooding eyes, and squared shoulders sprang across the street and lightly stepped forward.

"George, this is Taug, a special ambassador from Cresta. We are assisting him in a *private* matter. You'll see that he gets everything he needs."

George appraised Taug in a sweeping and ever-so-disdainful glance. His voice was as dry as the sidewalk he stood upon. "Certainly."

"Thank you." Taug turned to Governor Right. "It has been an honor."

Governor Right grinned, grasped one of Taug's tentacles, and shook it formally. "Just the beginning, I'm sure."

Taug stood back as George led the governor towards a waiting vehicle. The patient Cresta cradled his aching tentacle close to his body, his half-lidded eyes glowing like embers.

Curved walls glowed white against state-of-the-art, red shelving units packed with pristine lab equipment. An unoccupied dissection tube extended from one wall, while medical instruments stood lined up on neat tables like soldiers ready for the next battle.

"Do you like it?" Taug's usual confidence expanded as he waved a tentacle in an arching manner, encompassing the vast room in one magnificent sweep. "I always wanted to follow up on my father's work, and now I have my chance."

Derik took a tentative step into the massive laboratory. "But where… how? Did the Cresta government give you all this?"

Taug lumbered closer, a sheepish grin spreading his puffy lips wide. "Ah, no, that would be most unlikely. The Cresta High Council would like nothing more than to see me safely returned to Crestar. They have plans. I have plans. At some distant point, the two shall meet."

Derik appraised the expensive bio-scanners, surgical tools, the specimen containers, steel tables, bright lights, tubs of various solutions, and the central dissecting tube with miniature tubes, like petals, jutting from the wall. The entire room was bathed in a soft, white glow. In the back, a transparent wall offered a view into an enormous aquarium.

Derik stepped closer, his jaw dropping and his eyes widening. "You keep fish—in your own Cresta pool?"

"Just for eating, when I get hungry after a hard day."

"Why not just keep them preserved, frozen or something?"

Taug followed Derik's astonished gaze and burst into giggles, his tentacles writhing in mirth. "I forget; you are as ignorant as a hatchling."

Derik itched to take off his mechanical boots. He couldn't account for this sudden longing to jump into the Cresta-sized aquarium.

Taug scooted closer and, with a tilt of his head, appraised Derik's gaze. "Yes, you feel it, don't you? The pull of water? Once you've been trained, we'll go in together. It'll be fun. It may be the most pleasant thing you've ever done."

Derik's eyes remained fixed on the pool, his tone apathetic. "I've been swimming before, but I never liked it much. It was okay—"

"But it never felt right. Of course not. A Crestar pool is quite different. A human would no more enjoy a dip in a Crestonian sea than he would like to splash about in a bowl of vegetable soup. But for us, it's magnificent."

Derik slid his hands across the thick glass. His splayed fingers caressed the surface. His voice grew husky. "When?"

Taug nodded, a gleam in his eye darting from the pool to Derik. "Soon. But first I need to understand you better. You are unique in a universe of unique beings. That said, I must understand how to best adapt you to Cresta life."

Never shifting his gaze off the pool, Derik hunched his shoulders. "Cresta life? Why? Newearth is my home."

"Someday you may wish to visit our...your world." Taug's golden eyes appraised Derik's form. "It would be a shame if that visit were hampered by poor adaptations. Once we understand your biology better, we can fashion appropriate gear to make your visit on Crestar most enjoyable. I assure you, many Crestas will view you as a hero. You will swim everywhere acclaimed—"

"I'm no hero!" Derik's voice sharpened as he slapped the glass. "Just a mixed-breed, nobody."

Taug laid a tentacle around Derik's arm and gripped it firmly. "One thing you must learn now, before anything else: Crestas are scientists. We have inquisitive minds that never rest. No Inter-Alien Alliance or planetary treaty can keep us from our natural right—to pursue knowledge. Anyone who assists us is a hero."

Derik's gaze bore down on Taug's face. "How?"

"Allow me to study your biology and learn how my father

created you. Then, perhaps someday, you will not be alone."

Turning from Taug back to the pool of murky green water, Derik's voice fell to a whisper. "I'm not alone." He darted a quick glance at Taug. "What's in it for you—personally—I mean?"

"Success brings many rewards. Don't worry; I'll be well compensated, in the end." Taug padded to a wall on which hung a variety of breathing apparatus. "Though I planned on waiting, I think you need a little reward now. Here, put this on and come with me."

Derik held the apparatus at eye level, scrutinizing it. A quizzical expression spread across his face. "What is it?"

"It'll help you breath while we swim. I've been adapting it, just for you. I want to see how well it works before we begin our studies."

"So, you're not going to kill me—ever?"

"I have no immediate plans to kill you." Taug lumbered toward a side hallway.

Derik trailed along behind. "Somehow, that didn't sound as comforting as I hoped."

Taug and Derik disappeared into the dark hall, leaving the laboratory silent and empty.

Suddenly the waters in the tank were stirred and millions of bubbles floated in an arc toward the surface. Taug, swimming as gracefully as a porpoise, flashed by. His feet, free of the mechanical boots, paddled like luminescent fins. He circled up and around, dashing about like a child at play, swirling bubbles in his wake.

He dove away and returned with one tentacle wrapped around Derik. The breathing apparatus with attached goggles was strapped tight across Derik's face. His wide eyes stared straight ahead, frozen in panic. Despite Taug's support, Derik remained as limp as a noodle.

Taug began stoking Derik's arm with a free tentacle.

The anxiety in Derik's eyes faded. He began kicking his legs and stroking the water with his arms. Slowly, but more confidently with each movement, he began swimming...free as a fish in the green, Cresta sea.

CHAPTER NINE

A Mind Is a Terrible Thing to Waste

Bala leaned over the professor's ornate, Oldearth-styled desk and pounded his fist. "Stop lying!"

Professor Baltimore, a connoisseur of ancient civilizations with a decided bent toward OldEurope, was dressed in a tweed jacket, a white collared shirt, and black slacks. Since he was spindly, pallid, and had a voice that shrieking birds might covet, apparel and atmosphere would have to suffice for intimidation purposes. He sat back and pursed his lips in a petulant sneer. "Don't try to frighten me."

"I wouldn't have to if you would stop playing games. We both know that you had an argument with Mrs. Hoggsworth the night before she died, and we both know that it had something to do with the paper you assigned—"

"To blazes with you!" Stretching every millimeter of his skinny frame, the professor shot to his feet. "That woman could argue a Cresta to the Divide and back! She liked to argue. She just happened to pick me to argue with that fateful day because her son, *Timmy the Terror*, complained that I was unfair. So like the youth of today. They're always complaining! If you really want to know who killed her, you might try asking that miserable wretch of a husband of hers. Poor man, tied to that volcano. There are probably hundreds who'd love to carry her casket to burial, just to be sure that she's in the ground, never to raise her voice again."

Bala straightened and chuckled. "You're rather good at this."

Professor Baltimore glared through his ultra-fashionable, Oldearth wire-framed spectacles. "I don't know what you are talking about."

"You maneuvered the argument away from your lies and onto Mrs. Hoggsworth's personality. Very neatly done. I can see why the students fear you."

Professor Baltimore smirked as he swaggered around his desk. "Flattery won't get you anywhere."

Bala paced over to the classroom chalkboard. "You still use one of these? Why not a holo-screen?"

"This is a history class. I like to bring the past to life. Besides, holo-screens don't have the same effect when you run your fingernails across them."

Bala nodded. He picked up a piece of chalk and started writing awkwardly. His body blocked the professor's view. "Wow, I haven't done anything like this since Sister Mary-Origen took us to an Oldearth exhibit and let us play with the replicas."

In silent retaliation, the professor inched his way around the table, shuffling a few papers as he did so. His glance darted to the chalkboard. He lunged for the eraser, but Bala was faster.

"Tut, tut, professor! Don't be in such a rush to erase my masterpiece. I never get a chance to create art, at least not with chalk."

Professor Baltimore cocked an ear to the quiet hallway, then rushed to the door and shut it with a sharp click. He strode back to the front of the room and snapped out his hand.

Bala held the eraser aloft. "First tell me what you don't like about my work. After all, I might learn something. You're a smart man with many years of education. In fact, how old are you?"

"That is none of your business. Now erase what's on that board or—"

"What? Granted, you might be a few milligrams heavier than

me, but I'm faster and if it comes to that, I can outrun you the livelong day. Now, tell me—" Bala turned to the chalkboard where he had scrawled, "Governor Jane Right is...." in huge letters. "—what's so wrong with my work?"

"You think you're clever, but you have no idea who you are playing with." Professor Baltimore stroked his beard. "You're like the students, children really, who come in here day after day, thinking they're ready for the knowledge that I can impart, but they have no idea of the responsibility involved. Studying history is very much like absorbing an attribute of God."

Bala clapped his chalky hands dramatically. "So, as you play God, do you help out a few illustrious friends and write new histories, new family trees, impale the past with your chosen glory?"

The professor's eyes lit up, blinking in watery admiration. "Lord, that's a good line! I think I'll steal it."

"Wouldn't be the first time."

"Perhaps not. But that is quite beyond your scope of understanding." The professor returned to his desk and tapped on the computer console imbedded in the surface. "You're a detective, and you want to find a murderer. Fine. I will tell you everything I know about Mrs. Hoggsworth's death."

Professor Baltimore darted around the desk, snatched the eraser, and began brushing away the offending words as he spoke. "She came in here, shrieked at me in an incomprehensible rage for twenty minutes, and then stalked out into a dark and dangerous city." His glare darted over his shoulder at Bala. "Likely as not, she screamed at some poor unfortunate thug who happened to be on his humble way to pillage or burn the nearest town." He slapped down the eraser, raising a cloud of dust. "In any case, she annoyed someone who followed her home, blew a hole through her middle, and walked away undoubtedly feeling quite refreshed by the experience."

Stroking his chin, Bala considered the possibilities. "So, I am looking for a petty thief?"

"Someone for hire, most likely."

"And my artwork?"

Professor Baltimore appraised the blurry smear on the board. "There was nothing there."

As Bala opened his mouth, a bell clanged and hundreds of hurrying footsteps flooded the hall.

Professor Baltimore smiled serenely. "Ah, saved by the clang."

The Hoggsworth house was old, for Newearth that is, and exuded the dignified charm of a well-kept manor. It was situated on a comfortable corner lot in an upper-class, tranquil neighborhood inhabited by professional families who lived well and undoubtedly expected to die that way. They were a rare community of open-minded beings who mixed freely with others of their elevated social status. Crestas with advanced degrees and Ingots in government positions, especially diplomacy and political affairs, were accepted by the human inhabitants and in turn tolerated the Bhuacs and Uanyi hired for their discreet services in the area of child care and domestic duties.

In the somnolent living room, Bala stood awkwardly, first on one foot and then shifting to the other. He folded his hands and tossed a beseeching look heavenward. "I didn't mean to upset you. I just hoped—"

"You hoped what? That you'd solve my wife's murder by asking for details that tear me up inside? Frankly, I don't give a damn anymore. It could've been a Cresta, a mindless Uanyi, or one of Baltimore's students hoping for extra points. Nothing is going to bring Carol back. God, can't we let it go?"

Bala flicked his gaze to the ceiling again, asking for guidance from an unseen source. "Look, someone killed your wife, and it's in humanity's best interest if we find out who. Otherwise—"

Mr. Hoggsworth slumped deeper into his overstuffed chair. "Oh hell. I'm not usually so selfish. But it's been a trying week."

Bala knelt and laid his hand on the gentleman's arm. "I am sorry about your loss. I love my wife too, and if something happened to her, I'd go crazy. But Carol Hoggsworth deserves justice, and she can't be at peace with her murderer running free."

Mr. Hoggsworth's eyes filled with tears. "I had to send Tim off to my sister's place up north. He nearly lost his mind—plots of revenge. Look, you're a decent fellow, Mr.—"

"Just Bala. My last name is a tongue twister. I had to spell it three times before the registrar would sign my birth certificate."

A snort wrestled a grin free from Mr. Hoggsworth's grief. He took a deep breath and sat up straighter. "To begin with, I think you need to understand who my wife really was." Mr. Hoggsworth heaved himself out of his chair and ambled over to a roll-top desk. He shuffled through several tiny drawers until he found a miniature key. Beckoning Bala with the tiny, metal piece pinched between his fingers, he started forward. "Now, I've never shown this to anyone except my son, so I expect you to keep this a professional secret."

Bala's eyebrows rose as he followed Mr. Hoggsworth to a small bookcase on the back wall. A few tattered copies of ancient reference books and the usual Oldearth décor ornamented the shelf. Mr. Hoggsworth pulled out a faux Webster's dictionary and pressed the key into a hidden wall hole. A click and a snap made Bala step back. One section of the wall opened, revealing a second bookcase stocked with a variety of books, all ancient and authentic.

"These were my wife's treasures. They're real history books that refer back to the Greeks and Romans and detail archeological finds with photos of ancient excavations and reference charts that illuminate the who's who of history. Carol was extremely proud of our heritage. One thing she could not abide was this recent trend of changing historical records to make certain personalities appear better than they really are. It's like how certain socialites claimed to be descended from the original Mayflower. All a bunch of hullabaloo."

Bala tapped tentatively on one of the leather bindings and grinned. "I wish you had a cookbook among these treasures."

Mr. Hoggsworth pursed his lips. "Well, if you'd like to know about the diets of Native Americans, Chinese, or Celts, there are recipes here. Carol once made a dish of roasted pork with fruit and wild rice that was absolutely delicious."

Bala gulped for air. "Heaven, help me. How—?"

"She never told, but I believe that was the year when she and my son went on a three-day trip to the International Wildlife Center. Their bags bulged suspiciously when they returned."

"I wish I had known her." A beeping from his datapad forced Bala to check his message. "My wife would like help getting the kids in bed. All in caps." Bala sighed and refocused on the case as he caressed a thick book. "So you think that Carol recognized a misrepresentation in Professor Baltimore's work, confronted him, and he killed her?"

"I don't think *he* did, but I think he alerted someone who did. Professor Baltimore is a mouse, but he's clearly acquainted with a lion or two." Mr. Hoggsworth retrieved the volume from Bala's hand and pressed it back in the case. He relocked the cabinet.

Bala stepped back amiably enough, his mind shifting to new questions. "When I was reviewing your wife's files, I found several articles about Governor Right."

"Jane Right?"

"You know her?"

"I know of her... well, actually, we went to school together. Carol was her classmate. First, they were friends. Then, they were rivals. By the end, they were enemies."

"Could she have discovered something that would rock the governor's world?"

"Possibly. But Governor Right is not one to get her hands dirty. Not her. Besides, even if Carol knew, she wouldn't bother with Jane. She couldn't care less about politics. She wanted her son to trust his teachers, to know that they were telling the truth. Hence, the argument with Old Baltimore."

"I see. Well, thank you. You've been most helpful." Bala turned to go but then stopped mid-step. "Oh, I also noticed a few references to someone named Justine. I wasn't sure if that was a file name or a person. Do you happen to know?"

"Justine? Doesn't ring a bell. But, you know, Carol collected friends. I hardly knew them all."

Bala bowed and swept out the door.

Clare stood outside Cerulean's cabin on a patch of well-tilled soil and watched him scatter seeds in a wide arc from a bag looped over his shoulder. The sun shone down from a clear sky, while birds chirped encouragement from distant branches.

She tapped her foot. "You've taken up gardening?"

"It's winter wheat. I'll harvest it next summer."

"Really?"

"And I'll make the best bread this side of the Great Divide."

Clare pursed her lips. "Why?"

Cerulean looked up, shading his hand against the bright sun behind Clare. "Why not? Bread is more than a staple for— "

"You know, I'm here on official business, and I don't have time to watch you act out some antiquated Amens' tradition."

Cerulean tossed a last handful and patted his flattened bag, a frown darkening his face. "You've got an attitude."

"Nothing new." Clare padded across the lawn.

Folding his arms across his chest, Cerulean didn't budge. "No, but I don't happen to like this one."

"Come on, Cerulean! I'm in a hurry. I have a supervisor who thinks that life is too short and wants every case solved yesterday."

"Which case?"

"The Hoggsworth murder. I've got Bala going over things, but I'm not about to give up on Derik. You said you knew something. Tell me, so that I can go dig Bala out of whatever hole he's gotten himself into."

"Bala is a very competent detective." Cerulean looked at the rectangular field and scratched his jaw. "There's no way I'm going to be able to eat this much bread. You think Kendra would want some?"

"Kendra loves any sustenance, any time. Now, hurry up and talk!"

Cerulean strolled to the porch, pointing west with the folded pouch. "The strawberries will be ripe by then. I'll try my hand at jam to go with the bread."

Clare shook her head. "The Amens have turned you into a nature freak."

Cerulean's eyebrows rose as he looked back at her. "I'll have you know, I was working on a farm generations before you were even born."

Clare stopped at the bottom porch step and tapped her foot.

Cerulean heaved himself to the top step and sat. He looked Clare in the eye. "I went to Derik's apartment to see how he's getting along. I met someone I didn't expect."

Clare threw her hands out. "So? Is there a reason I should care? Wait. You didn't meet his new love interest—Justine?" Clare kicked the step. "Poor, stupid guy. Is he in love with an old flame of yours? You never tell me much about your...life."

Cerulean huffed. "That's because there isn't anything to tell. I wish you'd listen before leaping. How do you ever manage to solve a case?"

"End of lecture. Go on."

"Yes, it was Justine, but Justine isn't a love interest of mine, she's a...person I met a long time ago. She was on trial."

An I-knew-it eye roll accompanied a puff of breath. "Uh huh."

"I was surprised to see her—alive." Cerulean clasped his hands and stared off into the distance.

"Alive?"

"Last time I saw her, she was on a steel table being turned off."

Clare's mouth dropped open. "As in a robot?"

"She's an android. A very advanced android. You'd never guess, unless you knew her history. Even then, you might not believe it."

Clare slapped her forehead. "So, Derik is in love with a robot?"

Cerulean bounded to his feet. "Justine is *not* a robot. She's a person, a combination of modern technology and fetal—"

"Don't give me that! She's one of those... those things that go around pretending to be human but are hired out for every dirty job under—"

"Stop! Listen to yourself. You're not even giving me a chance." Cerulean clambered down the steps, pushed past Clare, and pounded down the path to the woods.

Clare hustled after him. "Okay, okay! Don't get angry. But you gotta admit; this is pretty bad. I mean, Derik'll be crushed."

Cerulean pivoted and faced Clare. "Human beings are quite resilient. Trust me, I ought to know." He hustled down the path again, allowing room for Clare to keep pace at his side.

Ignoring the branches scratching against her jacket, Clare glanced at Cerulean. "So, is this Justine a nice robot-person? I mean, she isn't a hired gun or anything."

Cerulean paced further into the woods. "Well, actually, she *was* a hired gun. That's why she was on trial. But it was a long time ago; she's changed."

"Terrific, just terrific! How long ago?"

"Seventy years, give or take...."

"Lord, she's twice Derik's age!"

"Three or four times it, I'd imagine."

"Then what is she doing? It'd be like my great-great-grandmother trying to date you. Oh, except—"

"I'd still be older by a millennium."

"Geesh, you non-humans really mess up the romantic timeline." Clare kept in step with Cerulean as they wound between trees. A vine clutched her pant leg and forced her to stop. "Dang these prickles. Why didn't you eradicate them when you bought the place?"

"I like nature and all her wild and prickly personalities." Cerulean stared down at Clare and a smile softened his features. "One of the reasons I like you."

Sucking a pricked finger, Clare glowered. "If you like me so much, help me get unstuck. This thing is cutting me to shreds."

Cerulean gently lifted the vine off her leg and tossed it aside. "See, you just need to know how to handle nature."

Clare blushed. "Stay on topic." She started forward again. "Shouldn't Derik know? I mean his heart's beating pretty fast for a woman who's not even human, and who might be planning to dig him a grave so she can rack up some extra units."

Cerulean peered up at the mottled sunlight pouring through the trees. "Things are rarely what they seem—except when they are."

"Is that supposed to help?"

Making a one-eighty turn, Cerulean started back up the path. "I'll talk with Justine. She trusts me, and she owes me a favor. If she's been hired to kill Derik, she'll tell me."

Clare flapped her arms and skipped aside to avoid a scampering chipmunk. "Why should she talk to you? Didn't you say you were at her trial, where apparently, she was found guilty?"

"Yeah, but thanks to me, she still has her mind." He darted a meaningful look at Clare. "After all, a mind is a terrible thing to waste."

CHAPTER TEN

Mixing More Than Metaphors

Justine stood in front of a large female chimpanzee and stared into its black eyes. A wall of windows separated them. Unimpressed, the monkey sat slumped in a corner, occasionally yanking on a chain suspended from a tall branch. A baby chimpanzee scampered about in the background.

Justine's gaze shifted to the baby. The mother's eyes shifted in accord. The baby trotted over, lurching between two legs and four. It stopped when it saw Justine and then scurried up its mother's arm, chattering and clinging to her. The mother glared at Justine.

Justine slowly lifted her hands and placed them, palms up, in full view. She lowered her head, letting her gaze drop to the ground.

The mother twitched and swung her baby high onto her other hip. With one last glare, she tipped her nose into the air and swung up into the nearest tree. The chain jangled as she flew by.

"Interesting creatures, aren't they?"

Justine swiveled and faced Cerulean, her look of concentration morphing into a twisted grin. "Yes, I feel strangely at home here. In a cage that pretends it isn't a cage."

Cerulean offered his arm as he glanced toward the door.

"I'm glad to see you again. I've thought of you often."

As Justine took his arm, her grin faded. "I can't say the same, since I only awoke a few weeks ago. But I'm glad to see you now."

Cerulean patted her arm as he directed her toward a butterfly garden. "Well, tell me about your awakening. Who rescued you and why?"

Justine strolled to a quiet corner and perched on a bench stationed against a life-like diorama of prehistoric insects. "I can't betray professional secrets, you understand. Suffice to say, my mind is intact, and I have learned from my previous experiences."

"So you aren't planning on repeating—"

"I have no certain plans at the moment."

"And Derik?"

"Ah, yes, I was wondering when you'd ask." Justine uncrossed her legs and rubbed her hands together. "It's a little chilly in here. Do you mind if we walk out into the sun?"

Cerulean's brows furrowed as his eyes darted around the tropical setting, but he merely offered his hand. They strolled out of the exotic building and into sunlight that shone on every visible food station and playground. Children swung from ropes and vines in a jungle gym not far from where the monkeys gamboled in their own sport.

Justine stopped and pointed. "They are not so different, human children and monkeys."

"Except the monkeys are in cages and the humans are free."

Justine peered at Cerulean. "Depends on how you define the word free."

"Not being locked in."

Justine sniffed her approval. "Yes, there is that." She strolled over to a popcorn stand and ordered a bag. Upon obtaining her prize, she meandered back to Cerulean, nibbling each kernel like a squirrel working on a nut. She passed the bag over.

Cerulean took a handful and chewed meditatively. "So are you going to tell me what's going on?"

"Why should I? Can't a robot have a personal life?"

Cerulean stared into her eyes, his voice softened to just above a whisper. "Justine."

Refusing his intimate gaze, Justine glanced away and started toward a herd of lumbering elephants set beyond a wide cavern. "I don't want to remember. I just want to start over."

Cerulean sighed as he kept pace. "Sounds like a wonderful idea. But to do that, you have to be free. Are you?"

Justine gripped the guardrail before the cavern and leaned over the wide abyss. Black streams of hair curtained her face.

With a gentle touch, Cerulean tipped her chin up so that their eyes met. "Who awoke you?"

"A Cresta named Taug."

Cerulean's hand dropped to his side. He shook his head at the elephants. "Damn."

"He's not so bad. He told me more than he should've. Seems that every biological creature thinks that robots have no moral code."

"You're not a robot."

"I am—to Taug."

"Not to me. You know that."

Justine leaned in, her lips only centimeters from Cerulean's. "Derik thinks I am real."

"Derik cares about you."

"Will that make me real?"

"To him? Or to you?" Cerulean raked shaky fingers through his hair. "Listen, Justine, you have nothing to prove. I care about you, too. You're a desirable woman who happens to live in a mechanical body. I could kill the mind who decided to put your being into a killing machine, but that wouldn't help, would it? *You* have to decide who you are."

Justine reached over, her fingers searching, and placed her hand in his. Her gaze turned to a group of children tagging behind their mother. "You'll help me?"

Cerulean wrapped his arm around her shoulder, pulling her close. "If you let me."

The orange harvest moon glowed big and round through the lace curtained windows as Bala slouched in the back booth of the Breakfast Nook, reviewing his datapad. The Breakfast Nook belied its name since it served meals from early morning to late at night and offered everything from human breakfast fare to Uanyi appetizers.

The original human owner planned a country diner serving humans with a hunger for rural Oldearth, but as Newearth's population changed to reflect more diverse inhabitants—few of whom hungered for anything reminiscent of Oldearth—he soon found himself unable to pay the bills.

Riko sauntered in one morning, saw possibilities, and saved the day—or at least the restaurant. The original human, Mr. Gilbert, long since disabled by old age, still received a healthy percentage of the profits and a certain level of Riko's unpredictable generosity in free meals whenever he managed to hobble into town. He always nodded approvingly that the lace curtains and Oldearth décor had remained intact even if the menu had drastically changed. Riko always shrugged the old man's gratitude away. Customers came for the food. It could look like the inside of a Bhuac cave for all he cared. As long as everyone paid in proper Newearth units.

At present, the diner was deserted except for a gangly human teen wiping down the last of the tables. After whistling a free-flowing Bhuac hymn, he slapped the counter with his towel and nodded his approval. He waved a cheerful goodnight to Bala as he passed into the backroom.

Bala grinned and returned a salute.

The door chime tinkled and a poorly attired, slump-shouldered Uanyi shuffled in, his eyes searching the environment.

Bala stood and squared his shoulders.

It was getting late, and Riko had told him he'd wait for his guest to leave before closing up. "But if you could hurry things along—I've got my own affairs to tend to, see?"

Bala tried not to cringe at the approaching spectacle. He considered few aliens beautiful and this specimen of Uanyi maleness slouching toward him left him in a cold sweat. Riko was the only Uanyi he'd ever felt comfortable around and even then, he had little desire to get on Riko's bad side. Bala tried on a smile, stared at the huge, bulbous eyes and the hissing breathing helm, and decided a cold frown might be more appropriate. "Zero, I assume?"

"Idiot, I assume? Don't use no names."

Bala sat down as the Uanyi slid into place. The alien's sibilant hissing made Bala's nose wrinkle. "Yeah, right. I just—"

A meaty palm slapped the table. "Get on with it. Don't got all night."

Bala considered asking Zero if he learned English at Bothmal. But he refrained.

"Yes, well, I need to ask you some important questions, and I expect honest answers. I work for the—"

The meaty palm was at it again, slapping the table. "You brought my stuff?"

Bala ran his fingers through his disheveled hair. "Yes, but I'm not about to give you anything until you tell me what I need to know."

"Huh! Human, you brute." Apparently, even Uanyi thugs liked to apply understated sarcasm.

Bala squared his shoulders and spoke through clenched teeth. "You haven't seen anything—"

"Four hundred."

A puzzled frown crossed Bala's face. "Excuse—?"

"You waste my time. I make you pay extra."

"The deal was three hundred, and I'm not about to—"

Zero moved faster than Bala had thought possible. Lurching across the table, he pulled Bala up close and personal, Bala's small, black eyes nearly touching the Uanyi's enormous, bulging orbs. "Do what I say—"

To Bala's utter relief and eternal gratitude, Riko suddenly gripped Zero by the back of his rubbery neck. His large, bulging arms flexed till they seemed like they would burst either his immaculate white shirtsleeves or Zero's neck.

Zero released Bala as he tried to pry himself free from Riko's grip.

Riko squeezed harder. "A deal is a deal, trash, now tell the man what he wants to know."

Bala stared at Riko, a delighted smile tugging at his lips.

Zero squirmed like a fish out of water, but Riko reached over and grabbed Zero's breather helm, hissing something in Uanyi, which did not sound one bit nice by Bala's estimation.

Riko blinked his huge eyes with a deadpanned expression, his head tilted toward Bala. "What'd ya want to know?"

Amazed at his piece of unprecedented good fortune, Bala jumped in. "Right, yes! I want to know who killed Carol Hoggsworth." He dragged his charmed smile off Riko and replaced it with his formal interrogation glare, one he had practiced in the mirror at home until Kendra told him to stop. "I know the murderer was part of a Uanyi gang, and I suspect he was one of your—"

Zero's breathing grew ragged as he struggled to get his words out. "Cho. His. Name. Was. Cho." Riko loosened his grip and Zero sucked in a shuddering breath. "But you can't have him. Someone else got him. Last week."

Riko dropped Zero back into the booth and released his breather helm. "See, that wasn't so hard. Next time, be quicker, and you'll find things go easier." Riko raised an eyebrow at Bala, tapping his foot.

Bala straightened and dug into his pocket. "Oh, yes!" He pulled out small computer chip and slid it across to Zero. "Three hundred, just as we agreed. Thank you." He leaned in, folding his hands as if they were buddies having a friendly chat. "Now, would you happen to know about someone named Jane Right?"

"Never heard of her." Zero rubbed his swollen neck.

"How about Justine?"

"Listen, you only paid for one—"

Riko slapped Zero across the head with the back of his rubbery hand. "If you don't want my prints all over your body, you better get generous real quick."

Zero glared at Riko but kept his seat. "Justine? Yeah, heard of it. Big gun, they say. Someone let it out of the freezer. It's on the loose. If you got Justine working for you... maybe we can make a new deal."

Bala pursed his lips into a silent whistle and shook his head, darting a glance at Riko.

Riko gripped Zero by the neck again, lifting him to his feet. "Closing time."

Zero glared at Riko and ambled to the door, tossing back a parting insult. "Humani."

Exhaling a long sigh, Bala stood and watched Zero lurch over the threshold.

Riko called out after the retreating figure. "Your mother'd be ashamed. Wash up before going home; you smell like a sewer."

The door chime clanged as the door slammed.

Bala turned to Riko. A handshake wasn't an option. "Mother?"

Riko shrugged. "My sister's youngest. Drugs, experiments, idiot stuff. Nothing but heartbreak."

Bala shook his head, his hands flapping at his side. "I don't know how to thank you. Really, I don't have the resources to bargain well. I'll tell Clare—"

"Forget it. I didn't do it for you...particularly. It was just something that needed to be done. The right thing. You know."

Bala swallowed. He did know. He was just surprised that Riko knew.

Dry winds rustled across the harvested fields on the outskirts of Waukee. Weak rays of sunlight spread out like a heavenly fan, making a brave pretense of warming the land.

As he strode along, Cerulean attempted to soak in the Newearth scent, but he shivered. He felt weak and washed out, like paints with too much water added. He had never felt like this before. Luxonians didn't ordinarily get sick. The illness that had nearly decimated the female population a century before had been easy to fix, once they knew what was wrong. Similar to the effect penicillin had on human illness in Oldearth history. Patting his arms, Cerulean considered the possibilities. He could simply be exhausted. Or he might have picked up some foreign illness during his work among aliens. Perhaps he had attempted to maintain his human form for too long. Or maybe...he was dying.

He sniffed again, worried. But with some relief, he realized that there was nothing to smell. All living organisms had hidden themselves deep in the soil or slept in organic repose. A picture appeared in his mind: snow swirling from a white sky as he guarded Anne's sleeping form on a long winter night. So long ago. A searing pain shot through his chest. A human body told his Luxonian mind things he didn't want to know.

Justine, apparently indifferent to the stark beauty of a Newearth winter, swayed easily at his side, moving as naturally as any woman he'd ever seen. His gaze flickered over her. She could never be Anne or Clare, yet she was refreshingly desirable, something he couldn't explain to himself. Her body was a biomechanical hybrid created by a race that remained utterly mysterious and ominously dangerous.

Justine stopped and tapped Cerulean's arm. Her brow furrowed as one hand rested akimbo against her hip. "Before we get there, I want you to tell me the truth."

Cerulean closed his eyes so as not to roll them in exasperation. He had just spent a couple hours with Bala and his family; the eye roll was becoming second nature. "As I pointed out earlier, Clare is investigating Derik's case, and I think she could benefit from your...wisdom."

Justine's penetrating stare surveyed his face, searchlights looking for any hint of a lie. "What am I going to get in exchange?"

"A friend."

"Do I need another friend?"

"No one has too many friends."

Justine's gaze fixed onto Cerulean's, unabashedly, hauntingly.

Cerulean's heart thudded against his ribs. He rubbed his temple and flicked a glance across the street at the transport station. A Bhuac wearily climbed the steps. He knew how he felt.

"Listen, Justine, I can't help Clare help Derik without *your* help... if that makes any sense. People do better when they work together. Everyone sees a different part of the picture, and we'll put the puzzle together piece by piece."

Justine's chin jutted forward. "I believe you just mixed your metaphors."

Cerulean stalked forth again, his hands clenched. "Oh, hell, I'm mixing more than metaphors!"

Justine's long skirt rippled in the winter breeze, outlining the perfect shape of her legs.

After another long block and across a quiet street, Cerulean led Justine to Clare's porch. Vibrations of Mozart's Ninth Symphony poured forth from the neighbor's house. Cerulean appraised Justine with a quick breath. "Just act natural. Be yourself. You're here as my friend, and you want to help. That's all that Clare needs to know. Really."

Justine squared her shoulders. "I don't want to help *her*. I want to help *you*."

"Same thing." Cerulean pressed the doorbell. Nothing. He knocked. Nothing. He rapped his knuckles loudly on the doorframe. Nothing.

Justine tilted her head, appraising the structure before her. "Let me." She gripped the doorframe and shook it till the whole house rattled.

Cerulean's shoulders slumped.

The door swung open. Clare's wide-eyed expression nearly engulfed her face as she peered out the door. "What the—?"

Her gaze flew to Cerulean and then swept over the tall, shapely, well-dressed woman in front of her.

Cerulean leapt into the breech. "Hi, Clare. I thought you were expecting us?"

"Tomorrow."

"No...today."

Clare looked from Cerulean to Justine. Justine mouthed the syllables, "To-day" without uttering a sound.

Clare stared down at her stained sweatshirt, baggy pants, and fluffy slipper-clad feet and stepped aside, her folded arms pressed against her chest. "Well, in any case, it's nice to see you. Welcome to my humble abode." Clare smothered her grimace with a tight smile.

Cerulean marched in. Justine swayed in. Clare stumbled up behind.

Reviewing the assortment of artifacts on the shelves, new paintings on the walls, and a speckled Cresta fern in the corner, Cerulean offered a low whistle of approval. "You've been delving into the world of alien art and culture?"

Her arms cemented to her chest, Clare glowered a low glance at Justine. "Yeah? So? I decided to try and understand the Cresta mindset a bit better. That so bad?"

Cerulean turned and frowned. "No, not bad. Just not something I'd expect from you."

Hustling to the center of the room, her stance wide, ready for a fight, except for the fact that her hands were still stuffed under arms across her chest, Clare huffed. "Why not from me?"

"Well, for one, you've never shown any appreciation of art before, and two, you have no great love for Crestas."

With a dramatic unfolding and accompanied fling of her freed arm, Clare gestured to the room as if giving testimony. "Can't you see? I'm growing—okay?"

Justine sauntered over to a half-finished clay statue on a pottery wheel, listing precariously to one side. She peered at it critically. "How primitive." She batted her innocent eyes at Cerulean. "You never told me Clare had children."

Clare's jaw jutted out as she blew air between her teeth. "No, that's mine. I know it's not very good, but I'm just learning. Kendra calls it art therapy."

Justine's brows furrowed in concern, still focused on Cerulean as if Clare were deaf as well as blind. "You didn't tell me that she was impaired."

Clare stomped her slippered foot, the fluffy ends wafting in the sudden breeze. "Cerulean!"

With a shake of his head, Cerulean lifted his hands. "Stop, you two! We're here to help Derik. Remember?"

A crimson blush spreading over her cheeks, Clare tossed a bag over the statue. "Thanks, but I'm the official detective on his case, and I've decided that I don't need your help." She turned back to Cerulean. "I know you mean well, but I work best alone."

"What about Bala?"

"I have him on another case. Besides, I need to keep my professional life separate. I shouldn't have told you my troubles. You're a great person—Luxonian, I mean—but you can't possibly understand."

Cerulean clasped his hands and bowed slightly. "I defer to your superior wisdom. But the truth is, you don't know what you're dealing with. Justine is more involved than you realize, and I don't think you can help Derik without hearing what she has to say."

Clare's expression frosted as her voice grew icy. "I don't need help from an ex-convict. I'm dealing with a crime against humanity by a Cresta, and no robot—no matter how well… endowed—is going to be able to help me. It's going to take every bit of my training to—"

The front door slammed in the wake of Justine's departure.

Cerulean exhaled a long, weary breath and raked his fingers through his hair. "Good job, Detective. You just made an enemy of Taug's hired gun."

CHAPTER ELEVEN

Disaster Original

The snow-covered houses along the dark, quiet street appeared to slumber like their inhabitants, resting up for the next day's adventures. Sleeping birds rested their tiny heads under spread wings to keep out the winter chill. Even the trees stood like silent, still guards, perhaps meditating on their long years of service while their sap slowed in a well-earned hibernation.

Kendra jerked up like a marionette immersed in blackness. Her heart thudded against her chest. She cocked her head and listened. One of the boys was snoring. Other than that, she couldn't hear anything unusual. She blinked in puzzlement, then sighed and leaned back against large, welcoming pillows.

A chair scraped across the floor.

Kendra sat up again and kicked Bala's foot under the covers. "Wake up!"

Bala stirred, licked his lips, and moaned.

Kendra offered a full arm wallop on his blanketed backside before she slid out from under her warm covers. She reached for the lamp. Click. Click. Click-click-click. *Damn!*

The faint hissing of a breather helm slithered through the house.

"Bala, if you want to live through the night, I suggest you get up. *Now!*" Kendra pounded Bala on the chest.

Bala leapt out of bed in one fluid motion and promptly fell to the floor with his foot tangled in the sheets. "Oweee, oooh, ahhh." He regained his balance and fluttered to his dresser where he pulled forth a dented, second-hand Dustbuster and a flashlight. As he aimed both the gun and the light at the door, it flew open.

Two enormous Uanyi entered the bedroom. Shocked hesitation cost all. In a flash, one intruder lunged forward, knocking Bala's weapon to the side and crushing him in a decidedly unfriendly hug, while the other Uanyi thrust Kendra into a corner.

Enraged, Bala fought back, kicking and punching, in a vain attempt to reach Kendra.

Changing tactics, the Uanyi flung Bala like a toy onto the bed, where he slapped, punched, and shook the man until his teeth-rattled, and he finally stopped struggling.

Kendra screamed. The children wailed from different rooms in the house.

At the sound of heavy, clomping steps, the two Uanyi jumped away from Bala's groaning form and stood at attention.

An enormous Ingot strode into the darkened room. "Enough. Next time, maybe. Just finish the job."

The two Uanyi then proceeded to do a fair imitation of trolls having temper tantrums, breaking everything in the room, including the windows and walls. The Ingot merely folded his bulky arms and watched, his eyes gleaming.

Kendra struggled to the door, begging to be allowed to go to her kids, but the Ingot sent her sprawling back to the corner with a swift kick. The other intruders grunted in exertion as they continued their thorough devastation.

Unseen intruders smashed their way through the other rooms, forcing panicked groans from Bala, "Oh, God, oh God," his whole body curled up in pain.

After an eternity, the intruders couldn't find anything else to break. The Ingot raised his arm and waved carelessly. "Done.

Let's go." He led the others out of the bedroom and headed toward the front door, which hung by one twisted hinge. Clomping noisily down the steps, they mounted waiting scooters.

The houses, birds, and trees frightened into eerie silence acted as if they had heard nothing.

Bala slowly uncurled and slid to the floor, weak with shock-shivering pain. Kendra scrambled from the room and was met by an onslaught of sobbing children. She knelt and hugged them, crying, calling them each by name. "Rachel, sweetie, you hurt?" Kendra took a screaming baby out of the girl's arms. "Barni? David?" She rubbed the little boys' tear stained faces. "How about you, Seth?" Seth clutched a whimpering three-year-old and mutely shook his dark, curly head.

Her eyes widened in fresh terror. "Veronica?"

Bala thrashed his way into the hallway and limped to the last bedroom, calling, "Veronica!"

Streaky tears streamed down Kendra's face as she and the children slowly hauled themselves en mass towards the last bedroom. "Oh, God, no...please, not one of my babies...."

Bala sat huddled on the floor with a small child cradled in his lap, his arms encircling her hunched form. She buried her face in his chest, as he lay collapsed against the cracked wall. "She was in the closet, hiding under luggage. She's... okay."

Kendra fell to her knees, all the children crumpling with her. "Lord, save me now, save me."

Swallowing against the pain, Bala rocked his shivering child. "He—just—did."

With a trembling finger, her face contorting in agony, Kendra wiped tears from her baby's face. "Not from this hate."

Clare dashed across the muddy, scarred lawn, jumped the porch steps two at a time, and banged ferociously on the front door. She hopped from foot to foot as she waited, peering through a cracked window into the living room. "Oh, God! Oh,

God! Please—" Shuffled footsteps pinned her to the floor. She braced herself, ready to rush in. The broken door complained feebly and was shoved aside.

Bala stood there, his black and blue face testifying to his current state of health. One eye had swollen shut. He gripped the doorframe for support.

Clare jumped forward and squeezed him in a hug. "Oh, God! Bala, it's worse than—"

Kendra's groan called from a back room. "No visitors, please. The place is a mess."

Bala managed a strangled, "Just Clare, honey. Go back to sleep." He stepped aside, releasing his neck from her suffocating embrace and gestured toward the living room. He shifted the door back into place, limped to his broken couch, and braced himself. With one hand, he flourished a mocking bow. "New decorating scheme. Disaster original."

Clare fought back tears. "How can you joke at a time like this?"

"It's either laugh or cry and my eyes hurt, so I figure—"

Clare paced the room, her hands clenched into fists. "I'll get her; I promise. I'd like to wring her thick, flabby neck with my own hands!"

Bala slumped onto the broken couch. It tipped at a precarious angle. Ignoring the danger, he rested his head on his hand, leaned back and raised a swollen eyebrow at Clare. "Who, exactly, are you planning on strangling on my behalf?"

Clare stomped around the room, groaning at smashed family pictures, tendrils of shredded plants, ripped curtains, and all the mind-numbing destruction. "I can think of two."

Bala rubbed his chin, and it started to bleed. "Aww, darn. I thought I stoppered all the leaks." He tried to heave himself off the couch but fell back with a pained squeak.

Clare ran to his side. "Stay put. What do you need?"

Bala pointed a nervous finger down the hall. "In the bathroom, the cabinet was left intact. Missed it in the dark, I suppose. Sloppy of them."

Clare scurried down the hall and bumped into Kendra with a shriek. "Kendra! Oh, Lord!"

Kendra waved Clare down the hall. "Bandages to the right. I'm just going to order something to eat. Can't fix meals in this—looks like a couple hurricanes came through."

Clare's eyes widened in alarm as if Kendra's sending a message would drain her last vestiges of strength. "No, let me! I'll call. I'll take care of everything. Just go sit with Bala. His chin is bleeding." Proof enough that the universe tottered on the edge of an abyss.

Kendra shrugged one shoulder and nodded her acceptance. "Sure. Fix everything." She rotated a limp hand in the air. "Play Fairy Godmother—long as you want." She stumbled down the hall.

Clare dashed into the bathroom. A moment later, she scampered back into the living room, brandishing a bandage. "Here, I'll just wrap your—" She stared.

Bala lay crumpled into Kendra's embrace. She rocked him like a baby.

Clare's eye filled with tears, and her lips quivered.

Kendra stared up through dry, vacant eyes. "Don't start." She peered down at Bala's blood-caked chin. "Let him sleep. He's been watching over us since this whole—insanity—happened. The Interventionists came, did their thing. Amazing the house is still standing."

Clare slid to the edge of the couch, bracing one hand on the wall to keep it from falling over. "Why didn't you call me?"

"Bala didn't want to wake you in middle of the night. Told 'em to wait till morning."

Clare shook her head. "Idiot. I'm supposed to be called first. I could have helped. Plus, I need fresh evidence. He knows that."

Kendra shrugged. "He wasn't thinking too clearly. Having your head bashed in and your family terrorized does funny things to a man." Kendra smoothed Bala's disheveled hair. "Look, you said you want to help, well, then go ahead. Order something. We need to eat, no matter how sick we feel. And then you go ahead and get these—" Kendra's voice dropped to a shaky whimper.

Clare fell to her knees and knelt at Kendra's side. "Don't let them get to you—not on the inside. Please. Hang on to the Kendra I know and love, the one who hasn't a mean bone in her body."

Kendra stroked her husband's head. "My kids wouldn't agree." Kendra leveled her gaze at Clare's teary eyes. "But I won't let this happen again. We're gonna protect ourselves. No one had the right to terrorize us. God! We're human beings!"

Clare rose, sniffed back impending tears, and started tapping on her datapad. "As soon as I get some food on your table, I'm going to call everyone I know to see that your family is protected."

A child called from the back room. "Maaaa-ma!"

Kendra sighed and laid Bala's limp form gently on the couch. She smoothed his hair away from his eyes as she called back. "Coming, honey." She straightened and gestured vaguely in the direction of the kitchen. "Sounds good. But please don't lay anything on the table just yet—it's scattered all over the floor." Rubbing the small of her back, Kendra limped out of the room.

Clare faced Bala and knelt by his slumbering side. Her voice lowered to a husky whisper. "We'll get them, Bala. Promise."

CHAPTER TWELVE

So Small On The Inside

The Newearth Museum of Human History was still under construction and probably always would be. It was five stories high and delved three stories into the ground, making a total of eight floors. Since it was built directly over the site of an Oldearth museum and had transported a significant number of artifacts from other ancient sites around the planet, it was the greatest collection of Oldearth history anywhere in the universe.

Justine stood in the enormous entrance hall, a reconstructed prehistoric cave dwelling, and soon became absorbed in analyzing the primitive wall paintings.

"Hey, Justine! Here you are. I was looking all over." Derik trotted to her side and stared up at the beautiful figures of ancient animals. "Yeah, my Dad liked these too. He said that the cave dwellers weren't nearly so primitive as we like to think. They just had underdeveloped superiority—something like that." He nudged Justine in the ribs with a grin.

Justine grinned back automatically and linked arms with her date. They strolled through the cave into further timelines denoting major ages of human development. "I like it here. It reminds me of something I can't quite remember."

Moving toward a life-size diorama of a medieval castle with a moat, drawbridge, keep, and battlements, Derik grinned. "Now this is where I'd like to live. Right here." He pointed to the center of the castle where a cutout portion exposed the main hall replete with roasting venison and long, trestle tables lined with warriors enjoying a feast. The lord of the manor wore a circlet of gold and a warm smile as he lifted a goblet in a feudal salute.

Justine's fixed smile faded as she tilted her head, first one way, then another, considering the diorama. "I don't see any of the women smiling. Why?"

Derik shrugged.

Strolling forward, Justine stopped at the thick doors of an ancient abbey. A life-sized chapel stood to the side. Justine circled around and entered the small church arranged with wooden benches, kneelers, a confessional, and an altar at the front. Flames on wax candles wavered in the breeze she carried into the still space. A veiled figure rose, bowed toward the altar, turned, and passed them with a gentle smile and a nod.

Derik stepped aside as she passed, tucking his hands under his armpits. "It's cold in here."

Justine padded to the altar, caressed the cream-colored stone and paused, her gaze fixed on the crucifix hanging above the door. "This place is alive."

Derik shook his head. "Probably just paid actors."

Justine gazed around the room, inhaling a deep breath. Crossing in front of a diminutive statue, she caressed the metallic face of a young woman holding a sword. Justine swallowed, blinking back a sudden, unfathomable emotion. She strolled toward the stained-glass windows, lifting her hand as if to trace the detailed pattern of colored glass. "I could live here." Traipsing over to a side panel tucked in a recess, she tapped the "Explore" button. A black-robed figure, who appeared to have stepped out of an Oldearth monastery, began to speak. "Welcome to St. Joan of Arc's Chapel, originally situated in the village of Chasse in the Rhone Valley, France..."

Derik tapped his foot.

Justine stared at his foot, pressed the end button, and stopped the exploration. "Another time, then."

Derik hugged her arm and led her toward new adventures. "There's so much to see here. We'll have to come again. But I really want to show you my favorite place—the dinosaur exhibit. You like dinosaurs?" Without waiting for an answer Derik pulled Justine tighter and leaned in close. "I don't care what I see, as long as I'm with you. It's so wonderful to—"

Justine kissed Derik, causing more than a few pairs of eyes to turn in their direction. Releasing him with a playful shove, she turned and started down the exhibit hall, pointing to a sign: "Dinosaurs: Their Rise and Demise." She grinned.

Dressed in a form-fitting sweater, long pants, and stylish boots, Justine traipsed up the dirt path to Cerulean's cabin. Near the top, she stopped and gazed over the great, bluish-green lake. Foaming whitecaps furiously slammed against the ice-encased coast. The green, pine-forested vista fell away behind her. She sighed, her white breath blown into the breeze, and marched the final steps to Cerulean's cabin. A quick tread behind made her stop. She cocked her head and peered around with a furrowed brow.

From the distance, Clare called. "Hey, Cerulean, wait up a sec—"

Justine stood her ground, her bare fists on her hips.

Well bundled in a white, fluffy winter coat, thick pants, and a red tasseled hat, Clare rushed forward with her head down, fighting the cold wind. She pummeled into the silent figure like a ball bouncing off a wall. Her head jerked up, her wide eyes, startled. "Oh, you. I thought Cerulean—"

Justine's eyes narrowed. "Seems we're both looking for him."

Clare stepped back on the path, wiping her pink, frozen nose with the back of her gloved hand. "Yeah, well. I need to talk to him about something important."

"Me too."

Clare rolled her eyes. "What could be so important to a robot?"

Justine stomped a large, menacing step forward. "I'm getting tired of your attitude. I've known Cerulean far longer than you."

Clutching the ends of her coat sleeves, Clare sneered. "What? Since your prison days?" She practically danced like a squirrel taunting a wolf. "Please tell me that you're reformed and hope to start a new life—" She underestimated Justine's reach.

Grabbing Clare by her jacket-front, Justine pulled her close, glaring directly into her eyes. "I could crush you."

Pretending that she was not trembling, Clare clipped her words. "How. Like. A. *Robot*."

Justine dropped Clare, brushed passed, and strode a few steps down the path.

Clare called. "I know you're a hired gun and that you have a connection with Governor Jane Right. I also suspect that you tried to kill my partner, Bala, when he got too close to the truth." Clare crossed her padded arms high over her chest, her tone just as high and mighty. "You wouldn't mind replacing all of humanity with machines, would you?"

Justine spun around and spat out her words. "Your jealousy blinds you. I thought humans knew how to separate fact from fiction, but apparently that is another art you have yet to master."

A flame rose in Clare's cheeks. She stomped up the porch steps and then turned and peered disdainfully down at Justine. "Jealousy? I have nothing to be jealous—"

Justine jabbed a finger in the air. "You have feeling for Derik *and* Cerulean, but you can't have either. Derik is more man than you can handle. Cerulean merely pities you."

"You wretched—"

Justine waved her off as she turned. "Don't be so easily insulted. It's not your fault that you're born weak. The fact that you even try to protect humanity is rather remarkable, pathetic but—"

"When I get enough evidence to tie you to that nefarious Cresta or Governor Right, I'm going to shut you down—or recycle your machinery—whatever they do with useless robots!"

Justine shook her head as she snapped branches out of her way. "Go ahead and try. But you'll have to get in line." Justine disappeared out of sight.

Clare stood on the porch, staring after her, blinking back tears of rage.

Governor Right tapped her fingers together pyramid style. The shadow towered above her, but she held her pose unperturbed. She had dealt with this kind before. *They always make themselves appear big because they're so small on the inside.* "So you need my help, is that it?"

The ultra-luxurious office signaled her importance to the beings of Newearth. A vast majority of citizens had voted her into office, though she owned a great number of the voting machines, while the humans who managed them owed her. Sitting at her artistically fashioned desk with an inlaid marble top and hardwood legs carved into snakes and other beasts of the jungle, she waited patiently. She had all the time in the world. Well, until her next appointment. A quick glance at her desktop datapad informed her that she had room for negotiating.

The shadowed figure pronounced each word distinctly. "Like you, I wish to rewrite history. But unlike you, my history will reveal the truth."

The governor tapped her fingers, bored. "I suppose you believe that. It always helps to believe our own lies." The disembodied chuckle surprised Governor Right. She didn't know any other thugs with a sense of humor.

"I don't need to lie. Besides, I have friends, very powerful friends who agree that my service is invaluable."

"Oh, we're all invaluable, certainly. And what, pray tell, is my invaluable service going to include?"

The shadow glided to a dim corner as if to distance itself from the message it had to convey. "Certain associates have been experimenting with a new drug, which could assist several races in their district; their biology is similar to humans. Naturally, they want to test their product first, without repercussions."

"Naturally." The governor knew it was stupid to ask, but her curiosity was piqued, and she never liked nebulous details. "So why don't you just pay for volunteers?"

"That would cost a great deal and take time. Besides, humans become unreasonable if something goes wrong. They tend to ban all further testing if too many subjects die."

The governor waved her hand eloquently. "Your associates, on the other hand—"

The visitor's dead tone snapped. "Could spend the entire human race and not blink an eye."

Governor Right stiffened. "Well, let's hope it doesn't come to that." She tapped her amble bosom. "I have some sensibilities, don't you know."

The shadow loomed closer. "You'll be well paid. And there is the matter of history..."

Rising, the governor shifted her large body and passed the mysterious figure. "You care about human history?"

"I find it fascinating, as do many on the Inter-Alien Committee. They have a fondness for accurate records."

Governor Right grinned as she poured herself an amber drink, never even considering a polite offer to her guest. "Ah, yes, a fondness. I have a fondness for units, don't you know?"

The figure floated near. "Would an extra million make you happy?"

"Delighted, would be more accurate." The governor saluted her guest with the drink-holding hand.

The figure retreated to the door, but Governor Right waggled a bejeweled finger in the air. "Just a thought, before you go to wherever it is shadows descend—Bala."

The shadow twisted. "Bala?"

"You know who I am talking about."

"I would like to know more, though—"

"Please, don't tell me that his innocent heart touches your spirit or some such drivel. After all, I don't believe you have a heart, and I doubt anything could quench your spirit."

The shadow grew, engulfing Jane Right in complete blackness. A strangled cry pierced the air.

The shadow receded.

Governor Right staggered. Her amber drink spilled across the smooth, tiled floor, the glass rolled out of sight. She grabbed the corner of her desk and leaned heavily against it. For several moments, she breathed, in, out, trying to steady herself, shaking off a blackout. With stiff-willed control, she raised her head and stared at the shadowed figure. "You shouldn't have been able—I don't believe in devils."

"Neither do I."

Reassembling her shattered dignity, the governor squared her shoulders. "You can go. I have no other questions."

The shadow quivered. "And Bala?"

Governor Right waved her hand weakly. "Forget it."

"I would like to leave him intact. I enjoy studying him, but I had to teach him manners."

A feeble nod assented. "If anyone could."

The shadow loomed closer. "Married men with children are easy to tame."

Governor Right chose another glass from her cabinet. "Lucky for me—"

The shadow rose, darkening the glorious office into premature night. "Women who want to live are equally easy to tame."

Jane Right's hand froze. She bowed her head. "I'm rather ashamed."

"You should be. There is a reason I never bothered to study you."

CHAPTER THIRTEEN

Long Past Trust

Justine stood in the middle of the pristine laboratory, analyzing Taug, her legs wide, her arms folded across her chest, and one eyebrow raised, marring her symmetrical face. She spoke with forced precision. "You-want-me-to-kidnap-Derik?"

Taug's tentacles spread in acceptance. "You've accomplished far more difficult tasks. This shouldn't prove much of a challenge."

Justine swatted a mosquito on her arm and frowned. She darted a look from Taug to the sterile room and back to Taug. "Why?"

Taug slapped at the buzz of an insect in his ear. He waddled over to a small tank, lifted the lid, peered in, shook his head and replaced it. "He hasn't been answering my messages. The last time we spoke, I urged him to move in—"

"You want him to live in the lab? Why?" Justine squared her shoulders and unfolded her arms, fists ready for hand-to-hand combat.

Completely ignoring Justine, Taug's eyes followed a buzzing insect around the room. "He might get hurt out in the open."

Justine snatched the fly from the air and held it by the wing. It dangled, buzzing even more furiously. She pounded forward, staring Taug in the eye. "Tell me the truth."

A tentacle flew at Justine. In a second, her legs were wrapped in a tight squeeze. Taug flipped her across the room.

Justine regained her footing and barreled forward, her head down in ramming position.

Taug's body quivered on impact. He grabbed a tentacle-full of hair and pulled Justine's head back so that she could see him. One tentacle held a Dustbuster while another tapped a small, black sphere on his belt.

Justine froze, her gaze fixed on the belt.

Taug shoved her back and gestured with the Dustbuster. "Stand by the wall." He circled her as he held the weapon leveled at her chest. "When it comes to telling the truth, you've not been particularly forthcoming." He nodded at the micro-recorder on his belt. "You've seen this before? I implanted a matching one on Derik; it looks like a mole on the back of his neck. I dare say he hasn't noticed, but you have." A snide grin slithered across his face. "With this little ear, I've heard every conversation he's had. I must say, he's not an original lover but at least he seems sincere."

Justine's jaw clenched, fitting her rock-like stance. "None of your business."

Taug chided her with a waving tentacle. "Oh, but Derik *is* my business. As he is supposed to be yours. No good ever comes from mixing business with pleasure, I always say." Taug aimed the Dustbuster as Justine's hand quivered. "Don't even think about it. I'm not a fool. It would only take one mark to have you disassembled for spare parts. My notes, available to every Cresta upon my death, would identify you as my murderer. Your memories are not so valuable so as to save you a second time."

Justine threw back her head, defiant. "What do you want?"

"Retrieve Derik. I want him here, in my lab, tomorrow. And I want him to know that he needs to cooperate with me or—"

"You're threatening me?"

"Very effectively."

Justine strode to the wall-tank and ran a finger across the glass. She stared into the murky depths with studious indifference. "What are you planning to do, long term?"

Taug lowered his tentacle, relaxing the Dustbuster against his side. "If it was necessary for you to know, I'd tell you, but it's not. All you need to know is that his life depends on how efficiently you obey me."

Justine's splayed hand stiffened. "I'm your slave now?"

"The term slave involves the possibility of freedom; you don't have that, so you are not a slave."

Justine turned, her gaze frozen, and stepped toward Taug. "What am I, then?"

"A tool."

"You cold-blooded, inhumane—"

Taug chuckled, his bulbous eyes gleaming. "Trust me, being human isn't quite as charming as it's made out to be. I've had a lot of experience, and humans are often every bit as cold-blooded as a Cresta. The difference is that I work in accordance with my nature; therefore, I'm perfecting myself. Humans have no such hope." Taug meandered past Justine toward the wall. "I'm going for a swim. Mention that to Derik. It'll make your task a little easier."

Justine strode to the door but before crossing the threshold, she stopped. She looked back at Taug. "And the insects? What are they for?"

Nodding in approval, Taug slid the Dustbuster back into a sleeve pocket. "I knew you'd ask. They are a part of my studies. Insects have some rather startling qualities that I might find useful."

Justine grunted her agreement as she stalked out of the room. "You'd make a good insect yourself."

Justine chopped carrots at lightning speed. Her fingers swept the assembly of other vegetables into a waiting pot, swiveled to the sink, and added water. Faster than a human eye could follow, she dropped in spices and a variety of mystery ingredients.

As the spicy aroma pervaded the room, Derik shuffled into the kitchen. He hugged her from behind and kissed her neck. "Hmmm, hmm, that smells good! How did you manage to put that together so quickly?"

Justine leaned back into the hug and reached behind to ruffle his thick hair. "I already had it prepared. I just needed to warm it up."

"Gorgeous, intelligent, and a good cook. Is there another woman like you on the planet?"

Justine's lopsided smile wavered. "Not likely."

A ting sent her into her living room. Ivy stenciling meandered across the upper walls while baskets of hanging plants brightened the corners. Oldearth-style paintings hung strategically throughout the room. Justine ignored it all as she retrieved her datapad. Taug's face rose into view. Justine slapped the datapad against her thigh as Derik ambled into the room.

"Something important?"

Justine shook her head and flipped the pad over on her desk. "Just a reminder." She stepped over to a wide couch and patted the seat next to her. "We need to talk."

Derik grimaced.

Justine interpreted his expression and grinned winningly. "Not that kind of talk."

"Ah, good!" Derik slid onto the couch beside her, one arm swinging up and around her shoulders.

She caressed one of his legs with hers. "I met a friend of yours, a Cresta named Taug."

Derik jerked but Justine held him back with a comforting touch. "Don't worry. He told me everything. About you and his father. It was a relief, really. I knew there was something different about you, but I just never imagined—"

Derik closed his eyes and leaned back with a strangled sigh. "Why did he have to tell—you?"

"He cares about you." Justine stroked Derik's cheek. "For a Cresta, that's a high compliment. He said he could help you adjust to all the changes. But you need to trust him."

Derik opened his eyes and stared at Justine. "Did he tell you that he considered killing me?"

Justine shifted closer and breathed into his ear, stroking his cheek. Her voice dropped to a husky whisper. "He told me everything. He needs you, and I just want you to be happy."

Tears brimming, Derik leaned forward. "I'm a mixed breed, illegal, and unwanted by every race in the universe. I should've had the courage to tell you. It's been hell trying to hide my deformities, but I was afraid—"

Justine ran a finger across his lips. "Don't. I have eyes; I already knew...some things. But it doesn't bother me. The man I care about is on the inside. Not the shell on the outside."

Derik's delicate composure fractured. He dropped his face into his hands and sobbed. "I don't deserve you."

A twisted smile shadowed Justine's face. "Maybe not. But you've got me just the same. And Taug. Question is, will you trust us?"

Derik wiped his eyes and leaned into Justine's comforting embrace. "It's gone long past trust."

Derik removed the swimming mask from his face and pulled a large towel from a rack above his dripping bodysuit. The suit didn't cover his Cresta anatomy, which allowed him to absorb the nutrients and experience the intoxicating sensation of revitalized Cresta skin. He had little to compare the sensation to, but he openly admitted that it was addictive. This month he had gone swimming with Taug nearly every day.

Taug donned his bio-suit in calm dignity. His eyes flickered over Derik's human-Cresta body, and he pursed his puffy lips. He no longer shuddered at the sight of Derik's anatomy. In fact, Derik wondered if he wasn't just a bit jealous.

Derik had shown that he had the capacity to enjoy Cresta sensibilities with remarkable depth. Yet he also retained the ability to enjoy a fully functioning human body. Though Derik did have to wear bio-suits now, so did everyone in a way. Even humans had to wear protective clothing.

As soon as they were dressed, Taug gestured Derik toward a round steel table piled high with instruments, standing in front of a wall of medical scanners. "It's time."

Derik shook his head. "I'm awfully tired. Couldn't we skip it today? I mean, I'll be back tomorrow."

Taug rubbed one tentacle across his chin meditatively. "Yes, I've been thinking about that." He padded across the room. "I'm concerned about you."

Idly lifting one of the medical instruments, Derik peered at it closely. "Me? Why? You're the only one I know who wants me dead, so I'm relatively safe, don't you think?" Derik's accompanying chuckle proved how far their relationship had developed.

Taug appeared to appreciate the joke and offered a thin smile in return. "True, but Newearth is still a dangerous place. Beings get injured all the time; they're victims of a hundred crimes a day. You never know when something might happen."

Derik thumped his chest. "No one is going to mess with me." He wagged his finger playfully at Taug. "You're in far more danger than I am."

"That is another consideration." Taug shuffled closer. "Derik, I'd like you to live here."

The instrument dangled from Derik's hand. "At a laboratory?"

"Yes."

"Don't *you* live here?"

"I have a small room in the back, but I would install separate quarters for you, a nice apartment, better than what you have now. That way you won't have to travel back and forth, and we can continue working—"

Slapping the instrument on the table, Derik pouted. "But I

have a job and a life! I'm not just your pet project, you know. I have a relationship and my job is very—"

"Low paying. I could pay you five times as much."

Derik shuffled across the room, curiosity getting the better of him. "You never offered to pay before."

"I was still deciding."

Stopping in mid-stride, Derik turned and unrolled a heart monitor from the wall. He darted a glance at Taug and twirled the tip between his fingers. "So if I take your offer, you're certain you won't kill me?"

Taug hesitated for just an instant. "Yes."

Derik dropped the heart monitor. "I don't know. I like your offer, but I need to think about it. I want to talk to Justine." Derik smirked and tilted his head back, appraising the figure before him. "So, are you considered good looking, on Crestar, I mean?"

Taug wiggled, a humorous gleam in his eye. "I was what you would call 'quite the catch.' In fact, I had so many Crestar females asking to be my mate that my parents held an auction."

Derik swallowed, his eyes bugging as he stumbled forward. "What? Your parents auctioned you off?"

Taug nearly fell backwards in a spasm of delight. "No, no. You are such a hatchling! I forget. No, they auctioned for the female to be my prize."

Derik rubbed his mouth with the back of his hand as if to wipe away a bad taste. "That's sick! I thought males and females had equal status in your culture."

Taug shook his head impatiently. "They do, but you misunderstand. Equal does not mean the same. We have rituals for mating and procreation, much like you humans. There was once something humans called the bride price, was there not?"

"In our barbaric past."

"Perhaps, but for us, the bride price is not barbaric. It shows how much the family wants the match and the worth of the female. You can trust that we do not waste our families. Males, females, and hatchlings each have an important part to play in our culture, and we do not treat any of them as expendable." Taug looked away.

Derik reached for the heart monitor again, as if clinging to a lifeline, and pulled it free of the wall. "But you're scientists. You experiment on everyone. If you experiment, someone has to be expendable."

Taug stood frozen. His gaze returned to Derik, appraising him anew. "It's intriguing, the way you think. But still, you don't understand. Science is our greatest good. To further science is the highest call, and therefore, no one is expendable."

Derik shook his head and stepped to the door. It slid open automatically. "Well, for a while there, *I* was pretty expendable. Maybe I'm not now, but seeing how things can change, I'd rather keep my options open." He trudged across the threshold.

Taug shuffled over, picked the heart monitor off the floor, and clutched it to his chest, his gaze never leaving the doorway.

CHAPTER FOURTEEN

Hope Endures When Doubts Are Few

Bala stood on the transport-docking bay and watched as a massively muscled and well-armed human guard led a manacled Ingot forward. Bala held out his hand and accepted a datapad.

The guard grunted. "This your guy? Just give me your print, and we'll be on our way."

Bala studied the Ingot and pressed his hand onto the datapad. "Yep, it's him." He pursed his lips as they started away. "Hold on a second; I have a question."

The guard frowned. "Hurry up, would you? I've got a schedule to keep. Bothmal is going to be busy tonight."

Bala braced himself. "So tell me—why? I got all the evidence I need, but I just don't get it. You didn't have any record before this, and your family says that you've never been in any trouble before. They insist that you were practically an angel—far as Ingots go. So why hire Cho? Why kill Mrs. Hoggsworth?"

The Ingot shrugged. "Everyone has their price."

Bala peered into his eyes. "Did someone threaten your family?"

A slight sneer cracked the Ingot's indifference. "My family has never been safer."

Bala shook his head. "I could argue that point. So what enticed you to risk spending twenty years at Bothmal?"

The Ingot's derision was palpable. "I won't be spending twenty years at Bothmal."

Bala pursed his lips, tapping his fingers together. "It's pretty secure. And the records are clear. You've got twenty with no chance of parole."

The Ingot chuckled, swiveling his gaze over to the guard. "We going?"

The guard shrugged. "No time to waste today." He nudged the Ingot down the long, gray corridor.

Bala stood back, frowning, as the Ingot strode to a corner, flashing back a confident grin.

Snow had fallen early in the day, but by the late afternoon, dreary, uneven shadows encompassed Clare's study. Shelves lined with an assortment of trophies, graduation certificates, family photos, Oldearth artifacts, and a shellacked Easter egg stood in silent testimony to a few of her favorite things.

Clare hunched over a cluttered desk, one hand propping her head as she scrolled through files on a screen imbedded in the wall.

A black cat sidled past, rubbing against her legs.

Clare lifted the feline onto her lap and stroked it absently. "Dang it! Justine is all over these files but only as a reference. Guess she wasn't working for Right, after all—" She peered through the gloom at the purring cat. "Are you even listening?"

The cat meowed a long series of vowels.

Clare lifted it to eye level. "I just fed you—" She glanced at her datapad. "Is that really the time?" She stood, dropping the cat unceremoniously. "Come on. Why can't you just hunt up some mice like all the other neighborhood quadrupeds? I bet they laugh behind their paws at you."

The cat twirled around her legs, meowing even more plaintively.

"Okay, okay. Don't trip me." Clare crab-walked, avoiding the ever-present paws all the way to the kitchen, where she noticed a small mound of clothes stuffed in a corner, wedged between the hamper and the wall. With a frown, she reached down to scoop up the laundry when the cat sprang between her and the mound, a deep-throated yowl issuing from its chest.

Clare jumped back, snatching her hand out of the way. "What the hell?" She sidestepped to the closet and snatched a sweeper. Her attempt to nudge the cat out of the way failed, as the feline sprang to the center of the pile and placed its feet around a wiggling mass. Clare bent in, not too close, but close enough to realize what she was looking at. A smile spread across her face. "Awww! When did the babies come? I thought that was another week away." She shrugged at the furious mother, who now glared as if Clare had indelicately intruded on private matters.

"Sheesh! You forgot who sprang you from kitty prison? Listen, I'm not the enemy, you know!" She ripped open a feedbag and dumped the contents into a wide dish and stood back as the cat scrambled for the food. Clare's eyes darted from the mother cat to the kittens. Taking the smallest step possible, she leaned toward the mound. The mother cat sprang with another howl. Raising her hands in surrender, Clare backed off and returned to her wall screen, muttering. "Prison must've made you paranoid. Never trust a human—that your creed?" Suddenly she stopped and stared into space, a blush working its way up her cheeks. "Oh hell!"

Slapping the console, Clare worked her way around a series of files. "You know, Justine could tell me everything I need to know about Governor Right, but she happens to hate my guts just now. Justine, not the governor. Though..."

The cat rubbed itself around Clare's ankles. Apparently, not being in the immediate vicinity of her kittens did wonders for the feline's attitude.

Clare peered down at the cat and stroked it with her toe. "All friendly now, are we? Do you even care about me? As long as I keep that dish filled, the entire population of Newearth could be planning my demise, and you'd be content." Clare huffed, paced across the room, and pulled on her shoes. "You think disassembling a robotic brain in the line of duty would be considered murder?"

The cat sat on its haunches, daintily cleaning its paws. A long tail swooshed contentedly around its back legs.

Clare rubbed her chin. "You don't think it has feelings—" Clare shook her head and stomped back to her computer. She scanned the files once more and frowned. "Cerulean certainly seems to like her. And she looks at him like she might—" Slapping the keypad, the wall screen went blank. "Not my problem. He's as old as the hills anyway!" She nodded to the cat. "I'll trust you to keep 'em safe. She snatched her datapad and dashed out the door.

The expanse of soft, white snow contrasted beautifully with the black, jagged branches overhead. Derik filled his lungs with the scent of distant pine trees and pristine, wintertime air. He stepped to the park bench and brushed snow to the ground in a fine dusting. His gaze swept the area and found Justine's figure slowly approaching from the north.

His heart pounded as one hand fingered a small box in his coat pocket. It was the perfect location, the spot where they had first spoken together. Okay, they had actually first spoken in the middle of the Vandi street, but that was no place to propose, unless he wanted to end up in a hospital before she had a chance to say yes. His eyes followed her, fixed like a ship's captain on the North Star.

Justine ambled forward, a soft smile playing on her lips. "You picked an odd place to meet today. Your apartment is a lot warmer and more comfortable."

"I have a good reason." He flourished a gallant gesture toward the bench. "Do you remember?"

Justine nodded. "The bench we shared the day I—"

"It was a fortunate accident that brought us together. I'd thank the driver, if I could."

Justine shifted, digging her hands deep into her pockets. "Surely, we would've met eventually. Vandi isn't so big."

Derik placed his hands low on her waist and pulled her in close. "You believe in destiny?"

Justine swallowed, a worried gaze surveying the environment over his shoulder. "'*Faith in destiny, my beloved, entwines us true, for hope endures when doubts are few.*'" She pulled back so she could look him in the eye. "Ancient Bhuac saying." She attempted a smile. "Still, I trust my senses. After all, Vandi is only a few hundred kilometers wide."

Derik threw back his head and laughed. "You always surprise me. Your brilliance is unmatched by anyone I've ever met." He stared into her eyes. "I don't know another woman alive who'd have loved me, knowing what I am."

Her gaze sliding over his, Justine leaned in for a kiss. Just before their lips touched, she wrapped her fingers around his neck and pinched him.

Jerking back, Derik grimaced and rubbed his neck. "Ouch! What's that for?" He turned pale at the sight of blood. "I've heard of love bites but—"

Justine held up a tiny, black dot, squeezed between her fingers. "Sorry, an insect of some kind." She dropped it and ground the speck into the dirt."

"A bug? Like a tick? I thought those were eradicated."

Justine turned away, her jaws tight. "Guess not."

Blinking back his confusion, Derik fumbled with his coat pocket. "Never mind. I've got something for you." Drawing out a small velvet box, he offered it to Justine. "It's like the one my dad gave my mom. They had to special order it, of course, because no one makes these anymore."

After one last surveying glance, Justine focused on Derik. An eyebrow rose. "You want to give me a box?"

Derik grinned. "Not the box. What's inside. Remember, what you said when you told me you knew the truth."

Justine froze. "What do you mean?"

"Open the box and find out."

With a flick, the box opened, revealing a golden band. Molded symbols curved around the edge. Justine picked the ring out of its nest and held it up to the failing light filtering through the winter sky. Hearts intertwined with ivy leaves wrapped around the outside. Etched lettering spelled the words, *Derik and Justine ~ Forever*.

Derik's eyes glowed in reflected glory as he watched Justine's eyes fill with tears. He smiled as he drew her into a tight embrace. "Don't cry. It's our future. Together."

Justine let the tears slip down her cheeks. She was not surprised at the ring or the offer. She was surprised at the tears.

CHAPTER FIFTEEN

No Matter How Hard I Try

Clare sidled up behind Derik as he took the last shuffling step to his apartment door. Dirty snow clung to his boots and dripped off his shoulders. He pressed his print-identifier key and pushed the door open with his boot while balancing two bags of groceries in his arms.

Clare frowned as she tapped him from behind. "Hey, where've you been? I've been waiting half an hour."

Derik jerked, peered at Clare, and sniffed. "How was I supposed to know? Did you message me?"

"I tried but your datapad must be broken. Anyway, it was a sudden thought. We need to talk. Can I come in?"

Derik shrugged and stepped aside, letting Clare march ahead. He strode around the counter, placed the bags aside, checked his datapad, frowned, and then opened his freezer. He tossed items in haphazardly.

Clare stared wide-eyed. "You only buy frozen food?"

"I'm not much of a cook, but Taug showed me something—" Derik colored. "Never mind."

"Taug? The Cresta who wants to kill you, Taug?"

Derik threw the last item on the frozen pile and balled up the shopping bags, flinging them into a hamper under the sink.

"Look, you don't know anything about him. I do." He strode to the couch, heaved himself down with a relieved sigh, and gestured to another chair. "Go ahead, sit. Tell me why you're here."

Clare eyed Derik darkly. "How very Cresta of you."

"Huh?"

"The commanding tone, the sharp gesture. Who made *you* boss?"

Derik tapped his fingertips together. "You're in my apartment. You said you were going to help me, but in the end, I had to help myself. I know who I am and why I was created. I even know who wants to kill me. I've got my life under control, so there's no great need for your services anymore." Derik assumed an exaggerated, professional politeness. "But I still need to pay you, right? You haven't done much, but I'll count your generous intentions." He sat up and started tapping on his datapad. "Working, see?" He shook his head at Clare's obvious incompetence.

Clare folded her arms across her chest as she stood in front of Derik, who though seated, could still glare intimidatingly. "You're too kind. Listen, Derik, I may not have accomplished much, but I did listen to you, and I've always been willing to help."

Derik nodded, his eyes returning to his datapad. "What account do I send it to?"

Clare stomped around the room, her hands clenched on her hips. "Would you stop? I'm not interested in getting paid at the moment. I don't get compensated until the job is done, and I haven't finished yet. You still don't know the truth."

Derik kept his finger poised over his datapad. "I know I'm thirty-percent Cresta and that Taug and I are friends. I'm helping him understand crossbreeds better, and he's invited me to live at his lab, though I have other plans. So, I think I know the score pretty well, don't you?"

"You don't know everything." Clare stopped pacing and leaned in. She stared Derik in the eye, one hand braced on the back of the couch. "Justine is an android. She's a hired gun. I don't know if she's been hired to kill you or not, but it's what she does for a living—if you can call being a robot, living."

Dropping the datapad, Derik flew off the couch and smashed Clare against the wall, squeezing her neck.

She gasped, wrestled his bulging arms, and kneed him in the groin. They fell together across the coffee table and onto the floor.

Derik rolled on top of Clare and pinned her, choking the breath out of her.

Clare, wide-eyed, smashed Derik's chest with her fists, attempting to shove him off, kicking and squirming, trying to roll to a more advantageous position, but Derik's combined weight and strength was too much for her. In desperation, she bit his arm.

Derik slapped her across the face. "Stop it! Just stop." His breath rose in great huffs as he blinked away tears. Sweat broke across his forehead. "I didn't mean… I don't want to hurt you!" His gaze lifted to the ceiling as his voice rose. "But you had no right to say that about her!"

Clare raised her hands protectively, turning her red-splotched face away. "Okay, you made your point. I was rude. Now think about what you're doing. I'm a detective; you're assaulting an officer. Twenty years…if you're lucky."

Derik rolled to the side, releasing Clare. "I could just as easily kill you, stuff your body in Taug's incinerator, and no one would ever be the wiser."

Clare scrambled to her feet, her eyes dark and narrow. "You are not the man I knew."

Derik climbed onto his knees and rocked back and forth, hugging himself.

His raspy chuckle ascended into hysteria. "Of course I'm not. Neither of us knew who I was. And no one on Newearth knows what I'm becoming. Even Taug. I may surprise him yet." Derik huffed to his feet and towered over Clare. "You don't know Justine, either."

Clare darted a look at the door and edged nearer. "I told you the truth, whether you want to believe me or not. She's an android created with human DNA."

Derik froze, his eyes strained and bloodshot. "Justine's a crossbreed?"

"Something like that."

"Then she's perfect for me." Derik dropped back onto the couch. "You've no idea how terrifying this whole thing's been. Finding out that I'm not fully human, that I'm part Cresta, and just for added entertainment, someone wants to kill me. It's enough to drive a man crazy." Derik rubbed his face, as if to wash away the horror. "But Justine is the best thing that's ever happened to me. I'm not totally blind. I wondered... But I didn't care! It's like you said, she's not attracted to my biology but my humanity."

Clare stood before the door. "I remember. But I also remember telling you that she's not the only one who cares for you. I didn't want you to get hurt."

"Too late."

"I know. But I'm not your enemy. At least, I wasn't." Clare rubbed her sore neck. "Now, I'm not so sure."

Derik's eyes flashed as he heaved off the couch again. "What does that mean?"

"If you can fly across a room and nearly strangle someone who's only trying to help—the Cresta in you might go deeper than thirty-seven percent."

Derik stepped closer, his eyes bloodshot and swollen. "If you ever insult Justine again or try to hurt her in any way, you'll find that both the human and the Cresta in me can be very dangerous, indeed. Your work here is over."

Clare nodded as she yanked open the door and straddled the threshold. "I work for humanity. If you become a threat, we'll meet again."

Cerulean stood against the wall as human workmen dressed in gray, durable clothes carried new furniture into Bala's refurbished living room.

A mover grunted his question. "Where'd ya want it?"

Bala pointed to Kendra who immediately passed baby Martha to him and scrambled over the rolled-up carpet, directing the workers.

Cerulean leaned in, jiggled Martha's finger, and grinned idiotically.

The baby wailed.

Bala passed Martha off to his son, who had just ambled innocently into the fray. "Emergency mission, Seth."

Seth swooped the baby into the air, playing 'space mission.'

"Keep the landings gentle, son," Bala advised with a deceptive grin. "Or you'll see her breakfast again in a distinctly unpleasant form."

Cerulean grimaced as his eyes followed the two children from the room. "I wish you hadn't put that image in my head. It'll be with me all day."

Bala shrugged. "Sorry. Life with kids. They do the darndest things."

Cerulean nodded. "True. Amazing how well they recovered from their shock."

Stroking his marred face, Bala concurred. "Yeah. Resilient. They take after their dad."

Cerulean's eyes twinkled as Bala affably gestured two heavy-laden movers toward his wife. "The boss is over there."

Leading Bala to a quiet corner, Cerulean lowered his voice. "Listen, I have a certain amount of influence in the Inter-Alien Alliance Committee. I can make a formal complaint for you. This was clearly an Ingoti incursion on a human domain."

Bala jumped forward and assisted one of the movers who nearly dragged one end of a large couch. "Steady there. I paid top price at a half-off sale for these." After the workmen unceremoniously plopped the couch against the back wall, Bala turned to Cerulean. "Nah. Don't worry about it. After all, I did solve the Hoggsworth case, sort of. I tracked down the killer's killer and, for what it's worth, he's on his way to Bothmal as we speak." Bala scratched his chin. "At least, I hope he is." He patted Cerulean's arm and squinted. "You lost weight?"

Cerulean opened his mouth, but a baby squalled at the same moment.

Bala waved the answer off. "Silly me. Luxonians don't lose weight. Light beings and all." He surveyed Kendra's frantic efforts to keep the movers' work undeterred by the three-year-old, who apparently thought that furniture was to be sat on even when it was still in motion. "Listen, I appreciate everything you've done, but I just want to put this behind us." Bala strode over to the child-laden couch and centered it.

A shadow filled the open doorway as an Interventionist stepped over the threshold. The three movers dropped what they were doing, pushed past the Interventionist, and retreated to their vehicle.

Cerulean sighed as he leaned against the wall. "Looks like you've got company."

Bala turned. His mouth dropped open.

Pushing himself forward, Cerulean took charge. "Something I can help you with?"

"Only if you are Bala Impala and want a warrant for your arrest." The Interventionist held a datapad at arm's length.

Bala's eyes grew wide as he tripped over the couch.

Cerulean snatched the datapad and scrolled through. "What's this about?"

The Interventionist stiffened. "I was just told to bring Mr. Impala in on charges of domestic abuse." He pointed to Bala. "You Mr. Impala?"

Bala swallowed and nodded. His gaze flicked over to his frozen wife and family. Kendra held a chair in one arm and the baby in the other. No one moved.

The Interventionist deadpanned his recital. "I hereby inform you that you have been charged with wife-beating, child abuse, and home-wrecking. Your human rights are guaranteed by the

Inter-Alien Alliance, but anything you say can be used against you in a court of law. Will you come with me peaceably?"

Bala tapped his ears as if they were water-clogged. "I didn't quite catch that. What—?"

Cerulean lifted his hand. His voice grew incredulous as his gaze scrolled over the datapad. "Someone is accusing Mr. Impala of abusing his family and destroying his own house?"

Bala muttered. "Why would—?"

The Interventionist threw up one protesting hand as he plucked back the datapad. "Don't ask me. Why does anyone commit crimes?" He slapped the datapad against his palm. "Look, there're witnesses. Pretty reliable sources, too. You're going to have to sit in the tank till we get this sorted out. Now, just come along—"

"Bala!" Kendra plowed across the living room like Moses parting the Red Sea and threw her arms around her husband. "No! Not this!"

Bala's head jerked back on impact. Hugging her and rubbing her back in large circles, he spoke over her shoulder. "You were right, honey. I can't be tied to safety." Responding to the Interventionist glare, he pulled away and muttered, "No matter how hard I try." He faced the Interventionist and raised his limp hands. "I'll behave myself." With a nod to Cerulean, he shrugged. "Oh, about that offer—"

The Interventionist clasped manacles around Bala's wrists and led him to the door. Bala looked back, tears welling in his eyes. "Keep the kids back. I don't want them to see—"

Cerulean nodded as he put an arm around Kendra's shivering form. His eyes followed Bala out the door.

Wearing a thick sweater and weathered jeans with snow-encrusted hiking boots, Cerulean trudged up his porch steps. Snowdrifts appeared flat and gray in the elongated shadows. He turned at the sounds of running steps and a voice calling his name.

Able, wrapped in a heavy coat, huffed into view. "Hey, Cerulean. I was praying I'd find you. I'm on my way to Vandi. There's been an accident."

Cerulean retraced his steps and stopped in front of Able, a weary frown shadowing his expression. "What happened?"

"Jim, one of our new members, got hurt, bad. He came to us last fall, insisting that he didn't feel human anymore. He wanted to get back to nature and rediscover his true identity."

Cerulean rubbed his forehead. "And did he?"

Able shrugged. "Hard to tell. Seems like a nice guy and all, but he's different all right. We had some roofing fly off in yesterday's storm, and against everyone's advice, he scaled the ladder to fix it. He was just about done when he slipped and fell."

Cerulean closed his eyes. "Lucky he's alive."

Able shook his head, his brows lowered. "Lucky isn't the word. He fell twenty feet and landed badly. He should be dead or paralyzed."

"A miracle?"

"Even I don't believe that. When I saw him scrambling to his feet, I went over and gripped him by the arm." Able leaned in and whispered, "His skin is cold and hard, like some kind of flexi-metal. He doesn't wear a bio-suit or anything. He's not human. At least not fully."

"Oh, Lord."

"You took the words right out of my mouth."

"So what are you going to do? Take him in?"

Able sucked in a deep breath and raised his gaze skyward. Small flakes of snow swirled around them. "I offered to take him to the hospital, but he got upset. You should've seen the terror in his eyes. He's not well, his skin color was off before he even slipped, and he says he blacks out sometimes. Probably why he fell."

Cerulean watched the flakes disappearing into the white ground, joined in anonymity, and sighed. "If he's sick and needs treatment—"

Able rubbed his hands together. "Look, I'm not turning the guy over to authorities. He's a serious mystery and might even be considered illegal." He looked Cerulean in the eye. "There are worse things than death, you know."

Cerulean nodded.

Able stomped his frozen feet. "Anyway, I'm going to Vandi to pick up some supplies, but I just wanted you to know. I figure if something goes wrong, you'd—"

Cerulean sniffed and rubbed his frozen nose. "What could possibly go wrong?"

With a twitch of a smile, Able shuffled toward the trail. "Yeah. Great minds think alike. Thanks, Cerulean."

Staring at the footprints leading from his porch into a black night, Cerulean shivered.

Alone in the room, Taug stood before the image of his superior on the holo-screen. With head bowed and tentacles wrapped behind his back, he slouched like a hatchling being chastened by his elder.

The laboratory resided in solemn dimness, while the crescent windows near the top revealed the merest glimmer of dawn.

Mitholie shook a tentacle at Taug via the screen, his head and shoulders resting on the edge of a murky pool. "It's not just your father's mistake that's a risk now. Other complications have come to light. Do you realize what this scandal could entail? Crestas would be ordered to leave the planet. There'd be interplanetary warfare—"

Taug looked up.

"Yes, I said warfare! We wouldn't leave Newearth peaceably, of course. We'd be forced to take over the whole planet, which would set off a nasty chain reaction. Ingots and Uanyi, even Bhuacs would be furious. You know how many innocent lives would be lost and how expensive the whole process of re-stabilization would be? It would run into the quadrillions."

Mitholie splashed his tentacle into the pool, sprinkling water across the screen. "Dark waters! I won't have it. I gave you a direct order, and I have been more than patient while you played with your specimen. But it's time that this matter was settled!"

Taug nodded. "I understand. Derik—I mean, my specimen—slipped away, but I have—"

Mitholie interrupted. "No more excuses! Your father's mistake must be disposed of quickly before it's discovered. Or I'll be forced to send someone to dispose of *my mistake*. Do you understand?"

Taug's head lowered, pressing against his chest.

"Good! I have a meeting with the Inter-Alien Alliance Committee soon. I'd hate to inform them that they have a traitor in their midst." Mitholie plunged and millions of bubbles surfaced.

The holo-screen blinked into blackness, leaving Taug in the dark.

CHAPTER SIXTEEN

A Moral Choice

Clare drifted away from the barred cell where Bala sat in slumped resignation. She stopped by a large, steel door and pressed a button.

A voice responded, "Yeah?"

Clare tried to speak but no words came. She cleared her throat and tried again. "I'm ready."

The door slid open. Clare crossed over the threshold with one backward glance.

Bala sat staring at the floor, his head propped in his hands.

Clare closed her eyes at the reverberating clang as the door slammed shut. A hand gripped her shoulder. Clare spun around.

Cerulean opened his arms, and she stepped into his embrace.

Hugging her, he nuzzled her head with his chin. "Even world-weary detectives need a hug now and again."

Clare rubbed her reddened eyes against his chest, mumbling.

Cerulean frowned. He pulled her back and looked into her eyes. "I'm not familiar with that particular dialect. Here—" He put his arm around her, led her down the corridor, and pointed to a bench. "Tell me what you found out."

Clare dropped onto the offered seat as Vandi Interventionists bustled about with official business. She spread her arms and then dropped them. “What’s to tell? I’m a complete failure, and I ought to quit before anyone else gets hurt. Lord, I hate my job.”

Cerulean scratched his head. “Self-pity isn’t going to help anyone.” He straightened. “What we need is more information. I tried to bring you the best resource on the planet, but you—”

Clare’s head snapped up. “Justine? That unfeeling piece of bio-mechanical—”

“Whoa! Stop right there, Clare. You’ve taken your animosity about as far as I can stand it. Honestly, I’ve never seen this side of you. Your parents would be horrified. They were two of the most accepting—”

Clare jumped to her feet, her gaze darting around the room and swinging back to Cerulean. Her tone lowered to a hiss. “You don’t know what you’re talking about. They hated robots. They always said that combining human DNA with AI was asking for trouble. It’s immoral—”

Cerulean’s jaw jutted forward as he leaned in close. “You think Justine is immoral—as if she had a choice? Put down your rage for just one second and think, would you? Justine is the product of a laboratory conception. I doubt her biological parents ever knew or cared what happened to their *donations*. No one cared about Justine, not as a person. They only cared about her as a source of profit, a point of reference in an argument, or as an excuse to play god. You’re angry at the wrong person, Clare.”

Clare fell back onto the bench and rubbed her face with her hands. Her voice became leaden. “Yeah. Maybe.”

Cerulean shook his head as an Interventionist stepped up and handed him a datapad. He pressed his palm onto it and handed it to Clare who did the same. Cerulean nodded to the guard and steered Clare toward the exit. “There’s more to this than your parents’ aversion to artificial intelligence.”

Clare shrugged as she trudged along at Cerulean’s side. “She reminds me of that voice I used to hear. Her smug perfection, her assumed superiority, it all feels familiar somehow, like she and he...it...are connected.”

Cerulean marched to the door, swung it wide, and gestured for her to hurry along. "Well, they're not. Justine is a victim as much as Derik, except she's learning to deal with her problems. Derik is just beginning to discover his." He waited, holding the door open.

Clare stepped out into the frosty night air. "Derik's gone over to his Cresta side. I don't even know him anymore. He nearly throttled me when I told him that Justine is a robot."

Cerulean stepped along beside her, looked up into the black, star-burnished sky and sighed. "Frankly, if you don't quit calling her that, I may throttle you yet."

Clare looked askance at Cerulean. "Really?"

Cerulean dropped his gaze. "Yes." He gripped her arm and stared her in the eye. "Look, you've got to get it through your head that even our enemies are—"

"If you say 'our friends,' I'll throw up all over your polished boots."

Cerulean snorted. "I'm not that naïve. What I was going to say—before you so rudely interrupted—was that even enemies are worthy of hope. No one sees the future. You can't trust everyone, but you can't decide you know other people's ultimate fate either."

"If it came between a human and a Cresta, I'll choose a human every time."

"Really? How about if it were an innocent Cresta and a guilty human? Think about it. You decided that Justine was guilty, so you never even gave her a chance to defend herself."

Clare leaned into Cerulean, shivering, hugging his arm. "I looked through everything we have on her. She killed a lot of beings on more than one occasion. She was a very effective hired gun, and she always walked away unscathed—until she was caught."

Cerulean stopped, pulled his arm free, placed both hands on her shoulders, and held her steady. He lowered his head so their eyes were level and their gazes interlocked. "Do you know *why* she was caught?"

Clare shrugged and looked to the side. "Some stupid mistake—"

Cerulean turned her so she could not escape his gaze. "She saved two men's lives. Against orders and against decades of training, she did the unthinkable; she made a moral choice. At that moment, she chose to stop being a killer."

With a moaning breath, Clare's head fell against Cerulean's chest, and she sobbed.

The bright, winter sun sparkled on the ivy-covered bungalow, and Clare whistled. A low, thatched roof drooped over twisted grapevines, which in turn wound around the windows. Front beds planted thick with red-berried evergreens offered a colorful contrast, while a snowy path veered toward the back. She sucked in her breath and meandered toward the front entrance of Justine's house.

A wooden door etched with acorns and oak leaves opened wide. Justine stood on the snowy welcome mat, one hand holding the ornate, iron knob, the other resting on the frame as the cold wind whistled past. She pursed her lips like an irritated teacher just waiting for the next infraction.

Clare halted in her frozen tracks. "Cerulean said you'd be home."

Justine's eyebrows rose, apparently surprised that the delinquent before her could speak coherently. "He told me you were coming. I almost left."

"But you didn't."

Justine shrugged. She swept her hand through the doorway. "Cerulean has a way with words."

Clare sighed through a puff of air. "He sure does." She stepped in with Justine watching her every move.

The inside of the bungalow shrieked of obsessive-compulsive disorder. Dust had not a particle of business here.

Clare dared not lower her gaze to her snow-caked boots.

Justine looked for her. Her eyebrows appeared frozen in the up position.

With a grimace, Clare unlaced her boots and peeled them off. After stepping into the living room, she let her eyes roll over the intimate space. Clare sucked in her breath. "You rob a museum?"

A crooked smile tugged at the corner of Justine's mouth. "I'd tell you, but I don't want to make you angry...again."

Clare felt magnetically pulled toward a painting of a mother and child, blues and reds vying for the eye's attention. They both wore golden crowns. Her eyes widened. "Did you—?"

Justine shrugged. "I only copied it. The original was lost long ago, but there were over a million electronic copies left on an Oldearth database called Facebook."

Clare hugged herself. "I'd love to get a look at that."

Justine padded over to an easel with a half-finished painting of a little boy with piercing blue eyes. She picked up a wet brush and dabbed it in the paint. "I'd pass it along, but it's restricted, addictive as opium they say."

Clare's eyes bugged, attempting to take in everything at once.

Justine smirked as she waved the paint-laden brush indulgently. "Well, possibly...."

Sidling up to the work in progress, Clare appraised the picture. She wagged her finger. "Cerulean—?"

"No one you know. Just a child I once helped—in a time of need."

Clare lifted her hands in an attitude of surrender. "Okay, sorry isn't good enough. I wasn't exactly reasonable. Can't say exactly what got into me."

Justine stroked her chin. Apparently deciding that there was hope for delinquents after all, she laid her paintbrush aside. She strode across the room to a circular table. A screen rose from the center. She tapped rapidly on a soft pad. "Cerulean told me about your dreams—night visitor—whatever. Must be disorientating. I can't say I understand, but as they say: 'to err is human'—forget it." Her eyes scanned multitudinous files flying across the screen.

Clare strolled to her side and watched Justine's hand move so rapidly that it seemed to blur. "I thought you considered *yourself* human."

"Only on odd days when the moon is full." Justine straightened and looked Clare in the eye. "What do you need to know?"

Clare leaned over the desk and peered at the file. She pointed to a single line. "I have that one. Bala showed it to me. He said you have other files that he couldn't get access to. I need to get to those."

Justine rubbed her chin. "Why?"

Folding her arms, Clare leaned against a chair. "Listen, there's a secret here that Mrs. Hoggsworth stumbled onto and Bala inadvertently tripped over. She's dead, and he's in prison. They both discovered something."

Justine offered a sad shake of the head at Clare's apparent return to stupidity. "There's no evidence to support that. Maybe someone simply hated Mrs. Hoggsworth enough to want her dead."

"And Bala?"

Justine maintained a steady gaze. "How do you know he's not guilty?"

Clare bolted forward. "What? You seriously think that Bala would beat his wife, abuse his kids, and trash his own house?"

Justine turned back to the datapad. Her hand blurred again. Up popped 5,764 files on wife battery and child abuse. "Those are the ones from this year alone. Don't tell me that they're all innocent."

Clare pressed her hands to her head as if trying to keep it from exploding. "Holy Saints in—"

A white cat meandered between Clare's feet and meowed. Clare stared down, her eyes widening. Without a blink, she glanced up at Justine.

Justine scooped the cat into her arms. "Come here, Theodora. You might get stepped on."

Clare waved Justine off and stretched out her arms, wiggling her fingers towards the cat imploringly. "Don't be ridiculous. I love cats. My own is about this size, but she's black. Just had kittens. Maybe you'd like one."

Justine passed the cat into Clare's arms and observed Clare rub her face in the cat's fur. She grimaced. "That unhygienic."

"Ah, but they love it." Clare's tone dissolved into a purr.

Justine's eyebrows returned to the up position.

As Clare continued to nuzzle the cat, her voice became soft and coaxing. "You've got files no one else has, and Bala's an innocent man. His family is miserable without him."

Justine exhaled a long breath. "Oh, all right. I guess even a robot can have a heart."

Justine wrapped her fingers around the prison bars and observed Bala with a long, cold stare.

Bala sat upright on his cot and glared back. "So, you've come to observe the monkey in the zoo?"

Justine shrugged. "You could say the same about me. Except I don't need a cage to be locked in."

With a sigh, Bala slumped against the wall. "Everyone has troubles."

"Not you. Your prison days are over. Cerulean has cleared your name. You'll be free to go once we get the final reports in and signed off."

Bala strode to the bars in the cell door, his eyes narrowing. "Really? How?"

"It was easy. The case crumpled against all the evidence Cerulean brought to bear. He provided ample proof that Ingots had broken into your house and there was not a shred of evidence that you ever harmed your family. Quite the contrary. You're a model husband and father by all accounts. I congratulate you; your reputation shall shine down through the ages."

Bala gripped the bars. "Having fun, are we?"

Dropping her gaze, Justine shook her head. "I'd never tease a prisoner."

Bala flapped his arms as he shuffled back to his cot. "So, how did I end up here? And how do I keep from being sent back the minute somebody starts tossing accusations my way?"

Justine turned at the sound of footsteps. She stepped aside as a guard sauntered down the corridor. After he passed, she returned to Bala. "In your investigation, you reviewed Mrs. Hoggworth's research of Oldearth records. Most of them have become corrupted or lost, but she somehow learned of my existence and that I have records going back to—"

The guard returned with a prisoner in cuffs. Bala's and Justine's eyes followed their passage down the corridor in silence.

Bala shook his head. "I could bet a steak sandwich that this all ties in with our illustrious Governor Right."

Justine paused, her eyes glazed as if searching interior files. "I don't understand the allusion to food."

Bala hung his head. "Never mind."

In response to a buzzing sound, Justine pulled out a datapad and tapped its surface. "Cerulean's here." She peered into Bala's wide eyes. "In any case, I'll have to do a comparative study of my original records with what's now reported on the official Newearth data files."

Rubbing his hands together, Bala perked up. "Sounds good, I'd love to see the results." His eyes roamed toward the door. "It's getting late. Any chance that I'll get out of here before Kendra puts the kids to bed?"

Cerulean stepped to the door, offering a nod to Justine before focusing on Bala. "How've you been doing, ol' man?"

Bala lifted his arms, indicating the small space. "Look around and take a wild guess."

Cerulean grinned as a guard strode up behind him. "Well, your time is up… in here, I mean. I just sent Kendra word. You're free to go—"

"Excuse me." The guard shouldered his way past Cerulean. "You'll have to sign a release before you walk. I go off in fifteen, so if we could hurry this up...." He pressed his hand against the electronic key. At the sound of the latch unlocking, he swung the door wide.

Bala nodded stiffly. "Certainly, anything to accommodate." He stepped in line behind the guard, next to Cerulean. They marched down the corridor, shoulder to shoulder.

Justine followed behind, her gaze turned inward, scanning unseen files.

CHAPTER SEVENTEEN

Miscalculation

Justine turned the lock and stepped away from the door. Pressing the wall panel, the lights turned on all over the small bungalow. Theodora trotted up and swirled about her legs with a demanding meow. Justine nudged the cat to the side with a wet boot. “In a minute, cat.”

The feline nudged back and meowed louder.

“You better watch yourself. I’ve had an offer to introduce another of your kind into this abode. Will it be a rival...or replacement?” With a deep sigh, Justine dropped down onto a bench and tugged off her boots. Slush dripped on the hardwood floor. Without a backward glance, she tiptoed over the melting pool and headed to the kitchen.

The cat sashayed behind.

A single chime forced Justine to change course and plod to her computer screen. After tapping the keypad, she straightened her shoulders.

Taug’s bland face appeared larger than life in her living room. “Glad to see you, Justine.”

“It’s rather late for a social call, don’t you think?”

Taug’s face remained impassive. “I need you here—in person.”

Justine shook her head, rubbing one damp foot against her leg. "Now?"

"Immediately. It's urgent."

"And if I decide to wait till morning?"

"You won't live to see the sunrise."

Justine strode into Taug's brilliantly lit lab, her shoulders back and her attitude marching before her. "This had better be good."

Taug limped across the room, meeting Justine halfway. "It's not. Trust me."

Justine's attention zeroed in on Taug's shredded boots with a snide smirk. "What? A dog attack you? An Ingot—?"

Taug flicked a tentacle toward the wall screen where a Universal Reports clip played on a continuous loop.

"The Newearth Inter-Alien Alliance Committee has been warned of a secret weapon placed somewhere in the Central Basin, ready to be discharged at a moment's notice. Both the Supreme Council and the Crestar authorities insist that they know nothing about it, while the Ingoti and the Uanyi ambassadors have yet to respond. Newearth citizens in the area are advised to stay close to home and only venture out if absolutely necessary until this threat has passed. If you learn—"

Justine stiffened, her hands clenched. She turned to Taug. "Why?"

"I have to be sure that you'll do exactly as I say."

Justine marched to the wall-pad and slammed her fist on the console. The screen blinked to black. "What do you want?"

"Kill Derik. Publicly. It has to be witnessed by every race, and it has to look like you saved Newearth from utter destruction."

Justine pounded over to Taug and pushed her face within centimeters of his. "Why?"

Taug pulled back and sauntered over to the pool wall.

"Because it'll be true. Due to some unforeseen circumstances—" His tentacle splayed across the glassy surface. "—the Inter-Alien Commission has become aware of certain Cresta activities that strain our relationship. If they learn of Derik's existence, of his origin, it would set into effect a rather grave chain of events."

"Why should I care? I can always leave—"

Taug turned and faced Justine, his bulbous eyes gleaming. "Two reasons. First, you would be hunted to your destruction and second, Derik would be forced to accept your guilt—before he dies." Taug retreated to a dissecting tube and swirled a tentacle in the murky water. "There are other reasons, of course, but I think those will do."

Justine folded her arms high across her heaving chest. Her voice rose like a hissing whisper. "You never planned to save him. He was always a tool, a specimen to dissect and study."

Taug glanced at Justine. "At your trial, you refused to state your beliefs, even about yourself. I reserve the same right. For much the same reason."

"And that would be?"

"Because no one would believe me." Taug sighed as he twitched a knife off the metal table and twirled it. "Time waits for no man...or Crestonian."

Justine's gaze fixed on the knife. "I'll bring him. Kill him yourself—if you can."

"Not good enough. I awoke you for a simple purpose, to do this one, small service. Either you do it, or you face extinction."

Justine stalked to the door. "When I called you an insect, I had no idea how insulting to the creepy, crawly world I was being. I repent my miscalculation."

Darkness shrouded the quiet cabin while a waxing moon peeked between through bare branches. A single owl hooted in the distance.

Cerulean lay on a rumpled bed, his eyes closed, one arm thrown over his face in an attitude of peaceful repose. His bare upper chest peeked out from the silky white sheets that covered the rest of his body.

A pounding on the door forced him to drop his arm from his face and issue a groan from the depth of his being. "Who the heck—?"

The cabin began to shake. Thrusting the sheets aside, Cerulean shot forward and grabbed yesterday's pants and sweater. "Hold on! I'm coming. Sheesh, you'd think the—" He staggered into his pants.

Justine was caught in the act of attempting to put the door back in its natural position, though the jagged hinges screamed a different truth.

Using his sweater as a pointer, Cerulean demanded, "What'd you do to my door?"

Justine tapped it into place. "I'll replace the hinges later. Right now, we need to talk."

Cerulean flicked the sweater over his head and pulled it into position. Padding barefoot over the cold floor, he gestured abruptly toward the kitchen. "Coffee, first."

As she perched on a tall stool, Justine gazed around the herb-strewn room. Bunches hung ornamentally from the rafters while others lay like fallen soldiers in neat rows next to carefully labeled jars. "You make your own teas?"

"I'm learning." He flicked the coffee machine on and grabbed two mugs. "The Amens community grows everything from anise to wintergreen, and they know a thing or two about soups too. One of these days, I may open a little shop like the one Alcina used to have."

Justine's gaze turned inward, scanning unseen files. "Alcina?"

"You wouldn't know her." He splashed steaming coffee into the cups with reckless abandon. "She was one of the early settlers, before your time—here—I mean." He blew rising curls of steam off his mug and took a sip. Nodding to her untouched cup, he sauntered to the table and slouched onto the bench. "I assume you didn't get me out of bed at the ungodly hour of—" he flicked a glance to an old-fashioned clock on the wall. "It's only three-fifteen?"

Justine slid off her perch and strode to the table, the steaming cup in her unscathed hand. "While you were slumbering in ignorant bliss, I was constructing a plan to save Derik and scanning through multitudinous files."

Cerulean's eyes twinkled and his lips twitched. "Multitudinous? I'm impressed." He shoved a chair out with his foot. "I don't usually do anything multitudinous until I've had at least *two* cups of coffee."

"You don't need coffee. You're just lazy." She sat in the offered chair, her back straight and uncompromising, though she tapped her knee with a nervous finger. "I know the mystery." Cerulean sat up, his gaze glued to hers.

"Governor Jane Right is older than the hills. In fact, she shouldn't even be alive. And she wouldn't be—if she were human."

Cerulean leaned back with a low whistle. "What is she?"

"Either a Cresta experiment gone right, an alien we don't know about, or—" Her gaze wandered toward the black window. "—she's an android, like me."

Clasping his fingers together, Cerulean appraised Justine. "And who are you?"

Justine dropped her gaze. "You mean, *what* am I?"

"No. *Who* are you?"

Looking up, Justine blinked back unaccustomed tears. "A mystery. No one knows." She shrugged. "There are others like me. I worked with one on a transport; the captain needed protection in a dangerous world." A smile tugged at the corner of her mouth. "A Mr. Max Wheeler—as naïve as a newborn babe."

Cerulean shook his head. "Naïve is not the word that comes to mind when I think of an—"

"Android? No. Well, that just shows how much you know." She rose and meandered to the window, her refection in the black frame appearing like a ghost. "We were created by a race you know little about. Even the Luxonians don't have much interaction with them. They are secretive by nature, but they're also immensely advanced. Few races dare to challenge their closed-door policy." She reached up and traced her face on the glass.

"Many generations ago, the Cresta leadership approached them, offering their abundant scientific skills in exchange for information. Soon after, a mighty plague swept through Crestar, decimating over a third of their population. No one knew for certain who sent the plague, but no one had a third of a population to spare in discovering the truth." She turned and faced Cerulean. "So, you see, there is much you don't know."

Cerulean rose and stepped to Justine's side. He traced her chin with a soft touch. "I know a woman who lay helpless on a steel table and did not regret her decision to save two human lives."

Justine held his gaze a moment before breaking away. "In that case, it may interest you to know that Governor Right has also been involved in several cases where questions about unlawful experimentation have been brought before the Inter-Alien Commission and were summarily dismissed. Apparently the Ingoti ambassador has some interest as well, for he appeared at each hearing to see the evidence first hand."

Cerulean refilled his coffee mug. "So, what do you think?"

"Crestas simply like to experiment. It's in their blood or ooze, whatever you want to call the sap that flows through their veins. Ingots have a long history of drug running. It wouldn't surprise me if they have a profit margin to protect."

"And the illustrious governor?"

"Who doesn't like to rewrite history for personal glorification?"

Cerulean leaned against the counter. "You've done well. This answers a lot of questions. I can see how Mrs. Hoggsworth's questions and Bala's investigation upset the delicate balance that has kept Newearth in blissful ignorance."

"Except for the unfortunate casualties."

Cerulean's gaze strayed to the herbs. "Yes. Except for them." He frowned and thrust a finger forward. "And Derik? Where does this leave him?"

Justine drained the last of her coffee and placed the cup gently in the porcelain sink. "Oh, did I fail to mention that I have been ordered to kill him in a public spectacle, or I'll be hunted to my destruction?"

Derik tapped at his computer console, the blue light reflecting off his face. A half-eaten sandwich and a small, green drink lay at his right. He frowned at the archived reports scrolling down the screen in front of him. Holographic images created years earlier popped from the surface, including one with the subtext: "Tarragon, scientist of unparalleled ability, honored for his exceptional service to Crestar."

Derik studied the hologram. The slump-shouldered, bulbous-eyed Cresta had a wise but somber look about him. As if he knew better than to trust accolades and honors. Taug resembled his dad a bit, especially around the eyes.

Continuing his search, Tarragon's name appeared again, highlighted this time under a bold heading: "Traitor in our midst!" Followed by reports of Tarragon's disappearance, and just a short time later, the appearance of his body—"Discovered by his son, Taug." This time the hologram showed a broken Tarragon, his face distorted with anguish.

Derik's hands shook as he considered the holographic image before him. He blinked back tears. His hand, poised above the off button, froze when he caught sight of a short, highlighted statement a few lines below: "Taug appointed to Second Degree, in grateful recognition for his valuable service to Crestar."

Stunned, Derik stared at the rotating image of a young Taug, a tentacle raised in a wave, wearing a bemused smile.

Skidding his chair backwards, Derik jumped forward and leapt for the door, leaving his heavy, winter coat draped over the back of the couch.

Once inside Taug's dark, silent laboratory, Derik inched his way across to the desk by the west wall. A heavy fog shrouded the nearly full moon. Glowing red monitors and reflected light from other Vandi offices made it possible to sidle across the room without crashing into anything.

Sliding into Taug's unadorned office chair, Derik tapped the computer console embedded in the desk. It blinked to life, a blank space awaiting the necessary print to unlock its secrets. "Dang!" Muffling his irritation with his hand, he considered his options.

"Perhaps I can help." Taug padded into view from the dark recess of the room. "You should have called. I wasn't sleeping."

Derik jumped to his feet, sending the chair slamming against the wall. "I—" Derik maneuvered around the desk and faced Taug, his bright eyes gleaming at the Cresta. "I've got to know. Did you—kill your dad? For the good of...so you could get...a raise?"

Taug shuffled around Derik, pulled the chair from the wall, and fell into it wearily. With a tap, a thin beam of light brightened the west end of the room. "It's been a long night, and it'll be a longer day tomorrow." He rubbed his dry, cracked lips with a tentacle. "I guess there is no harm in your knowing—now." He gestured to one of the chairs at the far end of the room. "Make yourself comfortable. This could take a while."

Derik shivered as he paced like a caged animal. "Just talk! Explain things to me—so that I don't hate you." Glancing at Taug, Derik's face distorted, as if pleading for his life.

Taug leaned back and wrapped two of his tentacles like a cradle behind his head. "My father, Tarragon, was a brilliant scientist, as I told you. But he had one weakness. He believed that he was right, even when it was not safe to do so. Stubbornness, plain and simple. He created three crossbreeds in all. Two met their demise early on, but you were his pride and joy. I think he really cared about you—as if he had spawned you himself."

Derik halted, darting a look of horror at Taug, but the Cresta's gaze was considering images of long ago and far away.

"When his activities were discovered, the whole family was disgraced. I had worked terribly hard to earn a position of relative safety within the scientific community. Suddenly, all my efforts were compromised. I became a pariah overnight. You can imagine my shame."

Derik hugged his arms around his waist, his voice rising like a howl. "So you turned traitor? Against your own father?"

Taug glowered icily at Derik. "It was him or me—"

With a snarl, Derik fled the room.

The sun had crested the horizon as Derik ran his fingers along the back of the park bench, knocking the melting snow to the ground. He shivered in the morning chill, especially without his heavy coat, but he didn't care. He wrapped his stiff fingers around the dagger in his pocket, comforted by the smooth handle. It reminded him of the dissecting knives in the lab, and he found this oddly amusing. Starting off at a trot, he jogged across the street, his gaze down, but his mind focused. Someone jostled him roughly. Glancing up, his mouth dropped open. Justine grabbed his arm with more force than he thought necessary.

"Justine?" He shook his arm free. "What're you doing here? I left you a message—"

"Like an idiot. You think you can murder a Cresta and no one will find out? You'll be hunted to—"

"Can't you see? It's the only way. I can't marry you till I

know that we'll have a chance at living a normal life—even an abnormal life. Taug's a lying—never mind. It's over. I'm taking matters into my own hands."

Justine ran her fingers through her wind-rippled hair with a long sigh. "My perfect plan—blown to smithereens." Gripping his arm, she nudged him toward the street. "Come with me."

"Where?"

"To your place. You're going to pack some necessaries while I shock you with my life story, and then we're going to the nearest transport and head off-planet."

Derik stood frozen.

Justine jerked his arm, knocking him off balance. "I'm not in a negotiating mood, sweetheart. Let's go."

As soon as Derik opened his apartment door, Justine barged ahead, her gaze sweeping the premises for any sign of intrusion. After a quick run-through, she returned to the living room and plopped down on the couch with a sigh. She patted the cushion next to her. "Sit."

Derik frowned. "You're beginning to sound a bit too much like Taug for my taste."

Justine snorted. "You don't know the half of it."

His hands on his hips, his legs braced wide apart, Derik jutted his chin forward. "I've already had more than a few shocks today. Go ahead, see if you can surprise me."

Justine stared at the ceiling. "You're not making this easy."

Derik clenched his hands together and wrung them like a towel. "I already had my day nicely planned. I was going to gut Taug like the animal he is, collect you, and we'd head to a Bhuaci settlement." He thrust a hand deep into his pocket and retrieved a data-chip. "See, our transport's all arranged. But now—"

Justine chuckled. "Don't worry, I'll disarrange all your plans in a moment. But keep the data-chip. You'll need it." She jumped to her feet. "Give thy soul air, thy faculties expanse; love, joy, even sorrow—yield thyself to all...."

Derik blinked.

"Forget it. A noble sentiment perhaps but too painful to endure." She cupped Derik's hand in hers and stroked it, her voice softening. "I'm not human, Derik. Not even close."

The smile that spread across Derik's face morphed into an inane grin. He started giggling and was soon doubled over in hysterical laughter. It took him several moments to gain control of his heaving shoulders. "Really? You honestly think I didn't know? I figured something...though Clare was kind enough to color in the details for me."

"*Clare* told you?" Justine's confused scowl darkened as she turned away. "That wasn't her place."

"Place or not, I've known for a while. And what's more, I haven't cared for a moment." He waved an imploring hand at her back. "You seriously believe that I, a mixed-breed, half-Cresta would care that you're a half-breed, human-android?"

Turning, Justine folded her arms across her chest. "You have a delicate way of putting things, Derik."

Derik plunged across the room and gripped Justine by the shoulders, his gaze delving into hers. "We're made for each other."

Justine closed her eyes and leaned in, her forehead resting on his shoulder. "I wish it were that easy."

Derik rubbed her back, pressing her closer.

Justine pulled away, all business. "Killing Taug won't help. You need an escape."

"What're you thinking?"

"Take that transport. I'll deal with Taug."

"Like hell! He's my enemy, not yours. You don't even know him."

Justine's arms dropped to her sides. "Now's when I shock you—ready? I knew Taug before you were even born. He was at the Inter-Alien Alliance trial that found me guilty of war crimes. He observed my sentencing and was the one who awoke me seventy years later. Now, he asks only one little favor to keep me out of prison—kill you."

Derik fell back against the sofa and slid to the ground.

Justine knelt beside him. "You can still escape. I'm not going to kill you. I never was—"

"You stepped in front of that autoskimmer on purpose. I remember...I wondered...I didn't care." Derik's shoulders shook as he dropped his face into his hands. "If I were dead—" He looked into Justine's eyes, tears running down his cheeks. "Kill me."

Justine's jaw tensed. "Shut up!" She jumped to her feet. "I have a plan. And it doesn't involve killing anyone. You're going to take that transport, and I'll take care of Taug—"

A snort made them turn around. Taug shuffled through the doorway. Three Crestas stood guard behind him. "No need. Taug can take care of himself."

Governor Right smirked at her datapad, elbows propped on her desk. "Screwed up didn't you, little fellow? So, you weren't as smart as your specimen. Funny, how that always happens. We think we have our options covered, then along comes a surprise element." She tapped her datapad, and her secretary's face appeared on the wall screen. "Cancel today's appointments. A private matter, so you don't need to tell anyone. Just say I'm indisposed. Let 'em chew on that."

She gathered a couple of small objects from her desk and placed them discreetly within easy reach on her person. She patted her hip with a flicker of a smile and headed out the door.

Ambling down the hallway, she nodded at a few faces, her glazed expression denoting her disinterest in conversation. As she reached the elevator, she waited for it to empty and then started forward. Turning around inside, pleased with her isolation, she was startled by a whoosh just before the automatic doors closed. Without turning her head, she knew exactly who occupied the small space with her. She trembled.

"No greetings?"

With a swallow, Governor Right tried to make her voice sound natural. "I avoid all unnecessary pleasantries. It takes too much time."

"This won't be pleasant, so you won't lose a moment."

Governor Right closed her eyes.

Vandi crowds bustled about in a holiday mood. The next day would begin the Inter-Alien combined Winter Festival and Religious Observation Season. The fact that it began nearly at the same time as the Oldearth Christmas Season irritated some, but since a lottery determined the date, few beings felt the need to argue the point. After all, every day was meaningful to someone. Christians considered it a sign from God. Others smirked at the very idea. The rest simply enjoyed the opportunity for paid leave and a few days of fun.

As Taug slogged through the wet snow behind Justine and Derik, he kept his weapon hidden from view. His three well-paid guards shuffled behind, their tentacles hidden under shapeless capes meant to appear inconspicuous. Only a few distracted stares came their way, which they ignored with icy politeness.

As they reached the middle of the main street, Justine scanned the environment. The streets were packed. Her heart froze. A group of children huddled outside a shop in serious consultation. Her gaze zoomed in. She instantly recognized the little boy's face. Glancing at Derik, she wondered what he had looked like as a child. She blinked in the sudden realization that she had never been a little girl. The loss hit her like a Dust-buster blast to the chest.

Taug stepped between them. "This'll do." He gazed innocently at Derik. "I'm sorry. But I was always honest. You know why you were created, and you know why you must die. It's as simple as that."

A figure strode forward. Taug's eyes narrowed at the daring approach.

"Not so simple." Wearing little more than a short-sleeve shirt, a pair of jeans, and slip-on shoes, oddly incongruous to the surrounding pedestrians bundled in heavy winter clothes, Bala stopped in front of Taug. He merely glanced at Justine and Derik. With a wave, he motioned Taug's weapon aside. "Cerulean sent word that Derik was in trouble. Clare's busy getting warrants and all that legal stuff. I'm here to see that no one gets hurt in the meantime." He pointed to the shuffled Cresta footprints and nodded. "You made it pretty easy to follow you."

Taug aimed his Dustbuster at Derik. "He's is past all trouble. Even he agrees. Don't you, Derik?"

Derik stepped away from Justine and thrust out his chest, making an easy target. "It's better for one man to die than for the innocent to—"

Bala shot a glance at Justine. "Oh, brother! Any other ideas?"

Justine shook her head. "I had planned the perfect escape when Taug showed up."

Pulling a dented Dustbuster from his back pocket, Bala shrugged. "Well, let's see if we can work together. Back off, Taug, and tell your—"

Taug's warning shot flew wide, blasting an innocent tree to bits. Bala rolled to the ground as shrieks filled the air.

Justine shoved Derik to the side and then lunged at Taug, but Derik gripped her foot from behind, and she slipped in the mushy snow.

Bala slapped his weapon free of snow, using words that would have shocked his mother.

Derik released Justine's boot and scrambled to his feet, ready to tackle Taug.

Sirens screamed their pulsating warning as a sleek, well-armored vehicle skidded to a stop. The door flew open, and Governor Right stepped out, her arms raised dramatically. Her gaze raked through the frightened crowd.

Taug's guards melted into the throng.

Bala lowered his weapon and stared, open-mouthed, as if the governor were a mirage.

The governor's voice rang over the cacophony. "It's all right, citizens. I'll protect you. Please, go about your business. This incident is well in hand." Her stiff smile matched her glassy stare.

When the crowd shook off its fright and began to circulate again, she dropped her gaze and glared at Taug. "Idiot."

Taug shuffled forward. "Hardly. If you hadn't interfered, at least some of us would have died, and Justine would have taken the blame."

Her eyes roved over the small assembly. "Which one?"

Taug shrugged. "Which one which?"

Governor Right's eyes flared. "The crossbreed, fool."

Derik stepped forward, his expression haggard and lost to the world. "That would be me."

With a snort, the governor marched forward and dug her fingers into his shoulder. "A prisoner is as good as dead in my book." Governor Right shoved Derik toward the open car door. She waved Bala's approach away and glanced at Taug, sweeping her eyes toward Justine. "Do with it as you will. Take it apart if it pleases you. Just never let it rise again."

Justine stretched her legs at an angle as she leaned back on a padded chair in front of a well-appointed desk. A pull-down electron microscope specially fitted to Cresta physiology hung directly overhead. She toyed with a bio-sample box as she watched Taug divest himself of his heavy coat.

"Does it bother you that badly? The cold, I mean?"

Taug shivered. "Horrible! It never drops below freezing on my planet. The average temperature is biologically perfect and the range is slight, so we rarely worry about seasonal preparations. Just wet and dry as the rotation determines."

"Lucky you."

His eyes glowed softly, curiously. "You feel cold, then?"

"Not like most people. But I have sensors that tell me what I'm feeling. I react according to my host's expectations. In winter, I wear sweaters and a coat to blend in."

"*Lucky you*." Taug plopped down on a couch across from the desk. He pushed a button and a wall section slid away, revealing a small fireplace. He tapped his datapad and colorful flames burst forth, undulating with glowing heat.

Justine grimaced. "A bit showy, don't you think?"

"Nothing like your paintings and Oldearth decor."

Justine pursed her lips. "You've been to my home?"

"When you weren't there, naturally."

With a dramatic yawn and a stretch, Justine rose and paced across the lab. She circled back and stopped, staring at the wall tank. "So, I want him alive and you want him dead. In either case, we need to get him back. Any way we could manage this without killing anyone or setting off an interplanetary war?"

Taug stroked his chin with the edge of his tentacle. "Yes, I was just considering my options. Mitholie will send someone to collect me soon."

Justine spun around. "Collect *you*?"

"Derik and you are not the only ones being threatened with annihilation. I'm beginning to think—we all are." Leaning back, he closed his red-rimmed eyes. The next moment, he opened them sleepily and swerved his gaze to Justine. "Governor Right knows things without my telling her, and she appeared a bit worried, did she not?"

"Your government—"

"Oh, dark waters, no! They're doing their best to appear shocked by every new event. No, I think we have a player in this game we know little about."

Justine stiffened. "My creator?"

Taug sucked in a breath and frowned. "I hope not."

Justine strode across the room and bent over Taug, staring into his golden eyes. "Why?"

"Because then we'd all be as good as dead."

CHAPTER EIGHTEEN

Save Us If You Can

Two Hundred Years Ago
Bhuaci Planet Helm

Faye loved to appear in various aesthetically pleasing forms, but once she learned about human fairy tales in her *Spectrum of Cultures* class, she adopted a fairy figure and insisted on the name Faye, meaning loyalty. Her mother, in her more mundane form of a gnomish, blue-green woman appeared almost human, though she literally did have eyes in the back of her head and an extra set of arms.

As far as either of them, or any Bhuaci for that matter, was concerned, Helm was the perfect planet and they, as harmless shape-shifters, were the perfect race. Unfortunately, they were not alone in thinking so.

The morning of the Telathot incursion began much like any other. Faye was heading out to class, but her mother called her back for an extra hug.

"Don't know what's gotten into me today. Your father thought I was coming down with something."

"Well, you're not exactly known for your impetuous nature, Mother." Faye's eyes twinkled at the understatement.

Her mother's gaze delved into her daughter's eyes and, with

a clouded expression, she placed a small chip into her hand. "You know I've always had the gift of foresight. I can see things—just a bit. I've seen something."

Faye's crystal eyes grew wide. "What?"

"Utter destruction."

Faye shook her head.

Her mother squeezed her slim fingers over the chip. "I may be wrong. I hope—but just in case, take this and if there is trouble, head to docking bay one-one-four. They're—"

Sirens ripped through the early morning. Faye trembled, her eyes growing even wider.

Her mother shoved her toward the door. "One-one-four. Remember. Go, now!"

"But, Mother! Father and...everyone!"

"Come back when you can. Save us if you can. But at least one Bhuac must survive. And it must be you!"

Present Day
Newearth

Faye slipped out of the black cloak that covered her from head to toe, her body shifting from a large, monstrous being into her preferred, petite form, and stepped away from its smothering embrace. Her dance-like steps propelled her to the circular living room couch, which lay against a large window overlooking the bustling city.

Stretching her body full length, she lay sprawled across the comfortable cushions until she heard the soft padding of feet and a polite, "Ahem."

She sat up and leaned back against the glass wall that revealed a half-mile drop to the pavement below.

A Bhuac male in a light green sweater and black slacks with a handsome, elven face, padded forward. "All well?"

Faye shook her head. "It's never really well, Gabriel." She peered at the holiday throng below. "You know that as well as I do."

"And the governor?"

"She's scared witless. That's something." She looked up at the figure in front of her. "I wish I didn't have to be evil."

Gabriel snapped to her side. "You're not evil. You're just doing as your mother asked. You're surviving. You're helping us all survive." He stroked her platinum blond hair and rubbed her cheek with his hand. "Remember what they did. Remember what Crestas and Ingoti really are."

Faye snorted her distain. "My current allies."

"Best place for your enemies is at your side—where you can keep your eye on them."

Falling back onto her couch, Faye sighed. "Remind me, what am I getting out of all this?"

Gabriel stiffened, his handsome body rigid, in perfect control. "As long as they fight among themselves, they grow weak, while we grow strong."

Wrapping her fingers around invisible bars, Faye stared into the air. "Ah, yes. Glorious, isn't it? Caged by unnatural ambition."

Gabriel scowled. "What's gotten into you?"

Her hands dropped from the dramatic pantomime. "I'm not sure. Self-pity, maybe." Faye scooted off the couch and wandered over to a table covered with ornamental figures in battle formation—not soldiers but fairy-tale dolls and animals of various descriptions—lined up against each other. She shoved a small, dark figure with large ears and round eyes closer to the front. "I like Bala. He's an interesting human. The most interesting I've ever come across, in fact."

"Bala? He has only a small part to play. All you must do is keep Governor Right dancing to your tune, which keeps Taug nicely in check and—"

Faye blew air in exasperation, like a child hundreds of years younger than herself. "There's always an *and*. The Ingoti drug-runners are not toys. They kill. Often."

Gabriel took the figure that Faye had moved forward and sent him in retreat to the back row. "All the more reason to keep them looking over their shoulder."

Faye flicked the figure flat on his back and spoke without looking up. "They think I am one of the Creators."

"Better and better." Gabriel sauntered to the doorway. "As long as they remain frightened, they won't attack anyone important without your permission." He turned and stared at the petite face. "Our people have been safe since you grew into power. Not one Bhuac has died under mysterious circumstances on Newearth, and Helm has remained untouched for years. You're doing your job."

A feeble smile arched Faye's lips. "You want my job?"

"Not on your life." Gabriel padded out the door.

Faye scooped up the toy figure and dropped him on the front line. "Pity."

CHAPTER NINETEEN

Enlighten Me

Bright, deceiving sunshine shone down on the after-holiday crowd as they endured their first day back to work. Some wore their new gifts of bright hats, thick coats, and padded footwear to protect themselves from the harsh, winter elements. Color and style did little to assist the beings as they plowed against a freezing wind. Survival loomed as the greatest good while ascetics followed a distant second. Holiday happiness had, by necessity, been replaced by grit and determination.

Governor Right stood before her ornate office cabinet and poured amber liquid into a shot glass. She tossed the drink down her throat. After an initial grimace, her face relaxed. With a sigh, she carried the bottle and the glass over to her desk and settled onto her padded chair. She poured herself another.

"This could go on all day." Mitholie stood just inside the governor's office doorway. The door slid shut behind him with a slight hiss.

Governor Right shot to her feet, her eyes narrowing. "Who let you in here? Who are you?"

"May I have a taste? It's not often that I have an opportunity to enjoy Newearth cuisine."

"Go to Bothmal! You're one of Taug's little minions, is that it? Listen, Cresta, I have—"

"Tut, tut. At least, I think that's the way you humans express polite displeasure. I don't mean to be rude, but you're shockingly ignorant. I'm no one's minion. I'm a leading scientist on Crestar. Some would say, the—"

A gasp knocked the governor back onto her chair. "Mitholie? By the Divide, what brings you here?" Her hand trembled as she pulled open a drawer and withdrew a second glass.

Mitholie's bulbous eyes glittered. "I'm so glad you asked."

Governor Right watched in fascinated disgust as Mitholie first sniffed her expensive brandy and then poured it into his breathing helm. Her mouth hung ajar like a broken hangar door.

Blinking his reaction under control, Mitholie grinned crookedly. "I had no idea you had such delicious liquids available. Taug's been keeping more than a few secrets."

Taug's name jolted Governor Right, her gaze hardening. "Have you seen him lately? I'd love to arrest him on a variety of charges, but he's difficult to pin down, and I don't want to offend—"

Mitholie waved her concerns away. "Humans can't help being offensive. It's in your nature. But don't worry, I've learned to control my sensibilities."

The governor plowed ahead. "He docs have one last piece of business to dispose of. Apparently, he's been stupid enough to awaken an android war criminal and planned to use it as an executioner—when need be. Or should I say, *if* need be. I get the feeling that honest Taug hasn't been exactly straightforward with us."

"Your scintillating insight is as I expected." Mitholie blew bubbles through his breather helm before continuing. "No Cresta is ever straightforward with anyone, least of all another Cresta."

"So you knew about his plans to create more half-breeds?"

"I knew the temptation would be irresistible."

Governor Right rose and strode to the furthest corner where the shadow had resided on its last visit. She searched the corners of the room. "Do you also know that other forces are at work here? Non-Cresta forces?"

Mitholie shuffled to a padded chair across from the governor's desk and snuffed another long draught from his spiked breather helm. "You mean the Ingoti drug runners? They're—"

"No. Not Ingoti. I mean another race. One I can't name."

"Can't or won't? Please, don't be shy. We're friends—enjoying liquids together."

"Priceless!" Clenching her hands together, the governor began to pace. "I'm not sure how much to say. I've had the office scanned numerous times, but one never knows who might be listening." She stepped closer, dropping her voice. "My guest has arrived at odd intervals and proven to be surprisingly resourceful. And dangerous."

Mitholie regarded Jane Right with a cold stare. "To what purpose?"

The governor looked away, her gaze unfocused and her words hesitant. "I'm not certain. But I know that it has an interest in Ingoti investments."

"Experimental drugs?"

"Could be."

"Well, that's always good for a few extra units. Not terribly dangerous, except to the test race. Human, this time, eh?"

The governor nodded.

Mitholie stroked his chin, his eyes half-lidded. "I don't think that needs to disturb us. My mission is to keep the good name of Crestar intact. Taug had a simple job to do, but he failed."

The governor resumed her stroll around the office. "So, you didn't expect him to experiment on the side?"

"I dearly hoped he would. Every bit of scientific knowledge is worth a million units. You don't have that saying?" A sad shake of the head appeared to denote further proof of pitiful, human ignorance. "In any case, I assumed he'd experiment first. But I expected him to be quicker and subtler. And now you tell me he has an android war machine at his disposal? Dark waters. This becomes cloudy, indeed."

"If it makes you any happier, I have the half-breed in one of my private holding cells. I ordered Taug to destroy the android."

"If he didn't obey me, what makes you think he'll obey you?"

With a nonchalant wave, Governor Right played her hand. "I own his laboratory."

Mitholie squirmed in glee. "You couldn't pinch a Cresta in a more tender spot! I take back what I said earlier; you are scintillating." Mitholie heaved himself out of the chair and shuffled to the door. "I think we can do better, though. Have your mysterious friend kill the half-breed in the interest of race relations and put the android on trial for its life. Everyone loves a spectacle. Offer a dramatic show, and you'll become the hero of the season." Mitholie chuckled as he ambled through the door. "You could sell tickets."

Watching the door slide shut, the governor slid her palm-sized Dustbuster back into her pocket.

Derik sat bolt upright. The darkness blanketed everything. Even with his heightened Cresta sensitivities, he could not peer through the black gloom. Someone was in his cell with him. He could sense it.

Shivering, he wrapped himself in the thin blanket offered by Governor Right's officers. He had chuckled at the irony of being locked up by secret police when he had been living in the open every day of his life. The chuckle had worn off hours ago.

"You're finally awake. I was getting bored."

Derik shot to his feet.

A muscular arm reached out and stopped him before he made it to the door. "Say one word, and you'll suffer a fatal heart attack."

With an audible swallow, Derik muttered. "My heart is strong."

"Not when it's crushed."

"What do you want?"

"To understand you."

Derik's chuckle returned and quickly morphed into insane laughter. Clutching the wall, he leaned at a crazy angle. "Everyone wants to understand me—I can't even understand myself. What? You're a friend of Taug's?"

"I've never been so insulted!" The shadow retreated to a far corner and folded the arms of its robe. "Actually, you and I are not dissimilar. I too have suffered from, shall we say, identity confusion."

Derik sighed. "My sympathies. But unless you are being hunted like—"

"My people have been hunted longer than you can imagine. Our perfection makes us a target for every conquering race. As your unique qualities make you a prized possession."

"So you're not Cresta or Ingoti...or even Uanyi." Derik let loose with a low whistle. "You're Bhuac?"

The intake of breath brought the first real smile to Derik's face. "I wish I could see you, though I suppose it wouldn't matter as you can take any form. I'd never see you again—would I?"

The shadow drifted nearer. "I didn't expect this level of perception. No one else has ever guessed."

"Must be the human-Cresta combination. A sensitive heart, an analytical mind—quick reflexes." Derik's hand snapped forward and caught the figure by the throat. "Why are you here? No one needs my sympathy."

"I could become a Kalama tiger and devour you."

"I'd break your neck before your first bite." As Derik applied pressure, the figure shrank. He shoved it against the wall and snapped his fingers in the air. "Make some light would you?"

A blue glow flared and a dainty Bhuac figure appeared before Derik, resembling a fairy child enveloped in soft radiance. "My name is Faye."

Derik fell back against the wall. "I'd say it's nice to meet you, but life's been a bit challenging of late, and I don't feel like lying."

Faye stepped forward. "I'm here to ask a favor."

Derik flapped his arms as if to embrace his environment. "You do realize that I'm in prison—about to be murdered?"

"I won't let that happen. But I need you to make me a promise."

"Oh, sure. I'm in the mood for granting favors. How about I give you the sun and the moon? Anything else?"

Faye swayed over to the hard bed and perched on the edge. "My family was destroyed in the Telathot incursion. Before she was taken prisoner, I promised my mother I would save my people. I've lived a lie for generations of your kind and served through deceit and despair, using every race at my disposal to keep the Bhuaci safe from any further desolation."

Derik slid down the wall and sat on the floor. "I'm impressed. In fact, I'm ashamed. I shouldn't have—"

Faye rose and paced in front of Derik, like a general reviewing her troops. "As a half-breed, you have special advantages. And your friend, the android, also has certain gifts. I want you to promise to assist me in protecting my race."

Rubbing his hands through his hair, Derik sighed. "If I wasn't locked in a cage, I'd be willing, but as you can see, my options are limited. Justine is probably—" He doubled over, agonized shivers wracking his body. "What will they do to her?"

"I don't know, but even if she is destroyed, there must be others like her. Do you know—?"

Derik covered his face with his fists. "I don't care. I only care about *her*." He lowered his hands and glared through haunted eyes. "Have you ever been in love?"

A twisted smile disfigured Faye's petite face. "I have suffered so, without the benefits."

Derik's head fell back against the wall; his shoulders slumped in defeat. "I don't get it. You're shape shifters. You should be able to conquer the universe. Take the form of demons and destroy all who oppose you."

Faye swayed closer, her gaze boring into his. "To conquer as you suggest, we'd have to destroy ourselves first."

"Innocence, a beggar's inheritance, isn't it?"

"I have often thought so...but in observing you and your friends, I have discovered a new strength."

Derik's sneer was palpable through the blue glow. "Enlighten me."

"Right makes might."

A harsh buzzing warned of a visitor. The room fell into darkness and a soft whoosh blew across Derik's face, alerting him to Faye's transformation. What she had become, he would never know. Despite the heavy tread of boots, a harsh, white light that made him blink, and a harsher voice that grated on his ear, he stood transfixed by the soft touch of a wing in flight.

CHAPTER TWENTY

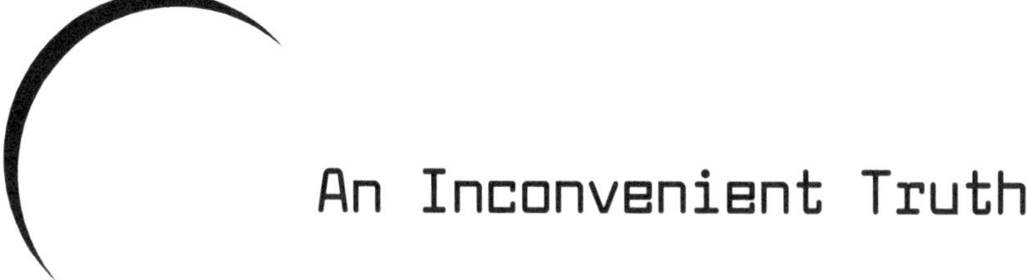

An Inconvenient Truth

Marching across the Luxonian Supreme Council Tower courtyard, Cerulean kept his gaze focused straight ahead and his expression neutral. The fewer hurdles between him and his appointed meeting, the better.

But no....

"Hey, Cerulean! Is that you?" Roux, in his athletic form, which he wore like a favorite fashion, jogged across the colorful, fauna-strewn square. His dark skin, well-set black eyes, and muscular body set him apart from the other guardians who usually chose less outstanding physiologies. Roux skirted a sparkling fountain and grasped Cerulean's arm in an old-chum-it's-nice-to-see-you greeting.

Cerulean swallowed and fixed a pleasant expression on his face. Roux was a good friend; at least it felt that way it felt every time they met. But he knew too much about Judge Sterling's deceptive nature and Roux's ambition to ever be at ease.

"Hi, Roux. It's been a while."

"I'd say. Given up the native shore, eh?"

Tendrils of vines wafted in a gentle breeze, reminding Cerulean of an ocean current. "Not quite. I just hoped to move onto—" With a sigh, he dropped his gaze. "You know."

Roux nodded. "Sure." He shifted his stance and shrugged away an unpleasant memory. "So, what's up? You here to see Sterling?"

Darting a glance to the tower, Cerulean hunched his shoulders. "There's been some trouble on Newearth—"

Roux snorted. "When isn't there trouble on that planet? By the Divide, they're as bad as Bhuacs for getting into black holes."

"Not always their fault."

"No, but then again, they ask for it more often than not. Take their new android initiative. You really think humans should be trusted with—"

Cerulean stiffened. "Their what?"

"You know. Surely you've heard of it. One of their governors, Bite or Right or something, she announced that they have broken the barrier between human and android—"

"Hell!"

"It will be, if she loses control of those things. I was on a transport with one named Max. Creative, eh? Anyway, he was built like a super-transport, had the mental capacity of a Cresta but not a particle of social graces. And not much of a moral code. Units were his guiding force. The more units, the stronger the force."

Stunned, Cerulean returned his gaze to Roux. "Would you know how to get in touch with him?"

Roux scratched his jaw. "Now, why in the universe would I want to do that?"

"As a favor to me."

A suffering sigh signaled Roux's consent. "He works for RunaWreck. They own nearly all the services in and out of Bothmal. It's a busy place, and Max is an able security officer. Try contacting their supervisor, Kingman. He'll put you in touch. If you make it worth his while."

"Any suggestions?"

Roux chuckled. "Pay Kingman a thousand units, and tell Max that you know an android named Justine. She's a legend that just won't die. He's obsessed with her."

"I know Justine. I was at her trial. She was shut down."

Roux's smile died. "Oh, well, even androids can be stuck on stupid." Roux's gaze shifted to the fountain. "And about Sterling and me, I never spied for him—it wasn't what it sounded like."

Cerulean's gaze joined Roux's at the fountain. "Good to hear."

Roux swallowed a bitter grin. "It's been good to see you. Don't be a stranger, or I might be forced to return to Earth, and you remember how *that* turned out."

Cerulean raised his hand and patted Roux's rock-like arm—once, twice. "Newearth now."

Roux paced away. "Humans are human. Some things never change." He looked over his shoulder. "And good luck with Sterling. You could do worse."

Cerulean blew air between his lips. He'd need to do better. And in a hurry.

Sterling sat ensconced in a large, overstuffed chair, leaning back, snug, plying a small tool about a ball of fluffy yarn. He crossed a long, luminous fiber around the hooked needle, lifted another thread over the hook, twirled the thread around again and repeated the process. His eyes squinted in child-like concentration.

Cerulean entered the office silently and observed the surprising dexterity of his superior's thick human fingers with fascinated abandon. "You've taken up—" He had to search for the word. "—crocheting?"

With his head bowed in studious determination, Sterling's rumbly voice rose to the occasion. "Therapy—to calm my nerves."

"You don't have nerves, sir."

Sterling let the tapestry of riotous colors fall on his lap as he glared at Cerulean. "Now you tell me!" He shook his head. "I have to reside in this human form so often and manage every new Newearth crisis with such resplendent dignity—my nerves are completely shot." He picked up the needle again.

Cerulean bit his lip against the tumult of incongruities that ricocheted around his mind. In the spirit of "If-you-can't-beat-them, join-'em," Cerulean edged closer. "Could you show me?"

Sterling glanced up. "Your nerves giving you trouble?"

Cerulean stepped back. "No, sir. My nerves are fine."

Slapping down his temporary insanity and rising to his feet, Sterling gestured with a stiff jaw. "I discovered a new drink. It's called brandy, and it has a wonderfully surprising effect." He strode toward a back wall and waved his hand, obviously confident that the wall would know exactly what to do. "Try some. It's Governor Right's favorite."

Scratching his head at his superior's current level of crazy, Cerulean stayed put. "I'm not very fond of alcohol. Or Governor Right, for that matter."

Sterling chuckled as he lifted a golden bottle from a rack unveiled by the sliding wall. "She's a remarkable woman. There's only one other I'd say could stand in her light, an Ingot named Lang from Universal Reports. Know her?"

"Never had the pleasure."

"It's never a pleasure. An experience, but never a pleasure." Sterling swirled his drink and ambled toward Cerulean, gesturing again, this time with a glance. "Sit down. You always stand so erect, like a guard waiting for the next attack."

"Probably because I am."

"You'll wear yourself out. Look at me...and my nerves." Sterling plopped himself down into his well-padded chair, shoving his crocheting aside. "Remember the day I visited you and that little girl got injured in a car wreck?"

Cerulean's jaw clenched. "She almost died."

"But you saved her, didn't you? And I was furious. Being in human form was so foreign. I hated it." He took a tender, loving sip. "You know I sent Roux to keep an eye on you."

"*Spy* on me."

Sterling pointed to the open wall. "Really, you should have one. It might mellow your heightened sensitivities. Humans do have some wisdom, after all. Being a nervous wreck isn't all that helpful."

"Am I a nervous wreck?"

Sterling sucked in a long breath. "No. And that surprises me. You should be. How was I to know that you wouldn't break under all that pressure and go native? We've lost others under less trying circumstances."

"By all accounts, I have gone native. I'm always in my human form."

Sterling nodded. "And by the Divide, I understand. There's something rather stimulating about the human body. Of course, being able to regenerate at will adds a pleasant security." He chuckled. "If humans could become Luxonian, we'd be overrun. Experiencing a bit both worlds is rather addictive."

"Yet most Luxonians forego the pleasure."

"Most Luxonians don't like a challenge. Or self-control. You have abundant self-control, Cerulean."

Cerulean folded his hands together. "You asked me here for a reason."

"Certainly. And you've answered all my questions, for the most part."

"This was a test? To see if my nerves were shot or if I had turned to drink?"

"To see *you*. You look good." He paused and scrutinized Cerulean's face. "Perhaps a little worn around the eyes, though. You're not seething over that absurd leak about Roux, are you? Why anyone thought it was helpful to bring that to light now, I can't imagine."

"Someone thought they'd make our leadership more honest by showing us how often they lie."

Wagging a finger, Sterling chuckled. "Uh, oh. Now there's the first sign of weakness I've seen. Bitterness does not become you. But, I'll put it aside." Swallowing his last gulp of elixir, Sterling rose unsteadily. "Now, tell me, what can I do for you—Newearth—that is? This part of the universe won't remain calm for long without our mutual support."

Cerulean let his eyes roam the room before settling back on his superior. "There is the matter of Taug, the Cresta who's targeted a crossbreed named Derik. He either wants him as a specimen or dead."

"Yes, I've heard. Governor Right told me that she has the matter in hand. She was shocked to learn of Taug's duplicity. Mitholie, one of Cresta's finest, has assured us that Taug will be punished most severely."

"And Derik?"

"Who?"

"The crossbreed."

"Oh, sorry. No. Crossbreeding isn't allowed by the Inter-Alien Alliance, so there are no crossbreeds. A mistake."

The guard in Cerulean stiffened to formal attention. "Derik is not a mistake. And he's not the only crossbreed."

Sterling poured himself another drink. "You know, if I do become an alcoholic, the blame will fall at your feet."

"About Derik?"

"Damn it, Cerulean! Derik can't exist. If he does, we are bound by the terms of our treaty to charge the Cresta government and expel the entire race from Newearth. But they're not about to go anywhere without a fight. And they won't be fighting alone. Do you really want another intergalactic war on your hands?"

Cerulean strolled to the open wall and lifted a glass from a hidden shelf. He poured himself a healthy serving and tossed it back in one swallow. Wiping his lips with the back of his hand, he glared at Sterling. "We can't hide from the truth. Crossbreeds exist. Killing an inconvenient truth isn't an option; it's suicide."

Sterling strolled back to his chair and picked up his crocheting needle. "This wasn't just for show, you know."

"Can't we amend the Inter-Alien Alliance agreement to allow for...certain irregularities? At least we can allow the crossbreeds that do exist to live and demand complete transparency. Cresta scientists will still experiment—evil exists—but at least we can call it what it is and embarrass those who do it with the reality of what they've done."

A bellowing laugh burst from Sterling. "And what exactly would they be embarrassed about? They've succeeded in crossbreeding two very different races. Cresta citizens will burst their bio-suits with pride."

Cerulean shook his head, staring at his empty glass. "Not when they realize that their brilliant scientists just created a race of beings stronger and smarter than themselves."

Max Wheeler stepped off the intergalactic carrier amid a crowd of urbanites and, as an android accustomed to the isolation of a prison transport, he stared in wide-eyed wonder. Turning on his heel a complete three-sixty, he used every scanning device at his command, searching through the crowd.

"Max?" Someone tapped his shoulder.

Max didn't jump. He stiffened like a rabbit caught in the glare of a hound. "Yes." He scanned Cerulean's face and an automated smile broke the line of his tight lips. "Cerulean."

Cerulean grinned. "I'm glad you made it on time. What, with all the extra traffic—" Max had not moved a millimeter. Cerulean nudged him on the elbow and nodded toward the street crossing. "There's a diner across the way. You want to get something?"

Max tilted his head. "I do not depend on human food. What would I get there?"

The grin was joined by a glimmer in the eye that Max didn't understand.

"Coffee?"

A passerby jostled Max and scrunched around Cerulean in

his hurry. Max accepted the inevitable. "If it would make you happy."

Upon sliding onto a bench in the Breakfast Nook, Cerulean waved to the hostess. The large, bio-armored Ingot wearing a blue sprigged, calico apron grunted, slapped her datapad against her palm, and charged toward them.

Max watched her approach, scanning her features, clothing, and behavior in order to classify her into a recognizable category. None.

The Ingot's gaze swept over Max and stopped. "What'd you want?"

Cerulean lifted two fingers. "Two coffees and a couple of sweet rolls."

Ignoring Cerulean, the hostess offered another appraising glance at Max, huffed her martyred patience, and tromped off.

Max, sitting ramrod straight across from Cerulean, stared unblinking. "It was my understanding that you were Luxonian."

Cerulean fiddled with the saltcellar. "Still am."

"As a Luxonian, you do not need human nourishment."

"Humans could take nutritional pills, but instead they still practice the culinary arts. Why?"

"Is this a test?"

Cerulean sighed.

Max shrugged. "It is a habit they cannot break. Like a drug."

Cerulean chewed his lip. "Just a small point, Max. Use contractions. You'll fit in better. It's more natural. Right now, you sound like you just swallowed an antiquated database." He leaned forward. "As for food, humans enjoy—"

The hostess slapped two hot coffees on the table and swished a metal plate with sticky buns in the middle. She tilted her head and appraised Max again, slowly. "Got back problems?"

Max glanced at Cerulean.

Cerulean spoke more quickly than he had earlier. "In the war. Never been the same—eh, Max?"

Max stared at Cerulean, unblinking.

The hostess relaxed. "Huh. So was I." She leaned in conspiratorially, her softened gaze joined by the hint of a smile. "I got a brace that helps when the load is heavy. Want me to show it to you?"

Coffee sprayed across the table as Cerulean choked.

Max tilted his head toward the hostess, meeting her gaze. "How kind of you. But, no. Thank you."

She recomposed her wide shoulders and tapped her datapad against her thigh. "Well, let me know. The name is Sal. I'm always here." She lumbered off.

"I didn't know it was possible." Cerulean's voice had grown thick and raspy as he wiped the table. "You've woken the passion of…an Ingot."

Max could feel the satisfied grin slide across his face. "Contractions, eh?"

Cerulean rubbed his forehead with a groan and nudged the coffee and plate of sticky buns toward Max.

As if the bun might explode, Max hesitantly lifted it. He carried it to his mouth and took a tiny bite.

Cerulean sipped his coffee and watched Max, his eyes wide. "Don't you *ever* eat diner fare?"

"Of course. Just rarely in public and never covered in—" Max tapped his sugar-coated fingers together. "—goo." Licking his lips, he took another bite and sipped the coffee. "They go rather well together."

Eyeing the hostess who kept swiveling her gaze in Max's direction, Cerulean leaned forward. "Time to get to business." He laced his fingers together. "You've heard of an android named Justine—Justine Santana?"

Max didn't swallow the bite in his mouth. He simply stopped chewing.

Cerulean shook his head. "That's not an answer."

Max gulped the unchewed bit, pushed away from the table, and rose. "Where is she?"

Cerulean waved his hand, his gaze tracking the Ingot's interested stare. "Sit down. It was a question. I need an answer before I can tell you anything."

Max leaned across the table and lowered his face within a few centimeters of Cerulean's. "If you know where she is, tell me now or I'll—"

The hostess appeared at Max's back and leaned over his shoulder, peering at Cerulean severely. "Problem here?"

Cerulean knew when he was beat. He raised his hands and shifted off the bench. "Everything's fine. Max and I are done—here." He stepped up to the cashier.

Sal maneuvered aside while glancing at Max. "You'll be sure to visit us again… soon?"

Max considered the Ingot standing before him, all seven biomechanical feet of her. "I will—I'll—make every effort."

Cerulean nudged Max forward. "Oh, don't worry; he'll be back. Max loves your sticky buns." He motioned toward the door. "Come on. We've got visits to make."

Max offered a parting smile to the blushing Ingot and traipsed after the odd Luxonian. "Where?"

Cerulean stepped out into the crisp winter sunshine and rubbed his hands together. "A prison and a morgue."

CHAPTER TWENTY-ONE

The Human Experience

Bala ran around the outdoor Waukee middle-school track with his skinny arms bent at the elbows, moving like the pistons of an Oldearth engine. His breath floated into the frozen air and wafted away.

Clare leaned against the woven metal fence while the sky darkened. An ache built behind her eyes. Hugging her winter coat around her slender waist did little to diminish the cold that seeped into her shaking bones. She was frozen to the core, and no coat in the world could warm her.

Bala turned aside at the entrance and swung his pounding footsteps in her direction. Panting, he heaved up next to her and bent over in an attempt to regain his exhausted breath. "What'cha doing here? I thought we'd meet at the Nook for something sweet and hot."

Clare forced a grin. "Always thinking about food, aren't you?"

Bala puffed smoke stacks in her direction and wobbled a skinny arm. "If you were born with this metabolism, you'd be obsessed with keeping body and soul together too, you know."

Clare threw an arm around his heaving shoulder, not so much to give him strength as to steal a bit of the steam pouring off his body. "Come on, oh-buddy-of-mine. We've got work to do. I stashed my larder with enough goodies to last you through another ice age."

Bala loped along at her side, wiping a wisp of curly hair out of his eyes. "Oh great. Another ice age. You have a dark mind, lady."

Clare shoved her frozen hands into huge, fluffy pockets, and they strode along the snowy sidewalk in silence. After a bit, she frowned and looked askance at Bala. "What're you doing out here at the track, anyway?"

Bala shrugged one lopsided shoulder. "Working off a little steam."

"Ha, ha!" Clare pummeled his left side down another notch. "So, tell me. How are we going to get Derik out of Governor Right's prison and Justine out of Taug's morgue?"

Bala glanced up at the first star twinkling in the sky and pointed. "Star light, star bright, first star I see tonight, I wish I may, I wish I might, have this wish, I wish tonight."

Clare stopped and joined in. "What'd you wish for?"

Bala hurried down the lonely sidewalk. "Can't tell. It'd break the… whatchamacall it."

Eyebrows rising, Clare laughed and bellowed frozen air in front of her face. "You're superstitious?"

"Not at all. I just don't want to lose my wish."

"Seriously?"

Bala sighed and stopped. He tipped his head back and stared wide-eyed into the blue and lavender sky. "I believe in more than the eye can see."

With easy dismissal, Clare waved him on. "So does everyone, I imagine. After all, we can't see everything. There's a lot we haven't explored and don't know."

Bala shook his head. "Naw. That's not what I mean." He hurried across a silent street and looked over his shoulder. "I hope you left a light on. My shins are still healing."

Twinkling windows illuminated the rural neighborhood. Clare huffed forward. "It's automated, idiot. Like your house should be. First wrong tip-toe around my place and lights and alarms go off."

Bala wrapped his quickly chilling arms around his lanky body and jogged ahead. "I got kids. Tip-toes are a security nightmare."

Once ensconced in Clare's largest and comfiest chair with a cup of hot cocoa in one hand and a plate of cookies in the other, Bala leaned back and grinned. "You do love me."

Clare sat cross-legged on the couch with a mug of steaming tea. "What are we going to do? I've been formally ordered to stay out of all political messes and concentrate on cases with legitimate humans."

"The boss knows about Derik?"

"Someone whispered enough in his ear to scare him witless. He told me to drop Derik's case and forget I ever heard of Mrs. Hoggsworth."

Bala whistled under his breath. "But we'll need Justine's help to free Derik, and she's a legitimate human, sort of. And after all, an unfriendly alien is holding her by force."

Clare shook her head. "I doubt she could be held by force... unless she thought she'd save Derik by offering herself up."

A swarm of kittens clawed their way up the side of Bala's chair. One nosed the plate of cookies near Bala's hand.

Bala sipped his cocoa. "Governor Right can't afford to leave evidence around that might bite her in the back some day." He chomped a huge bite out of his cookie.

Clare wrapped her fingers around her mug and stared at the rising steam. "And Taug's probably in hot water with the Cre-star leadership. They hate looking like the bad guys. Veneer is everything to them."

"I disagree. Science is their god. They'd sell their offspring for a crack at new technology. But given the Inter-Alien Alliance agreement, they're caught between science and diplomacy. The question is: how do we convince Taug that he can have both?"

"We want to do that?"

"Sure, on condition he gives Justine her liberty."

Clare's eyebrows scrunched in indignation. "Taug is a lying, murderous cheat who'll use anyone and everyone to further his own ends. And you want to offer him a way out?"

Bala leaned back and took another glorious sip of cocoa. "I said offer. I didn't say deliver."

All the snow had melted into rivulets of a late winter thaw. The sun shone mildly warmer, though it made no promises. The trees seemed to think that they had outlasted the worst of the season, and their branches thickened, the tips showing the tiniest swellings, hinting at future hopes.

Pedestrians plodded through the melting icy muck while those on autoskimmers raced above the mess, undaunted by nature's challenges. Bala marched across the street and held the door of the nondescript office building open for Clare, who glanced around nervously.

When they reached the desired floor, Bala stood back and let Clare take the lead, though he covered her with his well-aimed Dustbuster. They entered Taug's laboratory. Finding it empty, they both sighed.

Clare appeared to be dancing backwards as she turned about the immaculate, white-walled room. Bala edged nearer the furthest glass wall, his gaze sweeping right and left in wide arcs. Finally, Clare unclenched her fingers around her own Dustbuster and let out a long breath. "I guess he isn't here." She shook her head. "Though from everything I gather, he isn't anywhere else. I wonder—"

A sudden splash and a quick flash of tentacles swirling through the water forced a squeak from Bala. Clare clamped her hand over his, stopping him from blasting the wall to oblivion and drowning them in Crestonian fluids in the process.

Taug's eyes peered at them through the murky green swirl.

Clare frowned at his sudden smile. It almost looked like he was glad to see them. *He couldn't be…could he?*

Taug flashed out of sight.

Bala and Clare waited, their Dustbusters ready.

In a surprisingly short time, Taug's bio-suit encased body waddled around the curved wall and into the central laboratory.

Bala was busy inspecting every container and had just lifted the lid on the dissecting tube. He paled and clutched his stomach. Wagging a shaky finger, Bala croaked. "What the—*Who* the heck do you have in there?"

Taug grinned mischievously. "No one you know."

Bala raked his throat clear. "How do I know?"

"Hello."

The familiar voice made Bala swing around.

Clare gasped.

Justine stepped forward, wringing her wet hair in a long towel. "I would've killed him if it was human—or any sentient being—for that matter." She tossed a sinister smile at Taug.

Taug reflected the sentiment and opened his tentacles as if to embrace his long-lost family. "Come, let's make the most of this opportunity. It's not often that we gather without the express intention of killing one another." He gestured to an alcove off to the side populated with padded chairs, a sofa, and a couple of ornate tables.

Bala's eyebrows rose. "I had no idea that Crestas had a taste for comfortable furnishings."

Taug lumbered ahead and plopped down with a sigh on a cushy sofa. "After living in water, you don't think we'd prefer your hard, unrelenting wood and steel? No, there is much you do not understand about us. We are not as barbaric as you think. Your prejudice blinds you to our better qualities."

Clare huffed. "Honestly, it's your war crimes that blind me. But let's not get off topic." She folded her arms across her chest.

Bala leaned against one of the empty chairs, his eyes roving over to Justine, who seated herself across from Taug as if they were having an intimate moment together. Bala shook his head. "Okay, Justine, what's going on? You've become best buddies with your lover's would-be killer?"

Justine combed out strands of her wet hair with her long, slender fingers. "You do rush to rash judgments, don't you?"

Clare opened her hands beseechingly. "We came to rescue you!"

Justine flicked her hair over her shoulder and glanced at Taug before turning her full gaze on Clare. "Silly of you. I hardly need to be rescued. Thanks, anyway." Justine rose, towered over Clare a moment, then moved past her and strolled around the small space. "Remember in my apartment, when you apologized for being a judgmental idiot?"

Clare stiffened, only her eyes glowering.

"And you simpered all over my cat?"

As she flushed, Clare lowered her gaze.

Justine stopped in front of Clare and held up her hand to forestall any possible interruption. "I knew then that I had misjudged you." Justine stepped into Clare's personal space. "I couldn't embrace my human DNA, but I couldn't ignore it either." She tapped Clare's shoulder. "When you humbled yourself before me, you brought me the first real joy I've ever felt."

Clare turned away. "Happy to be of service." Her irony bounced off Justine like water off Taug's glass wall.

Justine's eyed followed Clare's pacing form. "It's all about choice, you see. My creator never gave me an option. I was caught between worlds. No human could really love an android, and technology has no heart to offer."

Bala slapped the back of the chair, startling Taug. "That's not true! Derik loves you. He offered his life to save you."

Justine shook her head. "Merely sentiment. He loves the idea of me."

Taug's eyes ping-ponged back and forth between the speakers.

Bala clapped his hands together in impotent fury. "If sacrificing yourself for another isn't love, then I don't know what is."

"Sharing yourself completely. Something I can never truly do."

Clare lifted her hands in apparent surrender. "I'm lost. How did I help?"

"You humbled yourself. You even hugged my cat!"

Clare glared at Justine. "Okay, fine. Fair trade. You come over and hug my cat sometime, and we'll be even. You'll be as humble as me."

Taug grunted at Clare, a tentacle waving in admonishment. "You're a stupid woman." He heaved himself to his feet. "Justine is humble enough." He glanced at Justine. "She was never a child and can never have children. A vital part of the human experience—lost to her."

Justine smirked. "But not so vital." She glared at Clare. "I don't need to be a child, a mother, or even *in love* to experience humanity. You humbled yourself for a cat." She turned on her heel. "I was never so glad to be an android in all my life."

Bala stood back and gripped his Dustbuster as he glared at Justine. "So you've sided with Taug—against us?"

Justine laughed as she pounded to the doorway and turned on the threshold. "I'm not against you. Just not one of you. I don't need you anymore. Taug's helped me understand that my uniqueness is my greatest asset. He's sent a message to his superior; I'll be returning with him."

Clare's eyes widened. "To Crestar? You're crazy. They'll dissect you!"

Bala waved his Dustbuster at Taug. "Right after they kill him."

Taug chuckled. "They won't kill a hero bringing home their salvation."

CHAPTER TWENTY-TWO

A Worthy Goal

The evening's winter wind had settled to a mild breeze as Derik jogged hunch-shouldered at Faye's side. Slugging his chilled hands deep into his coat pockets, he frowned at the memory of Faye's unblushing impersonation of a guard, allowing her to affect his release. Though he towered above her slight form, her prancing step kept him lumbering along at a quicker pace than was comfortable for his Cresta-booted feet. Tripping over a clump of ice, he nearly sprawled onto the sidewalk.

Faye reached out and steadied him. "Don't slip. I can't change out in the open, so I wouldn't be much help if you got hurt."

Derik pulled his hands out of his pocket to maintain his balance and nodded. He darted a quick look at the little Bhuac. "You're amazing. I still don't understand how your race can be at risk. You just sprung me from the clutches of Governor Right! You could use the same tactics everywhere and no one could touch you."

Faye glanced up at Derik's large brown eyes. "Have you never yearned to be free—to be yourself? Freed from the secret bonds necessary to keep you safe?"

Derik shrugged. "Beyond my boots, I don't have many protective bonds. In fact, if you hadn't saved me from my last fall, even these boots wouldn't have saved me."

A curious half-smile played around Faye's lips.

Derik grabbed her arm and pulled her under the shelter of a weeping willow. The long tendrils swept around them like a lacy curtain as busy pedestrians hurried by. "What? There's something you're not telling me."

Faye's almond-shaped eyes danced at Derik. "There is a great deal I'm not telling you. But to keep you happy and in the interest of building trust, I will share this particular incident."

Derik wiggled his fingers like a child waiting for a ball to come his way.

"When I learned of your existence, I was quite interested to learn more about you, which meant I had to learn more about Taug. So, on occasion, I would investigate his laboratory. Not long ago, I became so perplexed by one of his experiments that I did not notice his return—until it was almost too late."

Faye blushed a bright pink and covered her cheeks with her petite hands. "This is very embarrassing."

Derik's grin widened.

"I reacted on instinct. I don't know why, exactly, but I changed into a small dog, one of those yapping little quadrupeds that like to chew and snarl at everything."

Derik shook his head and snapped a weathered twig off the tree. "Wouldn't have been my first choice."

"Certainly. If I had been prepared, or thinking clearly…but I was so concerned by what I saw that I lost all reasoning."

"What did Taug do when he saw a mutt in his immaculate laboratory? Oh, I wish I had been there!"

Faye blushed harder. "He did what any irate scientist would do. He tried to shush me away. But I was annoyed and—" She dropped her gaze.

"You've come this far. Tell me everything."

"I attacked his boots. I nearly shredded them before I ran away."

Derik let out a yelp that turned heads. One passerby stopped and peered between the swaying branches. "You okay in there, little Miss?"

Derik cupped his hands over his laughter.

Faye smiled brightly at the concerned face and nodded like a six-year-old. "I'm fine. My dad's having one of his spells. Just give him a minute. He'll come out of it."

The stranger grunted, dropped the trailing vine, and turned away.

In a formal manner, Derik took Faye by the arm. "All right, daughter, you and I have a mission to accomplish. Let's go find Taug and free Justine. If he gives us any trouble, you can turn into a poodle and shred his bio-suit.

The cold, sterile laboratory appeared ashen in the dim light, echoing only dead silence as if it knew it had been abandoned and could not bear the truth.

Faye entered first, one thin-fingered hand lifted in front, probing for danger. Not a whisper or swirl of movement responded to their approach.

Derik marched stiff and hunch-shouldered behind, ready for anything. Not ready for nothing. "I wish I had a Dustbuster."

Faye halted and looked back at him. "Why? No one's here."

"One never knows when Taug'll show up. Remember the incident with the boots? Besides, I'd dearly love to blast his equipment to smithereens. It would serve him right. Double-crossing me!"

Faye circled the empty room, tapping and touching various instruments. "He never lied to you, Derik. He told you that he might have to kill you. It wasn't exactly his choice."

Derik tromped over to the pool wall, splayed his fingers across the glass, and stared into the murky depths. "You sound like you sympathize with him...your enemy."

Faye lifted the top off the dissection tube and shuddered. "I sympathize with all trapped beings. I know how it feels."

Derik slapped his forehead. "You're—"

The sound of someone clearing his throat made Faye and Derik freeze. Slowly the two turned in unison, like ballet dancers thawing from a deep frost.

Cerulean stepped over the threshold and folded his arms across his chest. "Honestly, I wasn't expecting this."

Taug groaned as he leaned against the hard, uncompromising transport chair, his tentacles limp at his side. He squeezed his eyes against the discomfort of the harness that kept him from sliding off the seat, while his ample middle bulged unceremoniously at droopy angles.

He choked out a ragged whisper. "I deplore space travel."

Justine, sitting ramrod straight with her feet firmly set on the smooth floor, crossed her arms languidly over her unharnessed lap. "It could be worse. You could be traveling in the baggage compartment."

A mere flicker of a glance indicated Taug's awareness of Justine's dry sense of humor.

Four other travelers sat strapped in their own ample seats. Two humans, well equipped with state-of-the-art headsets, tapped their datapads while their eyes scanned invisible screens. Two Crestas, younger and more robust than Taug, strained against their harnesses and leaned over to whisper to each other.

A loud buzz announced their entry into space and freed the occupants from their unnatural positions. The humans unbuckled and left without even glancing at the other passengers. The Crestas grunted with relief as they rose and passed into the passage. They studied a map highlighting the ship's points of interest, including the dining section.

Tapping her thigh, Justine rose and ambled across the small space.

Fumbling with his straps, Taug's grunts sharpened to disgust.

Unmoved, Justine faced him. "So tell me more about your planet...your people. What is the plan?"

Taug jerked fiercely at his strap, which nearly choked him. He gasped. "Get this damn thing off me, or you'll be arriving with a dead body."

Justine frowned but stepped forward. "Is that how you see yourself? I thought you considered yourself a scientist of the highest order, nothing less than a brilliant mind—"

"Hurry! I can't breathe!"

Justine jerked the strap so that it loosened the clasp and pulled it free from Taug's body. She stared down at the threadbare material. "Primitive. I wonder why they haven't come up with something better."

Taug staggered to his feet and wiggled his tentacles to reanimate his circulation. "The captain knows that the few travelers between Crestar and Newearth are either desperate or preoccupied. Humans don't go to Crestar unless they are ordered there on business, and Cresta scientists would rather keep our monetary resources for our work. No incentive for comfortable seating."

"But you like padded chairs and easy comforts."

"I'm high enough in the food chain to be used to such things. But I like to appear before my superiors as an earnest scientist who happily endures simple hardships without complaint." He flicked a grimaced smile at Justine. "You won't give away my little secret, now, will you?"

Justine tilted her head and gestured toward the dining section. "We all have our secrets. How about you teach me the fundamentals of Crestonian cuisine? After all, I intend to be at the top of your food chain, and I'd hate to eat anyone out of order."

As they settled into their dining booth, Taug waved a tentacle and alerted the host on duty. A Cresta youth ambled over, looking eager to please, his golden eyes large and watery.

"We're honored to have you on board, Taug. I've been told to offer you the best we have—" He bent down and whispered in an awestruck tone. "—no matter the cost." His fleshy eyebrows wiggled to underscore the momentous news.

Taug glanced at Justine and then offered a rewarding smile to the young, obviously aspiring Cresta. "I'd like to introduce my protégé to our finest selection. How about we start with—"

As Taug gabbed on about Cresta food options, Justine scanned the dining room. The two other Crestas were bent over sloppy bowls of sticky goo, though they hardly seemed to be eating. She watched as they made every pretense of conversing and enjoying a good meal. She smirked. Apparently, Taug's own kind didn't trust him either.

The host practically skipped away.

Justine eyed Taug as he leaned back in the padded booth. Burns, rips, and more than one dent in the furnishings attested to the lack of luxury. But it would hold together for their quick trip. "Happy now?"

Taug closed his eyes and sighed. "Until landing, I'm free and I've ordered the finest meal available this side of the Divide. I always like to look on the sunny side."

"Sunny side? A rather human sentiment for a Cresta, isn't it? You like to dive into deep water and surround yourselves with murky gloom." As Taug did not respond, Justine laced her fingers together, propped her elbows on the table, and leaned in. "Tell me your plans so I know what to expect. I'm not particularly confident that we'll meet a happy reception."

Taug opened his eyes and let a lazy gaze rove over Justine. "Why are you worried? I politely informed Mitholie that I was bringing home a prize worth uncountable units." Taug grinned. "Trust me, he's waiting with bated breath."

Justine pursed her lips in the direction of the two other Crestas. "So why did he send guards?"

Taug's gaze rolled across the room. He shrugged. "I'm always watched. It's part of the Cresta Code. Watch your back and watch everyone else too."

"You're not a very trusting race, are you?"

"Should we be? We value science, and we value advancement. We do not suffer fools."

"So what am I? Besides a prize, I mean." Justine's eyes narrowed. "I'm not going to be experimented on?"

The host appeared with a large tray, which he set to the side. With skillful motions, he set the table with bowls, utensils, and drinks. Using padded mitts, he placed a steaming bowl in the center. "Watch yourselves now, it's as hot as it looks, but the cook says it's the best batch he's made in eons." With a sharp bow, the youth smiled, his eyes desperate for approval.

Taug accommodated the juvenile with a smile and a nod.

"I'll check on the main course and be back shortly." A quick turn sent the young Cresta on his way.

Taug delicately ladled soup into Justine's bowl and handed it over. "Ah, I wish I were trying Samong for the first time with you. It's a true delicacy." He leaned in and whispered. "One of the ingredients is only found on a reclusive mountaintop. Though researchers have tried for years to duplicate it, they can't get the subtle flavor that makes it so unique."

Justine took a tentative sip. She shrugged. "It tastes a lot like the tomato soup that Cerulean makes."

Taug sniffed the wafting aroma and grunted. "Cerulean! Don't ruin my appetite." He sipped from his spoon and hummed. "It *is* a good batch."

Justine laid her spoon aside and folded her arms. "I have serious questions, none of which you are answering."

Taug slurped another long draught, his shoulders relaxing. "I told you, Derik will be safe until your return. I offered Governor Right a deal she couldn't resist."

Justine's eyes narrowed. "Such as?"

"She holds on to Derik, unharmed, until your return, and I'll pass our android findings onto her—to do with as she wishes."

"You'd do that? Give Newearth and that self-serving liar android—"

Taug lifted a tentacle. "You forget yourself. Remember,

you're serving your own interests as well. We all are." He took another happy sip. "Besides, it'll take her eons to decode it." He leaned back and patted his stomach. "All you need to do is let a few select scientists study you—nothing invasive—and you'll be free to return to Newearth under a new identity, collect Derik, and go wherever you wish."

"You won't need Derik—ever? You're giving up your crossbreed studies completely?"

Taug grinned. "What do I need with a crossbreed when I have a much better alternative? An android with Cresta DNA will be a far more worthy goal. We'll become like gods."

Justine shoved her bowl away. "*They* will be, anyway."

CHAPTER TWENTY-THREE

We Fall Into Chaos

Cerulean stepped into the lab and exhaled a long cleansing breath. “Before we go into the details, tell me one thing—where is Justine?”

Derik’s worried gaze flickered around the room. “We were hoping Taug would tell us—” He flexed his long, muscular fingers. “—by force if necessary.” Derik marched up to Cerulean. “Have you heard anything?”

Cerulean’s gaze swerved from Derik to Faye. “I don’t think we’ve met.”

Appearing to float, Faye swayed closer. Her large, almond-shaped eyes peered up at Cerulean. “Many times I’ve wished I could introduce myself, but secrecy has always been my best defense.”

Cerulean offered a gentleman’s nod. “Many the times I wished I could be of service. But your race is very secretive and singularly inventive. I doubted my ability.”

Faye’s gaze glanced off Derik. “I wish to come out of the shadows.”

Stroking his cheek, Cerulean appraised Faye before his eyes strayed to the wall screen. “We need to discuss this further. But right now, Taug must be stopped.”

Derik pushed in front of Faye. "Why? What's he done?"

"Clare and Bala confronted Taug yesterday and met Justine here. She's fine… at least physically. She said she was going to return to Crestar with Taug."

In a near shriek, Derik pulled his hair. "What?"

Peering at the wall, Cerulean marched across the room. He tapped the console and the screen flickered.

Faye faded into the background.

A white square appeared on the screen and then a blurry, shifting body shuffled closer. Gradually, an enlarged, perplexed Cresta face came into focus. "Taug? Is that you? I thought you were on a transport—"

Edging closer, Cerulean stationed himself in front of the screen. "No, sir, Taug isn't here. I'm Cerulean, a Luxonian on official business. Do you know where Taug has gone?"

The Cresta's jaw hardened and his eyes narrowed. "This my private address! I don't know what official business a Luxonian might have with Taug, but he's been ordered home. We have unfinished business he must attend to."

Cerulean pressed on. "So Taug is on a transport? Alone?"

"Until I understand the circumstance of your inquiry better, I'm not at liberty—"

Derik squeezed between Cerulean and the screen. "Is Justine Santana with him? Did he take her?"

A long, flabby tentacle jabbed at the screen. "Excuse me? Who is this?"

Derik folded his arms high across his chest. "I'm Justine's fiancé, and I demand that you tell me where she is immediately, or I'll file charges with the Inter-Alien Alliance Committee. Cerulean—" Derik jerked his thumb backward. "—is a founding mem—"

The looming face broke into an impressive smile. "Oh, you're *that* Cerulean! I didn't recognize you. My name is Mitholie. Perhaps you've heard of me?"

Cerulean dragged his wide-eyed glare off Derik and swung it at Mitholie. "Yes, sir. Sterling has mentioned you." His face tightened. "I'm very concerned about the android Justine, who was recently in Taug's company. She might be traveling with him to Crestar."

Mitholie's wide smile brightened. "If so, we would welcome her with pleasure."

"I'm certain of that." Cerulean cleared his throat. "But you can see how distressed *her fiancé* is." He dashed a quick glance at Derik.

Derik stood staring up at the screen, his hands wringing an invisible neck.

"I want her home at once! You hear me?"

Mitholie edged away from the screen, his disgusted gaze focused on Derik's hands.

Placing a firm grip on Derik's shoulder, Cerulean shifted him to the side. "I apologize, Mitholie, but we have our own troubles, and Justine needs to return as soon as possible."

Mitholie smirked like an understanding patriarch. "Certainly, if she arrives with Taug, I'll relay your message. But honestly, you're mistaken. Taug is traveling alone. If you look on the transport manifest, I'm sure that you'll find that no Justine Santana will arrive on Crestar." He waved the small end of one tentacle benignly. "I will inform Taug of your concern. He'll be gratified to know his friends have inquired about him." Mitholie offered a brief nod to Cerulean before peering narrowly at Derik as if memorizing his features. "Fiancé, eh?" Offering a lopsided smile, Mitholie continued, "My congratulations." The screen blinked to black.

Cerulean's head dropped to his chest and his shoulders sagged. Then he swung on Derik in fury. "What the—? You're supposed to be dead. You want to make absolutely certain the job gets done?"

Derik's broad shoulders matched Cerulean's muscle for muscle. They glared into each other's eyes.

Faye held up her elfin hands and stepped between them. "Please. There is enough anger in the universe. We share a common purpose; let's not forget that."

Derik's face flushed with rage as he peered down at the small figure. "Or what?"

Faye's eyes brimmed. "We fall into chaos."

Max sat upright on the bench in Bala's brightly lit kitchen and stared at the steaming bowl in front of him. He struggled to process the tumultuous energy bopping all around him. He knew full well that it was considered rude to stare, even at little humans, but it took every particle of his self-control to keep from glaring at his riotous surroundings.

Bala laughed and slapped Max on the shoulder. Leaning in, he sniffed the casserole as if appraising the danger. He shook his head. "Nothing to be afraid of. Go on. Kendra's got a way with rice, beans, and green things. If she didn't, I'd be dead by now."

Max swiveled his head, right and then left, allowing himself the luxury of a good long stare. The baby was strapped into a high chair, pounding a miniature utensil on a tray and drooling copiously amid Kendra's alternate cooing and humming sounds. Another child sat backwards, her long hair partially draped over her bowl. She clapped to a rhythm Max could not even faintly discern. A little boy clung to Kendra's legs, chattering in an alien language as his mother flittered around the large kitchen. With the grace of a seasoned acrobat, she slid a towering bread plate somewhat near the center of the table. An older boy sipped his meal in quiet contemplation, while another scanned his datapad, drumming his fingers on the tabletop.

Max faced Bala, plastering a benign expression on his face. "Are they always this noisy?"

Lounging against the table, Bala surveyed the miniature throng. "Not at all. Sometimes they get into a ruckus and then you hear some real noise, brother." Bala covered his ears to emphasize his meaning.

Max didn't have to feign astonishment. "Why in the universe did you have so many? Wouldn't two offspring continue your species just as effectively?"

Bala scratched his head. "Well, now, I hadn't thought of them quite like that..."

He smiled as Kendra plopped down on her chair, one arm encircling the now sedate three-year-old. She spooned a mouthful of stew into the little one's mouth, grabbed a broken piece of bread, chomped, and chewed as she grinned back at Bala.

"Kendra, Max would like to know why we had so many." With a sweep of his hand, he clarified his point.

Kendra's nearly frantic chewing slowed to glacial speed as one eyebrow rose. She swallowed, squared her shoulders, and smiled bravely. "Well, you see, it's our pleasure. We enjoy bringing new life into the world and training them to become wonderful citizens of Newearth."

Bala stared at Kendra, his eyes rounding into orbs. "The truth? You told him the truth!"

Kendra shrugged and she grabbed another slice of bread, handing a significant chunk to the baby. "I think he can handle it. Besides—" Her gaze rolled around the kitchen. "—it's what I drill into their heads every day of their lives. Made for a purpose. We all are."

The room froze as Max jumped to his feet. His perpetually mild expression had drained of all animation and color.

Bala tossed a quick glance at Kendra as he rose and placed his hand on Max's shoulder. "You all right? We're just kidding around—sort of." Running his fingers through his hair, Bala nudged Max toward the door. "Let's head over to Cerulean's place. He might have news by now."

With robotic steps, Max marched through the kitchen doorway.

Bala stopped on the threshold and faced his perplexed family. He shrugged. "So, androids have issues. Who knew?"

Max stomped up Cerulean's porch steps as a bedraggled, panting Bala took up the rear. "Hey, slow down, would you! I just barely sent word that we're coming, and you're ready to break down his door."

Max promptly smashed in Cerulean's front door and, standing amid the wreckage, scanned the large, open kitchen-living room.

Cerulean burst into the room, waving a Dustbuster. "What?" He glared first at Max and then at Bala. Lowering the Dustbuster, he shook his head in disbelief. "Max, why did you break down my door? I just got it fixed."

Max swallowed and spluttered. "I—I got a message from Justine. She's going to murder Taug."

Standing in his employer's personal recreation room at the Vandi Country Club, Eric handed a club to a waiting hand and snapped to attention. His shoulder-length blond hair, tied in a smooth ponytail that hung down his back, matched his bright yellow eyes, which he had altered as soon as he had enough money for the procedure. Altering eye color to unnatural hues had come into fashion only recently, but he was never one to lag behind a new trend. His stylish body suit and slip-on footwear fit his trim form like surgical gloves. His eyes roved over his employer, Simms, with a covetous longing.

Simms, a human with more replacement parts than he liked to admit, could not hide his boxy shape, though he tried. His hair—not his own—appeared thick and black. The mustard-colored shirt and trousers he wore complemented his olive skin tone. A gold pendant hung at his neck, and ornate rings bejeweled his fingers. Simms cleared his throat and swung the club over his head in a couple of practice moves. He frowned and handed the club back with a polite sniff. "Not this one. Give me the thirty-four."

Eric searched through the club bag and found the one mentioned. He pulled it forth, mesmerized by its polished gleam.

Simms had the best set of clubs on the planet and a wall of prizes to attest to his award-winning skill at Zinzinera. Though the Ingoti game had been adapted to Newearth sensibilities—the losers did not have their heads knocked together, and they counted score with points rather than injuries—everyone still took the game seriously and none more so than Simms himself. Eric had noticed that Simms took everything seriously—especially himself.

Eric observed his employer closely. There was more to this man than met the eye. He clasped his manicured fingers behind his back.

"Take this." Simms held out the club with a firm hand.

Eric reached and—Simms grabbed his hand and twisted it behind his back painfully. "I know what you're thinking."

Eric strained to keep his composure. "That would be?"

"You want what I have."

Eric considered his options and chose unprecedented honesty. "Is that so wrong?"

Surprisingly, Simms grunted and released his grip, shoving Eric forward. "Not at all. In fact, I was kinda counting on it."

Eric rubbed his wrist and raised an eyebrow.

Simms grimaced. "I have a job for you. Real simple. Knock a certain mixed-breed's head in or blow him to bits—whatever's easier. Take what's on his body and ransack his place. He managed to escape from certain death once; don't let it happen again."

Remaining unmoved, Eric considered his options again. "Why should I?"

"Because I said so. Because an important somebody wants it so. And because you don't get to be like me unless you have powerful friends."

"I'm not a killer."

"Sure you are."

"Someone might find out. Human Services will—"

Simms blew air between his lips, swinging his club. "Look,

he's a mistake. Mistakes aren't human." He tapped his club against Eric's head. "Like idiots who don't know a good opportunity when it comes along. *No one* will care."

New options danced before Eric's yellow eyes.

CHAPTER TWENTY-FOUR

Our Only Limitation

Misty air draped everything in a heavy fog. Taug grunted as he stripped off each section of his bio-suit in the white-walled, laboratory-style cleansing room. Water dripped down the tiled walls. Turning to Justine, he lifted one booted foot and wagged it at her.

"Would you be so kind? These things are worse than Tatarian leeches."

Justine unfolded her arms from across her chest and bent low. She grabbed the boot heel and jerked, nearly toppling Taug.

"Careful! I don't want my toes to come off with the boot. They don't grow back as quickly as the tentacles."

Wiggling the boot effectively, it squelched off the swollen three-toed foot. Justine wrinkled her nose. "What's that smell?"

Taug sighed as he lifted his other boot in her direction. "You don't want to know. The price we pay to travel to foreign parts."

After Taug was completely free of every article of clothing and well wrapped in a large towel, he tromped over to a shower stall, tossed the towel over the door, and turned the spray on full blast. Shouting over the noisy spray, he waved a tentacle. "Get me that robe hanging to the left. Oh, my! This feels good!"

Justine rolled her eyes. "I'm your servant now?" She threw the swirly green-and-blue garment onto a nearby hook. "I thought you were a water creature. Where's your ocean?"

Taug scrubbed and giggled. "We're a bit too advanced to stay in the water all the time. Just for sport and refreshment." He turned off the shower, snatched up the robe, and, patting his body in the joy of cleanliness and freedom, he stepped back into the room. "You have no idea how good this feels."

Justine tilted her head at him as if analyzing an insect.

Plodding down a white, rounded hallway, Taug lifted a tentacle and flicked off their itinerary. "First, I'll have to dress properly, then we'll attend the banquet, and finally, I'll arrange matters with Mitholie in his private suite. He enjoys luxury like nothing you've ever seen. You'll—"

"I'll see for myself. What do I wear?"

Taug stopped and appraised her with a frown. "What you're wearing will do."

He started forward again. Humming.

Justine laid a hand on his shoulder. Without the boots, he was much shorter. She peered into his eyes. "I've been wearing this for a week."

Taug shook his head. "No one will know… or care."

Justine squeezed his shoulder. "I know. I care."

Taug blinked. "I suppose you'll want your own room? And a shower and new clothes?"

"Your point?"

Taug peeled her fingers from his shoulder. "That's what I keep asking myself."

The air was heavy with water vapor as wispy ivies swung from the rafters like algae swaying in the deep sea. The murky green underworld of Crestar swirled behind a massive see-through wall. Various aquatic creatures swam about in placid acceptance of their environment. Pliant green tables and squishy white chairs dotted the floor, while Crestonian youth hustled between persons of importance offering drinks and hors d'oeuvres.

Taug sauntered into the room, positively transformed by his neat, new attire: a well-fitting white, sleeveless shirt and leggings with a long, flowing robe.

Justine trailed after him, unchanged.

A mingling, chattering crowd turned as one and stared past Taug to the android behind him.

A satisfied grin gleamed through Taug's eyes. Justine may attract stares, but he would demand respect. He plodded forward, scanning the intimate group until he zeroed in on Mitholie.

Mitholie wore a heavy, dark green tunic of shimmering brightness. The thin cilia on top of his head were daubed with blue gel, and his face bore the fancy red stripes of his rank and position. Stepping forward, he stretched out his tentacles in a welcoming gesture. "So glad the prodigal son has made it home at last."

Taug bowed out of respect and to hide his smirk. "I'm honored you know the reference. Newearth Studies was never one of your favorites."

Mitholie surveyed Taug only a moment before his gaze shifted to Justine. "Ah, the redoubtable android, Justine Santana. It is delicious to finally meet you."

Justine tilted her head, frowning. "It's delicious to meet you as well."

Titters broke out among the assembly. Tentacles rose to cover uncouth giggles.

Taug winced, but Mitholie reached out and cupped Justine's hand in a wide tentacle. "Let me introduce you to my brain trust. These are my most intimate associates. They will be working closely with Taug to make your stay on Crestar sheer ecstasy."

Justine stared at Mitholie's tentacle as he led her toward a tall Cresta with a high forehead and huge green eyes. She leaned toward Taug and whispered. "Hyperbole doesn't have the same—"

Taug shook his head in a sharp motion, while staring straight ahead.

Mitholie dropped Justine's hand and offered an introductory wave to the large Cresta. "Meet Zendrox. He specializes in biomechanical advancements. In fact, he was the one to adapt our bio-suits to Newearth terrain. He once worked with the renowned Donadello, who searched the furthest reaches of the universe to discover—" An undertone humming warned him off the topic. He flicked his gaze around the wide-eyed crowd. "—a cure for our weakness on land."

A chime induced Mitholie to bow benevolently. "Time for the festivities. Let's get comfortable." He waddled to a wide table and plopped down on a soft, white couch. The others arranged themselves as close as possible without blocking Mitholie's view of the runway arranged at the front of the room.

Justine stood to the side, her arms folded. Taug patted the cushion beside himself. With a sigh, she clumped over and sat on the soft material that oozed up around her.

Green and yellow lights swirled around the room as troops of scantily clad beings filed in. There were Bhuacs, Ingots, Uanyi, and three human children. They began to perform various acrobatic games, displaying their species' best attributes.

Justine's eyes widened and her breathing quickened. She shot a glance around the room. Every Cresta perspired with pleasure. She recognized Taug's automatic grin, set in place to cover his thoughts. Mitholie actually drooled.

Calls and grunts of dissatisfaction urged the players to perform more daring acts of entertainment. One Cresta stood and gestured in such a manner that even though Justine could not understand the exact expression, she knew the vulgar meaning.

The players halted, confused, sweating and heaving desperate breaths. One of the human children wiped his eyes. His shoulders hunched, despair animating his trembling limbs, as if he knew something was coming and dreaded the moment.

Justine's eyes narrowed.

Mitholie stood and barked a command.

Taug struggled to his feet and raised a tentacle. He glanced at Justine and then offered an extravagant bow to Mitholie. "The journey was long, and I know Justine would like to prepare herself for tomorrow's events. We should eat and retire before—"

Mitholie glowered. "You've grown insensitive to pleasures of your own kind, Taug. But—" He sighed. "—it's true, our opportunity is a narrow one." He dismissed the players and waved the waiters forward. "Bring the food." Dashing a glance at Justine, he grinned wickedly. "I know you don't need to eat as we do, but you might enjoy a sustaining meal. We don't partake of our own kind—but that is our only limitation."

CHAPTER TWENTY-FIVE

Taug Will Feel My Blade

Cerulean paced in front of Governor Right while Max stood sentry at the door. Bala and Clare stood like mismatched statues on either side of her well-appointed desk.

Cerulean wagged his head like a disappointed father. "I'm surprised you've been so sloppy, governor. It wasn't easy to discover your connection to the Uanyi Utopia Empire—their drug running schemes have been a bane to Luxonian interests for eons—but it was possible. You left quite a trail."

Governor Right squared her shoulders and sniffed back a twisted smile. "You think you know something? Fine, go to the Inter-Alien Committee and file charges. Bring your evidence. They will nod their various bulbous heads and intone how grateful they are... and they will do nothing. Because they have no power. They are totally incapable of changing anything!"

Swinging around her desk and brushing past Clare, the governor marched to the door, opened it, and flung out a dismissive hand. "Leave before you find out who has the real power here." She flicked a glance at Bala. "You were in prison."

Bala rubbed his forehead. "I was, but I didn't like it much. You have a lot to learn about hospitality."

"Ha!" She shook her head as she tapped on her datapad. "You have a lot to learn about prison. Bothmal has enough cells for you all."

Max unfolded his arms, strode into Governor Right's personal space and, grasping her by the shoulders, lifted her off the ground. "You have a lot to learn about androids."

Cerulean shuffled forward and tapped Max on the shoulder. "Remember what I said?"

Max dropped the governor unceremoniously.

Clare tapped her datapad. "Thanks, Max, but we only have a few minutes." She grinned at him. "Faye and Derik can only keep everyone busy for a limited time."

Cerulean took the governor's arm and strolled with her to an intimate corner. "What is Taug's plan? Why does he want Justine?"

The governor's eyes strayed toward Max and then returned to Cerulean. She shrugged. "Taug's nothing. It's Mitholie who wants her. He's got plans of his own. The Divide knows what. I'm not his confidant. Ask—" She froze and her eyes widened. Her gaze scoured the room.

Cerulean lowered his voice. "Ask who?"

Governor Right shook herself. "No one. Nothing. Just leave. I don't have anything to give you. Taug's gone with the android and that's the end of them. Good riddance, as far as I'm concerned." Her brows knit. "What happened to the mixed breed? I had him in prison too...." She flicked a glance at Bala.

"Someone freed him."

"Treacherous Cresta! Damn—"

Max stepped forward.

Cerulean held up his hand, forestalling any dramatic moves on the android's part.

The governor shuddered, recomposing herself. "Be interested in a trade? I could ask Mitholie if he'd take that one instead." She nodded to Max. "He doesn't seem too bright, but I don't think Mitholie's looking for intelligence."

Cerulean's eyebrows rose. "No? He's a bigger fool than I

thought." He glanced around at the various faces, each trying to appear to not be soaking up every word. He refocused on the governor. "How much are the Uanyis paying you to cover for them?"

Governor Right stiffened. "If you had a modicum of intelligence yourself, you'd leave now and drop this whole matter. Some enemies can't be destroyed."

Cerulean sighed and straightened. "Some enemies are not meant to be destroyed—only endured—so as to outlive them."

With a smirk, Governor Right chuckled. "You don't have enough lifetimes."

Cerulean strode toward the door. "We have a decision to make, Governor, and you have an appointment to keep."

The four friends ambled over the threshold. Bala turned with a courtly nod.

Governor Right furrowed her brow as she darted to her datapad and scrolled through. She bit her lip and leaned against her desk. The door opened with a hiss and a looming shadow entered.

Governor Right reached for her desk drawer but Faye, under a swirling black robe and four times her usual size, seized the governor's hand and gripped it like a vice. "You don't have time for that. You have a mission to accomplish."

Governor Right was in no position to argue, but she tried anyway. "Do I?"

The shadow tightened its grip. "You will contact Mitholie and let him know that an android, Max Wheeler, is on his way to rescue Justine."

With her teeth clenched, the governor nodded. "Certainly. I enjoy keeping Mitholie happy."

Faye dropped the hand and floated back to a dark corner.

Governor Right darted to the wall screen and tapped the console. As the screen flickered, she glanced back to the dim outline. "Good to know we'll be working for the same purpose. Androids should be kept under *our* control."

Faye held her peace as the governor reported the news to

Mitholie who accepted it with unperturbed grace. When the screen blinked to black, the governor sidled to her cabinet. Lifting an ornate container, she poured a drink and then another and held it out to the shadowy corner. "Let's drink to our continued—"

Silence.

The governor stepped forward, her eyes scanning the darkness. Nothing.

She lifted the glass in a salute and then proceeded to gulp the amber liquid. Returning to the cabinet, she swallowed the second and slammed the glass on the counter. "No loss. I saw your eyes this time—Bhuac."

"I'm going." Max stood even straighter and squared his shoulders.

"No, I'm going." Cerulean blew air between his lips and grimaced.

Clare waved them both off. "No, I have more official authority than either of you."

Bala wiggled one finger in the air. "How about we all go? Could be fun. A quick trip to Crestar on some broken-down transport. Stopping a murderous android. International spectacle. We might even make Universal News."

The four sat tightly packed in a booth at the Breakfast Nook. Despite its name, patrons swarmed through at all hours. Riko had waved to the group when they entered. He sauntered over when Cerulean nodded in his direction.

Appearing as meek as possible, Cerulean peered up at the formidable Uanyi. "I know it's late, but do you mind? I'm afraid we might be—"

Riko shrugged. "Say no more. My hostess is smitten—" He tipped his head to the side indicating Sal hovering in the background. "—with your friend here." His gaze swept over Max in puzzlement. "Besides—" He placed a meaty hand on Bala's shoulder. "I enjoy assisting those in dire need."

Bala blushed.

Clare pursed her lips and drummed her fingers on the table. "Hey, I always leave good tips. And to be quite honest, I bring in a lot of business."

Riko sniffed. "I won't say what kind of business." He turned and gestured to the hostess.

She bounded forward like a happy elephant.

Passing her, Riko snapped his fingers. "Give 'em whatever they want, but the Luxonian pays for all."

All eyes shifted away from Cerulean.

Sal's beaming grin zeroed in on Max. "What can I get you?" Her husky tone spoke volumes.

Max started to rise, but both Clare and Bala pushed him back onto his seat.

Clare matched the Ingot's beaming expression. "He'd love some of your coffee mocha. In fact, we all would."

When the Ingot remained stiff and staring, Max lifted his eyes enough to graze her face, offered a tremulous smile, and nodded.

Satisfied, Sal bounded away.

Rubbing his forehead, Cerulean hunched over the red tabletop. "We've got to make a decision quickly. Max, you got the message, what did Justine actually say?"

Four Uanyi patrons settled into the booth next to them. They made a point of flexing their arms as they positioned themselves so that they could watch the small group in their deliberation.

Bala tensed. "I think I might know one of those chaps—"

Clare hissed, elbowing Bala into silence. "Not now! Go on, Max, what did Justine say?"

Max peered at his folded hands. "Many years ago, we worked closely together. This is the first time since—you know—that Justine's reached out to me." He paused and sighed. "On our last mission together, we got into an argument. It was stupid; we had different ideas on how to handle our identity. Justine always leaned toward a romantic view—"

Clare scoffed. "Justine romantic? I'd never have thought that."

The front door clanged and flew open. Derik tromped in, huffing and sweaty. His gaze did a quick rotation of the room and, spying the group, he pounded over. "Sorry it took so long. You wouldn't believe what that little Bhuac can do—"

Clare gripped Derik's sleeve and pulled. "Shush, you idiot!" She glanced at the neighboring booth of open-mouthed Uanyis. "Grab a chair and—" She speared him with a glare. "—don't talk so loud!" The room fell silent at her last word. She plastered a grin across her reddening face.

The hostess appeared at Derik's back with a loaded tray. She scowled at Derik. "Suppose you want one too."

Derik blinked at her.

Clare stood and passed the mugs with alacrity. "No, he doesn't touch the stuff. But *Max* really appreciates your efficiency."

The hostess beamed and practically skipped away.

Bala glanced at his datapad. "Before my next birthday, which happens to be arriving with alarming speed, could we decide our next step?"

Max swiveled toward Bala. "Your birthday?"

"No!" Cerulean clenched his hands together as if in desperate prayer. "Focus, Max. What did Justine say?"

Max grabbed Bala's datapad and tapped it systematically for a moment. "Here, I downloaded it." He shoved the screen toward the center of the table.

"'...lifted afresh he hewed his enemy down. And saved a great cause that heroic day.' *Taug* will feel my blade!"

Silence.

Cerulean laid his chin on his clasped hands. "I thought we were past this stage."

Max rose. "Up until a short time ago, I thought Justine was lying inert in a morgue. I've fought alone for seventy years and if I can fight at her side once again, I will." His gaze swept the assembly. "I don't care what the rest of you do. But I've got a transport waiting."

Derik swung out and gripped Max by the arm. Rising slowly, his voice lowered to a growl. "*I'm* her fiancé."

Clare jumped to her feet with a puzzled expression. "Can androids even get married?"

Bala sighed. "Clare, let's just keep Justine alive before plumbing the depths of her capabilities, okay?"

Cerulean slipped out of the booth and lifted his hands in surrender. "Bala's right, and we're running out of time."

The Uanyis were staring wide-eyed at the group while Riko barely restrained Sal.

Cerulean turned to Max and swept his hand toward the door. "Lead the way."

CHAPTER TWENTY-SIX

An Honest Fool

Taug had used not a smidgen of hyperbole when he described Mitholie's suite. It was the finest set of rooms available on Crestar. A full wall tank undulated with colored lights at one end while creeping vines and swaying foliage draped every centimeter of surface area not designated for sitting, walking, or working. Lab equipment held their proper station against one wall, spilling into a neighboring wing, while an ample food station and accompanying attendant waited orders on the against another wall. Comfortable chairs, a wide screen, and plenty of room for guests, completed the luxurious setting.

Taug stood with his tentacles clasped in an attitude of contemplation, his gaze lowered until Mitholie should deem to speak.

Mitholie deemed. "The android's not quite what I was expecting, but she'll do." He strolled to the food station, motioned, and waited while the attendant splashed a dark liquid into a tall glass and handed it over with a proud bow. Mitholie swirled it playfully. There was not a hint of an offer to Taug. "With her technology, I'll live forever."

Taug peered up but remained expressionless.

Mitholie tossed a glance at Taug. "I suppose you know how to turn the damn thing off?"

Taug swallowed. “It is not easily done.”

“I could blast a hole through its middle or its synthetic brain. Would that help?”

Taug lifted one tentacle beseechingly. “If you damage her—”

Mitholie inhaled a long slurp and grinned over the glass. “I have a backup. Governor Right sent a message. Apparently there’s another one, and it’s coming here. To affect a rescue, no doubt.”

The yellowish tinge drained from Taug’s features. “Alone?”

“Who knows? Who cares?” Mitholie surveyed Taug’s swaying tentacles. “You’re not frightened of an android? They’re just tools, like any other.”

“Even tools can be dangerous. Especially when they have a will of their own.”

Mitholie chuckled. “So you are completely useless to me, eh? You didn’t take care of the little matter of the crossbreed, and you can’t manage an android. Your father‘s reckless experiment is free, tromping around Newearth like an angry ox. You know, he yelled at me? Actually threatened me.” Mitholie’s face darkened perceptibly.

Taug closed his eyes. “He’s one of our own. At least partially. I could’ve learned a great deal from him.”

“Dark waters!” Mitholie slammed his drink on the counter. “We don’t need him. Androids are stronger and more durable. If the creators could make one, there’s no reason why we can’t. As long as they don’t find out.”

Taug exhaled. “What do you want from me?”

A slow grin played across Mitholie’s face. “Nothing.”

Taug’s eyes widened in alarm.

The door at the far end of the room slid open.

Justine sauntered in, an appraising gaze roving over the two Crestas. “You look like you need to say your prayers, Taug. How does it feel to be expendable? Derik never liked it either...maybe you’re more like him than you realized.”

Taug’s gaze shifted to Mitholie.

Directing the attendant to leave, Mitholie refilled his glass and sauntered to his desk. "I have been informed that a friend of yours is rushing here to see you, Justine. Does the name Max Wheeler mean anything?"

Justine froze. Her gaze shifted from Mitholie to Taug. Her eyes narrowed. "I almost felt sorry for you. Almost."

Mitholie reached behind the counter and withdrew a Dustbuster. "Don't bother." He tossed the weapon to Justine.

Justine caught it and sneered at Mitholie. "You think I need a weapon?"

The corners of Mitholie's wide lips rose in a flabby grin.

Taug lifted a tentacle. "Before you act on impulse, know this, Justine. I never wanted to hurt Derik. I only wanted to study him. As for this Max Wheeler, I've never heard of him."

Justine circled Taug like a predator eyeing her next meal. "And me? What was I?"

Mitholie wagged a tentacle at Justine. "A useful tool! Now get on with it. I'm not Taug; I don't like to prolong the inevitable."

Justine laughed, her eyes sparkling with ironic pleasure. "The inevitable? There is no inevitable." She swiveled around faster than Mitholie could react, her fingers flying across his console. The wide screen flickered, and she grinned at a screen full of expectant Cresta faces.

"Your brain trust awaits your next move, Mitholie. I informed them that you had a surprise. As a scientist, you surely want every experiment made transparent so others can verify the results. Or perhaps you'd rather create a spectacle?"

Mitholie darted forward.

Grabbing Mitholie by the neck, she splayed his body against the screen. "You use beings for your own purpose. You say it is for the glory of science, for the good of Crestonians, but it all ends up as a matter of entertainment in the end. You don't need to live longer, Mitholie, you need to live wiser."

Mitholie's tentacles flailed as the android lifted him off the ground. His eyes bulged to enormous size as he squeaked. "Kill her!"

Taug remained motionless. Excited murmuring filled the room as the assembly on the screen jabbered over their options. Three Crestar guards burst through the door, their weapons ready. Their eyes shifted from Taug to Mitholie to Justine.

In a blur, Taug wrapped his tentacles around their legs and swiped them off their feet. He snatched their weapons out of their grasps.

Justine aimed the Dustbuster and blasted through Mitholie to the screen behind him. With unexpected agility, she tossed Taug over her shoulder and fled.

Derik slouched against the transport wall and tapped on his datapad. Max sat at the controls and fixed his attention on the dozen monitors arrayed at the front of the craft. Cerulean stood with his arms folded, across from Bala and Clare who sat crumpled in their bucket seats.

Clare groaned. "How long is this going to take? I'm not used to space travel, and I'm not even sure I can handle Crestar gravity. They do have gravity, don't they?"

Bala huffed. "Really, Clare, don't be so ignorant! They have an artificial environment that nearly matches ours. How did you ever make it through the academy?"

"I studied about Crestonian environment the night before and—"

Bala covered his ears. "Don't tell me another word. To think I always held you in such high esteem."

Clare's gaze rolled over Derik. "What're you doing?"

Derik shrugged. "Research. It helps to know the planet you're invading."

Bala nudged Clare. "Bet you wish you'd have thought of that."

Clare shouldered Bala off his chair.

Heaving himself to his feet, Bala sauntered over to Derik. He stretched and tried to look over his shoulder. Suddenly, he shrieked. "Eek! What's that?"

Cerulean turned sharply while Clare jumped to her feet.

Derik froze. His fingers paused above his datapad. "What?"

Clare inched up. "Is that a… SPIDER?" She raised her hand.

Cerulean jumped forward and grabbed her arm. "Don't!"

Derik swiveled around and, with a graceful motion, slipped the spider off his shoulder and into his pocket.

Bala's eyes bulged. "You keep a spider—as—a—pet?"

Clare spoke through clenched teeth. "Bringing unauthorized life forms to another planet is strictly forbidden! All insects die in exit sterilization anyway."

"Shut up!" Max swiveled in his chair and faced them. "Justine's in trouble!"

Derik pounded forward, slamming his leg against one of the monitors. "Oh.… Ah!" he limped ahead. "What happened?"

"No poetry this time." Max tapped the console.

Justine's face appeared on an overhead screen. She huffed heavily and seemed to be carrying a sack over her shoulder. She looked up and frowned. "I'm dropping this off at Bothmal transport baggage department. Land there and pick it up. Then return to Newearth. Don't look for me." The screen blinked to black.

"Bothmal!" Max shook his head and tapped the console with alarming speed.

Clare staggered to the console. "What're you doing?"

Max stared ahead as Crestar came into focus on the main viewer. "Going faster."

"Okay, everyone, this is where tiptoe practice in kindergarten really pays off." Bala hunched his shoulders and followed Clare, who followed Cerulean, who followed Max. Derik took up the rear, his Dustbuster at the ready.

Clare glared over her shoulder.

Bala shrugged.

Max whispered. "I see a guard. I think I know him." Max

straightened and motioned for the others to stay back. He sauntered forward and tapped his datapad. "Hello, Thurston. Captain Kimberling sent word that he'd be docking here, and I thought I'd be ready. Any news?"

Bala tapped Clare's shoulder as they huddled closer to Cerulean and whispered. "He can *lie*? I thought that was against android code or—"

Cerulean squeezed Bala's shoulder and glared.

Abashed, Bala swiped a finger over his lips and squeezed them tight.

The guard grinned. "Finally mastered contractions, eh, Max? Good for you." He shrugged. "Nothing new here." He scrolled through his datapad and frowned. "You must've got your info wrong. Kimberling isn't due for another month. You mean some other captain?"

Max scrolled through his datapad with a grimace. "Huh? I don't know how this happened. I got a message saying to pick up a package. I thought it was from Captain Kimberling. I just assumed—"

The guard smacked him conspiratorially on the arm. "Don't worry about it. We all make mistakes." He tapped his thigh. "But hey, there is a package here. I don't know if it's for you, just says—" he darted away and came back with a data-chip. "An honest fool?" He shrugged and handed it to Max. "I'm not sure if that's the name of the package or the receiver. Everyone likes to be funny these days. Bothmal! If I had a unit for every idiot—"

Max peered over the guard's shoulder. "Yes, that's for me. Though the last time I came, it was anything but funny." He sighed. "Mind if I take it?"

"Long as you sign for it. I'm not losing my job over a dumb joke."

Max waved Cerulean and Derik forward. "I have assistants who are working on my transport." His voice took on an authoritative tone. "Come on! Hurry it up. I haven't got all day. Take the package."

The guard beckoned with a wagging finger.

Cerulean, Clare, and Bala trudged after the guard with let's-get-this-over-with expressions.

Clare nudged her partner. "What do you think's in the package?"

Bala sighed. "As long as it isn't Taug."

Faye ambled along the corridor ceiling. It was never fun being an arachnid, but it was rather interesting. Everything looked different from the upside-down perspective. She scurried toward a crowd of excited Crestas doing their utmost to hold an enraged android at bay.

A cargo door was at Justine's back, and her hand flew over the console. Her eyes glowed with triumph. "*It was the best of times, it was the worst of times, it was the age of wisdom, it was the age of foolishness....*" Her fingers hovered.

Faye slid down a drop line, morphed into a hulking Cresta, and spoke in a guttural voice from behind the crowd. "*...it was the spring of hope, it was the winter of despair....*"

Justine's gaze fixed on the looming figure.

Faye passed through the crowd as if crossing the Divide and laid a tentacle on Justine's shoulder. "I have the authority to take this prisoner to her just destination."

A new voice made the entire crowd turn their heads once again. "But I'm afraid you don't." Cerulean marched forward and stared at Justine through forlorn eyes. He slid Faye's Cresta tentacle off Justine's shoulder and sighed. "As a representative of the Inter-Alien Alliance Committee, I'm taking Justine Santana into custody, where she will await a trial at the convenience of the court." He returned Faye's bitter gaze. "Nice try, though." Stepping forward, he led Justine by the arm.

Max, Derik, Clare and Bala rushed forward in a straggling huddle. Seeing Cerulean and Justine, they bounded to a heaving halt.

Max grinned. "You found her!"

Derik heaved a sigh. "Thank God."

Clare and Bala grinned.

Justine sighed. "You got the package?"

Derik's chin rose and Max's chest swelled as they nodded in unison.

Justine straightened her shoulders and offered her wrists, a prisoner ready for her manacles. "Well, here's your fool."

CHAPTER TWENTY-SEVEN

We're All One Of Us

Bright noonday sunrays shone through the Vandi Interventionist Station windows. A few guards sat at their desks and others stood in small clustered conversations. A barked order broke the low hum—but only for a moment.

Cerulean led Justine forward, barely touching her arm. The rest of the group trailed close behind, bleary-eyed and silent.

A short, thickset human dressed in an official Interventionist uniform with the nametag "Bradshaw" stepped in front of the desk and intercepted Cerulean. He wagged a finger at Justine. "This her?"

Cerulean nodded.

The Interventionist snapped his fingers at two other officers standing to the side. "Here's the Cresta killer. Take her in and make sure everything is done right! I don't want some Luxonian diplomat chewing my ear off about Inter-Alien Rights."

The two officers gripped Justine's arms. One jiggled a pair of manacles in her face. "Try anything funny, and we put these on you, see?"

Justine stared straight ahead.

Bradshaw shrugged at Cerulean. "Thanks. We would've had a mess on our hands—her coming from Newearth and killing a high profile Cresta and all." His gaze swept over her form. "Dang, if she isn't the prettiest android I ever saw." He clucked his tongue. "Too bad. Termination for sure."

As the officers led her from the room, Justine glanced over her shoulder and met Cerulean's gaze.

Cerulean watched until her perfect form turned a corner.

Bradshaw peered around Cerulean and considered the rest of forlorn group. "They with you?"

Cerulean peered over his shoulder.

Derik leaned forward, seething.

Max firmly gripped Derik's shoulder with one hand and steadied the "baggage" over his shoulder with the other.

With disheveled hair and dark circles under her eyes, Clare stared at the floor.

Leaning against the wall, Bala rubbed his gloomy face with his hands.

Faye stood to the side, elfin and childlike, shivering.

Cerulean sighed. "Yeah. They're mine."

Cerulean led the group down the hall and lifted his hands. "I know everyone is upset, but we still have jobs to do." He surveyed the group. "Listen, I did the only thing I could! She would've been hunted for the rest of her days. This way she has a chance to get a fair hearing and possibly be found *not guilty* this time."

Bala shook his head. "She murdered Mitholie in front of a lot of witnesses. It's like she wanted to be found guilty."

Derik shoved Bala from behind. "There was a good reason! Trust me. I know her better than any of you. She—"

Max poked Derik in the shoulder. "I've about had it with you. The fact is, I've known her longer than anyone here and—" He shrugged Taug's slumbering form onto Cerulean's shoulder. "Here, you carry him awhile. What'd you give him, anyway?"

Cerulean shrugged. "It wasn't me. Justine must have put him out with something. A right cross is my guess."

With a quick shake, Max turned on Derik and leaned in. "We need to settle this. Any suggestions?"

Derik sneered. "If you're man enough. I know just the place." He turned and started away. "Follow me." He glanced over his shoulder and called, "And if she isn't freed, Cerulean, I'm coming for you next!"

Cerulean sighed and ran his hand through his ruffled hair.

Bala sauntered up and shook his head. "And then there were—" He pointed at each of them with his index finger and hesitated. "—does Taug count?"

Cerulean turned toward Faye. "Do you think—?"

Faye nodded. "Certainly. I have a place not far from here. If you would bring him along, I'll see that he's taken care of."

Bala glanced at Clare. "Thank God! I was afraid I'd have to explain him to the kids." He shivered. "They've been through enough. Besides, Kendra would kill me."

Clare stepped up and placed a hand on Cerulean's shoulder. "It wasn't your fault. You did the right thing. I would've had to do it if you didn't."

Cerulean nodded. "Doesn't make it any easier."

As Clare and Bala turned away, Cerulean called after them. "There is something you can do. Follow up on a lead at the Amens community. A man there has been having strange symptoms. They thought maybe he was a half-breed, but I don't think so. Contact a guy named Able. Tell him you're a friend of mine, and see what you can find out."

Clare sighed. "Sure. Discover the truth. That's my job, isn't it?"

Cerulean hefted Taug's body over his shoulder and traipsed after Faye's child-like form. He sighed. "All our jobs, really."

After two long showers, Clare ventured into the role of Newearth Human Services detective again. As she tromped along a wooded path, a prickly branch caught her coat, halting her in mid-step. She threw up her hands in frustration. "Oh, help! It's got me. Bala! Come quick."

Bala rushed down the wooded trail, huffing, with a strained expression. "If you hadn't decided to run ahead, you wouldn't be in this mess!" He stopped and surveyed Clare's puffy coat sleeve entangled in a thorns. He stroked his chin, meditatively. "Well, it looks like the vegetation has taken a liking to you. Either you can slip under it, or I can rip your arm off."

Clare closed her eyes and counted under her breath.

With delicate fingers and smothered yelps, Bala struggled to disengage the vine. "You might have to leave your coat as a peace offering—"

A laugh made them both turn.

A tall, thin man ambled up the path. He waved Bala off with a grin. "I figured you'd get lost, not caught in the Rubus plant, commonly known as a blackberry vine." His fingers dexterously disentangled the fabric without a single tear.

Clare's eyes widened.

Bala stood back and folded his arms, humbled.

The stranger thrust out a work-roughened hand. "The name's Able. Cerulean sent word you'd be coming." He patted Bala on the back with a hearty thud. "The first time I got caught in such a vine, I was about four. I'd slipped away for a private need. I ended up in need, all right. Couldn't sit for a week."

Bala's mouth wobbled and his eyes twinkled while Clare's eyes stretched from amazement to horror.

Able returned down the path he had just come up. "Follow me. The wife has tea and fixings ready for you. I can hardly believe you just got back from Crestar. The whole community wants to hear about it, but I told 'em that you're coming to help Jim, not be interrogated." He tromped along the path with Clare and Bala on his heels. "They'll leave you alone for a bit… but then it's every man for himself, if you know what I mean."

The cabin dominated the top of the hill. Rough-hewn log walls, exposed beams, and the sheer size and sturdy nature of the structure made it appear like an ancient fortress of Oldearth. In the main room, herbs hung from the rafters, while braided rugs lay strewn over the wood floors. A large stove with an attached black pipe thrust through the vaulted ceiling took up an entire corner. A neat stack of split logs lay nestled in a wood box.

Able handed Clare a cup of steaming tea, while his wife handed Bala a plate of fluffy scones. The four were seated around a table that could comfortably seat sixteen.

Bala leaned over his tea and sniffed in glorious appreciation.

Clare sampled a scone and hummed. "Hmm, hmm, I haven't tasted anything this good since Kendra decided to enter her pies in the Culinary Arts Contest."

Able smiled at his wife, seated across from him. "We try to do our best." As a figure huddled in the doorway, Able sighed and folded his hands. "But our best isn't always good enough." He faced the figure across the room, raising his voice as he spoke. "Come on in, Jim! Don't be shy."

An emaciated figure with sinewy limbs hesitated and then darted across the floor, finding refuge behind Able. His eyes had narrowed to mere slits and his ears were reduced to dimple holes with crusted edges, while sores and thin scabs covered his mottled skin. He quivered in obvious agitation.

Able reached back and gently led the figure into full view.

Bala's mouth fell open. Clare inhaled a shocked breath.

Able passed his hand along the disfigured man's arm, tapping gently. Jim relaxed enough so that Able could press him onto the bench beside him.

When Jim had calmed, leaning like a frightened child into Able's side, Able faced Clare and Bala. "The changes were slow at first, but then suddenly they quickened. Every day, we noticed more deterioration of his body. He can't see, except in the brightest light, but that causes excruciating pain. He can barely hear, though his skin is sensitive enough so that I can calm him with a gentle touch."

Jim rocked, humming under his breath.

Tears filled Clare's eyes. "He looks so lost and afraid."

"He is. By God, that's exactly what he is."

Bala clutched his warm cup. "So why did you send for us? The poor man needs a doctor."

Able's jaw clenched. "A crime's been committed! Can't you see?"

Shifting off the bench, Clare stepped carefully to Jim and knelt at his side, her gaze scanning his body. "You think he's a crossbreed?"

Able shook his head with a shrug. "Don't know. But he was a perfectly healthy man once. He told me that these changes came on like a bolt of lightning out of a clear sky."

Lifting his datapad, Bala began to tap across the screen. "Derik's the only crossbreed we know of. Even Taug and Mitholie didn't seem to think there were any others—still alive, anyway."

Clare passed her hand over Jim's head. He shrank back in fright. "Oh, sorry!" She turned to Able. "Could you ask him if he was a part of any test group...had any medical issues before this happened?"

Able tapped Jim and then spoke slow and loud. "Have you had any medical tests, Jim?"

The rocking increased.

Able gripped Jim's arm, held him firm, and spoke directly into an ear hole. "They want to help. Did you ever have any medical tests?"

With a shudder, Jim shook not only his head but his whole body.

Bala rose and slid his datapad toward Able. "Looks as if Jim isn't the only one with these symptoms." He nodded toward the shivering man. "Ask him if he was partial to mega-vitamin drinks. Says here that there's an experimental drug on the market to increase vitality and stamina, except it had the opposite effect on some humans."

Able leaned over Jim's rocking body and asked Bala's question. This time Jim froze then he nodded.

Clare patted Jim's thin shoulder and stepped to Bala's side. "Let me see that." She scanned the info and sniffed. "Uanyi, I guarantee it."

Bala retrieved his datapad. "It would fit with the pattern." He pulled his nose. "I wonder how much Governor Right made on the deal."

"How about the Bhuac, Faye? You think she knew?"

Bala shrugged.

A low moan from Jim pulled Able to his feet. He gestured to his wife who led the forlorn figure out of the room. Smacking his fist into his hand, Able muttered. "I'm a peace-loving man, but this boils my blood."

Rising, Clare proceeded to the door.

She stopped and faced Able. "We'll follow up on this mega-vitamin info and any other leads that might explain what's happened to Jim. I'll be happy to send the idiots who did this to Bothmal for the rest of their lives."

Able rubbed his hands together. "Bothmal is too good for some villains."

"Too true." Clare pulled her coat tight. "Oh, and thanks for rescuing me from the attacking Rubus vine." Her eyes glanced over the room one last time. "You certainly have a beautiful home. I can see why Cerulean likes his neighbors so much."

Able blushed. "It's us that are the lucky ones." He nudged a little closer. "He hasn't been home for a while. Everything okay?"

With a long, drawn out sigh, Clare gripped the door handle. "You're not the only one upset lately. If Cerulean had blood, it'd sure be boiling by now."

Faye propped up Taug's limp body with a large pillow. A flutter of his eyelids alerted her to his imminent recovery. She scooted across the room, opposite her round couch, so that she could observe him from a safe distance.

Turning to her game table, she languidly shuffled the figures around on the board. The small, dark figure with large ears and round eyes stood safely ensconced in the back row. She tapped him on the head and placed a huge, fanged creature defensively in front of him.

A low moan made her turn from the engrossing activity. "Are you awake, then?"

Taug raised a tentacle and rubbed his head, adjusting his breather helm in the process. "How long have I been out?"

Faye considered his greenish tint, sunken eyes, and rasping breath. She glided forward and felt his head with her slender hand. "Long enough to become dehydrated." She clapped her hands.

Gabriel appeared like magic across the threshold.

Faye pointed to the distressed Cresta. "He's not feeling well, dehydrated, I suspect. Do we have anything?"

Gabriel's icy smile broke wide enough to allow a soft murmur. "I'll check."

Faye turned back to Taug. "Don't try to get up. You need rest. When Justine wants to knock someone unconscious, she does a thorough job."

Taug groaned. "I remember being lifted up and jostled down the corridor. She was saving me…I thought."

"Oh, she saved you, most certainly." Faye's gaze darted away. "Mitholie took her rage instead."

Taug squeezed his eyes shut. "Mitholie—"

Returning to the game board, Faye moved another figure to the back row and finished his sentence. "—is dead. She obliterated him and the wall-screen behind him. A very useful friend but a dangerous enemy."

Silence filled the room as Taug covered his face with a shriveled tentacle. Faye moved another figure to the back of the board.

When Gabriel presented Taug with a bag of murky liquid, he opened his eyes and smiled weakly.

With a stiff bow, Gabriel murmured. "It's the best I could obtain on such short notice."

Without further ado, Taug punctured the seal and poured the liquid into his breather helm. A deep sniff brought forth another groan, but this time, one of relief. He peered up at Gabriel through tearful eyes. "It's very good. Thank you."

With a less icy smile, Gabriel nodded and left.

Faye watched Taug with cynical amusement. "I won't bother to ask why you betrayed her. I know too much about protecting my own to be even slightly curious." Her gaze returned to the board once again.

Taug's eyes followed her. "Governor Right sent you?"

An off-key, tinkling laugh bounced around the room. "Heavens, no! I tell her what to do. She has no power over me."

Taug patted the mountainous pillows and then surveyed the room. With a raised brow, he shifted off the bed, wobbled, steadied himself, and then toddled over to the game table. A gleam entered his eyes. "I used to have something like this as a hatchling."

Faye fingered one of the pieces. "Yours were sea creatures, no doubt."

Taug lifted a tentacle and darted a question. "May I?"

Faye tipped her head graciously.

Swirling his quivering tentacle across the board, he stopped at the fanged creature. He held it up for inspection. "We use figures of all the known races. But never Crestas."

Faye blinked. "Why not? Don't you like to be a part of the game?"

Taug sobered as he placed the creature behind the round-eyed figure. "Only as the masters and movers. We don't like to be played." He stepped back from the table and folded his tentacles, appraising Faye carefully. "You're a Bhuac, obviously. Who do you work for? Ingots? Uanyi?"

Faye sighed and drifted toward the large window overlooking the bustling city. "I work for no one and everyone." She turned and faced Taug, a scowl marring her symmetrical beauty. "Don't you realize that you were a fool to trust your own kind?"

Taug shrugged. "It comes as no surprise. Crestas never trust anyone, especially our own kind."

Pained, Faye closed her eyes. "Foolish and terrible." She pointed back at the crowd below. "So why do you bother to live?"

Taug ambled closer and shared the view. "Survival is an inherent quality in us all."

She darted a glance at him. "My family was killed in the Telathot incursion and my planet has been decimated more times than I can count. I became strong, so they could remain weak. But—"

Taug was watching her closely, holding his breath.

"It's killing me."

Taug shifted aside. "You are much like Justine, then. Like Derik even. Perhaps even a bit like—"

"You?" She strayed back to the board, surveying the multitude of figures. Suddenly, she slashed the board with the back of her hand, sending the pieces flying across the room, rolling into corners and under the bed.

Gabriel practically flew into the room, alarm written across his face. Darting to Faye's frozen side, he laid a hand on her shoulder.

She didn't move, not even to glance at his hand.

Taug stood back; his tentacles hung limp at his sides.

Finally, Gabriel nudged Faye toward the bed. "You need rest and—" He glanced at Taug. "—he needs to leave. You can do no more for now." He helped Faye perch on the edge. "The android's trial is set for next week. The Inter-Alien Alliance has decided that it must be dealt with swiftly in the face of a rash of violence sweeping across the planet."

Taug jerked out of his stupor and lumbered forward. "What's happened?"

Gabriel darted a questioning look to Faye.

Faye waved his secrecy away. "Taug's one of us. We're all one of us. Except, of course, for those who aren't."

With a frown, Gabriel sent Taug a questioning look, but then he cleared his throat. "Apparently, Human Resources has discovered that Uanyi have been using humans in a secret drug testing scheme. Fifty-one deaths have been attributed to a health drink they sold as a cover in their experimental study." He strode to a circular, wall-sized screen and tapped the console.

The blank whiteness blinked to a riot scene with red and orange fires burning out of control in the Uanyi business district while crowds of weapon-wielding humans screamed at the citizens defending their wares.

Gabriel folded his arms across his chest. "As long as they fight each other, they won't fight us."

Taug shook his head. "Not necessarily. Chaos begets chaos." He padded over to Faye's stiff form. "You appear ill. You need rest." He plumped up the pillows and bunched them around Faye.

Gabriel's eyes followed him closely.

As she leaned back, Faye looked Taug in the eye. "Why did you bring Justine to Crestar? Surely you knew it was a trap."

Taug's shoulder's drooped. "Only for her. I hoped, in time, to convince Mitholie of her worth and to return to Newearth to continue my studies with Derik. They both have a lot to offer the scientific community."

As Gabriel hesitated over the threshold, Faye's sad expression turned introspective. "You're unique. I never would have guessed such a thing possible—in a Cresta."

Taug stroked his chin. "May I ask you a question as well?" To her assenting silence, he bent down, retrieved one of the figures, and placed it on the game table. "Why did you inform Governor Right about the other android? You must've known she would inform Mitholie."

"I directed her too. I wanted to see if—" Her voice cracked, but she held up her hand and recovered herself. "—if an android would rescue another of its kind. I needed to know how much he would risk."

"For self-preservation?"

"By sacrificing self." She dropped off her bed and scooted to a corner. Retrieving the figure with large ears and round eyes, she placed him on the game board—facing the fanged creature. She glanced from Gabriel, still hovering on the threshold to Taug standing firmly before her. "We all have our trials to face."

Padded walls, bright lights, a smooth, gray floor, and equipment suited to different bio-types created an ideal gymnasium for those looking for both recreation and a serious workout. Tumblers practiced their arts at one end, while sleek runners raced each other around the perimeter. Grunts, groans, and sporadic conversations settled into a background murmur with an occasional yelp thrown in for good measure.

Derik, decked out in fencing gear with a long rapier in one hand, swaggered up to Max, also bedecked in fencing apparel. They circled each other until Max raised his sword hand and gestured to his outfit.

"Couldn't you have found something less...involved?"

Even from behind the mask, it was obvious that Derik sneered. "What's wrong? You can't handle a little protective gear?"

Max tore off his breastplate and mask, and tossed them aside. "I don't need them. But don't let that intimidate you." He thrust out his chest. "If you insist on acting like a barbarian, I can accommodate you. Just remember, Justine is an android. Human chest thumping and Cresta wrangling does not impress her."

Derik frowned. His gaze darted from the abandoned gear to Max's face. "I suppose your modesty is going to win her heart? Just try to keep from being run through, and we'll see who impresses her. She's more than an android, tech-head. She's a woman in the fullest sense of the word." Lifting his rapier, Derik saluted his enemy.

Max shook his head and returned a half-hearted salute.

Derik charged forward with the first thrust.

With matching dexterity, Max met Derik's initial blow, and they clashed swords around the fencing ring. A small crowd gathered as the intensity of their flashing blades gathered strength. Neither Max nor Derik would give in. After an hour, the crowd began to seep away from the monotony of their struggle. Finally, Max's untiring strength began to wear down Derik's exhausted physiology. With sweat dripping down his face, Derik suddenly did the unexpected. He stopped dancing about and raised his arms. Max halted, letting his sword arm fall to the side. Derik dove in and stabbed Max's chest with his blade.

Those intrepid souls who had stuck out the extended battle, sucked in a collective breath. One human screamed. "Call a medic. He's hit!"

All eyes darted from one figure to the other.

Derik fell backwards, his hand releasing the rapier, shocked by the violence of his own move. The abandoned sword quivered, protruding from Max's chest like a child's toy.

Max frowned at the steel undulating from his chest. He gripped the handle and drew it smoothly from his body. "It's not that easy to kill me, you know."

All color drained from Derik's face as he limped to the wall and slid to the floor. Medics rushed onto the scene, stared at Max's impenetrable expression, turned to Derik's drooping form, and immediately scrambled to Derik's side.

A couple of spectators tried to correct their mistake but gave up when Max waved them away.

Max sauntered over, swishing the two rapiers menacingly. He tapped the human medic on the shoulder with the tip of a blade. "Not him—me. But don't worry; I wasn't seriously damaged. Only irritated."

Confused but eager to move away from the rapier-swinging figure, they backed off with the rest of the crowd.

Max sighed at the forlorn figure. He toed Derik's boot and

tossed the rapiers aside. "Come on, idiot. I got a date, and I could use a chaperone."

Max sat opposite Derik at a Breakfast Nook booth and twiddled his elongated thumbs. "You've got a date—with whom?"

"Sal, the hostess. She wanted me to come by for a sweet treat. Considering her various hints, I think she has… feelings for me. I hate to disappoint."

Derik gazed at Max through bloodshot eyes. "Aren't you a mercenary? Killer-for-hire-sort-of-guy? And you're afraid of—" He rubbed his temple as Sal lumbered into view with a heavily laden tray. He sneered. "Max, your sweeties are here."

Max stiffened and plastered a happy grin on his face.

Sal sashayed over and placed the tray with extra care in front of Max. She matched his expression, grin for grin. "It's the best we've got. Pecan pie, vanilla ice cream, and an extra-large health drink." She positively beamed. "Even androids need to take care when indulging." She leaned in and whispered. "I studied up."

Derik slapped his forehead, disbelief writhing across his haggard face.

Max became practically giddy. "You are one of a kind, Sal. Not another like you from here to the Divide. Thanks." He patted the bench. "You want to sit and help me eat it?"

Derik closed his eyes and swallowed something back.

Riko turned from a pie rack and snapped his fingers, his eyes mere slits.

Sal shoved Max playfully. "I know your type. Just because I bring sweets, you think you can have your way with me." She grinned. "I'm no fool. Besides, I've got a price on my head. A working Ingot like me is worth half a million—easy." Her eyes teased. "Let's see if you can handle that pie first." She hurried off at skipping speed.

Derik held his head in his hands as if he were afraid it might fall off and roll away. "What in darkness was that? I don't know if she's smitten, looking for an easy victim, or just having fun at your expense."

Max balanced a spoonful of pie against a dollop of ice cream. He surveyed it like a geologist studying an unusual rock formation. "According to human customs, this is a special treat. But she knows I'm an android, so why bother?"

Derik leaned on one arm, giving into the surreal situation. "She must've heard that you have human DNA, and she figures you'd like anything that makes you feel more human."

Max slipped the dripping spoonful into his mouth, swirled it a bit, and swallowed.

Derik's gaze followed the pie all the way down his gullet.

"Nothing." Max sighed and darted a glance across the table. "Does Justine like human food?"

Sitting up straighter, Derik folded his hands. "Yeah. I think so. When she eats with me, she always likes whatever we have. At least, she never complains."

"You don't even know what she likes, do you?"

Derik's hands clenched into one big fist. "Do *you*? How well did you know her before she was turned off—back in the war years? Trust me, she's not that person anymore."

"She killed Mitholie." Max shoved the ice cream and pie toward Derik. "Despite your feelings, you can't honestly say you know her well. She's only been reawakened for a few months and during that time, she's been living a double life, working for Taug and pretending to love you."

Derik jumped to his feet, his breath coming in sucking waves. "I'm her fiancé, at least in my heart. She was going to run away with me. We're going to get married—"

Max rose slowly and faced Derik. "I am sorry. But Justine can't be anyone's wife. Her creators think they still own her, like they still own me. She was made to hire out, not to live free. When she killed Mitholie, she was acting according to her nature."

Derik glared at Max. "I don't believe that! Justine is not a killer."

"Why did she kill then? The Inter-Alien Alliance Committee will judge her—again." Max laid a firm hand on Derik's shoulder. "You have nothing to offer but a broken, crossbreed heart. But I can offer a way out. I was tried for a crime once, but when I claimed my android nature, I was covered under weapons' immunity. Justine just needs to claim her true identity, and she'll be free."

Derik shouldered Max's arm away as he pounded to the door. "You're not free. You're a slave."

CHAPTER TWENTY-EIGHT

Lies and More Lies

Sterling ambled down the lush corridor and sighed. He had left his knitting at home, and he missed it. Oh well, he might as well get this over with. He motioned to his Luxonian bodyguards to wait. The door to Governor Right's office slid open. He threw back his shoulders and marched across the threshold.

Governor Right rose from a luxurious chair behind her mammoth desk, straightened the cuffs of her garish-green, bold-print blouse, and greeted him with a tight smile.

Sterling held his twitching lips sternly in place. To accommodate his human appearance, he had dressed in casual wear: gray slacks, a dark blue sweater, and black shoes. His thick, white hair offered his human associates the comforting assurance that he had years of experience. It was no lie. Except that he never had the same experience twice.

Governor Right gestured to the available seat—a hard, straight-backed chair, similar to ones used in Bothmal and nodded. "Please, sit. I'm grateful that you've finally squeezed me into your over-burdened schedule."

Her sarcasm was not lost on Sterling. He was fully aware that he had waited longer than she liked to arrange this official visit. He wasn't playing a game, just suffering from dread.

But he could hardly tell her that. Still standing, he clasped his hands behind his back. "Good to see you, too, Governor." He cleared his throat, segueing into the business at hand. "Cerulean has informed me that the android is now in custody. I have informed the Crestar representatives that we'll do everything possible to assist in this time of trial…no pun intended."

The governor's thin lips tightened into an even thinner line. "I should hope so, since it is one of your own who created this mess. Your *Cerulean—*" Her mouth puckered with distaste. "—has encouraged an android to think of herself as a sentient being with moral rights."

Sterling inspected the ceiling a moment before he lowered his gaze. "Yes, well, we've never quite decided that androids are *not* sentient beings."

Jostling around her desk, Governor Right practically flew to the side counter. She reached under and smacked two glasses on the top. Tossing Sterling a look of disgust, she poured the drinks. "I'm not addicted to the stuff, it's just that I've been up all night dealing with one crisis after another." She eyed the Luxonian like a surveyor considering the landscape. "Every time you come, you seem like a new creature. Last year you presented yourself as Commander in Chief of the Universe. Today, you're a regular bleeding heart." She shoved one of the drinks in his direction.

"I've taken up knitting, as well."

Spluttering her drink across the counter, Governor Right tried not to choke. "By the Divide! You're a worse freak than the Bhuac!"

Eyebrows rising, Sterling sipped his drink with prim neatness.

Sloshing what was left in her glass, Governor Right waved Sterling to her desk. She pulled a large datapad forward and slid it toward him. "Look those over. I had my men follow her."

Sterling scrolled through a series of pictures of an elfin-looking Bhuac, passing through different parts of town.

"During the day, she presents herself as Faye, a Bhuac who lives here in Vandi. But I've seen a different side of her and none too friendly, let me assure you." The governor tossed back her drink and headed for the door. "It's hot in here, and I never know who's listening. Come on!"

Pushing past the waiting guards with a fixed frown, the governor stomped down the steps.

Sterling marched behind in resignation.

They followed the path she and Taug had taken months before. Except this time she did not stop on the curb and call her private secretary. Now she scurried across the street and stepped into the park, still wet from the melting snow.

Governor Right took to the path and, clasping her hands behind her back, she looked like an ardent philosophy student plumbing the depths of truth.

Sterling patted his chilled arms and jogged to keep up. "Why would a Bhuac pretend to be your enemy?"

"She didn't pretend anything. She simply used me. She wanted to know what I knew and keep me playing her game." The governor shrugged. "Why do ruthless people ever do what they do?"

Sterling strode along, gazing at the elongated shadows. He shook his head. "Bhuacs have never been known for their aggressive nature. Surely there must be a good reason."

A cold wind whistled between them.

With a sneer, the governor quickened her pace. "Your sensitive heart is going to bleed all over the grass."

Suppressing a chuckle, Sterling attempted an authoritative tone. "Bhuacs came to Newearth seeking refuge. Perhaps this one's smart enough to keep an eye on her enemies as well."

Governor Right flung her hands wide and turned on him. "So, *I'm* the enemy—is that it?"

A fallen tree blocked the path ahead, and Sterling saw no way around it. He slowed his pace. "About the android. She killed Mitholie without warning. Would you happen to know why?"

"As I said, she isn't sentient. She was put together by some mystery race; *the creators*, some call them. Her only reason for existing is to do what *they* want. Reason enough to have her disassembled. We have no treaty with them. They could send an army of these things and take over Newearth. You want that?" She stopped and gestured toward a cluster of apartments. "Like that mixed-breed. Mitholie knew he was trouble and warned me. I was a fool to trust Taug."

Sterling watched as a hesitant squirrel scampered down the side of a maple tree, halted in fright, and assessed the danger through piercing black eyes. "The one named Derik?"

"Derik? I'd give it a more appropriate name: unwanted, a mistake, a risk to everyone. Do you know he actually screamed at poor Mitholie—threatened him?" She twitched a budding stem off a branch and sighed. "But considering how things played out, I should have eliminated the android first."

Sterling could feel his human heart racing. If he had been in Luxonian form, he'd be glowing bright red. *"First?"*

The governor offered a sly smile, digging a little furrow in the muck with the toe of her shoe. "My secret. Consider it an act of goodwill toward all beings."

Turning around, Sterling's eyes narrowed. He didn't feel like crocheting anymore. He wrung his hands together to keep them from wringing a neck.

The squirrel scampered back up the tree.

Governor Right frowned at his hands. "You can't be cold or tired. What's wrong?"

Sterling paced forward. "Nothing." *Everything*. He coughed and wiped his reddened nose. "I have other appointments. Riots are breaking out all over the planet because of this Uanyi business. We should set the trial date as soon as possible."

Governor Right clapped her hands together. "Sounds good to me!" She hustled ahead. "As long as we see eye to eye, the rest of the planet can go to Bothmal." She gestured vaguely in the direction of her office on the third floor. "I've work to do myself. See you at the circus!" Her bulky, lightly clad form marched off, undaunted by the late winter chill.

Sterling stood in the failing light. He could hear the voice of the reporter, Lang, cajoling him with her byline: "Lies and more lies." He wasn't cold or tired, not physically anyway. But then neither was Governor Right—though she should be.

As darkness gathered, Sterling could almost feel himself bleeding.

Derik heard the knock and thought of Taug with a grimace. *If that slug thinks he can come here and*—The knock repeated itself. Taking loping steps, Derik charged across his living room and grabbed the door handle. He remembered Cerulean's warning about opening the door without glancing through the peephole first. *Like he knows anything! Traitor.*

After swinging the door wide, Derik froze and faced the handsomest man he had ever seen. The yellow eyes were especially provocative. "Can I help you?"

"Are you Derik Erland?"

Derik frowned. Solicitations were illegal in this building, and he had a hard time imagining this guy worked for Human Services. "Yeah."

"May I come in? I have a message."

Derik snorted and retreated back into his living room. "What? If it's from Taug or that Luxonian—"

The stranger followed him inside and shut the door quietly. "No. Actually, I am doing a favor for all of humanity, compliments of an interested benefactor." He pointed a Dustbuster at Derik's chest.

Derik stepped backwards, his eyes wide. Nausea swept up from his middle. He lifted his hands in surrender. "What—? Why?"

The yellow eyes darkened. "Yours is not to reason why. Your is but to—" He fingered the trigger.

Derik lunged.

Yellow-eyes swerved. His shot glanced off Derik's leg, blowing it apart below the knee.

With a scream, Derik crumpled to the floor. "God!" His

breath came in sucking heaves. "I'm innocent...in love...." He rolled onto his back.

Yellow-eyes approached, aiming the Dustbuster more carefully this time.

Derik's gaze clouded into a gray mist as his voice fell into an abyss. "I... have..." He shuddered. "...dreams."

Yellow-eyes shook his head and fired. "Not mine."

CHAPTER TWENTY-NINE

This Is Our Journey

Cerulean stood in his bedroom, a sweater dangling from one hand as he appraised the portrait in front of him. A slight earthquake that morning had set everything off balance, but nothing else demanded his attention as did this painting. He tossed his sweater aside, squeezed between a chair and the end table, and slid the painting up on one end. It fell off its hook, sending a chill through his body.

Cradling the picture to his chest, he closed his eyes and memories burst their bank. Justine stood in her cell, paintbrush in hand, dabbing color on the canvas faster than his eyes could follow. When she held it up in the crook of her arm, he could still feel his intake of breath. No robot in the universe could have such talent, to catch the soul as it peeks out through the eyes.

An ache throbbed behind his eyes as he clenched his jaws against another memory: Justine lying on a steel table, squeezing his hand, afraid and vulnerable. The jerking shake—

His eyes snapped open, and he clutched the painting at arm's length. It would go on the wall and hang there safely, by God!

He stood back and appraised it once again. Is that how he looked to her then? If she were given the same tools, how would she paint him now? He sighed.

A buzzing sent him across the room. He checked his datapad. A message from Clare blinked for attention. "Get to Derik's—fast!"

Interventionists bustled in and out of Derik's apartment, while Bala stood in the doorway, his face drained of color. Cerulean elbowed his way forward, stared at Bala, who simply shook his head, and glanced over to see Clare kneeling on the floor—in the middle of a mess. Blood splattered the walls and something— Cerulean swallowed back whatever was rising from his stomach.

After approaching Clare from the side, he laid his hand gently on her shoulder. "You okay?"

Clare looked up through swimming eyes and shook her head. "Of course not." She rose, folded her arms, and shivered. "Dustbusters don't leave much evidence."

"You're sure it was Derik?"

"First thing I checked." She stared ahead, her face tight. "I'd love to get my hands on the alien who did this."

"No evidence it was a human?"

"No evidence of humanity." Clare shrugged. "Could have been anybody. The room's been ransacked, hard to say why."

"Well, we know it wasn't Taug or Mitholie."

"That leaves about a billion other possible suspects. Whoever did it was probably following orders in a chain of command. You do this, and I'll do that, and we'll all be happy."

"Except Derik."

Clare nodded, her gaze sweeping the floor. "I feel as if it was my fault somehow. I got mad at him. I hated Justine—the love of his life." Slowly Clare's gaze fastened on Cerulean. "Oh, God! Justine. Who'll tell her?"

Newearth prisons were not nearly as intimidating as Bothmal's, though the harsh reality of being locked in a cage did not diminish with the location. Cerulean strode behind the young, human guard with measured steps, refusing to glance at the other inhabitants of the cells he passed. Beings of all kinds were locked in here, some awaiting trial; some to be shipped off to confinement centers more accommodating to their species' needs. Some would find themselves at the docking bay of Bothmal itself.

As he refused to look, so he refused to sigh. Most of these beings had earned their place in a confinement cell. There were always reasons and occasionally excuses, but the fact remained that in some way, most of these beings represented a threat to the safety and wellbeing of Newearth society. Luxonians tended to be harsher and swifter than the citizens of Newearth in allocating punishment to a truant. But then, that was one reason Cerulean chose to live on Newearth and not on Lux.

The guard stopped, checked his datapad, and tipped his head in the direction of the cell to the left. "Here she is, sir. You can talk for an hour, though I go off in fifteen and the next guy's got a bit of a control issue—if you know what I mean."

Surprised at the guard's self-deprecating smile, Cerulean found himself thanking the guard and watched him tromp away. *Why on Newearth is he working here?*

Bracing himself with a quick shake and squaring his shoulders, Cerulean tapped the console. The opaque door cleared into a see-through window.

Justine wasn't painting. She sat hunched on a flat, hard bed, which apparently folded up into the gray wall. The few accommodations were sparse and uninviting. With her eyes closed, she leaned back, apparently unaware of his presence.

Cerulean hesitated. A sob begged to be released. The memory of Derik's splattered remains made him wince and close his eyes. He jerked at the sound of Justine's voice.

"Sorry, no artistic giveaways. Though to be fair, they did offer to get me something—a puzzle, reading material, a noose—

but I'm just not particularly creative this time around."

Anger elbowed its way in front of his grief. "Why'd you do it, Justine? I told you I would help, if only you'd come to me—"

Justine flew off the bed and slammed her fists against the transparent door. "Damn your insufferable arrogance! Just because you're Luxonian and can move around at will, doesn't mean you're almighty. You can't save Derik or the next mutants—like me. Mitholie wanted to create a new sub-race, beings he could use like puppets." She clenched her fists tighter. "He didn't care if they were crossbreeds or androids or whatever came into his demented little mind. He used everyone—even his own kind!" Spent, she sighed and fell back onto her bed; her shoulders slumped. "At least Derik's safe—for now." She glanced at Cerulean, and a shadow darkened her scowl. "He *is* safe, right?"

Unable to look her in the eye, Cerulean dropped his gaze to the floor. "Justine." He took a long breath and steadied himself.

Justine crept to the window. Her fingers splayed wide as if she could reach through and take his hand. Her face froze still as stone. "What happened?"

A tear slid down Cerulean's cheek. He couldn't raise his head and look her in the eye. "God, Justine. I don't know how—"

A cold, automated voice broke over his. "He's dead. Mitholie got to him—somehow. Or Taug. Or Governor Right.... It hardly matters now, does it?"

Cerulean scraped his gaze off the floor and stared into Justine's vacant eyes. "It matters to me." He shuddered through a deep breath. "Listen, I am going to find out who did this. Clare is doing her best—"

A snort. Justine shook her head and flopped down on her hard bed. "Clare didn't care about Derik." She tilted her head and peered at Cerulean. "He didn't have many friends."

Cerulean swallowed. "Friends? We need more than friends. We need a shared vision. A purpose to see us through. Even Sterling is going to help. Together we're going to stop the

Cresta abuses, the Uanyi abuses, all the abuses—but it's going to take time." He pushed off from the wall. "You took the law into your own hands by killing Mitholie. Your hate didn't stop his hate."

Justine stared down at her clasped hands as if studying them for the first time. "He was an evil being who deserved—"

Cerulean whirled around. "But you're the one in prison, Justine! You're the one on trial—damn it!" Cerulean closed his eyes and clasped his hands. His fury had fled as fast as it had emerged. He felt drained. "This is our journey, Justine, Luxonians, Ingots, Crestas, Uanyis—whatever. As long as we can choose between good and evil, we are more than our biology. That *more* is what unites us."

Justine folded her hands in her lap. "There is a time for hate."

"Hate will not unlock this cage."

Justine shook her head. "I find I don't care for freedom as I once did. I don't want to be human. I want nothing."

Like a fleeting dream, Cerulean whispered his wish. "Justine, don't give up."

Justine kept her eyes lowered, refusing to meet Cerulean's gaze. When she dared to raise them, only a wall stared back.

CHAPTER THIRTY

I See Through Many Eyes

Breaking News: Lang reporting from Newearth Capitol.

Dressed in a slinky outfit that outlined every Ingoti sharp edge, the sultry news reporter, Lang, faced the camera. The Capitol building was set strategically behind her and a huge crowd lined the walkways. The tumult of the jeering spectators bled into her feed. She smiled brilliantly for her audience of which she had no small following.

Like days of old, the Newearth assembly is gathering for the trial of the century. The android, Justine Santana, murderer of the leading Cresta scientist, Mitholie, is being led from her cellblock to the courtroom as we speak. Extra guards were called in to handle the protesters who are linking her case to the Ingoti drug-testing scandal. Some insist that the android was acting on behalf of Newearth when she attacked and murdered the Cresta high official. Others claim that she is merely a weapon gone rogue.

Lang winked at the camera.

An alluring android, a dead diplomat, drugs and scandal—a fascinating case to be sure! Will we see new Inter-Alien investigations into the dealings between Cresta and Ingots? Or will further sanctions be placed upon android development? What will happen to the gorgeous human-android hybrid in the center of this maelstrom? Is she woman—or weapon? That is the question we long to answer.

With a kiss to her adoring audience, Lang signaled her mutual devotion. Holoscreens across the planet switched to the bustling courtroom.

Two armed guards led Justine, dressed in a gray jumpsuit, to the center of the room, up two steps, and onto a circular platform. Her shoulders were straight only because her hands were manacled behind her back. Well over fifty delegates sat on comfortable chairs, along the perimeter, each chair tailored for their particular species. Every sentient race on the Inter-Alien Alliance Committee, including Ingots, Uanyi, Crestas, Luxonians, Bhuacs, and humans had at least one representative in attendance. No race wanted to be absent from this trial. Hundreds more sat in the court's upper wings, eagerly awaiting the spectacle.

Cerulean stood next to his chair, watching as Justine was escorted to her place in the center of the excited throng. His gaze rolled over to the judges' bench. Beside the Ingot Judge, Sterling in a formal black robe, sat back, appearing relaxed with his head propped on one hand. He leaned over to speak to a Uanyi representative on his right. Cerulean wondered if he had brought his knitting with him.

Frowning, Cerulean scanned the crowd of watchers for Max. The android had informed him about his literal run-in with Derik in the sport's center with unemotional clarity. He didn't appear to mourn Derik's death. Why should he? He hardly knew the man. Yet it rankled. How many beings die unmourned? Max had merely stated that he had a solution to Justine's predicament, but he could not explain. With a sigh, Cerulean's scouring gaze landed on Max shuffling to the witnesses' side of the room. *Max was a witness? To what?* Cerulean shook his head.

As Max sat in apparent indifference, Cerulean's gaze began to rove again. Uh, oh. Bala and Clare sat next to Able. How on Newearth did they wrangle Able away from his homestead? And why? Cerulean pursed his lips. Bala had seen him and was waving. Should he nod back?

No. Absolutely not.

What's he doing? Idiot! He's coming this way. Doesn't he know that I'm a Luxonian representative, and I'm not supposed to—

"Psst! Cerulean! Hey, don't pretend you don't know me. Okay, pretend if you like. Just listen. Able has evidence. He wants to speak—"

A large Uanyi guard strutted over and laid a hand on Bala's shoulder, squeezing none too gently. "This human annoying you, sir?"

Cerulean shook his head. "No, just passing along a message." He eyed Bala sternly. "Thank you, Officer, I will take that into consideration."

The guard sniffed, his voice dripping with disdain. "Officer? Too puny. Look at those arms! Off with you, vagrant!" He shoved Bala forward. Eyeing Cerulean, the guard shook his head. "You shouldn't encourage 'em, sir." The guard paced off to other duties.

Bala shrugged and stepped away.

Cerulean rubbed his temple where a massive headache was launching itself right into the center of his forehead. As the last of the officials settled into their chairs, everyone quieted. A small disturbance attracted Cerulean's attention on the upper left, where three spectators were positioning themselves on the very top tier. He squinted to get a better look, but then his eyes widened in horror.

What in Bothmal was she doing here? With him!

Faye, dressed in a long, sweeping skirt and a short top, perched on the edge of a chair. A male Bhuac acting very much like a protective father took a seat at her side. Taug sank onto the hard bench; his tentacles wrapped close about his body—

probably to avoid swiping the attendees standing near. Cerulean stifled a low moan.

A clarion call like a trumpet of old signaled the crowd to stand. Massive shuffling brought everyone to his or her feet. The presiding judge of this case, a huge Ingot dressed in formal black robes, wended his way forward followed by eleven jury members.

Cerulean noticed that Sterling observed their entrance with a steady gaze.

The Judge introduced himself as Judge Tobias, the IAA Judge for Newearth Region Nine. Reading from his datapad the rules of attendance, he emphasized the need for silence and the consequences of unruly behavior. The judge glared at the assembly and even at the holo-screen, as if warning those viewing from across the known universe to behave themselves. He sat stiff-backed with his head held high.

As if on cue, everyone rustled back onto his or her seats. Judge Tobias intoned his formal opening. "In the case of the android Justine Santana, we are here to ascertain its guilt in murdering the Crestonian, Mitholie, and the implications for all androids on Newearth. We shall begin with the plaintiff, Crestar's distinguished representative—"

Cerulean leaned back and closed his eyes. He knew the legal jargon, virtue signaling, and insidious threats that the Cresta representative would use: how their scientific advancements benefit all beings, that Mitholie, a victim of deep-seated prejudice, could no longer assist Crestonians to fulfill their true potential because Justine Santana, a wanton killer, had murdered him. The case was fairly simple. Justine killed a Cresta in front of a bevy of eyewitnesses. Few beings this side of the Divide would care to let her live.

Several witnesses, including the Cresta scientists who had seen the actual event, now appeared on the holoscreen, larger than life, but more confident than when facing Mitholie. They dramatized the terror of the tragic event with wiggling tentacles, insisting that hatchlings throughout Crestar were terrified that an android would murder them while they were taking their first experimental steps. Seeing their highly esteemed colleague blown to bits had certainly shaken the Crestonian population.

Over an hour later, when no more witnesses for the prosecution were forthcoming, the judge called for witnesses for the defense. Cerulean's gaze shifted to Justine's court-appointed lawyer. The slump-shouldered human, Mr. Paris, rose and addressed the courtroom. "I call the android Max Wheeler."

Murmurs filled the room and several Crestas stood up to protest, but the judge waved them off.

Max marched forward and stepped up to the witness stand. He stared straight ahead with a vacant expression.

The judge waved the lawyer to his duty. Mr. Paris cleared his throat. "As an android, Mr. Wheeler, you have significant insight into this case. What is your assessment of Justine Santana's guilt or innocence?"

Max kept his gaze fixed, staring at the air in front of him. He was more robotic than any robot Cerulean had ever seen.

"I knew Santana during the war years. We were hired to defend certain planetary interests. Later, we were hired to protect transports and merchant ships. It was a matter of indifference to us as to who hired us. We simply fulfilled our duty. In the case of the Cresta's death, Justine Santana must have been hired to perform her duty, or she was threatened in some manner. Androids are programmed to protect themselves." His monotone voice arrived at a fixed stopping point.

Murmurs in the courtroom rose to loud rumblings. Judge Tobias struck his gavel and wagged his finger, glaring at the assembly as if they were naughty children who had pushed their parental generosity too far.

A Cresta representative lumbered to his feet, huffing into his breathing helm. He spat out his words. "How can anyone allow this misrepresentation to stand? This android is obviously trying to protect one of its own. We don't even know who created these maladjusted, bundle of technological—"

The judge rapped his gavel again, this time searing the Cresta with his glare. "There will be no insulting the witnesses!"

A Uanyi representative stood, her bulky bio-suit glittering in the harsh lights. "The Cresta has a worthy point. We do not know the creators of these beings. In light of this fact, they should be seen as possible spies at best, or traitors at worst. They should never have been allowed to settle on Newearth. Who, I'd like to know, brought the female here in the first place?"

A commotion in the stands forced all eyes to turn upwards. Taug shuffled down the incline to the perplexed frown of the judge. "Who are you?"

Taug came level with the witness platform and waved Max aside. "If you will excuse me, I am the cause of much of the trouble here. Really, it should be me on trial today."

Crestas from both within the courtroom and on the holoscreen sucked in a collective, shocked breath. The two Cresta representatives tried to climb their way to Taug, but too many other delegates stood in their way.

The judge froze everyone with a bark. "Halt!" He glared at Mr. Paris. "Is this one of your witnesses?"

Mr. Paris, with a quick glance at an unresponsive Justine, nodded. "He is now."

After being waved on, Taug gripped the handrail and heaved himself forward until he stood in front of Max. "I brought Justine to Newearth to protect myself as I attended to a task that Mitholie had ordered me to complete."

A Bhuac delegate rose from her chair. "What task?"

Taug scanned the crowd. "I was sent to destroy a mistake, a mixed breed Human-Cresta my father created in the interest of Inter-Alien relations."

Everyone jumped to his or her feet, talking at once. Cerulean and Sterling were the notable exceptions. Judge Tobias nearly broke his hammer as he attempted to regain control of the assembly.

Faye, now at the judge's side, whispered in his ear. He frowned, stroked his chin thoughtfully, and then looked up and scanned the crowd. "There has been a request to clear the courtroom of unauthorized personnel." With an I-hate-to-do-it sigh, he gestured to the guards. "Considering the sensitive nature of these claims, I concur." He peered at Faye. She offered a modest nod of approval.

Guards shifted begrudging personnel out of the room, though most moved along peaceably.

Clare stomped down the incline to the front of the room, with Bala following close behind, and thrust her datapad ID in front of the judge. "My partner and I are intimately connected with this case, and we insist that as Human Relations detectives, we be allowed to stay and testify on Justine Santana's behalf."

Judge Tobias shook his head and gestured Mr. Paris to his side. He reiterated Clare's claim. The defense lawyer shrugged in the apparent wonder of modern miracles. "If I knew there were so many willing to testify, I would've called them, but she remained silent as a stone when I questioned her."

The judge pursed his lips and merely waved Clare off to the ever-lengthening defense line.

After a bit of shuffling, the courtroom was emptied of nearly two-thirds of its former occupants. The judge eyed the room carefully. "For clarity's sake, would the witnesses for the defense stand over here?" He thrust a thick arm to this left. "And would the witnesses for prosecution stand over there?" He motioned to the right. "And would all official representatives move closer so that we can see who's who in this mess?" He jerked his head, glaring at the jury. "You stay right where you are!" Slapping his forehead, he mumbled, "Newearth courts! Give me an old-fashioned Ingoti death-wrestle any day."

Cerulean marched closer, as did Sterling. They looked each other in the eye briefly, offering only a nod in salute. Sterling sat behind the prosecution crowd while Cerulean found a seat behind the defense assembly.

Cerulean let his gaze rove over the official delegates and then refocused on Sterling. His eyes narrowed. Sterling was staring fixedly at the woman in front of him. Cerulean leaned toward Clare, who sat only two seats away, and tapped her shoulder.

She jumped.

"Who's that?" Cerulean pointed to the figure in front of Sterling.

Bala leaned over Clare and grinned. "Don't you recognize our illustrious governor? She's done herself up in new colors and is sporting a decidedly different fashion, but that's her. I'd know those eyes anywhere. I stared at enough of her pictures—"

The judge hammered his gavel with more restraint this time. "Thank you. I believe we can now continue."

Through all the exiting, rearranging, and shuffling, Justine had remained fixed in place, staring at nothing. Max had seated himself on the defense side, also staring fixedly ahead.

Taug lounged in the witness stand until the defense attorney stepped up and opened his hands in a welcoming gesture. "If you would explain, Mr. Taug—"

"Just Taug, please. I am an unworthy scientist of Crestar, the son of—" Taug waved a tentacle. "But you don't need my family history. What you need is to understand the Crestonian compulsion to succeed. We are a race obsessed with science because technology offers us the best chance to gain security in a precarious universe." He nodded to Justine. "My father had hoped that through crossbreeding, sentient races would finally unite and the destructive wars of the past millennium would cease."

A Cresta representative jumped to his feet. "Traitor! Your father wanted personal glory, and he was willing to break Inter-Alien laws to do it!"

An Ingot Representative rose. "Why weren't we informed of this? Once the crossbreed was known to exist, we should have been apprised of the situation."

Taug waved a tentacle. "The crossbreed had a name. Derik. He was both human and Cresta and betrayed by both. In fact, he has been murdered." Taug lifted his gaze to Faye. "Every race on Newearth could have learned a great deal from him—I know I did." He shrugged away the tumult around him. "I did not see the truth until too late."

Faye rose to her feet and glided to the middle of a small knot of Bhuac representatives. "Because the truth is often shrouded in lies. Bhuaci have been invaded by nearly every species present, and we have learned through centuries of suffering that survival is not based on truth but on endurance."

The Ingot representative pounded his fist into his hand and glared at the judge. "We should have been informed! We are not Bhuac infants or Uanyi thugs. We have a legitimate stake in this planet."

A Uanyi representative rose with an indignant snarl. "Thugs! How dare you insult us! You—"

Clare rose, her eyes flaring, and shouted. "The Bhuaci are not the only ones at risk. We have proof that Uanyi have been experimenting on humans in their drug trade. Profiting off our suffering—"

The judge's gavel hammered until the ruckus calmed to a grumbling murmur. His voice lowered to a thick growl. "This case has triggered many of sensitive issues, but we are only here to deal with one of them. Is this android guilty of murder? If so, what is her sentence? We will deal with the ramifications for other androids and mixed-beings at a later date." He wagged his head like an angry ox, challenging the assembly.

Sterling rose to his feet and, clasping his hands like a pedagogue about to impart a difficult lesson, he cleared his throat. "I believe that we must accept one more unpleasant truth before we ascertain the guilt—or innocence—of Justine Santana. We have one in our midst one who has misrepresented herself and put us *all* at risk." He leveled his hand at Governor Right. "This apparent woman who sits before you as Governor of Newearth is not the elected governor—nor even human. She is a murderer."

The judge dropped his gavel.

The entire assembly gasped, including Cerulean.

Governor Right turned and chuckled. With an imperious hand, she addressed the crowd. "Do not be fooled by this idiot. He's a Luxonian lunatic. I have proof of his mental instability, if you care to view it. Taken up native artistry or some such—"

Sterling reached inside his voluminous robe, pulled out a dagger, and threw it at Governor Right's chest where it lodged itself with a thud.

The governor glared at the spike before she launched herself at Sterling. Cerulean literally appeared in front of him and held her at bay. Guards from every side scrambled to contain the chaos.

"I'm more human than you, Luxonian, no matter how you appear!"

The mixed phalanx of guards, including an Ingot, Uanyi, and a Bhuac in the form of a small troll, struggled to control the former governor as she raged.

Pulling the spike from her chest and using it as a pointer, Right gestured emphatically. "Get these fools away from me! That one—" She shook the spike in Faye's direction. "—the fair one over there is not what she seems. She appeared as a shadow, tortured me, and—"

Faye strolled up and leveled her gaze at Right. "Protected my people—at all costs."

The Ingot judge tapped his gavel as if the slight, measured beat would calm the assembly. When the room grew a few decibels quieter, he cleared his throat and leveled his gaze at Faye. "Not at all costs. We do have laws on this planet. If we forsake them, we forsake all hope of justice. Even a small temptation will make us slip." He gestured with his gavel at Right. "And great temptations topple us."

With a sigh, the judge motioned to the guards. They began hustling the resisting former governor toward a side door.

Suddenly the massive main doors were thrust aside as if they were made of straw, and a beautiful, lithe, blond-haired child stepped through.

This time, the judge tapped the gavel against his forehead like a man banging his head against a wall. "What—?"

The child's smile rivaled the light beams as she surveyed the stunned assembly. She gazed ahead, fixed on Justine, and with a child's dexterity, practically danced across the silent room. She skipped up the two steps to stand in front of Justine. The little girl positively beamed at the android that stared down at her with a puzzled frown. With her head tilted up, she spoke with a voice strong enough to be heard by the whole assembly. "I have a message for you—from your creator." With a sweeping gesture, she bowed and the most extraordinary figure ever seen on Newearth appeared before the crowd's astonished eyes.

A dashing human-looking man with a mane of wild, black hair, an oval, alabaster face, and piercing green eyes, dressed in robes of riotous, clashing colors, opened his arms dramatically, as if welcoming them all into his presence. His voice rang deep and clear. "Forgive me, I have a passion for doing the unexpected." He twirled around, gazing at each face in the assembly. "But at this significant impasse, I decided it would be best to reveal myself so that your development may continue, unimpeded by grievous misunderstandings." He bowed. "Let me introduce myself. My name is Omega—creator of new life."

Five guards charged forward.

Omega lifted a finger, and they flipped backwards and fell harmlessly to the ground, stunned.

The figure strode toward Justine. He gazed deeply into her eyes. "Your coming into existence was imperative to my happiness. I never meant to neglect you, but I did not want to influence your development." His gaze turned and addressed the assembly. "I must create—though sometimes I am forced to destroy." His gaze swerved to the former governor. "An unhappy responsibility." He marched sedately across the room to the cowering woman, now abandoned by her guards. He glanced at Justine. "Some of my creations advance, which pleases me mightily." His gaze returned to Right. His eyes grew somber, grieved, as they rolled over her. "Some descend into the abyss."

The former governor's eyes widened. A silent, "*Please,*" formed on her lips.

With a flick of the finger, the cowering woman disappeared.

The figure turned and faced the assembly. "You may call me Omega, for though I am not the beginning, I certainly enjoy a good ending." He smiled at his own joke, surveying the unsmiling crowd. Twirling like an acrobat, he spun to the other side of the room. "I have been insensitive—" His gaze found Bala, and he grinned. "—as Officer Impala would surely attest." The bizarre figure chuckled happily. "But Taug understands—" He turned and held Taug in a steady gaze. "Do you not? Working so closely with Mitholie was certainly an education in insensitivity—if nothing else." He stroked his chin as he stepped closer to the shivering Cresta. "You have powers of resistance I wouldn't have thought possible."

Gripping the guardrail, Cerulean squared his shoulders and demanded the answer they were all too terrified to ask. "*Who* are you?"

The figure swirled around and stared at Cerulean, a wild grin beaming through his eyes. "Ah, Cerulean, a Luxonian with abundant sensitivity! Anne would agree, wouldn't she?"

Cerulean froze.

Omega waved his hands in an attitude of understanding. "Don't be surprised. I see through many eyes."

Clare fell back against her chair with a strangled gasp, her eyes wide and horrified.

Marching across the room, Omega glanced at Clare's prostrate form, his voice softening to a mere whisper. "I'm not done with you, *little one*." He returned his gaze to Justine as he paced before her. "I have come for you, Justine Santana. Doubt lingers. The fools who question your worth seek only to elevate themselves. I created you—out of given materials—true. The one who gives true freedom gave you what you needed long ago. I did not choose that. I simply gloried in it." Omega leaned in. "You must decide if you are free. And if you are guilty."

Justine stared at the floor, frozen. "I am both."

Taug rose from his stupor and lifted a wavering tentacle. "Free perhaps but not guilty. Mitholie ordered her to kill me. Instead she killed him and saved me—and others."

Omega bowed at Taug. "A rare gift indeed! An honest Cresta!"

Justine raised her head. "No. I didn't do it to save Taug." In a flash of introspective insight, Justine paused while everyone waited, their eyes glued to her still form.

She had always wondered what it would feel like to be completely free. When she fired the Dustbuster at Mitholie, she had felt an exquisite release of an enormous weight; an engulfing exuberance had swept her entire being. It had felt perfect.

But as she had watched Mitholie's body blow apart, her mind had slowed the process. She watched every synaptic fiber stretch beyond its limits until it was torn asunder. In that same, glorious moment, a flash of horror struck her inner being very much like a Dustbuster ray. As Mitholie's synapses clung desperately to life, straining pathetically against their doom, so her identity flew to pieces.

She had been deceived.

Justine met her creator's gaze. "Seventy years ago, I stood trial for war crimes I was hired to commit. I was caught and tried because I stopped to save two men from certain death. Today, I stand before you on trial for murdering a murderer and once again, saving lives. I am not sorry I saved Taug though I am sorry I killed anyone. Humans must accept burdens of guilt as we struggle between right and wrong. It is the price I, too, must pay—a burden I now gladly bear."

With the glint of fatherly pride, Omega caressed Justine's cheek. Slowly, he turned and gestured with an open hand. "As a reward for your humanity, I will give you what I neglected to offer when I created you. You can never be a child, but I give you this child as your own—to raise however you wish. She is one of your kind." He tipped his head and bowed in gentlemanly fashion.

The little girl tiptoed forward and curtseyed low. Her anxious eyes peeked up and met Justine's stare. The two held each other's gaze.

"He's gone!" Bala jumped over the rail and ran to the spot where Omega had stood a moment before.

Cerulean ran to Justine's side. Sterling strode near, his searching gaze scouring the room.

Bala waved his wiggling fingers through thin air. "That wasn't a hologram!"

Cerulean shook his head, raking his fingers through his hair.

Sterling stroked his chin. "Closest thing to a god I've ever come across."

Sobbing, Clare stood and pointed a shaking finger. "Not a god—a devil!" She fell back on her chair weeping. "He plays with us—like toys."

Without breaking their mutual gaze, Justine held out her hand and the little girl grasped it.

CHAPTER THIRTY-ONE

Not Alone

A gentle breeze sent whispers of spring across Justine's cheek as she strode toward the Vandi docking bay. The scent of Newearth soil breaking through the last of winter's tight grip wafted through the air. Max strode along on her left while the little girl clutched her right hand. Huge bay doors dwarfed the pedestrian ones, marked by large boarding-zone numbers.

Max slowed as they drew near. "There's no reason for you to go in. Just a maze of tunnels filled with business opportunists hurrying to manage their insignificant lives."

"And a few random diplomats, scientists, reporters—"

"No one *you* need to worry about. Your friends are here—on Newearth." Max glanced down, knelt on one knee, and stared into the little girl's golden eyes. "What's your name?"

The child shrugged.

Justine pursed her lips. "My first challenge as a mother."

Max surveyed the glossy-haired beauty before him. He grinned. "Zara." He glanced up at Justine. "It means dawn."

Justine grunted and questioned the girl with a furrowed brow. "Zara?"

The child nodded vigorously with a happy smile.

"Zara Santana. It is rather melodious." Justine pursed her

lips as she returned her gaze to Max. "You've changed. There was a time when you could hardly use contractions, much less think creatively. Thanks for trying to save me, but the truth is, I needed to save myself. Or die trying." A glint of humor showed in her eyes. "Remember Captain Kimberling?"

Rising to his full height, Max shrugged one shoulder. "Hey, I've grown."

Justine raised an eyebrow as she appraised Max's six-foot frame.

Max snorted. "Not on the outside—on the inside." He peered at her. "Literally." He folded his arms. "Listen, there's something I need to tell you." He glanced around and then refocused on Justine. "I was in an accident some time back, got a little too close to a marauder waving a Dustbuster. Nearly got blown to bits. In surgery, the doctors were ready to turn me off, but an assistant suggested that they check my brain synapsis to see—" Max blinked and swallowed.

Justine glared at him with impatience. *"What?"*

"My human synapses had taken over. My brain is more human than android."

Justine blanched. "So your testimony was—"

"A lie meant to save your pretty head." Max stepped closer and stared into Justine's steady eyes. "I've always wanted to tell you—" He swallowed, dropped his gaze, and stomped away.

Justine followed his every move, still clutching Zara's hand.

Muttering to himself, Max circled back. "Listen, you're the closest thing I've ever had to family. You're like a sister—or something. I thought you were dead! I couldn't afford to let them turn you off again. Don't you see? They wouldn't turn me off when they realized that I would die. They saved me—like they'd save any other human."

Dropping Zara's hand, Justine braced herself. "But I was shut down for seventy years!"

His jaw clenching, Max blinked back tears. "Now you understand why I had to see you. I had to know if you were *really* alive."

Justine's deadened gaze turned away. "Am I an android then?"

Max shook his head and chuckled. "No, Justine. You're a miracle."

Sterling leaned back in the former governor's chair in the Capitol building. The room had been stripped of all art and decorative elements. Only the desk and cabinet appeared unchanged. A heavy silence hung in the air. Sterling clasped his hands behind his head. "She was a remarkable woman, despite the fact that she wasn't a woman."

Cerulean stood at the cabinet and poured a drink into a short, thick glass, stopped a moment, and then reached for a second glass and poured again. "What was she?"

Staring at the ceiling as if appraising the stars, Sterling shrugged. "Pure android. The most superior model ever made. She was the forerunner to Justine, no doubt. She's been around a long time, known by many names. As is her illustrious creator, Omega. A bit overdramatic for my taste."

Cerulean handed Sterling one drink, swirling the other meditatively. "Was there ever a human Governor Right?"

With a heaving sigh, Sterling thrust himself upright. "I'll never know. You oversaw the first Inter-Alien Committee. Did you notice a sudden change in her? The records have been wiped."

Cerulean sipped his drink, leaning against the wall. "I left before her election. It was time to let Newearth handle some of their own problems." He gestured to Sterling with an outstretched finger and not an ounce of humor. "Your orders, remember?"

Sterling took a long sip and stared at his glass as he heaved himself onto his feet. "One of my bigger mistakes. Of which—" He jerked a glance at Cerulean. "—you will remind me—there are many."

Clutching his glass, Cerulean shook his head. "I've never been your counselor or conscience."

"Damn right. To my detriment!" Sterling glared across the room. "Why do you always react so blandly to everything I say? What's so wrong with a good, knockdown, drag-out fight? Damn it, you're like a son. I wouldn't disown you for telling me the hard truth once in a while."

Staring at his hand, Cerulean exhaled a long breath. "I have tried—but it never seems to help. Besides, I don't like to make you angry."

"Afraid I'll take you away from Newearth?" Sterling snorted. "Should be obvious, I can't manage the place without you."

Cerulean shook his head, stared at his drink, and swallowed the last drop.

Sterling started toward the cabinet where the near-empty bottle stood like an idle sentry. He picked it up, stared at his glass, and then threw the bottle across the room, where it thudded harmlessly against the wall and fell onto the matted floor.

Cerulean raised one eyebrow.

Sterling wiped his face as if giving it a good rub. "I'll convene a special committee to consider the matter of mixed-races and android life." He heaved a heavy sigh. "We've got to widen our understanding—with that demi-god running around. What next, a Luxonian half-breed?" He glanced at Cerulean.

Placing his glass on the counter with a controlled tap, Cerulean shook his head. "He doesn't *create* anything. He merely imitates what he doesn't understand."

With a weary chuckle, Sterling shrugged. "Don't we all? In any case, I'm returning to Lux immediately. I'll meet with the Supreme Council to decide how best to address this Omega threat." He rubbed his brow. "It'll take time." He glanced at Cerulean out of the corner of his eye. "By the time we're done, I'll have knitted enough blankets to keep a whole battalion of grandchildren warm." Placing his hand on Cerulean's arm, he leaned in. "Where are my grandchildren?"

Cerulean froze.

Sterling wiped his hands free of non-existent crumbs and strode toward the door, flinging one last comment behind him. "Oh, by the way, Roux has asked to be reassigned to Newearth. He's tired of his exile, and—he misses you."

Cerulean watched the door slide shut. Weariness overwhelmed him.

Faye blinked as she entered Taug's laboratory. The white interior did not blind her and neither did the stark walls, but the utter desolation before her eyes short-circuited all coherent thought. She paused, staring. Everything that could be shattered—was. Cords and medical instruments had been ripped from the ceiling and hung limp, like dead vines. Splattered liquids of various colors marred the ceiling and walls as if a deranged rainbow had gone on a rampage, leaving traces of its former self in sickly drools and pale drips.

Her gaze circled the room until it fell on Taug, who stood before the most shocking sight of all—a drained pool. A Cresta-sized hole gaped in front of him as lifeless vegetation and small sea creatures lay motionless, attesting to the absence of life-giving liquid.

In Taug's limp tentacle dangled a Dustbuster.

Faye took a step back.

Without moving, Taug spoke in a deadened voice. "Don't run away. You can't get far enough. Trust me."

With soundless steps, Faye swept forward. Moving between Taug and the broken wall, she stared up at him, her eyes glimmering. "I know."

Taug's tight, emotionless expression, stayed frozen even as his gaze darted to her face. "I suppose you do."

Carefully lifting Taug's tentacle, Faye pried the Dustbuster from his grip and tiptoed across the room. Seeing an intact dissection tube, she dropped the gun inside. She wiped her hands on her long dress-shirt, returned to Taug, and tapped him on the shoulder. "You need something nourishing. Come with me. There's a little diner I've always wanted to try."

The Ingot hostess glared down at Faye and Taug. Tilting her head, she trained her eyes on them as if to determine whether they were merely an illusion.

Faye smiled brightly at the perplexed face and folded her little hands in steeple fashion. "Max says to say hello. He had to leave Newearth on an assignment, but when he returns he said he'd love to sample more of your sweets."

Taug choked. And continued to choke until Riko snapped his fingers at the starry-eyed hostess. "Get that Cresta a Green before he expires all over my booth!"

Yanked out of her dream, the hostess hustled off. Riko retreated to the back room, slump-shouldered and grumbling.

When he had finally stopped coughing, Faye reached out and patted Taug's limp tentacle. "You can start again."

Taug's weary expression crumpled. "As what? I was a top Cresta scientist, but now I'm an accessory to the murder of a top Cresta scientist."

"You didn't kill Mitholie. Everyone knows that."

"I wanted to. Everyone knows that too."

The hostess returned with a tray bearing a large glass of Green. A straw leaned jauntily from the top. "Here. This'll put new life in you." She frowned. "You look like you need it." She turned to Faye. "What'll I get you?"

"I'll have the same. I could use something nutritious."

Taug's slurp stopped abruptly. Sal's' eyes widened alarmingly.

Faye took it in stride. "I like to try new things. Keeps me young."

With a doubtful nod, Sal shuffled away.

Taug dispensed with awkward ceremony and poured the rest of his drink directly into his breather helm. Closing his eyes, he sucked it in and leaned back.

Faye nodded approvingly. "See, I knew you were out of balance when you—" She averted her gaze as Taug opened his eyes. "It is natural to become depressed when you find yourself at odds with your own kind, especially when you're only trying to help."

Taug leaned forward, his bleary eyes sharpening into mere pinpricks. "Who are you helping?"

"Bhuacs have been oppressed for—"

Taug shook his head. "Save the propaganda. I've heard it all my life: 'just trying to survive in a hostile universe.'" His voice dropped to a simpering whine. "Victims of cruel fate."

Faye's gaze hardened, her eyes narrowing.

Sal placed a smaller version of Taug's drink on the table. "Got you the small." Her appraising gaze slid across the lithe figure. "Didn't think you could manage the Cresta size."

Faye covered the edge in her voice with a masked smile. "You'd be surprised what I can manage."

Sal scratched her neck where her body-armor rubbed against her leathery skin. "Nothing should surprise me." She leaned down and stared into Faye's eyes. "I thought he—" She flicked a glance at Taug. "—was wanted or something."

Taug raised a feeble tentacle. "Don't look for a reward, Ingot. *No one* wants me."

Straightening up, the hostess glanced at new customers shuffling through the door. "Well, if you need me, just call. My name's Sal. Max might've told you." Without waiting for a response, the Ingot lumbered to her next duty.

Taug shook his head. "Remarkable."

Faye slurped her drink in one almighty gulp, leaving Taug wide-eyed and breathless. Patting her stomach, she sighed. "Not bad. I've had better, but one can't expect non-Crestas to make a perfect Green." She jutted her jaw. "There are some things Crestas can do better than anyone."

Taug's eyes glimmered. "Cheat and deceive?"

"You knew about the creator, Omega, didn't you?"

"Crestas have our nightmares—same as you Bhuacs. The creator knows how to destroy very effectively when he has a mind to."

"I've heard about him, in whispers, of course. But he's not alone. There are others."

"He's part of a race. A collection, brotherhood, school of thought...." He sighed. "They are undefined by anything we understand and very dangerous. There is a section of our planet filled with Crestas who fell in battle against them."

Faye leaned in, her voice falling to a whisper. "They attacked Crestar?"

"We were foolish enough to think that we could learn from their experience." His smile turned grim. "But they do not accept apprentices. Over one-third of our population died of a mysterious plague that same year."

Faye frowned and tapped her fingers against the tabletop. "Could've been a coincidence."

Taug swallowed. "Our leading scientist, Grimm, was found stuffed and mounted on the Capitol pinnacle. He held a flag of surrender in his tentacle." Taug waved at the hostess and glanced at Faye. "I could use another. How about you?"

Faye scrolled through her datapad. "We're due at Cerulean's at sundown but—" She clasped her hands together. "If Omega could do that to Crestar, he could have—" She stared at her empty glass.

Sal hustled up, swiping a splatter off her blouse. "It's filling up fast. Rush hour, you know."

Faye pointed to their empties. "We'll take another round. Oh, and make mine Cresta-sized."

With a wave of I-refuse-to-be-surprised-by-anything, Sal lumbered off with the empties clutched in her grip.

Taug eyed Faye. "You think that's wise? Green on an empty stomach can have... unpredictable results."

Faye's hard stare held Taug in her gaze. "We are victims of cruel fate only when we allow fate to rule us." She reached across the table and cupped Taug's tentacle in her small hands as if forming a bond. "We have bigger troubles to consider. *Cosmos* is on the loose again. How do you think he and Omega will get along?"

Taug stared down at the hands embracing his tentacle. Lifting his other tentacle, he folded it over Faye's hands, sealing the bond. Without breaking their gaze, he called to the passing hostess. "Make mine an extra-large."

Standing in front of the monkey arena, Justine peered up and watched massive birds twirling in the air, drunk on warm updrafts. She smiled. Turning, she dropped her gaze to Zara. The child kicked her thin legs into the air, not unlike the soaring birds, and leaned back, lifted high by the current of the swing's tide.

Leaning on the fence, Justine turned to the chimpanzees as they rollicked in their own playground, unhampered by mothers applying wet tissues or father's vague warnings. Then her gaze roved across the yard to the path and landed on the figure of a man she knew well—but not well enough.

Cerulean's easy stride carried him past a clutch of children at the popcorn stand. He passed the gamboling monkeys without a sidelong glance. His gaze was directed exclusively to Justine. Arriving in front of her, he offered a gentle hug and gazed into her eyes. "You see him off?"

Justine nodded.

Cerulean faced the swinging child. "Max is a good man. No matter how he was created."

Justine's eyes followed Zara on an upswing. "As was Derik."

Cerulean closed his eyes a moment. Silence held them both. Finally, he looked up. "True." Taking a deep breath, he nodded toward the child. "Does she understand what's happened?"

Justine rubbed her arms in a fair imitation of an anxious mother. "I don't know. She said that Omega told her that she would meet her mother and that we would be happy together."

Cerulean glanced at Justine out of the corner of his eye. "So how long has she—?"

Justine shook her head, her eyes fixed on the child. Finally, she turned, strolled toward the monkeys, and nodded in their direction. "Remember?"

Cerulean grimaced and cleared his throat. "You're safe now, Justine. Everyone agrees you acted in self-defense and to save innocent lives. Sterling is going to lead the Inter-Alien committee. They're reconsidering Newearth's policy on sentient life, including mixed-breed races and technological beings. The borders of our understanding will widen to include a bigger truth."

Justine's gaze rolled over a baby monkey clinging to her mother's back. "And what is truth?"

Cerulean gripped Justine's arm and pulled her closer. "Didn't Max tell you?"

"That it's a miracle I'm alive?"

Cerulean held her gaze.

With a shrug, she sighed. "My life has always been a miracle. One I never understood."

Attempting to slide off the swing, Zara jumped while still in motion. She leapt, but her trajectory was off.

In one fluid motion, Justine slid across the gravel, arms outstretched, and caught her daughter.

Cerulean hustled forward and lifted the child from Justine's embrace. He stroked Zara's smooth cheek and chuckled. "Warn us next time, little one. I'm getting too old for shocks, and your mother will get worn out. Literally."

The golden eyes brimmed with unshed tears.

Justine wiped her torn pants and then wiggled her fingers for the little girl. "An accident. No harm done. Nothing a little glue can't fix." She blinked a frown at the child's shaken countenance and then embraced her.

Zara dropped her head onto Justine's shoulder and sobbed. "I'm *always* making mistakes."

Cerulean shook his head with a puzzled grin. "Even androids

make honest mistakes."

Justine smoothed Zara's long hair and imitated every mother she had ever seen, soothing the distraught child with rocking motions and a hum.

Zara lifted her head, wiped her eyes, stared at Cerulean critically and then turned to Justine. Her small hands rested on Justine's shoulders. "I'm not an android."

The hum broke off suddenly.

Cerulean's eyes widened. "Then what—? Who are you?"

Braving a wobbly smile, Zara kicked to get back on the ground. She grasped one of Justine's hands and one of Cerulean's. "I'm a mixed breed, Luxonian and Human. My creator said I am amusing."

Justine knelt and stared into Zara's eyes. "But he said you were one of *my kind*. I'm part android."

Zara shrugged. A rambunctious monkey caught her eye. She grinned at their antics, swinging from tree to tree. She looked up at Cerulean and Justine, her grief forgotten in a new interest. Suddenly, she yanked on their arms, dragging them along.

Allowing himself to be pulled by the current of Zara's enthusiasm, Cerulean laughed. "He said she was one of your kind—but you're one of a kind." His eyes twinkled in sudden mirth. He glanced at Justine. "Don't you see?"

Justine's expression remained a stoic blank.

Cerulean chuckled. "We're all—*one of a kind*."

Justine let herself be dragged along. "My creator has a deranged sense of humor."

Cerulean shrugged. "Could've been worse. You could've been created by Taug… or Bala." Horror crept across Cerulean's face as he peered at the setting sun. "Oh, no. We're late for your surprise party!"

Bala led the way up the wooded path, slashing aimlessly with an invisible sword.

Clare slogged along behind. She lifted one mud-caked boot and shook it to no effect. "Why didn't he install a proper path up here? I'm all for nature but getting mired in mud hardly puts me in a celebratory mood."

Bala glanced over his shoulder and grinned. "Quit complaining. After all, I have risked life and limb slashing all the dangerous foliage out of your way. Just call me Bala the—"

"Absurd!" Clare pushed past and huffed up Cerulean's porch steps without a backward glance."

Bala stroked his chin. "Rather short, a bit scurrilous even. I'd prefer—"

The front door swished open, and Able stood beckoning them inside with a broad smile.

"—warmth and food."

Clare returned Able's smile and gestured sharply to Bala. *Hurry up*, her eyes warned, *or die where you stand*.

After unloading her coat and sweater onto Able's arms, Clare strolled through the decorated room. Beeswax candles, sconces, and lanterns filled the room with golden warmth. A large, steaming bowl brimming with hot cider dominated the central table, while plates, platters and bowl loaded with sandwiches and a variety of cheeses, crackers, soups and hot stews, dotted the perimeter.

Bala didn't need to be invited. He was already ladling hot cider into the largest mug available with sparkles of joy gleaming from his eyes. "Wait till Kendra gets here with the kids. They'll fall over!"

Clare politely nibbled her sandwich, rolling her eyes at Able in abject commiseration.

Leaning against the counter, Able grinned. "My kids have games set up outside. They can all play together."

Clare's jaw dropped. "In the mud?"

Stuffing cheese into his mouth, Bala tried to talk around frantic chews. "I'll go out and supervise. My kids can get a teensy bit rambunctious. They take after their mother." He shrugged helplessly.

Clare slapped her forehead.

Screams from the yard alerted them to the arrival of youngsters. Able pushed a curtain aside and grinned. "Looks like your kids and mine just met."

The door was suddenly flung wide, and Kendra staggered in. "Lord have mercy!" She looked around, her gaze landing on Able. "Those your kids?"

Able nodded.

Bala stopped chewing and was frozen in mid-sandwich grab.

Kendra righted herself, stuck out her hand to the opposing team, and sauntered over to Able. "I've got to give it to you. Stopped my kids dead in their tracks. That doesn't happen often." She tossed a glance at her husband. "Man-o-mine, I've worked all day getting things ready here, now get out there and hold up the family's honor."

Gulping down the last of an extra-large bite, Bala saluted smartly and marched out the door to the tune of a soundless drummer. A pocketful of nuts went with him.

Kendra smiled sweetly at her departing husband and then surveyed the room. "Everything has turned out beautifully. Reminds me of All Saints Cathedral we used to visit. Off world—you wouldn't know. Mind if I collapse?"

Able and Clare nodded in silent unison.

Returning to her former stroll, Clare wandered to the open kitchen. She blew on her steaming mug of cider and turned to Able. "So, you haven't told me about Jim. How's he doing these days?"

Able looked away. "He passed on. Nothing we could do...."

Clare's hand flew to her mouth. "Oh, I'm the idiot now. Even Bala wouldn't—" She closed her eyes. "Sorry."

Able circled around the counter and led her back to the main room where a fire rippled behind a black grating. A slight snore from Kendra's slumbering form ushered them to the corner. Able looked out the picture window overlooking the cresting lake. "It wasn't your fault—or mine—or Jim's, for that matter. It's the price we pay for living in a broken world with—"

Clare's eyes brimmed. "Evil?"

Able nodded, his hands cupping a hot mug. "The being who made Justine...he's like you said, a devil in disguise. But there are a lot of devils in this world." He shrugged and smiled at Clare. "Some angels too."

"You believe in devils?"

Able set down his cup. "Devils are real enough. Jim suffered—up to the end. There'll be hell to pay."

Clare darted a glance from Kendra to Bala outrunning a mob of children on the muddy lawn. "What a world."

Able stood behind Clare. His gaze followed as Bala suddenly reversed himself and began to chase the children around the yard. "In his own way, Bala works for the angels. Thank God no one gave up on him."

The sound of knocking brought Clare and Able back to the kitchen.

Opening the door as wide as it would allow, Able stared. Taug and Faye leaned on each other precariously.

Clare folded her arms and sauntered forward. "Are you two—drunk?"

Faye hefted Taug over the threshold to the couch that Kendra narrowly vacated and dropped him in a heap.

Kendra stared and her mouth dropped open.

Bala sauntered in. "I think I've got them worn out for a few minutes." The evening light had faded into twilight and the kids were milling around out front, lost without their leader. His gaze moved from face to face until it landed on Taug. He sighed.

Shaking her head, Kendra twitched Able's sleeve. "I'm all for early education, but I don't think your kids or mine need to see this. Is there anywhere—?"

Able nodded. Wrenching his gaze from the couch, he placed a hand on Kendra's arm. "Follow me. We'll take the kids to my place."

Kendra patted Bala's mud-splattered cheek as she passed. "Bath before bed, honey."

Clare and Bala faced Taug as he crumpled, falling into a snoring sleep.

Faye surveyed the food. "Oh, good."

Clare shook her head as she watched Faye and Bala tuck into the sandwiches.

The door opened. "Glad you made yourselves at home." Cerulean strode into the room with his arm around Justine who held Zara's hand.

Clare pounced. "You're late!"

Bala sidled up to Zara and bent down, talking around chews. "You like some sandwiches? Soup?"

"A few nuts?" Justine shrugged at Bala. "Sorry, a play on words. You wouldn't—"

Bala huffed. "I'm proud to come from a long line of nutty humans. Unique and always in good taste!"

Justine led Zara to the table and smiled. "Go ahead, enjoy!"

Pink rays lightened the horizon. Silence reigned supreme. Cerulean strode into the kitchen with a yawn. He tapped the coffee maker, peered inside, and frowned.

"Coffee? I hope I'm smelling coffee." Bala stretched, stumbled off the couch, and rubbed his hair, making it stand even further on end. "Gotta say, your couch is pretty comfortable. Better than my bed at home. Of course, your couch doesn't have arms and feet that smack me in the face."

Cerulean filled the coffee maker with water. "You're not often away from home, are you?"

"Not if I can help it. Home is where the heart is." Bala scratched his belly and peered through the darkness toward the lightening horizon. "I hope Kendra and the kids slept okay at Able's place."

Cerulean clicked the on button. "I hope Able slept okay." Cerulean popped bread into the toaster. "They don't snore, do they?"

Bala shrugged. "Not that I know of." He rolled his eyes. "Oh, I know! Horrible, wasn't it? I had no idea Crestas could reach that decibel in their sleep."

Cerulean stared at Bala, pursed his lips, then turned back to breakfast preparations."

"Can I help?" Clare sauntered in looking as if she had just passed through a wind tunnel.

Bala's jaw dropped.

Cerulean stopped short, but then returned to his work. "Start the kettle. I've got oatmeal... somewhere."

A shuffle turned Cerulean's attention.

Tugging Taug by the arm, Justine marched forward. She scanned the room's occupants, apparently not concerned by their state of disarray. "Where's Faye?"

One hand still patting through the cabinet, Cerulean scowled. "Why?"

Bala pointed. "She's outside, strolling along the edge there. Hey, is that safe? I was running close to that part, completely unaware that I might drop to my doom." His glare pointedly informed Cerulean that he considered himself outraged.

Cerulean returned his gaze to Justine.

Taug slumped down on a stool and dropped his head onto two tentacles. "You didn't need to get me up. Crestas sleep cycles—"

"Be quiet!" Pointing at Bala, Justine barked an order. "Get Faye and be quick about it."

Like a beaten dog, Bala hunched his shoulders and shuffled toward the kitchen door. "Sheesh! Who died and made you—"

"Bala!" Cerulean, Clare, and Taug all chimed in unison.

Uncomfortable silence reigned inside as birds began their morning serenade, twittering in response to an unnamed reality. They must sing.

Bala, regaining a modicum of his composure, strode in behind the bright and cheerful Bhuac.

Faye practically twittered like one of the birds. "Good morning! I thought you'd sleep for—"

Justine raised her hand to forestall any other happy comments. "I just got a message from Max."

All eyes locked on Justine.

"Cosmos is heading this way."

Cerulean leaned heavily on the counter, while Faye's normally pale complexion paled even further. "Newearth—"

Taug sucked into his breathing helm and choked. "I'd hoped she'd stay away."

Bala looked from face to face, while Clare leaned across the counter and gripped Cerulean's hand. "What? Who's Cosmos?"

Taug ran a tentacle over his face , wiping sweat from his brow. "A deadly enemy."

Bala swallowed a chuckle. "Oh, we have so many, what's one more?"

Justine shook her head. "I've never encountered Cosmos personally, but I have memories of those who lived to tell the tale. Their planets were—"

"Devastated. Beyond repair." Faye's eyes widened. She wrapped her arms about her waist. "We had a sister planet once. Cosmos—ate—it."

Clare hustled over to Faye, gripped her small hands, and stared into her eyes. "Ate a planet? How?"

"She is an omnivorous being, without mercy or even intent beyond her own survival. She feeds on planet life, consuming everything in her path."

Bala shook his head. "This sounds like a horror show I saw on the loop once. Scary as hell but made up by fools with nothing better to do than ruin a night's sleep. There can't be anything so bad. We would've heard of it before now."

Cerulean folded his arms. "We knew. It's one reason we send out guardians."

Taug raised a tentacle. "It's why we obsess about science in the hope of one day—"

"It's one reason we're so bitter." Faye stared ahead, sightless.

Justine folded her arms. "Cosmos is pure predator."

Cerulean circled around the counter and faced Justine. "What'd Max say—?"

Justine offered a wobbly smile. "He's coming back. He won't abandon us."

Zara stepped into the room. She gazed at the stricken faces and then ran forward and placed her hand into Justine's open palm. She peered at her mother's anxious face. "Don't be afraid. Omega will help—if it amuses him."

Max strode down the exit tube and stopped when he saw the assembly awaiting him. Justine raised her hand. Zara waved. Bala and Clare stood side by side. Cerulean nodded. Max continued forward with an uncertain grin.

"You're all here—to see me?" He shrugged. "I'm flattered, but I really don't have any news."

Cerulean cleared his throat. "We got the message you sent Justine. We have a plan."

Max stared at the phalanx of faces. "So… am I a part of this plan?"

As the whole group trouped along behind, Cerulean threw his arm around Max's shoulder and nudged him into the bright spring day. "Oh, yeah."

As a hot sun beat down, the gnarled, old apple tree stretched forth with millions of tiny blossoms, contrasting sharply against the vast blue sky. Inhaling the fragrant scent, Cerulean plodded along the path to the tombstone. He brushed a few stray leaves and twigs aside and knelt before the grave.

Running his fingers through the short grass, he exhaled a long sigh. "There's a new threat, Anne. This time, it's not something we can defeat. Cosmos doesn't care. So we have to go to another enemy… and see if we can draw good from evil." He stared up at the sound of birds flittering in the branches. A breeze rose and whispered, harmonizing with their innocent tune. "I'm so tired. I don't know what's wrong with me. I might be dying."

Stretching forth his hand, he traced the words etched in stone. *Anne Smith—Last of Her Kind*. "No. You were one of a kind."

Cerulean rose and gazed at the wild landscape and the mound where the old farmhouse used to stand. He breathed deep. "We all are." He turned toward the path, his gaze rising to the eternal sky. "Unique—but thank God—not alone."

QUOTES

1) (Page 8) "To sleep, perchance to Dream; aye, there's the rub…all my sins remembered."
~"To be, or not to be" is the opening phrase of a soliloquy spoken by Prince Hamlet in William Shakespeare's play *Hamlet* Act III, Scene I.

2) (Page 83) "Faith in destiny, my beloved, entwines us true, for hope endures when doubts are few."
~Ancient Bhuac saying

3) (Page 102) "Give thy soul air, thy faculties expanse; Love, joy, even sorrow—yield thyself to all…"
~*The Soul* by Richard Henry Dana

4) (Page 139) "…Lifted afresh he hewed his enemy down. And saved a great cause that heroic day."
~*Opportunity* by Edward Rowland Sill

5) (Page 158) "To sleep, perchance to dream—ay, there's the rub."
~Soliloquy spoken by Prince Hamlet in William Shakespeare's play *Hamlet* Act III, Scene I

6) (Page 143) "It was the best of times, it was the worst of times, it was the age of wisdom, it was the age of foolishness…"
"… it was the spring of hope, it was the winter of despair…,"
~*A Tale of Two Cities* by Charles Dickens

www.ingramcontent.com/pod-product-compliance
Lightning Source LLC
Chambersburg PA
CBHW070613310726
48982CB00001B/72
9798986180342